RAPTURE'S STORM

"Get out of my way," she demanded in a flat voice.

He shook his head, a lock of dark hair falling across his brow. "I want you, Brittannia. And I warn you: I'm not a patient man."

She had had enough of his arrogance. "Perhaps you'll find, Captain Barclay," she said icily, "that I'm a woman worth waiting for." Picking up her voluminous skirts, she attempted to brush regally by him.

Immediately she regretted her words. For with a swift movement he reached one strong arm out and spun her toward him, roughly pulling her lithe body against his lean frame.

"Don't play the coquette with me," he said harshly. "You're not in London anymore and I'm not one of your fawning beaux." With that he crushed her tender lips with a ruthless kiss.

Brittannia's gasp was drowned beneath his assault and she struggled against him holding her mouth tight against his searching lips.

When he broke the hungry kiss it was only to blaze a burning trail of kisses to the shell of her ear. "Admit it, Brittannia, you want me as badly as I want you," he demanded, his voice hoarse with desire.

She was boiling from within, fires burning in places she had never before experienced sensation. Of their own, her lips moved to form one word: yes. It was part moan, part plea, and when Dain demanded she repeat it, she gasped, "Yes, yes . . . damn you!"

DESIRE'S STORM

LINDSAY RANDALL

ZEBRA BOOKS
KENSINGTON PUBLISHING CORP.

ZEBRA BOOKS

are published by

Kensington Publishing Corp.
475 Park Avenue South
New York, NY 10016

First printing: July 1986

Printed in the United States of America

To my husband, Randy, for many reasons especially his belief in me when even I had none.

Chapter 1

"Sorry, dearie," a buxom, redheaded woman said through yellowed teeth that contrasted sharply with her bright red lip rouge, "the likes of us ain't allowed on the proud Cap'n Barclay's ship. Ye'll have ta wait yer turn in line with the rest of us girls."

"Bessie's right, luv," chimed in another garishly dressed woman. "We're formin' a line for this ship. We heard the boys made a handsome profit on this run and they'll be willin' ta pay a good price for their pleasurin' tonight. First come, first served!"

Brittannia Denning came to a halt as she coolly regarded the tastelessly showy woman who stood blocking her way. "If you don't mind," she replied calmly, "I've things to do." With a grace that came naturally to her, she lifted her sea-foam green skirts and without another glance in their direction, swept by them and proceeded up the plank of the *Airlee*.

"*EEK!* Look at her, wouldja? Sashayin' up there like

7

she was the Queen of England herself!" screeched the readhead and Brittannia turned only to see the old woman wipe a tattered red sleeve across her overly powdered nose. "Don't worry," she yelled to Brittannia, "ye'll ger yer arse booted off quick enough when the cap'n hears of ya!"

"Indeed?" Brittannia said under her breath. "The *Airlee* belongs to me and I'll see it sunk to the bottom of this harbor if it pleases me!"

She was angry as she stepped onto the deck of the ship. Without her knowledge her financial agent and life-long friend, Michael Delving, had invested the whole of her inheritance in the building and manning of the blockade-running vessel and she had traveled all the way from her Cotswolds home in England to see firsthand what her money had purchased. There was a determined set to her delicate chin and her full mouth was slightly pursed as her turquoise eyes, beneath their sooty lashes, flashed like two hard chips of ice caught in a brilliant sunshine.

"So, we meet again." The male voice came from behind her.

Brittannia whirled around and came face to face with a sailor with a gold loop through his left ear and a silk neckerchief tied loosely around his neck. He wore a tight striped shirt and baggy trousers, and upon his mouth, a jaunty smile.

"If I am not to think you're a dockside whore, then you would be wise not to venture out alone, especially aboard the ship I sail on," he said.

"Sir, you've obviously mistaken me for another. I've never seen you before in my life and I would appreciate you leaving me be."

8

The man laughed. It was a deep, guttural sound that caused the fine hairs on the back of her neck to stand. "Come on, honey. Make it worth my while." He took one slow step toward her.

Brittannia instinctively backed away. "Don't dare to talk to me like that!"

"I dare to do anything," he said boldly. "I'm a daring man; you have to be to run the blockade."

Brittannia drew in a deep breath, trying to steady her nerves. She looked around for someone who might help her, but there was no one. "Please move out of my way." She hoped she sounded commanding.

The jaunty sailor in front of her slowly rubbed the stubble of hair on his chin, making no attempt to move. "My guess is you like daring men. Why else would you frequent the waterfront? Don't tell me you're an admirer of ships, although you did seem mighty interested in her when I came upon you." He again moved toward Brittannia and this time he grabbed her roughly by the shoulders.

Brittannia gasped and tried to struggle free, bringing her arms up to push his away. His grip was forceful and she could smell liquor on his breath.

"I've a rich purse tonight and I'm willing to share it with you if you make it worth my while," he said as he pulled her closer and brushed his mouth by her ear and down her long, slender throat.

"No!" Brittannia protested as she turned her head away in disgust and pushed at his chest with all her might. The push made him lose his footing and he fell backward, giving Brittannia enough time to run out of his reach—but not for long. He jumped up quickly, and with the litheness of a cat, pounced upon her. His weight was too much for her to bear and she fell beneath him.

"Will!" a voice boomed from the distance. "What the hell are you doing?"

The sailor stopped his assault on Brittannia and scrambled quickly to his feet, leaving her sprawled upon the deck in a disheveled heap. "Nothing, sir. I—I mean, the lady and I were just having a bit of fun," he stammered, quickly straightening himself up to stand at attention.

The man whom the sailor had called "sir" strode purposefully toward them. Brittannia saw he was powerfully built and in his stride she sensed an aura of pride. He walked like a man who was sure of himself and his position. He wore a white billowing shirt that was opened to the waist, exposing a broad expanse of chest bronzed by the sun. His trousers were of tight fit and hugged his tapered waist and finely muscled thighs. Brittannia's cheeks burned as she realized where she had let her gaze travel and quickly looked to his face. His hair was ebony, tinged with burnished gold throughout the mass of dark, wind-tossed curls. His eyes were stormy gray. They reminded Brittannia of a cold, relentless England winter. He evoked a nameless fear in her.

The tall, dark man took in the scene before him. He looked at Brittannia. Her long, blond hair, pulled free of its pins in the struggle, tumbled down in lustrous waves, framing her face. He had seldom seen hair that color, only on small children. It was the color of bright sunshine, touched here and there by bits of gold. Her eyes were the color of turquoise; more blue than green. Her mouth, full and sensual, was a mouth made to be

10

kissed. She stood there in front of him, her eyes blazing, her chest rising and falling with emotion; she looked the temptress, he thought. She looked wild. He wondered briefly what it would be like to tame her in bed. The thought was pushed out of his mind, however, for there was work to be done and this female, no matter how beautiful, was obviously just a common whore.

"Will," he said in a voice hard as steel, totally void of emotion. "You know there is to be none of this aboard ship."

"Yes, sir. I know that, sir."

"Get back to work," he ordered sternly, evoking a slight shiver from the man before him. "I'll talk with you later."

With that, the man called Will scurried down the plank and onto the wharf.

Brittannia stood motionless, watching from beneath long lashes the man before her. She was once again alone with a strange man—but this man was not like the other sailor . . . this man had the power to make her heart hammer in her chest and her skin tingle from an odd mix of fear and intrigue. His feet were planted wide as he watched the other sailor leave the ship, and the slight breeze that ruffled his belled sleeves and night-dark hair did not a thing to cool Brittannia's suddenly burning skin. To her, his strength was not just something seen but something felt, as one would feel a raging tempest or a thunderous boom, and when finally, after what seemed to Brittannia deliberate, long moments on his part, he turned to her, she sensed the violence held in tight check behind the cool exterior.

She took in a deep steadying breath. "Thank you for

coming to my rescue," she said. Her voice, to her chagrin, sounded soft and breathless.

The stranger raised one dark brow at the gentleness of her voice. "Rescue?" he repeated mockingly. He folded his powerful arms across his chest as his cold, gray eyes slipped appreciatively down her figure then came back to meet her own gaze with a lazy arrogance.

Brittannia fought the blush that sprang from her anger. With a defiant lift of her chin she gave him a bold look, her blue green eyes flashing in the bright sunlight. This man was much too bold and his casual perusal of her was infuriating. "Yes, *rescue,*" she said.

He said not a word as he nodded his dark head, a slow smile spreading across his handsome mouth as he did so.

"Sir," Brittannia began, trying to keep her voice level, "you seem to be making assumptions about me tha—"

"No assumptions," he interrupted, his lazy, slightly Southern voice cutting smoothly into the warm air in deep rich tones. He unfolded his arms and with one hand reached over and pushed back the silky tresses of her hair that had fallen over her shoulder in a shimmering rain.

Brittannia felt her head swim as his fingers brushed gently by her cheek and ran through the long strands of her silky hair. His arm brought with it the masculine smell of the man; a wonderful, light mixture of tobacco and sweat. She stood animal-still fighting down the intoxicating sensations evoked by his nearness.

"I thought," he said softly, "it was made quite clear to you 'ladies of light virtue' there is to be no pleasuring of the men aboard ship. You're to wait until the men

12

are finished with their duties."

Brittannia very nearly laughed until she realized the depth of his insult. "I assure you, sir, I am not a 'lady of light virtue,'" she said indignantly. "I was only here to inspect the ship when that sailor attacked me for no reason."

"Inspect this ship?" He took a step closer. "I think a woman with your charms would be more apt to inspect the build of a man . . ." His voice lowered a note. "I don't think a woman as beautiful as you would care to know how well this vessel rode the waves. I'd think you'd be more willing to know how well a man could be ridden."

Brittannia, shocked and outraged by his words, turned to leave but his arms closed around her and brought her flush against his chest. She felt the heat of him as her soft breasts were crushed to his chest. A breeze had fluttered his shirt open and the fine hairs of his chest touched the naked skin at her low neckline. Her heart raced. She opened her mouth to protest but he took that moment to cover her lips with a kiss—a kiss that went on endlessly, searching, hungering, demanding.

No one had ever kissed her like this. Against her will, her body responded to the lips that were working over her own. She felt her knees grow weak, felt her senses come thrillingly to life. His lips, soft in their movements, expert in their quest held much too much power over her. He held the hypnotism of a snake. She was powerless, leaning into his arms, opening to his gentle assault.

The stranger felt her submission, felt her body go pliant in his arms and he pressed his advantage; his lips moving deftly over hers, his tongue probing caressingly as his strong hands gently massaged her back. After immeasurable time, his lips broke from hers and he whispered into the shell of her ear, "You see, it is not a ship you've come to seek this day. Admit it, lovely lady, and perhaps you'll be the one I'll let cool my desire."

His words brought Brittannia abruptly back to earth. "You cad!" she hissed. She brought her hand up and slapped him hard across the face. No sooner had her palm met his tanned visage with a resounding slap than his hand closed viciously over wrist. He towered above her, his eyes icy. Then he yanked her ruthlessly to him, his one hand still holding her wrist, his other going around her waist imprisoning her in a steely hold.

Brittannia's eyes grew wide with fear as she looked up into his unreadable face. Even in anger he was undeniably handsome. She must surely be going mad was her last thought before his mouth closed over her parted lips in a ruthless kiss.

There was no gentleness in this kiss and it was as if the rage of a sea-storm had swept inland and was now blowing around Brittannia and sweeping her up into the middle of its funnel-shaped fury. His insistent lips pushed hers farther apart as his tongue probed forcefully into her mouth, claiming and exacting from her responses she did not want to give but was unable to stop her body from giving.

He released her just as her body was coming to life again, and Brittannia stood dumbly, just inches from him. Her body had played the traitor and responded to the stranger's kiss like no decent woman would have.

She searched her confused mind for words but none were to be found, only sensations, sensations that tingled and even now yearned for more of the man's touch. She turned her head from him, ashamed of her own wanton response in his arms.

"Inspecting this ship indeed!" He laughed.

Brittannia jerked her head back toward him, her hair flying with the gesture. "Indeed I was!" she cried, forgetting her embarrassment. "I happen to be—"

The dark-haired man did not wait to hear her out, instead he interrupted her with, "There is a line down on the wharf. I suggest you get in that line. They're waiting for exactly the same thing you came on board to get." He nodded his head in the direction of the red-headed Bessie and her friends, then turned on his heel and was gone. Brittannia stared after him, her mouth opened wide at his insolence. After a moment she snapped her mouth shut and made her way down the plank and onto the wharf, her lips still burning from his passionate kiss.

"I told ya she'd get her uppity arse kicked off the ship, didn't I?" screeched the redhead in her high-pitched voice.

Brittannia glared at her as she walked by with her head held high. Her temper flared as she left the wharf and made her way to Bay Street. She should have boxed the man's ears! Better yet she should have him dismissed from his duties! Yes, that's what she would do. She would tell Michael—no, not Michael, she corrected herself. He would send her straight back to England if he ever learned of what happened. Michael Delving was not only her financial agent, but had been a close friend to her for as long as she could remember.

15

He acted like the older brother she'd never had and she knew for certain if he thought she'd even been looked at funny, he'd send her packing. Not that she would listen to him, but still, she didn't want to upset him. No, she wouldn't tell Michael. She would go straight to the captain of the *Airlee* and tell him of the abuse she had suffered at the hands of two of his men and then she would demand he reprimand them.

Glancing up from her thoughts, she noticed she had gone two doors beyond Michael's office. She backtracked her steps and brushed an errant blond curl from her face before entering the building of Henry Adderly and Company. Adderly and Company served as the Nassau correspondent for the fabulously wealthy Fraser, Trenholm and Company, the financial agents for the American Confederate government. Brittannia knew Michael had been offered a very nice position in Nassau by George Alfred Trenholm, himself. She hadn't heard any of this from Michael, who never told her very much about his business or her finances. It was the bookkeeper Delving employed for his London offices who had told her where her monies had been invested—after she'd badgered him for nearly two hours and emptied her purse into his greedy palm. He told her Michael had invested the whole of her inheritance into the building and manning of a blockade-running vessel. "The *Airlee,*" the man had said, "and she's running out of Nassau."

Brittannia felt a fresh surge of anger as she pushed open the door and stepped in out of the bright sunlight. A bell jangled sassily above her announcing her entry. After her eyes adjusted to the dim lighting, she approached a young gentleman seated behind a huge

16

oak desk to her left in the back of the room.

"Excuse me, sir. My name is Brittannia Denning. I'd like to speak with Michael Delving. I believe he is an agent for Fraser, Trenholm and Company."

The young man looked up from his work for an instant or so, then resumed what he was doing as he pointed a slim finger toward a door behind him. With a quick nod of her head, Brittannia stepped into Michael's office. The room was large and decorated in hues of brown and gold. To her right the wall was covered with maps of all sizes, most with many red markings on them. To her left a bookshelf ran the length of the room, laden with ledgers of all sizes, magazines, newspapers, and a few books which leaned precariously toward each other, threatening to topple off at any moment. In contrast to the cluttered walls, the huge oaken desk before her was bare except for an inkwell and a neatly piled stack of papers.

Brittannia cleared her throat in order to get the attention of the figure seated in the brown leather chair behind the desk. Michael Delving whirled around, lifting his feet from the ledge of the bay window he had been staring out when she entered.

"Mr. Delving," she said, placing emphasis on his title.

"Brittannia! What an unexpected pleasure! Please, have a seat." Michael rushed to her side, taking her slim gloved hand in his.

Had the sight of her brought a tremor of alarm to his brown eyes? She sensed his nervousness as he helped her to her seat.

"Really, Brit, you should have let me know you were planning a visit. I could then, at least, have made a proper welcome for you."

Brit. He had always called her that when she was a little girl. She had known him since she was nine years old. His father had been Lord Denning's London agent. Since the lord never traveled far from the Cotswold Hills, his agent traveled to him and Michael, eager to learn the business, always accompanied him.

"Surely you haven't come to Nassau alone. This is a wild town and I couldn't have you going about unescorted."

Now why was it always this way, Brittannia wondered. That tone of voice, she had learned to loathe it. It was the tone an older brother might use when reprimanding his errant little sister. It bothered her he still might think of her as a young girl who couldn't take care of herself. Since her mother's death years ago and her father's recent passing she had made a very conscious effort to be independent. "I have," she replied, "and there was no need to let you know of my arrival. I didn't want you forewarned of my visit, for you would have undoubtedly made up a clever story about where you have invested the whole of my inheritance!"

Michael walked to the bay window and placed his knee upon the cushioned ledge as he gazed out the dusty window. "Actually, Brit, I've been expecting to hear from you. I knew you would eventually take an interest in your financial dealings. I just didn't expect it to be so soon." He continued to look out the window, but what he could see through those dusty panes, Brittannia did not know. "I never would have kept it from you," he continued, his voice low and apologetic, "but there is a war going on and with war there are spies. It was risky to let you know."

He turned to her expectantly. She sat perfectly still, preparing herself for him to tell her a different story, for him to tell her he hadn't built a vessel with her money. She almost expected to hear him say he had lost her money in some foolish scheme. His words took her by surprise.

"My dear Brittannia, you are the owner of a blockade-running vessel. This vessel has outfoxed, out-run, outmaneuvered, and not the least of which, penetrated the Federal squadrons off the Carolina coast for the past fourteen months. All of this has made you a very rich lady."

"Michael, you have invested my money in a ship whose voyages are illegal!"

"Illegal? Ah, now, Brit. That all depends on how you look at the situation and whose side you take, although I prefer not to take sides."

"So if you prefer not to take sides, why are you investing in such an illegal adventure?"

"There, you've said that word again, *illegal!* Brittannia, a nation does not blockade its own ports. Blockade is a recognized agency of war only between independent nations."

"Are you saying the North sees the South as an independent nation?"

"On the contrary. They are not independent nations and that is why it isn't illegal. Brit, there are people in those Southern states who need what the blockade-runners are bringing in."

"And they pay a very dear price for it. Perhaps a bit more than what *you* paid for it."

"Perhaps a bit more," Michael admitted. "But there is a great deal of risk involved in every aspect of blockade running. Who can put a price on a man's life? One or all could lose their lives trying to penetrate the Federal squadrons."

"Michael," she began, her slim shoulders rising slightly as she took in a deep breath. "I came here today angry with you for not consulting me. Always in the past you've at least let me know you were considering something new to invest in and I know I've never shown a great interest in what deals you've made, but this time . . . I—"

"But this time," Michael interrupted, "you feel hurt because I didn't tell you and you feel hesitant because it has to do with a war that you know nothing about and is too far away to be a reality to you."

Brittannia looked down at her hands that were folded in her lap. She was angry at herself because she didn't know how she felt. Her anger at Michael had carried her from England to Nassau but now that she was seated across from him, her anger subsided. She should have known she could never stay angry with Michael Delving. Not Michael with his smiling brown eyes and his keen sense of understanding her. "I find it difficult to be angry with you for overly long," she said. "Tell me more about this vessel. What supplies does it carry to the Southern ports? What makes her so successful? What is the size of the crew?"

"Whoa!" Michael said, holding up his hand. "You surprise me, Brit," he said as he settled himself back into the huge leather chair behind his desk. "A woman isn't to be concerned with business ventures. You should be worrying about the latest fashions from . . . oh, whose house is that? You know, the one in Paris?"

He pondered his own question as he leaned back and placed his feet upon the desk. Brittannia frowned. "Ah, yes, the House of Worth," he added, obviously impressed with himself that he knew of the place.

"Remember this is me you're talking to," Brittannia reminded him. "I'm concerned with whatever is most important to me and I think this blockade-running vessel is *very* important to me. I've never been one to limit my world to fashions and needlepoint."

"And so you aren't. Forgive me for underestimating you."

Brittannia smiled at the crestfallen look that crossed his features and realized just how much she'd missed seeing him these many months. His straight, light brown hair was brushed back from his face and his brown eyes were just as merry as she remembered them to be. His amiable attitude and his inordinate good looks had turned more than one London lady's head. Michael, being a true *preux chevalier* was as ready for a dance as he was for a fight. The fact that many of the ladies were married hadn't stopped him from pursuing them.

"You're forgiven, Michael. And now, about the ship."

Michael looked her in the eye but Brittannia had the distinct feeling he wasn't even seeing her. When he spoke his words were slow and full of pride. "You should see her, Brit, long and lean, sleek as a cat. She's light draught, doesn't draw as much water as a Federal war vessel. She has three masts and two powerful engines, enabling her to move under sail or steam. She's a vessel truly built for speed. Her captain, he's a fine man. I've known him for years. Captain Barclay and the *Airlee* are one and indivisible. A fine team indeed."

"Captain Barclay," Brittannia repeated aloud, branding that name to her memory.

"I'll have to take you on a private tour of her as soon as the cotton and tobacco are unloaded. Captain Barclay reported the *Airlee* safely arrived earlier this morning. He said they stacked her with as much cargo as they could in Wilmington. It should be an all-day job unloading it."

"I'm in no great hurry for a tour," Brittannia said hastily, remembering her earlier episode aboard the *Airlee*. "But I would like to meet with Captain Barclay. Could you arrange that for me?"

"Certainly. Is tonight too soon?" Michael asked with a twinkle in his soft brown eyes. "There's a bit of a celebration planned for this evening. There always is when there's been a successful run."

"Tonight is perfect," she replied as she stood to take leave. She was anxious to relay her encounter with the sailors to the captain. "If I'm to look presentable for this evening, I must get back to my rooms and unpack my clothes."

"Brittannia, why didn't you bring Ella with you?"

"She's much too old for such a strenuous journey and it would be me watching out for her in this heat. Besides, I understand the conventions are more relaxed here and no one will look amiss at a lady without a maid."

"Well," Michael said as he came around the desk to stand beside her, "if you intend to walk about unchaperoned please be careful. There are ships just in from

22

running the blockade and profits are high. The men will be rowdy and that can be dangerous for a young lady out on her own."

Indeed, Brittannia thought to herself as she recalled what had happened earlier aboard the *Airlee*. She walked with Michael into the outer room to the main entrance.

"Are you staying at the Royal Victoria Hotel?" Michael asked as he opened the door for her. The small bell jangled above them.

She nodded.

"I'll send my carriage around eight o'clock for you then. Who knows, after tonight you just might be tempted to forget our fair England and stay in Nassau."

"I doubt that," Brittannia said as she squinted her eyes against the sun that splashed the world outside the door.

Michael laughed as she stepped outside. "Be careful, Brit. I'll see you this evening."

Once outside, Brittannia took a moment to adjust herself to the racking clamor about. She wondered if she would ever get used to such constant activity on the streets. Probably not, she decided and stepped into the flow of people, letting it push her along the street until she came upon a small market. She nudged her way closer to the stalls and then stepped out of the moving mass of bodies.

Heaped in piles atop rickety tables were mounds of fruit of all different colors and sizes. Yellow, scarlet, green, and orange were all thrown together, making Brittannia's mouth water. She approached a heavyset Negro woman and pointed to a dash of green among the mound, reaching into her reticule for a coin.

Just then a commotion caught her attention to her right. She turned to see a burly man take a blow to his face from another equally stout man. She gasped as teeth and blood splattered the air and the man careened backward toward her.

Before she could jump aside, the husky man had crashed into her. She felt the great force of his weight and her arms flew out trying to grasp something before she toppled to the dusty ground, pinned beneath him. From behind, strong arms wrapped around her midsection and whirled her in a half circle out of harm's way just as she heard a gun fire. With wide eyes, she peered over her rescuer's shoulder and saw the gaping bullet hole between the burly man's eyes. She felt her body shiver involuntarily and she turned her head away, trying to fight down the sudden nausea.

"Are you all right?" The man's voice was deep and draped in a light Southern accent.

She nodded, still not looking up, still not sure she wouldn't be sick. The man retained his hold on her, his large hands spanning her tiny waist. Brittannia took a few deep breaths and with her head still down, opened her eyes. She looked at the hands that held her. They were deeply tanned by the sun and the nails were clean and clipped. She felt a blush rise to her cheeks as she suddenly became conscious of the man's warm, intimate hold on her. Twice in one day, she thought wryly and took a step away, out of his reach.

"Thank you," she said, looking up. "I—" The words caught in her throat as she looked into stormy eyes that were nearly covered by a tumble of ebony curls, gold-tinged here and there. "You!" she thundered.

The dark stranger folded his arms across his chest

24

and said, "It seems, madam, you are forever being thrown to the ground by the men of this island. Perhaps in the future you would allow me the honor. I can assure you, the spot I choose will offer us more privacy than the deck or the middle of Bay Street."

Brittannia stamped her foot in anger. "You, sir," she replied icily, "will never have the chance."

"Ah, so the lady is feisty as well as beautiful!"

With one deft movement of her wrist, Brittannia lifted her skirts and turned away from him, intent on getting as far away from him as possible. But with two long strides he was beside her.

"I'll accompany you to your destination," he informed her as he walked beside her, the billowing sleeves of his white shirt fluttering in the slight breeze. "You don't object, do you?"

"I do!"

"I was afraid of that, but I'm not one to let harm befall a young girl."

Brittannia gave him an angry stare. She quickened her pace, hoping he would leave her, but he kept beside her, walking with that easy, graceful stride of his. Her heart was hammering in her chest and her stomach was all aflutter. It angered her that this man could have such an effect on her.

"A young girl? Is that how you view me, sir?" she asked as she came to a halt in front of a dressmaker's shop.

His eyes crinkled at the corners with amusement. "Would it bother you if I did?"

She lifted her delicate chin and gave him a level look. "Certainly not!" she replied.

"Good, because I do."

25

Brittannia's first reaction was to open her mouth wide and with hands planted on hips inform him she was twenty-one years of age. Instead, she gave a light toss of her head and shrugged her slender shoulders as if to say nothing he thought could bother her. Deciding it would be best if he didn't know where she was staying, she said, "I shan't be needing your company any longer. This is my destination." She turned to walk into the shop but his hold on her arm stopped her.

"When will I see you again?" he asked.

"You won't."

"Ah, now don't be hasty. I want you," he said, leaning his dark head toward her. "And I always get what I want."

Brittannia straightened with his words. He was too handsome and much too close for her to be able to think right. "I'm not something to be had," she informed him coolly.

He contemplated her words for a moment, the sun dancing on the burnished gold highlights of his hair as he stood in the bright sunlight. "I didn't mean to put it that way. You shouldn't be subjected to the manhandling of these Nassau brutes. You deserve better."

Did he still think she was one of the many women who sold their bodies? She was angry but at the same time felt a bit wanton knowing that he believed her to be practiced in the ways of pleasing a man. "And I suppose you fancy yourself better than the others?" she asked, willing to play her role of courtesan or trollop, whichever he thought her to be.

"Perhaps," he said, a devilish grin crossing his handsome features. "Why not spend some time with me and then you be the judge of that."

An unbidden smile touched her lips and even though she tried to turn it to a frown, she couldn't. She tried looking coquettishly up at him through her lashes. "Your good looks tempt me, sir. But I haven't the time today."

"I'll be in Nassau for a time. My ship doesn't make another run to the States for a while."

The *Airlee* is *my* ship, she thought. "Well, sir, if I want to be found in the near future, you'll find me." With that she turned and walked into the dim interior of the shop, being sure to make her silken skirts rustle seductively. Once inside, she moved directly behind a bolt of cloth and peered through the grimy window, watching, with a beating heart, the handsome seaman stride away.

Chapter 2

"We're almost there, Miss Denning," Michael's footman said over his shoulder before continuing to talk softly to the horse that pulled the elegant carriage up the slight incline to George Street.

Gone were the many drays that had banged about, gone were the throngs of people buying and selling merchandise. Gone were the loud voices of dockworkers and seamen. As twilight descended, a leisurely pace stole over the city. Voices, softened from the distance, drifted to her on a cool, perfumed wind that carried away the heat of the day. There was a magical, intoxicating air around her and she breathed deeply, closing her eyes.

Nassau was the farthest she had ever been from her home in the Cotswolds of England. Since her father's death, Ella, her governess, had taken on the role of overseeing all of Brittannia's doings. Only since her twenty-first birthday had Ella stopped trying to dictate her every movement.

She smoothed down the royal purple taffeta skirt of

her balldress and wondered what kind of people would be at Michael's party.

"We're here, Miss Denning." The footman swung the carriage door open giving Brittannia a full view of the wide staircase leading to the huge double doors that stood open. Lanterns were hung in symmetry near every other pillar along the wide veranda, casting a warm, inviting light about. Couples strolled leisurely in and out the huge double doors and she could hear the sound of music and laughter mingled together. She took the hand offered her and climbed down the carriage step.

"Brittannia, you look beautiful as always," Michael commented as he appeared, it seemed to her, from out of nowhere.

"Thank you. You look extremely handsome yourself." He did indeed look handsome in his striped trousers and matching gray vest. His top hat, a lighter shade of gray, was set at a rakish angle above his light brown hair. His long top coat of solid gray displayed expensive satin lining.

Michael smiled a very smug smile for he had spent a lengthy time preening in front of his mirror. He took her arm in his and proudly escorted her to his home.

Brittannia had to blink her eyes to become accustomed to the bright lights indoors. Michael guided her to her left and they entered a large ballroom lit with the brilliance of a thousand candles. There was a long table to her right filled with drink and food, and musicians to her left. In the many gilt chairs along the wall were seated beautiful women garbed in the latest Parisian styles.

"Michael," she gasped. "This is so very grand!"

He smiled as he led her down the three stairs to the floor of the ballroom. "May I have this dance, Miss Denning?" he asked, giving her a deep bow and then extending his arm.

"You could," she replied, "but there is no music."

"Ah, easily remedied, m'lady." With one flick of his wrist in the direction of the musicians, the tune of a favorite waltz was begun.

Brittannia laughed as Michael whirled her about the ballroom. Her crisp taffeta skirt billowed out in three generous ruffles and as she twirled beneath the arch of Michael's arm she could see the royal purple hue of it glisten in the light of the many candles. Her bodice of black velvet fit snugly and the puffed, off-the-shoulder sleeves showed to advantage her long slender throat. This night she felt beautiful, and as Michael and she danced around the room, she knew she was glad she had come to Nassau.

"Do you always throw such elaborate affairs?" she asked.

"In England, no. In Nassau, always."

She laughed. "You said Captain Barclay would be here tonight. If he has arrived I should very much like to meet with him."

"Always thinking of business, aren't you? Well, he hasn't arrived yet, but when he does you'll be the first lady I introduce him to."

"Are there other ladies waiting to be introduced to this captain?"

"Brittannia, he is a very rich man and his cool handling of running the blockade has made him very popular in Nassau. He's considered quite a catch for a husband . . . but then I hear I am also considered quite

31

a catch."

"Oh, I'm sure you are! I suppose all the scheming ladies are wanting to scratch my eyes out for receiving so much of your attention tonight."

Michael smiled. After the music stopped, he led her to the far side of the room, promising to return to her with a glass of champagne. Brittannia looked about her, her turquoise eyes scanning the length of the room. She caught sight of a tall, superbly built figure dressed in black. Her pulse began to race.

The figure need not turn toward her for her to recognize him. She need only to see that mass of dark, unruly curls touched lightly with burnished gold and the powerful stance of the man.

She quickly averted her eyes lest he look her way and catch her staring at him. She vainly tried to center her attention on something else; the intricate steps of the dancers on the floor, the way the candles along the wall flickered with the slight breeze in the room, anything and everything that was near to her and far from him. Try though she might, her gaze always returned to him, and though it was only for an instant, she took in every detail of his attire, his stance, his gestures, and the lady by his side. *She* was far too beautiful. Her dark hair, pulled back in a stylish chignon at the nape of her neck, shined with a glossy sheen and her dress of blue taffeta was snug against her ample bosom. She carried a light-colored fan and used it to advantage as she turned her head to one side and smiled up into the dark face of the man who had told Brittannia earlier that he wanted her.

Brittannia instantly disliked the woman. She seemed older and obviously knew how to flirt with a man of the world. She was the kind of woman men desired and women despised. She was everything Brittannia was not.

Brittannia was thankful when Michael finally reappeared with two glasses of champagne. She quickly took the glass offered her and downed half its substance.

"My dear, you are to sip it, not gulp it," Michael said teasingly and then took a healthy gulp out of his own glass.

"Has Captain Barclay arrived yet?" Brittannia blurted as her gaze again traveled the length of the room to the tall, stormy-eyed seaman.

"My, my, Brit. You're making me suspicious of your reasons for wanting to talk with our famous Captain Barclay."

"You needn't be suspicious, Michael. I just—I have some important matters to discuss with him. Matters I don't want to go into with you right now."

Michael slanted a look at her then shrugged. He looked about the room. "Ah, there is the guest in question. Come," he said, taking hold of Brittannia's hand. "I see he has brought the countess with him. She's a fascinating woman, recently out of mourning, though one would never know it."

"I'm sorry to hear that," Brittannia murmured—hardly paying attention to her own words as she realized where Michael was leading her. Surely, the tall, dark-haired man, the man who had implied she was a whore, could not be Captain Barclay!

"No need to look so distraught, Brit," Michael was saying. "The man was old enough to be her grandfather. He didn't last long, how could he with such a passionate woman sharing his bed? Oh, sorry," he added when he saw the blanched look upon Brittannia's face. "I didn't mean to be so blunt."

"Blunt?" Brittannia asked, repeating the last and only word she had heard him say. She was growing more distraught with each step they took toward the virile seaman and his lady friend. "Michael, just *who* exactly is this Captain Barclay?"

"*This* is Captain Barclay. Dain, good of you to come. Esmée, you look beautiful as always." Michael took the raven-haired woman's slender gloved hand in his. She replied something in a voice swathed in a French accent. Brittannia was trying valiantly to retain her composure. Surely this seaman wouldn't be so callous as to relay her embarrassing episode to Michael and the Frenchwoman?

"Esmée, Dain, I'd like to introduce a very good friend of mine and, I might add, the owner of the *Airlee,* Miss Brittannia Denning."

Brittannia smiled what she hoped was her sweetest smile as she nodded to the countess. She turned her attention to the captain. Hard gray eyes met bright turquoise ones. The ruggedly handsome features of his face showed no hint of recognition beyond the slight raising of one eyebrow and a gleam of amusement in his eyes.

Brittannia held her breath as he brought her hand to his lips, brushing it gently. She noticed how full those lips were, how square his jawline. He reminded her of a statue of Adonis. Yet, this man before her was no youth and his rugged features, though finely chiseled, could turn harsh, revealing a ruthless nature.

"I'm pleased to make the acquaintance of such a

beautiful young lady," he said gravely.

"Yes, and this beautiful lady has been waiting all day to meet with you," Michael said enthusiastically, a bit too enthusiastically for Brittannia's comfort.

"Has she now?" the captain drawled lazily. "All day, you say?" He turned to Brittannia and she thought she caught the glimpse of a half smile play across his too-sensuous mouth.

The musicians began to play another waltz and Michael asked the countess for a dance. She accepted, giving Dain a sideways glance as Michael escorted her onto the dance floor.

Brittannia stole a quick look at the man beside her only to find he was looking down at her through half-closed lids. She quickly looked away, wishing with all her might the floor beneath her would open up and swallow her, taking her down into its dark depths, shielding her from his penetrating gaze.

"May I have this dance?" he asked.

"Perhaps just one," she said. Anything to end the agony of the moment.

She felt his arm go around her waist, felt the warm band of steely muscles in it and her body went rigid. His words, the words he had flung so carelessly, came rushing back to her mind: "I'd think you'd be more willing to know how well a man could be ridden."

"Madam, if you would relax and listen to the music I'm sure we could circle the dance floor in a less ungainly manner."

She opened her mouth to retort but clamped it shut. She wouldn't rise to his bait this time.

"I must admit I was a bit surprised to see you here and on the arm of my good friend." He continued his one-sided conversation.

Oh, what a cad! "I'll have you know, sir, I tried to tell you that this afternoon, that I was not a . . . that you were under a misapprehension, but you were not in the mood to listen!"

"Yes, I suppose I rather jumped to conclusions this afternoon. I apologize and only hope you can forgive me." His tone was husky and it took Brittannia by surprise.

She looked quickly up into his face but encountered only hard, gray unfathomable depths with no hint of emotion mirrored there. She saw only a color; a gray the color of the mist that hung over a storm-tossed sea holding down its violent tempest. "Sir, shall we forget this afternoon and start anew?"

"Yes, I'd like that," he replied. "Now, tell me what it is you wanted to talk with me about so anxiously all day."

"Oh," she stammered. "Uh—I'm interested in what provisions you run through the blockade," she said hastily, "And—and if there are any repairs needed to be done to the *Airlee* while the moon is full?"

He smiled slightly, his full lips tilting up at one side. He looked enticingly handsome in his black top coat, matching trousers, vest, and immaculate white shirt. His skin, where it showed, was bronzed by the sun and Brittannia could almost feel the warmth of that sun upon her as she studied the man who held her so closely. As they whirled together executing an intricate step, he pulled her closer to him, his warm breath touching her cheek.

She could feel the abrupt curve he put to his mouth and she knew he was smiling, as he said, "No, Miss

Denning, no major repairs from this run. I pride myself on my skill of running the blockade."

They whirled once again and her skirts bellowed out with the movement, rustling as they did so.

"As for provisions, the *Airlee* is packed with the usual things: cigars, soap, pepper, coffee, wearing apparel, candles . . ." He let his voice trail off and be lost in the music as he pulled her closer still and led her in a graceful dance around the room.

He smelled faintly of musk and tobacco. It was a warm and inviting smell that seemed to envelop her and caress her senses. *This is madness,* she thought to herself. She wanted to stop, wanted him to stop holding her so close; so close she could feel his body press against hers.

The music ended. As he released his hold, she looked up into his face to see stormy eyes staring down at her.

"I feel the need for some fresh air. Perhaps we could talk outside. Would you join me for a stroll in the gardens?" he asked and led her toward the wide, double glass doors that led to the gardens.

The cool night breeze caressed her warm skin and blew back the tiny blond curls that surrounded her face. He led her, as one who had been the route numerous times before, through a maze of narrow paths. He didn't stop until they came to a small moonlit clearing with shrubs and vines pressing in on all sides.

Brittannia noticed, even if he seemed not to notice, the spot he chose was meant for lovers wanting to escape the lights, music, and other guests. She looked about her uneasily; wondering why he had brought her to such a secluded place. "Captain, I had no idea you wanted to bring me so far into the gardens for just a breath of fresh air. I demand you take me back this instant. I fear you still suspect me to be something I am not!"

He thought for a moment before speaking. "You're too quick to anger, Miss Denning. You might allow a person a chance to explain."

"You mean as you allowed me a chance this afternoon?" she retorted.

A glimmer of a smile touched his lips. *"Touché,"* he said. "But I thought we decided to forget this afternoon."

How handsome he was, she thought suddenly, with his unruly black hair tumbling down around his face. His broad, flat cheekbones and finely chisled nose gave him an air of aristocracy. Brittannia had never before encountered a man whose nearness affected her so. She wanted to run from him, but at the same time she longed for him to hold her and never release her. "Yes, we did," she replied. "But if someone were to see us here alone, what would they think?"

"Along with being too quick to anger, you also worry too much about what other people think. I merely brought you out here to talk in private and to enjoy the beautiful night with a beautiful lady. But if you would rather go back . . ."

The inviting coolness of the moonlit evening, or perhaps it was something in his deep voice, beckoned her to stay. Brittannia turned away from him and seated herself on a white stone bench, smoothing out her royal purple taffeta skirt. Her hands shook nervously as she arranged the glistening folds of material about her. She could feel his eyes upon her as he stood where she had left him, his legs spread wide and his arms folded in front of his broad chest.

"Well, Captain, what did you want to talk about that required such privacy?" she asked lightly. She couldn't let him know her inner turmoil.

He didn't answer her right away, but stood staring at her, an unreadable expression in his eyes. "I was hoping we could become better acquainted since, as Delving tells me, you're owner of the *Airlee*. Whatever concerns the *Airlee* concerns me."

"I was surprised that a captain such as yourself would not know who financed the building and first manning of his ship."

"This is a time of war, Miss Denning, and the names of such backers, financial or otherwise, are not spoken of freely. Perhaps that is why Michael did not tell you where your monies were being invested. You were in England and spies are everywhere in these turbulent times."

So, he knew Michael had not told her what he was doing with her money! How many other people knew? Perhaps even that French countess, the one with the green, inviting eyes; the bedroom eyes, she thought ruefully.

"No need to be upset, Miss Denning. Michael and I go back a long way. He's a shrewd businessman and knows when to keep his silence. If he judged it best to keep you in ignorance about where your money was being invested, then undoubtedly he had his reasons."

He sees into my very mind, she thought wildly then said, "Yes, Michael's a good man and friend. I trust him completely."

"At least we agree upon one thing," he said as he positioned himself upon the white bench beside her.

"Michael mentioned a female backer but no names were given. I assumed she was an old dowager reveling in the secrecy of it all. But now that I've seen you, I suspect Michael's reasons for not telling me about you were not all for the sake of secrecy."

He paused for a moment and Brittannia shot a quick glance his way. The color rose in her cheeks when she saw how penetratingly his gaze rested on her and she quickly looked away.

"You're very beautiful, Miss Denning," he said in a slow drawl. "A man could lose himself in such beauty, forgetting all else save his want to touch you and his need to possess you."

"You're much too forward, Captain."

One dark eyebrow quirked upward. "I say what's on my mind. To me life is today and tomorrow, no more."

Was there a note of bitterness in his voice? Low voices and the sound of female laughter drifted to them from somewhere in the distance. Fireflies lit the darkness near the foilage, glowing brightly then disappearing.

"Do you plan to stay long in Nassau?" he asked.

"Perhaps. I haven't decided yet."

"If you do, allow me to offer a bit of advice. Do not trust every person you meet. Out here there are those who would use you and enjoy using you." His voice was husky as he looked at her through half-closed lids. "A woman of such rare beauty and obvious innocence is a tempting prize."

"And would you, Captain, . . . use me?" she smiled coquettishly at him.

His lids lifted slightly and she could see raw desire in the smoky gray depths of his gaze. "If you would let me, yes."

Brittannia gasped, shocked. Her first thought was to leave, to return to the ballroom where there was safety from the captain and from the strange effect he had on her. But then she felt his warm touch upon her and it was too late. Her breath caught as she turned her head slightly toward him, and through sooty lashes, watched as his hand ran lightly across one bared shoulder. From there his fingers teasingly traced her collarbone. Brittannia knew she should protest, knew she should pull away, but she couldn't. His touch was too warm, too soft, and she welcomed it.

Her dark lashes fluttered upward as she finally brought her gaze up to meet his. His gray eyes were smoky, passionate, and their intensity caused a ripple of excitement through her. He leaned closer, his face inches from her own, and Brittannia's heartbeat quickened. She sat perfectly still. He dipped his dark head toward her, a few jaunty curls tumbling down to graze his brow as he did, and tenderly he brought his lips over hers.

Brittannia closed her eyes, giving herself over to her senses, parting her lips as his tongue found its way into the moist recesses of her mouth and gently searched. His kiss was slow, lazy and unhurried, and Brittannia felt as though she were floating on a gentle tide whose waters were warm and calm. He tasted faintly of fine tobacco and brandy. It was a wonderful, manly taste. She wanted him to never release her. Every fiber of her demanded completion. She felt his hand move along her velvet bodice, felt him softly touch her straining breasts. It would be so easy to let him continue, she thought lazily. So easy . . .

His lips upon hers made breathing nearly impossible, and when he slipped his hand inside her bodice and began to gently caress the soft fullness of one breast, she felt all breath leave her as her body trembled with hot delight. His strong fingers expertly stroked and caressed, tracing the pink nipple, teasing it until it grew taut beneath his fingertips. She quivered involuntarily as millions of stars burst within her showering beautiful sprays of intense feeling to all parts of her body. She felt the moan break from her parted lips as his hand tugged the velvet material away from her hot skin. His mouth left hers to travel first to the long column of her throat and then to the bared skin just above her breasts, which had now burst free of their black velvet prison.

Her mind could give no thought to her half-naked state, for all her mind could think of was how wonderful his touch was and how very badly she wanted her breasts to be kissed by this handsome captain . . . a man she barely knew yet felt she had known all her life.

With teasing, licking kisses he left a fiery trail upon her already burning skin, and with a swiftness that brought shivers of delight to Brittannia, he put his lips to her breasts and nuzzled her there. She strained toward him, forgetting everything but the exquisite sensation he seemed to draw from her.

He urged her back on the small bench, tugging at the off-the-shoulder sleeves of her gown, intent on having her body totally naked and beneath him. At first, Brittannia complied so caught up was she in the power of his touch, the spell of his kiss. But just as her back touched the cold stone, reality came rushing back to her.

"No," she breathed, pushing him away with great effort. Quickly she pulled her sleeves up and covered her breasts, tugging the bodice back into place. Her breath was coming in ragged gasps and her whole insides were in a confused state. "Please don't," she whispered. She wanted to be angry with him, but she could not, for she had let him take her as far as he had . . . and she had enjoyed every minute of it.

"I thought," he said slowly, his voice slightly husky, "you wanted me to treat you like a woman."

"I do." Her reply was barely audible.

"Do I frighten you, then?"

She could feel tears of humiliation spring into her eyes and she stood, turning her back to him. "I want you to leave me alone," she said. Picking up her skirts, she ran toward the lights of the house. She wasn't sure of her way, but she plunged forward anyway, pushing past the many vines that slapped sharply at her face and bare arms. Tears fell unbidden down her cheeks and she angrily wiped them away. There was an opening in the twisting path that led to bright light and she ran toward it blindly, not stopping until she ran full force into a hard lean figure that had appeared, it seemed, from out of nowhere.

"*Querido,* from what do you run so quickly?" The voice was thick with a Spanish accent. Brittannia looked up into coal-black eyes under a shock of midnight-black hair staring down inquisitively at her, waiting for an answer.

"Excuse me," she panted, nearly out of breath from her mad dash through the gardens. "I didn't mean to run into you." Nervously she glanced over one shoulder to see if Dain was pursuing her. She had to keep her distance from that man; she must never again be alone with him; she couldn't trust herself.

"You seem to be fleeing from something or someone," the man said as he too glanced over her shoulder and peered into the darkness there. "Perhaps I can be of some assistance. May I escort you back inside?" He extended his arm.

Brittannia stood for a moment, indecisive until she heard the sound of approaching steps behind her. She didn't want to chance seeing Dain, at least not until she'd had a chance to regain her composure. She forced a polite smile. "Yes, yes I think I'd like that." She placed her gloved hand on his arm and resisted the temptation to peer over her shoulder one last time before walking toward the house with him.

Caught up in her own tumultuous feelings, Brittannia missed the way the Spaniard raked his black eyes up and down her figure, missed the look of dangerous lust in those ebony depths.

Chapter 3

Brittannia sat on the tiny settee with her hands clasped tightly together, and as she tried vainly to still their trembling, looked up into the large gilt-framed mirror before her. She was astonished by what she saw. Large turquoise eyes, shining alive and bright, stared back at her. Her cheeks were flushed and she put a slender hand to her face, feeling the burning warmth there. Her fingers brushed lightly along her cheek and traveled to her lips. They too burned with the memory of that searing kiss, a kiss that had left her shaken and frightened of the man, yet inexplicably wanting more.

How could he take such liberties with her? Surely she hadn't provoked him in any way? Never before had she felt such tumultuous emotions that both excited and frightened her. She stood and turned her back to the large mirror, smoothing the many folds of her skirt, and then she pushed the last few stray locks of hair into place. Finally pleased with what she saw, she picked up her skirts and left the room in search of the dark Spaniard. Brittannia and he had separated upon entering the ballroom, he in search of refreshments and she to the powder room to regain her composure. She returned to the ballroom, the sound of laughter and music returning her mood to that of a more festive one.

"Ah, senorita, I have been waiting patiently for you," the Spaniard said, pressing a glass of champagne into her hand as he led her to one of the many chairs along the side of the room. "Since we have not been formally introduced," he continued once they were seated, "let me introduce myself. I am Sebastian Diaz and from this day forward one of your, how you say, admirers?"

Brittannia smiled. She liked the melodious sound of his voice, the way he rolled his r's. His rich Spanish accent and dark good looks intrigued her. "I'm flattered, sir, to have a man such as yourself as an admirer. My name is Brittannia Denning."

They continued their light conversation. Brittannia did not notice when Dain reentered the room, his eyes quickly scanning the crowd for her. She did not see the cold, steely glint in his eyes when he saw with whom she sat conversing. His hands clenched into tight, capable fists as he strode purposefully toward them.

"Dain, darling, where did you wander off to?" It was the countess. Dain gave her a cold look. *"Chérie,* you promised me a dance, *non?"* she asked in a silky voice. She had been chasing the rich captain of the famous *Airlee* for some time and was not about to let him out of her sight for long. Her brief marriage to the shriveled count and seemingly endless mourning had proved to be more than she could endure; she with her unquenchable yearning for a hard male body. She had come to Nassau to visit an old friend but what had kept her were the men. *Men.* Men of all ranks, men with money to spend, men who worked hard during the day and played harder in the dark night. Here in Nassau she had got her fill—or so she had thought until she had met Dain Barclay. Dain had not proved to be the easy conquest she had hoped for. He seemed oblivious to the seductive glances she cast him, the slight brushing of her full breasts against his arm as she passed, the purring of her voice as she spoke to him. His cool attitude toward her made her want him all the more. Dain had told her on more than one occasion he considered her a good friend and that was all. It had hurt when he said he would always be her friend but never her lover.

She followed his gaze across the room. A feeling of jealousy washed over her and her green eyes narrowed as she realized where that gaze rested. Her eyes had venom in them as she stared at the slim, young, golden-haired Brittannia. So, that little schoolgirl interests him, she thought. She looked to the man beside Brittannia and her eyes narrowed even more with recognition. She smiled a wicked smile. Sebastian Diaz, that ruthless man with a heart of stone. It had taken her but one tumble in his bed to realize what kind of man he truly was. She was sure he would prove too much for Brittannia; he with his tainted lusts and perverted ways in the bedroom. Why, she had even heard it rumored he dealt heavily in the selling of white women to the highest bidder. Perhaps she would not have to wait long for Brittannia Denning to be out of her life!

The musicians continued to play and Dain's nerves

became tight as a bow string as he watched Sebastian lead Brittannia onto the dance floor. He watched them circle the room, Brittannia laughing at something Sebastian had said. Esmée pulled gently at his sleeve asking him to give her the dance he had promised. His eyes flicked over her quickly as he gave her roughly into the arms of the approaching Michael, glad to be rid of her. The music ended only for a moment but Dain took advantage of the pause to come between Sebastian and Brittannia.

"I believe the next dance is mine." His tone indicated he would brook no argument.

Sebastian, however, would not release his hold on Brittannia. "Are you sure you want to dance with the captain, *mi pajaro de oro?*" he asked.

Brittannia saw the steeliness in Dain's eyes, saw the muscle twitch along his strong jawline. She felt the familiar thrill tingle along her spine that just his nearness caused and she knew she wanted to dance with him, wanted him to hold her in his arms. "Yes, I'm sure," she said.

Sebastian gave one last dark look to Dain. Then he pulled Brittannia's hand to his lips and planted a kiss upon the back of it.

"'My golden bird,' hah!" Dain mumbled under his breath as he watched Sebastian leave the dance floor.

"What?"

"That is what he called you, his 'golden bird.'"

Brittannia was going to smile but thought better of it when she saw the dark look in his eyes. "I didn't know, but it did have a nice sound to it," she said, her mind traveling back in time to her younger years when she would forego her language studies and instead race out

48

to ride her pony. Ella might throw her arms up in exasperation but her father would only laugh and tell Ella not to worry.

"Brittannia," Dain was saying, the steely tone in his voice bringing her back to the present, "I don't want you to go near Sebastian Diaz again, do you hear me? The man is not to be trusted."

Brittannia's cheeks flushed with anger. "I'm Miss Denning to you and I don't like you telling me what to do, Captain. I think Senor Diaz is every bit a gentleman and I'll be with him whenever it pleases me."

The music stopped and Brittannia turned to leave the dance floor. Dain grabbed her arm in a tight grip and whirled her around to face him. She gasped, bringing her hand up to pry his hand from her arm. "Please don't make a scene," she hissed as she turned to leave again. He gripped her arm with more force and she had to bite her lower lip to keep from crying out; a gesture that would surely bring more eyes upon them.

"You're hurting me," she said, her voice rising a note with each word.

"I mean it, Brittannia. Keep away from Diaz, for your own safety." His voice was low and his tone frightened her.

Dain looked away from Brittannia and glanced around the room. All eyes were upon them. "Damn," he muttered under his breath. He looked back at Brittannia and saw that her large blue green eyes were filled with unshed tears and her lower lip was trembling slightly.

Michael strode into the room and was at Brittannia's side in an instant. He took her arm as he motioned for the musicians to play again. His smile was wide but

Brittannia noticed it did not reach his eyes.

"Dain, old friend, what are you trying to do? Ruin the party?" Then he turned concerned brown eyes to Brittannia. "Are you all right? Has the captain upset you?" His gaze traveled back to Dain. "She's too young for you, Dain, you've frightened her."

Brittannia was very near to tears again, all she wanted was to be alone and sort through her thoughts. The events of the day had been many and the threatening tears were more from exhaustion and confusion than hurt feelings. How was she to explain to Michael how Dain made her feel when she wasn't even sure herself? One minute she was angry with him, the next she would thrill to his touch, to his voice, to his very nearness.

"Michael, I'm ready to leave," she said as they walked from the ballroom.

"Good," Michael replied, summoning his butler. "I'll have my carriage brought around and I'll ride with you back to your hotel."

Brittannia smiled to the passing guests silently hoping they would forget the episode on the dance floor. She seethed inwardly when she heard the voice of the countess coming their way. She told herself she was glad when Dain walked back to the ballroom with Esmée on his arm, glad he was away from her. *Then why do I feel so miserable?* she wondered as she and Michael settled into the carriage for the ride to the Royal Victoria.

Bright sunlight spilled into her room as Brittannia threw open the red drapes. She was usually an early riser but this morning she had overslept. Her stomach rumbled with hunger as she hurriedly donned a day dress of light blue. It fit her snugly through the chest and waist, the puffed sleeves and the abundance of material in the skirt enhanced the tightness. Her body rose slender and elegant above the mass of material and her shoulders and long, slender neck were shown to full advantage. She brushed back her riotous blond curls and caught them up Grecian-style with a blue velvet ribbon. She topped it off with a matching blue bonnet, ornamented with two large white ostrich plumes.

She hadn't slept well through the past night. Her dreams had been haunted by hard, gray eyes and whenever she had tried to move she had been deterred by some unknown force, a force that beckoned her to stay yet frightened her. She had awakened shivering, wiping the perspiration from her brow. Now the heat was stifling in her room and she longed for fresh air, longed to be back home in the coolness of her English Cotswolds. But she knew she couldn't leave Nassau—not yet. Not while Dain Barclay was here. There was a timid knock at her door and she hurried to unlock it, anxious for company after such a fitful sleep.

"Excuse me, ma'am. I'm to give you these flowers right away." The tiny girl was obviously an island girl, her large brown eyes as round as saucers as she handed a bouquet of red hibiscus to Brittannia.

"Why thank you," Brittannia said. She reached for her reticule to give the little girl something extra.

The young girl held up her hand in refusal as Brittannia tried to press a coin into it. "No, ma'am, the gentleman already paid me and said there is more when I tell him you took the flowers."

Brittannia watched the young girl run down the corridor and out of sight as she brought her nose to the delicate red petals of the hibiscus. She found a note tucked into the middle of the bouquet and anxiously plucked it out to read.

Dear Miss Denning,
Mi pajaro de oro, I missed saying good night to you. I hope you will meet me for luncheon today at your hotel. I'll look forward to seeing you.
Sebastian Diaz

He had called her his "golden bird" again. She didn't care what Dain had said to her the previous night. She thought it sweet of Senor Diaz to send flowers and she would meet him for lunch, Dain Barclay be damned!

The lobby of the Royal Victoria was filled to capacity. Brittannia marveled at the array of the many different people as she descended the last flight of stairs. Handsome, well-dressed men escorted beautiful women who showed off the latest fashions from "Godey's Lady's Book." They stood seemingly engrossed in each other's company, their jewels flashing.

In contrast to this flamboyant display were young gentlemen, some seated others standing along the walls, dressed in somber colors. They all looked haggard and each held his own sad story in his eyes. Brittannia's heart went out to these poor souls. She didn't know what had brought them to Nassau, but she was sure it was that damn war. It wasn't the prosperous side of war they had seen, but the ugly, all too-real side.

She felt a guilt rise in her, for she had never known such tragedy.

"Senorita, you look upset. I hope I am not the cause." Sebastian Diaz smiled as he took her arm and led her to the dining room. There a waiter led them to a small table in the corner of the opulent room.

Sebastian ordered for them and Brittannia couldn't help but notice how handsome he looked. His suit of dark gray broadcloth, white embroidered waistcoat, and satin cravat enhanced his dark, good looks. Brittannia found herself relaxing in his presence. The melodious sound of his voice seemed to be for her alone and his many compliments were nothing less than sincere.

"I hope you plan to stay in Nassau," he said as they sipped their wine. "I feared you had left the island this morning and I would never see you again."

"And would that be so terrible, never seeing me again?" she asked. She was enjoying the constant attention he paid her. He treated her like a lady, not a young girl as Michael and not an easy conquest as did Dain.

"*Sí*, it would."

The waiter returned to the table and replaced the jellied consommé with plates of large fantail shrimp. Brittannia looked up from the table—and swallowed unchewed the bite of shrimp she had just put into her mouth. In the doorway of the dining room stood Dain, his powerful frame dwarfing the small waiter beside him. Brittannia was again struck by his tanned handsomeness, his strong, lean body. A tumble of ebony curls grazed his brow, the gold highlights showing, and Brittannia found herself wishing she were beside him.

She shook her head as if to push such thoughts from her mind and turned her attention back to Sebastian.

"Is something the matter?" Sebastian asked as he too looked toward the entrance of the dining room. His dark eyes took on a dangerous look when he saw Dain. Before turning back to Brittannia, he masked his feelings and said, "I see Senora Rougeaux is here with Captain Barclay. They make a striking couple, do they not?" He nodded his head in the direction of Dain. He raised his glass to his lips, watching for Brittannia's reaction, then after a long sip of wine continued. "I hear they are seeing each other frequently. Esmée is known for her many affairs but some say this will be a lasting relationship."

His words had their desired effect. Brittannia looked back toward the door and saw Esmée, then turned her head abruptly away from the couple, her blond curls swinging from the swift movement. She drained the contents of her wineglass and gave Sebastian a dazzling smile as she asked for a refill.

"To what do we owe this sudden mood for celebration?" he asked as he quickly obliged to fill the proffered glass.

Brittannia brought her chin up. "Why, to my continued stay in Nassau and," she added as her gaze traveled to the table where Dain and Esmée were now seated, "to our newfound friendship."

Brittannia was growing bold. Seeing Dain and Esmée together had upset her more than she cared to admit. Had he noticed she was with Sebastian? What did he think? What did she care what he thought? She looked toward the tanned captain and gave him a bold stare. He looked up and their eyes locked. His stormy

54

look denounced her. Brittannia saw Esmée's hand reach across the table and rest upon Dain's muscular forearm. She also saw that Dain made no movement to stop the delicate, circular trail Esmée traced with silken fingers.

She took her gaze from him and returned it to her own table. Sebastian's eyes were upon her, black as a starless night and as full of its mystery. She shivered involuntarily. His piercing gaze seemed to penetrate her mind, searching its many recesses for the key to her thoughts, past and present.

She took another sip of wine wondering absently why she had a sudden urge to down the whole bottle. Dain was seated across the room with a beautiful woman, a woman who was world-wise and could offer a man that which he most secretly desired, a woman who was everything Brittannia was not. Brittannia was jealous and she hated the feeling but she could do nothing to stop it.

She cocked her bright head to one side and gave Sebastian a flirtatious grin. "So tell me, senor," she said, her voice light and coquettish, "how shall I fill my time now that I've decided to stay in Nassau for awhile?"

Sebastian leaned back in his chair and returned her flirtatious grin, a triumphant look in his black eyes.

Chapter 4

The bar room was smoke-filled and the smell of rum, sweat, and perfume hung heavy in the air. Drunken sailors and dockworkers called lustily for more drink while buxom, overly made-up women vied for their attention and any extra coin they might have. Most men leaned against the bar, others played toss-penny in one dimly lit side of the room.

Brittannia made her way through the crowded room and searched its corners for Michael Delving. She had gone to his office and was told he could be found at the Wooden Penny. Brittannia soon discovered the Wooden Penny was not a place a lady should enter. It was one of the many disreputable dives that lined Bay Street. But her need to speak with him urged her on and so, with a toss of her bright head, she had boldly entered.

"A few more days'n it'll be the dark of the moon and we can set out. Ya can be sure I'm lookin' forward to feel the roll of the ship beneath these feet of mine, for I'm no landlubber and I've nearly run out of money what with all these thievin' tavern owners and dockside whores!" said a heavyset man to her right. He had spoken so loudly Brittannia thought he had been addressing her, but when she turned his way he was not looking at her. Instead he was leering at the backside of a passing barmaid.

Brittannia felt a hand on her arm. She turned to look into the unsmiling brown eyes of Michael Delving. "Michael!" she exclaimed, "I've been looking for you."

"What are you doing here?" Michael tossed his head to one side and in that gesture succeeded in encompassing the entire room. "Here in such a place as this?"

"I came to talk with you."

"You could have gone to my office."

"I did and you weren't there. I was told you could be found here. Michael, please don't be angry with me. I need to discuss financial matters with you." She gave him a dazzling smile, then said, "Since we're here, would you treat me to a glass of wine?"

"I don't think they serve wine here," he said dishearteningly.

"I'll settle for rum," Brittannia said cheerily, ignoring the dour look on Michael's handsome face.

"You'll not have rum! I'll see if I can find you a decent glass of wine."

Brittannia smiled to herself as Michael escorted her to a small table in a far corner of the bar room. The smile quickly froze on her face when she saw who was seated at the table.

Captain Dain Barclay lounged lazily in his chair, sipping slowly from his tankard of ale and watching with heavy lids the couple approaching. He slowly rose to his full height as Brittannia and Michael reached the table. "Miss Denning, how nice to see you again." Dain pulled out one of the wooden chairs for her.

"Captain," she acknowledged with a slight nod of her head. He was the last person she wanted to be near, yet here he was and his very nearness was setting her pulse to racing. She could smell the musky scent of him; it was inviting, intoxicating, and she chided herself for finding it so.

"If you two will excuse me, I'm off in search of a glass of respectable wine," Michael said.

"Be sure they wipe the glass," Dain joked as Michael made his way through the rowdy crowd.

With Michael out of reach, Brittannia was at a loss for words and her stomach was full of butterflies. She felt very ill at ease sitting beside Dain. She started to stand but the sound of his voice stopped her.

"Miss Denning, I want to apologize for my behavior at Michael's home the other evening. I didn't mean to embarrass you."

She looked across the worn table into his gray eyes. They seemed not to look as stormy in this dim lighting, not as storm-gray as she remembered. They were a very light gray, almost hidden by a tumble of dark curls. Even though she despised the man for his casual treatment of her she had to quell the urge to reach across the table and push the unruly tresses into place.

"I'd rather not speak of our last encounter, Captain," she said, still not certain she should stay seated across from the man who held far too much power over her senses whether he realized it or not. She guessed he probably did realize the power he had over her and the thought unnerved her even further.

"I can almost see the wheels of your mind spinning behind that beautiful face of yours, Miss Denning. Are you trying to decide whether or not to forgive me? Or is it you don't really want to forget our last . . . what did you call it, encounter?"

She felt her anger rise, which proved to her again that she was quick to *any* emotion around this arrogant man. "I'm quite certain I want to forget our—the last time I saw you," she said with determination. "As to accepting your apology, Captain, I haven't yet decided. You are forever taking steps to cause my ire."

He laughed good-naturedly. "Yes, I guess I am, but if I promise to be nothing but a gentleman in the future, can you find it in your heart to forgive me?"

He was making light of the situation now, and although she tried to suppress it, a slight smile touched her lips. She said, "I accept your apology, Captain, but only as long as you keep your promise."

"Good." He returned the smile, raising his mug as if in toast to her. He took a deep drink of his ale, then set the heavy tankard down with a thud on the rough-hewn surface of the table.

Brittannia watched him, her pulse slowing to a normal pace. His eyes found hers and there was a long silence between them that soon became uncomfortable for her. "It will soon be dark enough to make a trip to the States," she said finally, remembering the conversation she had so recently overheard. "Are you planning to do so?"

"I wouldn't miss a run."

She knew very little of running the blockade. "Why do you do it? Why do you run the blockade and risk your life? I've read that any captain or pilot that is captured is considered too valuable to be exchanged and so they remain in Northern prisons. Aren't you afraid?"

He paused before answering her, as if he were pondering the question for the first time. "Yes, the consequences are frightening, but there is an unequaled excitement in running the blockade, to know you have helped clothe, feed, or doctor a few Southern men." His gray eyes became storm-gray and he took another drink, emptying the tankard.

She could sense she had hit a raw nerve and she wondered what his real reason was for running the blockade.

Michael returned to the table with a glass of wine in hand. "It took all of my charm to get this for you, I hope you enjoy it," he said, taking a seat to her right. "So tell me, Brit, what is it you wanted to talk with me about?"

"Actually, I'm low on funds. I didn't bring enough with me. I was hoping you could see to that for me."

"No sooner said than done. I should have taken care of that as soon as you arrived. For the past few days Dain and I have been seeing to the loading of the *Airlee*. It should be another profitable run for us all, eh, Dain?" Michael held his glass up to toast the captain.

Dain smiled to his friend, waiting patiently for a voluptuous barmaid to refill his tankard. She smiled saucily at him, giving her riotous brown curls a toss as she rubbed one shapely thigh by his arm. Dain seemed impervious to her bold flirtation and finally she gave a dejected snort as she moved on to the next table.

"Yes, it should be profitable," Dain answered. "Along with the meat, we've loaded up with more profitable and less bulky cargoes such as medicines, liquor, and silks. Once in Wilmington we'll stack the cotton wherever we can."

Brittannia was fascinated by him. He seemed not to fear the Federal men-of-war he knew were stationed off the southern coast filled with ammunitions and swiveling guns, ready to blow a gaping hole in the lead-colored hull of the *Airlee*. She admired his determination to get supplies to the southern men. She was glad to hear he would be carrying meat on this trip, for she knew it was badly needed on the front line. Most runners would let the meat rot on the wharves and instead choose more profitable cargoes.

"One of these days I want to make a run with you aboard the *Airlee*," Michael said, his brown eyes full of anticipation. "But right now I've too much work here in Nassau." He pulled an elegant gold chain watch out of his vest pocket checking the time and then replacing it as he hurriedly downed the rest of his ale. "Speaking of work, I've got to get back to the office."

He stood and turned to Brittannia. "Have all your bills sent to me, I'll see to them." He flipped a gold eagle onto the crude table; it rolled on its edge, stopping as it came in contact with Dain's tankard. "Thanks for the drinks, ol' friend. If I don't see you again before the run, I wish you Godspeed."

Brittannia watched Michael's retreating back as long as was possible, but he was soon lost in the throng of people. She turned her attention reluctantly back to the table. Dain's eyes were upon her, full of male appreciation. She absently smoothed one sleeve of her dress, all the while feeling his gaze upon her.

"Would you join me for dinner this evening?" he said.

"Certainly not," she replied, shocked. "How could I?"

"I see. You're dining with someone else," he said smoothly. "I'm told Sebastian can be very charming—to women."

"Captain Barclay," she spluttered. "I am not planning to dine alone with Sebastian Diaz or with anyone else. It wouldn't be seemly."

"Seemly?" One dark eyebrow shot up. "I'm afraid, Miss Denning, you will discover that very little is 'seemly' here in Nassau. You are no longer in London. I would advise you to both take advantage of that fact—and be wary of it."

"Spare me your advice," Brittannia retorted. "I assure you, I'm well aware of the differences between London and Nassau. It's one of the reasons I came here without a chaperone. I'm perfectly capable of taking care of myself."

"Then dine with me tonight." He leaned forward and took one of her hands in his. "Please."

Brittannia's brilliant turquoise eyes went wide. "But—but what would people say?" she said, futilely tugging at her hand.

Dain threw back his head and laughed.

Her cheeks turned pink. "Why are you laughing?" she demanded.

"You're delightful."

"I don't know what you mean," she returned crisply.

"No, I don't suppose you do." He was still grinning, his teeth white against his tanned skin. "What would you say if I told you that here in Nassau, when men and women want to dine together they do exactly that and no one cares one way or the other about it?"

"Well, I . . ." She lowered her eyes. "I . . ."

"And what would you say," he went on inexorably,

"if I told you that you won't find a finer meal in all of Nassau than you will in my home."

"Well . . . I—"

"And if I gave you my word of honor that your reputation will be none the worse for wear—er, none the worse on the morrow."

It was Brittannia's turn to laugh. "Well, then I would say I had better accept your offer and make the best of it!"

Later that day, as the sun was making a brilliant exit, Brittannia nervously let Dain lead her to the dining room of his elegant Georgian home on Queen Street. The ceiling of the dining room was very high and was of white plaster, the walls were paneled in a deep rich wood, the drapes and carpet of warm, mellow tones. The chairs, table, and other furniture were definitely Chippendale. The total effect was very grand, yet not intimidating.

"Would you care for a glass of champagne before we dine?" asked Dain as he motioned to his manservant. He pulled out a high-backed chair for Brittannia and the intricately carved scrollwork of it gleamed in the gaslight.

"Yes, thank you," she replied.

Dain expertly uncorked the quickly supplied bottle of champagne, the frothy bubbles spilling over the sides as he tipped it to Brittannia's proffered glass.

He looked very handsome in his top coat of dove gray and matching trousers. His dark curls were brushed back from his face, revealing finely chiseled features that were softened by the huge candelabrum that had been strategically placed in the middle of the elegantly laid table.

He leaned back in his chair, the movement one of leisurely grace. "You look very beautiful this evening, Brittannia."

He had used her given name, making it sound like the name of a goddess; light and golden. She did not remind him that she'd rather he called her Miss Denning. Tonight he could call her what he would. "Thank you," she murmured, all too aware of his handsomeness, the clean smell of him.

"You know," he said, pushing his chair away from the elegant table, "I'm really not in the mood to sit indoors and eat a large meal. Would you care to walk along the beach? I could order a basket packed with food and drink and we could take it with us."

Brittannia smiled. "Yes, let's."

"Good," he replied, and within the span of a few minutes she found herself walking along a darkened shore of Nassau on the arm of Captain Dain Barclay.

The moon was almost nonexistent, only the dull, half-seeable outline of the shore kept them from walking into the cool water. A breeze, borne out at sea, blew across them, cooling their warm skin, ruffling their hair and blowing Brittannia's white silk skirts about her ankles.

"Calming, isn't it?" he asked as he took her arm and placed it in the crook of his.

"Yes, wonderfully."

"There's a small hut up here to our right," he said as he guided her away from the frothy waves of the ocean toward a group of palm trees.

A small voice inside her warned to steer away from

65

the secluded hut that looked incredibly small against the huge, towering palms. But she kept her pace steady, keeping up with the virile captain.

"I sometimes sleep out here before a run when I'm too worked up to sleep in the opulence of my bedroom," he explained as he pushed the thatched door of the hut open.

The one-room hut was totally dark until he lit a gaslamp with one quick strike of a match. The yellowish, golden light revealed a feathered mattress with light coverlets upon it and a small crudely made table beside it. Nothing else adorned the small space. It was small and cozy and surprisingly tempting to Brittannia. He motioned for her to sit upon the makeshift bed and she did so without reserve, surprising not only herself but Dain as well.

"This is cozy," she said, bouncing once on the thick mattress then settling and smoothing her skirts about her.

He set the basket upon the rough table and pulled out a bottle of champagne. As he poured full two long-stemmed glasses, also procured from the large basket, she said, "I feel honored to be the first person you've brought here." She took the glass he offered and sipped the cool liquid while looking into his dark features.

The burning gaslamp threw soft shadows over his face and she felt beautiful beneath his close scrutiny. His storm-gray eyes didn't leave her face as he sipped the wine and sat beside her on the makeshift bed.

Suddenly, with his nearness and the realization of where she had let him lead her, Brittannia was uneasy. The hand that was now reaching up to stroke her hair made her acutely aware of her innocence.

"Gorgeous," he murmured as he ran his fingers through her hair, pulling out some of the pins.

She swallowed once as she moved away from him, out of his reach. She had gone too far this time. How was she to extricate herself from this situation? It was quite clear what he intended: the makeshift bed, the champagne. He intended to have his way with her—as he would with any willing, common harlot!

"I've upset you," he said into her silence.

She was nervous now; the room was too small, the champagne fuzzing her confused mind. "No," she tried to reassure him . . . or was it herself she was trying to reassure? She didn't know. "I—I should not have come here tonight, Captain."

He leaned back against the wall of the hut, his wine-glass in hand. His movements resembled those of a lazy panther and his ease only increased Brittannia's discomfort. "Call me Dain," he insisted. "No formalities tonight, Brittannia."

"I shouldn't be here," she repeated.

He emptied the contents of the fragile glass within his hand, then said huskily, "You want to be here, Brittannia. We both do."

There, he had done it again! He had succeeded in bringing her quick anger to the surface! She abruptly stood, roughly placing her half-full glass on the crude table. She had no intention of staying one minute longer in his company. She heard his laugh but she did not see his arm that snaked out to pull her to him, and before she could take a step toward the door, he had her elbow in a tight grip and was pulling her down upon the bed.

"Not so fast, Brittannia," he said, pulling her body

back and down, fitting it perfectly across his lap. His eyes were dove-soft as he looked down into her angry, flashing ones and he laughed at her struggles and the defiant pout she put to her lips. "Now tell me, wildcat, what is it you fear? Me? Or your own desires?"

At his words Brittannia struggled all the more, her hands pushing at his chest, and her legs beneath her many silk skirts kicked wildly. "Let me go!" she fairly screamed. "I've no more to say to you!"

He held her fast. "No," he said, laughing. "We have a lot to say, for you seem to think *I* think you are a loose woman."

She had a mind to sink her teeth into his arm but she deemed it too unladylike, not that being sprawled across his lap *wasn't* unladylike but that was nothing she could, at the moment, control. After long moments of struggling in his embrace, she ceased her movements and tried to calm herself, her breath coming in ragged gasps. "Well, that *is* what you think of me, isn't it?" she demanded, feeling terribly vulnerable in his arms. Her dress of white moiré silk was cut shockingly low—her breasts were very nearly about to burst from it as his hold on her was pulling the fabric down.

"I think that beneath that adorably innocent exterior you are a passionate woman—but only with me."

She stared incredulously at him, their faces only inches apart. "Don't flatter yourself," she said between clenched teeth, reminding herself not to struggle, for if she did she would regret it.

"Admit it, wildcat, you came here tonight secretly hoping I would make love to you."

She wanted nothing more than to rake her nails across his too-handsome, arrogant face. "And *you* brought me here hoping to make love to me!"

A rakish smile lit his features. "I did," he confessed. "And I still plan to do so."

"Oh no!" she rallied, pushing hard at his chest and squirming from his tight hold. It no longer mattered if the movement exposed her breasts, for if she stayed one minute longer in his embrace he would accomplish the task himself. "You've misjudged me, Captain," she said in a wild voice as she scurried from the makeshift bed and backed up against the far wall of the small hut. She was panting from her efforts as she tugged up her bodice and her eyes burned brightly like two blue flames. "I'm not what you think me."

"And what is that, lovely lady? A whore?"

She grimaced at the very word.

With quick movements he was up and off the makeshift bed, standing only inches from her, his powerful frame blocking any way of escape. There was a tenderness in his gray eyes as he looked down at her, and something else as well. Desire. When he spoke his voice was a husky caress, and although she willed the feeling away, that huskiness played along her sensitive skin. "Your response to our first kiss aboard the *Airlee* would tell me you are. So also would your eager compliance in Michael's garden. But truly, Brittannia, I don't think you've ever known a man." He put warm fingers beneath her chin and tilted her face up toward his own. "This night I'll take you to womanhood—if you let me."

Brittannia's knees felt weak and her head was swimming from her careening emotions. Where was her anger going? It was slipping quickly away while strange sensations were filling her body, making her weak and wanting the man before her. *No.* She refused to succumb to his charms. But in the next instant, as his lips sought hers and his arms entwined around her small frame and pulled her close, she felt her resolve melt away and she knew she could not resist this man. She felt her body lean against his in quivering response to his ardent kiss and when her breasts were crushed to his hard chest his hands traveled up her back and began to undo the many hooks of her gown.

Even though her body had weakened, her mind fought against this weakness and with his gentle undoing of her hooks, the mind won the tough battle. Her eyes flew open as she pushed against his chest. "Please," she said in a ragged whisper. She wouldn't admit it to herself but she actually didn't trust herself to be near him any longer, for she wasn't too sure she would be able to say no to his next advance. She turned to walk away but even as she made the movements, Dain was in front of her, blocking her way. "Get out of my way," she demanded in a flat voice.

He shook his head, a lock of dark hair falling handsomely across his brow making him look more virile than any man had a right to look. "I want you, Brittannia. I warn you: I'm not a patient man."

She had had enough of his arrogance. "Perhaps you'll find, Captain Barclay," she said icily, "that I'm a woman worth waiting for." Picking up her voluminous skirts, she attempted to brush regally by him.

Immediately she regretted her words. For with a swift movement he reached one strong arm out and spun her toward him, roughly pulling her lithe body against his lean frame.

"Don't play the coquette with me," he said harshly.

"You're not in London anymore and I'm not one of your fawning beaux." With that he crushed her tender lips with a ruthless kiss.

Brittannia's gasp was drowned beneath his assault and she struggled against him holding her mouth tight against his probing tongue. His kiss was fury unleashed and it left her breathless and weak. His hands were at her back, tearing at the hooks that kept her bodice together while his knee thrust between her thighs, pushing against her skirts. Her struggles continued as his tongue finally pushed past her bruised and swollen lips and when it delved deep into the moist recesses of her mouth she felt her head spin and involuntarily she leaned against him for support. He took her gesture as one of compliance and his arms tightened about her causing her to moan when she felt her breasts meet with his muscular chest.

When he broke the hungry kiss it was only to blaze a burning trail of kisses to the shell of her ear. "Admit it, Brittannia, you want me as badly as I want you," he demanded, his voice hoarse from throbbing desire.

"No," she breathed weakly. Still his kisses persisted and she felt her bodice go slack as her last hook was undone. Her mind was in a total state of confusion and her body was boiling within, fires burning in places where she had never before experienced sensation. Of their own, her lips moved and formed one word; yes. It was part moan, part plea, and when Dain demanded she repeat it, she fairly gasped, "Yes, yes . . . damn you!"

He loosened his hold on her and while peering into her turquoise eyes, thrilling her with the evidence of appreciation shown in those stormy depths, he pulled the gown from her shoulders, peeling the silky material from her ripe, young body. Brittannia was impatient, her skin hot from wanting, and she helped him by shrugging out of the silken mass. There was still more to be unfastened and Dain stood in front of her unfastening, unhooking, and placing moist kisses on her warm skin. Brittannia felt dizzy with the first awakenings of desire and now that she was naked, she wanted him naked also. Boldly, with trembling fingers, she worked his top coat over his broad shoulders and set to the enjoyable task of undoing the many buttons of his silk shirt. She pushed the thin material away to reveal his deeply tanned chest, and with a daringness that surprised and frightened her, she ran her fingers through the curling hair and planted soft kisses upon it. He was beautiful, warm and hard; and she desired him.

His hands caressed the curve of her bare back, then moved lower to cup her buttocks. He gave a low moan as he took a step back and quickly doffed his remaining garments. He stood before her like a proud animal, his male hardness causing exciting ripples through Brittannia's body. The lamplight threw soft shadows on the contoured planes of his athlete's body and as he stepped near to her she felt her heart thrill and her blood rush through her veins. He swooped her naked body into his arms and laid her gently on the makeshift bed coming quickly to her side and pulling her into his embrace.

"So beautiful," he murmured as he nuzzled the soft skin of her slender neck. He brought his lips to hers and when they touched worlds collided, crashing with great intensity. She felt the force, welcomed it, and searched for more. His tongue pushed past her moist lips and she met it with her own, touching, tasting, and enjoying. She was entrapped by her own passionate nature and all reason was gone to her. All she knew, all she wanted to know, was the feel of his body next to hers, the tickle of his chest hairs on her breasts, the hard maleness of him that even now stabbed at the soft skin of her thighs.

He worked his mouth down to her bared breasts and she moaned with pleasure as he took one taut nipple between his teeth and gently nipped it. He kneaded the soft flesh of her full bosom, teasing her with his tongue until her nipples rose to pink, swollen peaks. His mouth moved lower still, blazing a fiery trail over her flat stomach, down to her rounded hips, between her shapely thighs until he found the treasure hidden by the golden triangle between her legs. She gasped as she felt his moist kisses, his probing tongue, and when he gently pushed her legs further apart, she allowed it, giving herself to him, letting him pleasure her as she had never imagined being pleasured.

After long exquisite moments she pulled his dark head toward her. She wanted his mouth on hers, wanted his body on top of her. He brought his mouth down with an urgency and he kissed her passionately, releasing a new, surging desire within her. She tasted herself on his lips, those full sensuous lips that teased her, enticed her, pleased her. She pressed her nakedness against him and felt her heart tremor when she heard the small moan escape him.

Brittannia had never dreamed she could feel this way, so very wanton, so very desirable in the arms of a man she barely knew . . . a man who had labeled her a whore. Yet, here she was, succumbing to the carnal desires that had been awakened in her, giving all when just moments before she had been about to walk out of the small hut. With each dip and thrust of his tongue she felt reality slip away and became aware only of the gentle pressure, the soft fullness and moistness of his lips. No, she could not leave. Her fate was sealed. This night, the moon above would see her made a woman, and Dain Barclay was the man who would receive every charm she possessed.

He moved over her, pushing her thighs apart with one leg and then settling on top of her his fingers entwining in her hair, pulling out the few pins that still remained. He smiled down into her face, his eyes glittering darkly, full of passion. Slowly he brought his mouth to hers, ravishing, taking, and eventually giving. His roughness excited her—as it had when she first met him—and when she felt his throbbing manhood press against the softness between her thighs, she opened herself to him unable to do anything else. She craved his touch, his kiss . . . his penetration. He entered her swiftly, pulsating inside of her. Though she cried out at the first sweet pain of her shedding virginity, it was soon forgotten. He moved rhythmically within her and she writhed to that same, unheard ancient tune. She strived to meet every driving motion of his warm body, every kiss upon her throat and breasts and the soft murmurings he whispered, as her body rolled over and over in tumultuous rapture. She was moving with him, their bodies melding as one as they each strove for that faraway peak. She was spiraling upward, soaring to some unknown pinnacle. She arched and writhed under his arduous assault, giving as well as taking, until suddenly she shuddered as a great force gripped her and brought with it unequaled pleasure. Within her, she felt the greatness of his manhood, felt it throb as her tender flesh surrounded it. She felt him shudder, fill her, and slowly, oh so slowly she drifted back to earth.

It had all happened so quickly. She hadn't meant to let things get this far. Yet here she was, lying naked beneath the captain of her ship, her virginity a thing of the past. Her lids felt heavy, and her mind did not want to dwell on what she had just let transpire. She let her eyes close, let her drowsiness overtake her, his flesh still inside her. Perhaps when she awoke she would learn it had all been a dream . . . a very enjoyable dream, but still only a dream . . .

She awoke with a start, momentarily forgetting where she was but the roaring of the distant water and the makeshift bed beneath her brought reality abruptly back. She groaned as memories of the night before came rushing back. Dain was not beside her and she was glad. Quickly she got up and hastily drew on her garments wanting to get far away from the hut. Through the open door she could see him near the water's edge. He stood with his back toward her and from her position he looked small but strong standing alone on the endless stretch of beach, looking toward the sea. Perhaps if she was quick about it she could get away without his noticing it. She bent down to retrieve her slippers, grimacing as she had to lift Dain's top coat to get at them. Had she actually *helped* him undress?!

"Good morning." His voice was husky, coming from behind her.

She jumped from fright and dropped his topcoat as if

it were hot flame, turning toward him as the color climbed high on her cheeks. "Good morning," she blurted, not knowing what one should say in a situation such as this. Her embarrassment was furthered by the fact he hadn't bothered to put on his shirt. He wore only his trousers, which fit him like a gray shadow, and his chest rose majestically up from his tapered waist and muscle-rippled stomach. His hair was tousled, boyishly so, and the grin on his face reminded her of a cat that had gotten away with licking the cream. He looked incredibly smug, as if he had won the game. He had! At that thought she became irritated. "The least you can do is put some clothes on!" she snapped as she sat on the bed and jammed first one slipper and then the other on.

He leaned casually against the doorjamb, folding his arms across his tanned chest. "I suppose in this morning light the events of last night seem obscene and undignified."

Her slippers now on, she stood, smoothing her crumpled skirts. "I don't wish to speak of last night, Captain."

"And I, Brittannia, never want to forget last night. You're very good, you know, just think what a little prac—"

She brought her hands over her ears closing her eyes momentarily as she tried to keep her anger in check. He stopped his words but his laugh rang in her head. She took her hands from her ears, placing them squarely on her hips. "Last night was a mistake."

"If that was a mistake it was well worth the making."

"You seduced me."

"Did I? And here I'd been thinking it was you who

had seduced me!"

"You infuriate me!" she declared, blushing crimson. She turned from him to find her wrap.

"And you excite me beyond reason." He watched her for a moment, a smile playing on his mouth. "I've something for you," he finally said.

Wrap in hand, Brittannia gave a toss to her head, her hair flying over her shoulders with the gesture. "Payment for my services?" she asked coldly.

He shook his head. "Just something I want you to have." He dug deep into his trousers pocket and when he brought his tanned hand back out it was clenched tight into a fist. "I leave later today on a run to the States. In wartime, one never plans tomorrows so I'll give this to you today."

"Whatever it is I don't want it," Brittannia said.

He took a step toward her, the morning light behind him leaving his face in dark contrast. "Please," he said, taking her hand in his and pressing his gift into her palm. "It belonged to my mother."

Brittannia opened her palm and looked at the delicate gold chain with locket he had placed there. Grudgingly she said, "It's beautiful—but I can't accept it."

She held her hand out to him, but he shook his head. "Keep it . . . at least until I return. Then I'll have a gentlemanly reason for seeking you out."

"I want no reason for you to seek me," she replied, hand still outstretched.

Ignoring her, he reached for his shirt, shrugging easily into the silky material and quickly buttoning the front of it. Waves lapped the distant shore, birds overhead squawked, and the breeze rustled the leaves of the palms outside the hut, and still Brittannia stood there, her mind in turmoil. Why was it this man could always best her? Why did she always back down? He slung his topcoat over his arm, extending his other arm to her.

"Shall we go?" he asked, as if they were leaving for the theater.

She brushed by him and out the door, totally ignoring the arm he extended. She heard his laugh as he caught up to her and took hold of her elbow anyway.

Dain escorted Brittannia back to her room at the Royal Victoria Hotel and as he continued on to his home on Queen Street, he felt a great sadness to be leaving her so soon after discovering her. She intrigued him and he enjoyed her show of struggling against their passion. But he was sure of his skill of bringing the *Airlee* and its crew back to Nassau in one piece. Only seven days round-trip and he would be back to Brittannia.

He entered his home, passing quickly through the central hall. He took the wide stairs two at a time, his hands barely skimming the top of the polished, elaborately turned balustrade. His long strides took him through the high-ceilinged central hall of the second story and he shed his gray topcoat and unbuttoned his white silk shirt as he went.

His thoughts were of a turquoise-eyed goddess with hair the color of bright sunshine. So engrossed was he with his mental image of Brittannia that he did not notice the naked figure lying in a seductive pose upon his huge, four-poster bed.

"*Chérie,* it is about time you got here!" Esmée

Rougeaux said in a husky voice.

Dain looked up from the task of undoing his trousers. His shirt, now totally open, exposed the rippled muscles of his taut stomach. Esmée longed to run her long-nailed fingers across that smooth surface.

Dain raised one dark eyebrow, his gray eyes taking in the scene before him. "What are you doing here—no, never mind that. Just get dressed and get out!" he commanded in a steely tone as he shrugged off his silk shirt, tossing it carelessly to the floor.

Esmée ignored his command and fluffed the pillows up behind her, leaning back into their feathery softness. "So, do tell which lucky little creature had you warm her bed last night."

"What I do is none of your affair," Dain said as he stepped out of his gray trousers, leaving them in a crumpled heap. He grabbed another pair of gray trousers that were lying neatly across a chair. He quickly donned them, ignoring the raven-haired woman in his bed.

"Please, Dain, we have time before the tide is high. Won't you take me in your arms?" she asked, her green eyes alive and bright.

"I haven't the time and if I did, it wouldn't be you I'd take in my arms."

His words were cruel and she felt the familiar feeling of jealousy knotting in the pit of her stomach.

"Mon Dieu!" she nearly screamed. "Who *IS* she?"

Dain shook his head; he did not want to be witness to one of Esmée's blind jealous rages. "I haven't got time for this," he said and left the room.

"NOOOOO!" she yelled, flinging herself off the bed, dragging a sheet as she ran after his retreating back.

"It's that little blond ninny, the one at Delving's party, isn't it?" she screeched, wrapping the sheet around her body toga-style as she ran down the wide stairs after him.

He wanted to strike her for calling Brittannia a "little ninny," but he thought better of it. "I hope you're in a better mood when next we meet," he said as he opened the door and left, leaving a fuming Esmée standing in his front hall clad in nothing more than one of his silk sheets.

"Damn you, Dain Barclay! I hope the Federals get you!" she yelled to him and he smiled to himself, wondering where her French accent had gone.

Esmée stood at the door long after Dain had gone. She was trying to think of a plan to get Brittannia out of her way, for she was sure Brittannia Denning was the one Dain had referred to.

She looked up from her thoughts to see none other than Brittannia making her way toward the house. Esmée quickly shut the door, then thinking better of it, left it open a few inches and scurried back upstairs, a smug smile playing across her full, red lips.

Chapter 5

Not until she'd been alone in her rooms at the Royal Victoria had Brittannia looked closely at the locket Dain had given her. She was mad at herself for accepting it. She should have thrown it back in his arrogant face! She lifted the delicate chain from her palm trying to look indifferently at the heart that dangled from it.

With gentle fingers she pried the locket open and there, in a tiny daguerreotype, was Dain. A younger Dain by a number of years on one side and, on the other, Dain as she knew him now: dashing, smugly handsome with a smile playing across his lips. Just what she needed—a constant reminder of the man! She impatiently snapped the locket back together.

After a quick change of clothes and an even quicker repinning of her hair, she left the hotel for Dain's home. She had no intention of keeping his locket and she wanted to make it clear once and for all that she wanted nothing more to do with him!

She approached the home without a bit of timidity, boldly taking the brass knocker in hand, ready to push it against the great door, but seeing it was ajar she let go of the knocker and stepped into the huge hallway.

"Captain," she called. She heard the small rustling sound on the second story and she followed that sound, not caring if she had to step into his bedchambers.

Esmée heard the lilting voice of Brittannia and found herself wanting to claw the girl's eyes out. She suppressed the urge and instead continued rustling a few things about to lure Brittannia upstairs to Dain's bedchamber. When she heard Brittannia's light footsteps on the stairs, she jumped into Dain's already crumpled bed, pulling the thick covers around her slender neck and pretending to sleep.

"Captain, I've come to return—" Brittannia's words caught in her throat when she saw Esmée lounging in Dain's bed.

"Chérie, is that you? I miss your warm body against mine," Esmée said in a husky voice, opening her eyes as if awakening from a peaceful nap.

Brittannia looked around the room, taking in Dain's carelessly thrown silk shirt and gray trousers, the same garments he had worn the previous night. She noticed how haphazardly they had been tossed and her heart was wrenched from its place as her stomach knotted with the painful realization of what had transpired.

"Brittannia, what are you doing here? I thought you were Dain coming back for more," Esmée said with a wink. She sat up and let the covers fall from her body, exposing her full, rounded breasts.

Brittannia felt her whole world come crashing in around her. Dain had left her at the hotel an hour ago! Was she so lacking that he had to find pleasure in the arms of Esmée? Esmée who had warmed so many beds?

Brittannia felt a complete fool. More than that, she felt used—cheapened. She looked once more to the raven-haired woman and had to quell the feline urge to spit in her face. But in that same instant she realized Esmée could not have known what had transpired between Dain and her. No, Esmée was not to blame. It was Dain who was at fault.

"I'm sorry," Brittannia said in a barely audible whisper. Turning, she left the room and closed the door softly behind her.

"Good day and good riddance!" Esmée said as she snuggled deeper into Dain's bed, reveling in the inviting smell of him that still lingered there.

Brittannia angrily made her way to her hotel room, her heels clicking as she walked with a hurried gait. How could she have been so stupid? How could she have let that . . . that, louse use her as he did? Her humiliation was complete. Oh, how Dain Barclay must deem himself the handsome stud! He was probably even now regaling his crew with stories of his sex-filled night.

She picked up her hand mirror and threw it at the far wall, enjoying the sound of the glass smashing into tiny pieces. "Damn you, Dain Barclay!" she yelled into the room. Her shoulders slumped. She was confused. Why should she care if Dain had made love to another woman, she wanted nothing more to do with the man. But she *did* care, and it wasn't just the fact he had been with Esmée so soon after being with her—it was the thought of him doing the same intimate things he had done to her! Visions of the two sprang before her eyes and she groaned.

Dain Barclay meant nothing to her, she told herself, nothing at all. She had made a mistake in letting him have his way with her and now she must live with that mistake. She stood then, determined to put thoughts of the past night from her mind. But even as she tried, images of their lovemaking pushed into her mind and her traitorous body tingled again with remembrance of Dain Barclay's touch.

Brittannia dressed carefully that evening. She ignored the buzz of commotion around her as she descended to the lobby of the Royal Victoria, and more importantly ignored the warmth of the locket that hung about her neck. Why she had worn it, she did not know, only she had felt compelled to put it on. She told herself it was in the unlikely event she saw Dain and then she would have the pleasure of throwing it in his face.

Unfortunately Dain was already on his way to the Carolinas, risking his life to help the Southern men and to line his pockets. All the better to forget him now, while he is out of sight, she thought.

"Excuse me, Miss Denning?"

Brittannia looked up from her reverie to see a tall, brown-haired man staring down at her. His face was covered with a growth of hair, badly in need of a trim. His corduroy trousers were a faded orange and his leather jerkin was spattered with bits of dried mud. She had never seen him before and couldn't imagine how he had come to learn her name.

"You are Miss Denning?" he asked when she did

not speak.

"Yes, I am," she replied hesitantly. "Who are you?"

"Would you come with me, please?"

"Why?"

The man looked about him as if he were nervous, brushing a brown wave of hair from his high forehead. "There has been an accident, Miss Denning."

Brittannia felt her heart tremor. "An accident? What kind of accident? Who has been hurt?" she asked, leaning toward the man, her eyes large with worry.

The man's eyes continued to dart around the lobby. "Mr. Delving has been hurt and has asked that you come to him."

"Michael?" she asked. "Where is he? What has happened to him?"

"Please, Miss Denning, there is no real cause for alarm. Mr. Delving is being treated. Follow me."

Brittannia couldn't help but be caught up in a tide of worry. Michael was hurt and asking for her! To each other they were family. "What has happened?" she asked as the man led her from the lobby of the Royal Victoria onto the veranda and then through the maze of hedges to Parliament Street.

He didn't answer. He kept his gaze fixed straight ahead as he pulled her alongside him with a quick stride. He helped her into the awaiting, rust-colored carriage and, slamming the door, yelled to the driver, "Hurry, man!"

"Sir, you must tell me what has happened to Michael!"

"Sit back and keep yer mouth shut!"

Brittannia felt her blood run cold. The carriage moved at a rapid pace along the darkening streets of

85

Nassau. She could hear the sound of the horses' hooves hitting the road, could hear the creak of the conveyance as it was pulled at a breakneck pace down Parliament Street.

"Who are you?" she demanded as she pressed back against the cool leather of the cushion behind her. "Where are you taking me?"

The young man smiled. It was a slow, lecherous smile; one that turned her stomach. "Finally caught on, uh, miss?" he asked.

Why hadn't she been able to hear the coarseness of his voice before? The sound of it now filled the small interior of the carriage and it frightened her. "There is nothing wrong with Michael, is there?"

The man chuckled as he drew out from his shirt-front a bottle filled with a clear liquid. He uncorked the top and took a long drink. After an audible, "Ahh," he said, "I don't know who the hell Michael Delving is and I don't rightly care!" He laughed then as if it were all some great joke worth the retelling.

"Stop this carriage!" Brittannia demanded, her heart hammering with fear against her ribs.

The man plopped his feet onto the cushion beside her and smiled. "Soon enough. Until then, keep yer mouth shut."

Brittannia looked to the door of the carriage, considering jumping out of the moving conveyance if she could, but his long legs barred her way. With a quick, jarring motion, the carriage came to a grinding halt and Brittannia was flung across to the opposite cushion in front of her. Her captor pushed her back to her seat with one sweep of his arm, then with his other he swung the carriage door open. He jumped to the ground then turned to pull her out.

Brittannia stayed where she was, fear gripping her, making movement or thought impossible.

"C'mon, dearie, the senor is waiting."

The senor? Could he possibly mean Senor Diaz? She shrank back against the padded leather when his arm snaked in and grabbed her sleeve.

"Out with ya," he said as he pulled her out and onto the ground with one great yank. "Make a commotion and ye'll be sorry," he warned her then led her along the darkened street.

Beyond the dark buildings that loomed up beside her she could see the harbor and the dark outlines of the many ships that lay at anchor there. She could smell the familiar smells of the wharf and instinctively knew the man had brought her to one of the many warehouses along the quay.

She brought her slippered foot up and, with all her strength behind it, kicked the man sharply in the shin then pried herself loose from his hold and ran in the direction from where they'd come. She cursed herself for that wrong decision when she felt meaty arms go around her waist and spin her back toward the menacing warehouses.

"Got her, Johnson!"

"Let me go!" she screeched, hoping to get the attention of someone near. She felt a wet, heavy cloth descend upon her nose and mouth and though she tried to fight it, the heavy, black wings of oblivion overtook her.

She awoke to the feeling of a rolling ship and an

enormous headache. Her tongue was thick and dry in her mouth and she longed for some water. "Ohhh," she groaned as she partially sat up and leaned on one elbow.

"Brittannia, *querido,* are you all right?"

The form of Sebastian Diaz wavered in her sight until she could finally focus her eyes and look at him clearly. He was seated on a chair beside her. "Sebastian?" she asked, her mind still shrouded in misty oblivion.

"*Sí,* it is I. How do you feel?"

"Thirsty."

He smiled a knowing smile, then pressed a cup of cool water into her outstretched palm. She took a few great gulps of the water, then handed the cup back to Sebastian.

"What happened?" she asked.

Sebastian replaced the cup of water on a nearby table. "You do not remember?"

She shook her head.

"A few of my men came upon you, they said you were being abducted by some cutthroats. Not knowing what else to do they brought you on board the *Real Sangre.* I recognized you and ordered them to place you in my cabin." He reached for her hand and held it in a tight, reassuring grip. "Lucky for you my men were there."

Brittannia slowly raised to a sitting position, gingerly touching her fingers to her temples. Her head pounded unmercifully. "They told me Michael had been hurt. I believed them."

"Certainly you did, *querido,*" Sebastian said as he crossed the small space of the cabin and turned up the flame of the gaslamp. "You are a trusting person. We will be to Andros Island soon. I took the liberty of sending a man back to the Royal Victoria Hotel to pay for your board and bring your personal belongings to the *Real Sangre*. I don't want you in Nassau unescorted."

"Andros Island?"

"*Sí*, my home is there. I've sent word to Senor Delving that you have accompanied me so he will not be worried about you. You don't mind, do you, Brittannia? I felt it would be the safest place for you after what happened."

Brittannia hesitated. Andros Island? Why was he taking her away from Nassau without consulting her? She felt groggy, confused. "Sebastian, I—you don't have to do this. I'm quite capable of taking care of myself. There's no reason to take me to another island."

The dark Spaniard ran a forefinger thoughtfully along his black mustache. He was just about to speak when someone burst through the cabin door.

"Is she awake yet?" the gruff voice of the intruder wanted to know.

Sebastian immediately stood, his eyes going from Brittannia to the man in the doorway, back to Brittannia. Brittannia drew in a sharp breath at sight of the man. When she turned her eyes back to Sebastian they were full of shocked rage, for the man who had barged in wore faded orange trousers and a dirty leather jerkin. Brittannia waited for Sebastian's explanation as her insides churned with anger and fear. She was seeing Sebastian Diaz in a new light—seeing him as he actually was, and the discovery frightened her.

It was as if a grave mask had been pulled over Sebastian's features. Gone was his quick smile and the tenderness he'd worked so hard to make reach his unfeeling black eyes. He stood in the meager light looking as dangerous as a viper and when he spoke his voice had a hardness in it Brittannia had never heard.

"Leave, Johnson," he commanded of the intruder.

Brittannia did not take her eyes from Sebastian as she heard the man called Johnson make a hasty exit. "You know him," she stated flatly.

"Sí."

"He works for you."

He nodded.

Ignoring the ache in her head and the fear in the pit of her stomach, she pushed back the coverlet with a quick jerk of one arm. *"I demand that you take me back to Nassau."*

She was about to stand but Sebastian's arm reached out and held her in place. "No, *querido,"* he said. "You are staying with me."

"You're mad." Her voice was ice.

"I've wanted you since the first night I saw you, do you think I would let someone as beautiful as you slip by me?"

She pushed his arm away in disgust, then with a willful toss of her head, she said, "Take me back to Nassau. Now!"

He laughed then. A demonic sound of demented mirth.

She was through listening to him and with the quickness of a cat she sprang off the bunk and lunged for the portal. Her hand was on the latch and she very nearly had the door opened when all at once her head spun

90

violently and Sebastian's arm came around her waist, spinning her body back toward the bunk. She struggled in his hold but she was weak and her head felt light.

"I'll take you struggling or I'll take you submissive. Either way, I *will* have you," he whispered into her ear. And then with a vicious shove he pushed her onto the bunk. He was angry now, angry at her denial of him, and as he looked at her on the bunk, huddling into the corner like some scared animal, he felt his manhood rise. With her, he could always find pleasure whether or not she succumbed to him. She gave to him a feeling of power he enjoyed and suddenly it did not matter to him if she denied him. With the deliberate slowness of one sure of his plans, Sebastian fished into his overcoat pocket and withdrew a tiny bottle and then a handkerchief. "You shall rest now, *querido,*" he said coming toward the bunk.

Brittannia shook her head, a tumble of golden curls coming to cover her face from the quick movement. "No," she breathed, pulling her legs up to her body and placing her hands on either side of her body. She looked like a feline ready to pounce in any direction, and as Sebastian reached the side of the bunk and leaned toward her, she sprang.

He merely laughed as he reached one strong arm out and met her springing body with a vicious hit that sent her sprawling into the cabin wall. Her head hit the wood with a loud thump and before she could regain her balance Sebastian's hand was over her face, clamping the now-wet cloth over her mouth and nose, holding it there until she was forced to breathe. When she did, she felt a helpless feeling course through her, felt her arms and legs go slack, and suddenly her mind did not care whether she got up or not; it wanted only to rest as she went under the effects of the ether.

"Sleep, my beauty," Sebastian whispered, then quietly left the cabin.

When she awoke, she was alone in the cabin and the flame of the gaslamp was small, giving off very little light but still enough to bother her bleary eyes. Sitting up, she gingerly touched her temples, wincing from the pain that even that slight movement caused her. She closed her eyes momentarily, taking in a deep breath, then as she exhaled she opened them, hoping the room would not spin as much. It helped. Slowly she put her legs over the side of the bunk and tested standing up. When she felt she could walk without falling she started for the door.

What a fool she'd been! How could she have so misjudged Sebastian? She should have stayed away from him as Dain warned. But Dain had made her so angry and anything he said made her want to do the opposite. She had made a grave mistake in getting near Sebastian Diaz and she had yet to learn how grave this mistake was. She lifted the latch on the cabin door and stepped into the passageway. It was dark and she walked cautiously, not sure of her way. Once on deck, the night was pitch-black and the whole of the *Real Sangre* was but a dark shadow moving swiftly over the water. She dared not walk the deck for fear she might stumble and fall into the clutches of the waiting darkness; or worse yet Sebastian. She shivered involuntarily at the thought and pulled her light shawl more closely about her. A cool breeze touched her skin and with its coolness it brought the muffled sounds of low male voices. She could hear the steady pulse of the engines and could feel their vibration beneath her feet.

She thought of Dain then, sailing to Wilmington aboard the *Airlee*. Did he too feel closed in by the enveloping darkness? No, she thought, he probably welcomed it, for it was the darkness that cloaked his entry to the States. She sighed deeply, bringing her hand up her arm to her shoulder, resting her chin upon it. That was just one more thing that separated her from the gray-eyed captain; he found a friend in the dark when she could find only frightening thoughts. At thoughts of Dain she abruptly dropped her hands. Why was she thinking of him at a time like this?! She had a most pressing matter at hand and that was: how to escape Sebastian Diaz.

"Brittannia—"

She jumped at the sound of Sebastian's voice. She could barely discern his figure as he approached her. She wanted to turn and run from this madman approaching her but she had nowhere to turn to and she knew she must face him, must find some way to outwit him. With a deep indrawn breath she maintained her ground, putting up a brave front. "You can not keep me against my will, Sebastian," she informed him with a coolness she found hard to sustain.

He was beside her now, the whites of his eyes showing starkly against the darkness of the world. "You are like a wild bird, Brittannia. At first you will squawk loudly and flutter about your golden cage, but in time I am sure you will cease your willfulness and agree to things on my terms."

The man seemed utterly sure of himself, frighteningly so, and Brittannia's turquoise eyes narrowed with her deepening hatred of the man. "Never," she breathed, a look of disgust on her pretty features.

He laughed then, putting an arm about her slim shoulders. "I have ways, Brittannia, of making a woman want me."

Revulsion turning her stomach, she shrugged from beneath his arm. "Ways?" she mocked. "Must you rely on force to make a woman come to you, Sebastian?" Had there been more light, Brittannia would have seen the dangerous look that crossed the Spaniard's features, and known how delicate the ground she was treading. "You are but half a man, Sebastian Diaz, and you are wrong to think I will ever love you!"

Those were the wrong words to speak. Brittannia had only a second to get out of the way of the stinging blow Sebastian sent her, as it was she was not quick enough and the fist that slammed into her jaw brought with it a jarring force that put her to the deck, stunned.

She cried out from the pain of the blow and then cursed herself for the tears that immediately sprang into her eyes. She couldn't stop them; the pain was too great and her humiliation even greater.

"Get up!" he demanded in a metallic voice.

Brittannia wiped away her tears then tested her jaw, moving it back and forth, then opening and closing her mouth. Miraculously it was not broken. Slowly, she got to her feet, pushing a tumble of hair from flashing eyes that soon bore holes in the man opposite her. She now knew the feeling of true hatred.

"Get back to my cabin—wait for me there."

Her chin came up defiantly. "No," she replied, her voice dripping with enmity.

The Spaniard raised one black brow. "No?" he questioned then, his voice going mean, said, "You have no choice." He grabbed her roughly by the shoulders, intent on turning her body back toward the passageway, but Brittannia's arms came up, pushing his away and she turned and ran.

She ran blindly through the thick darkness, not knowing her way, not caring what she ran into as long as it was not the form of Sebastian Diaz. He was right behind her, yelling her name, but she blocked out the sound of his voice and concentrated on the sound of water hitting the hull of the ship. She would jump! She would jump into the dark waters and take her chances—anything would be better than staying in the clutches of the madman behind her.

Her slippered feet caught in a coil of rope. She fell forward, her arms flying out to break her fall. She felt a flood of relief when she realized she had fallen against the rail, her hands quickly grabbing hold of it as she lifted herself up. Just as quickly she disentangled her feet then lifted her skirts and climbed onto the wooden structure. The wind whipped her hair into her face and sent her skirts fluttering to one side as she stood, poised like a bird on a thin branch. She took in a breath, willing herself to jump, forcing herself not to think of what waited below; the wet, the darkness . . . the sharks.

She heard him behind her, heard him yell to crew members to grab her. No, she would not let Sebastian win! Without another thought she pushed off of the railing, aiming far away from the ship, going down into the water in a graceful arch. She felt her stomach flutter, heard the wind rush to fill her ears as she felt her body falling, falling. She could not tell whether her eyes were open or closed, for anything she did with them she was still met with total darkness, and when her body hit the water she felt herself go under, way under. The cold shocked her system and the feeling of nothing under her, nothing around her frightened her and she kicked her legs and thrashed her arms wildly, trying to get her head above water so she could breathe. It seemed a long, voidless eternity that she struggled for the surface, her arms and legs propelling her upward, her heavy skirts pulling her downward. When finally her head broke above the line of water she opened her mouth to breathe but was instantly met with a crashing wave that filled her mouth and nostrils with salty, cold water. She choked on the brine, her stomach muscles contracting and pushing upward more of the salty stuff. With water coming in and water going out she could barely catch a much-needed breath and when she did she was instantly hit with another forceful wave that took that breath right away. *So this is what it's like to drown* . . . The thought coursed through her mind. Nothing seemed real in this dark, cold, wet world she had hurled herself into. There was nothing to grasp onto, nothing to do but work to keep her head above water.

Another wave hit her, pulling her long hair across her face and wrapping the wet strands around her neck. Trembling fingers of one hand worked to push away the strangling tresses while the other worked to keep her body up, fighting against the constant pull of her heavy, sodden skirts. It was no use, her mind was screaming, she was going to die in the clutches of this great, wet monster! She heard her name being yelled and she tried to answer, not comprehending anything but her need to be free of the cold claws that held her. She spit out more sea water and willed her lungs to be free so she could speak. "Help!" It came out like a gurgle, heard only by her own ears just before her head went under again. She was going down now, powerless to help it, she thought, and her crazed mind brought before her visions of grotesque-looking seabeasts whose jaws were opened for her and whose claws were unsheathed and ready to pierce her flesh. The hand that grabbed her hair and pulled her up in her mind belonged to one of these beasts and she fought against it, her nails digging into the meat of it while she tried to scream and fight free of its death-grip.

Sebastian, angry at her for jumping and even angrier now with her still fighting him, swore under his breath as he yanked Brittannia up to the surface by her golden curls; it was the only part of her he could grab at the moment, so wild were the movements of the rest of her body. "Be still!" he yelled near her ear as he wrapped one arm about her chest then swam with sure strokes toward the small boat his crew members had lowered.

Johnson was in the boat and without ceremony he helped lift Brittannia's quivering, wet body from the sea and deposit her roughly into the bottom of it. This woman had caused too much trouble and he wondered why Diaz even bothered with her.

Finally free of her cold tomb, Brittannia rolled on her side and retched, purging the green water and foam from her insides. She was dizzy and her whole body shook from her own shock and the numbing cold of the water. She wrapped her arms about her sore body as she listened to the sounds of slapping waves and that of oars dipping into the water and coming back up. Finally her mind cleared and she realized who had "saved" her: Sebastian.

Right from the frying pan into the fire, she thought with despair. She wanted to cry . . . and she did.

The *Real Sangre* dropped anchor just off the northern coast of Andros Island before midnight but Sebastian decided to wait until daybreak before taking the small boat to shore. After what seemed an eternity to Brittannia morning came and the sky overhead was clouded over by huge gray clouds, their somber coloring matching that of her mood. She had not slept the past night, and even though Sebastian had left her alone in the cabin, she spent the night fearing he would return and do her harm. After pulling her from the water, he had not said a word to her, and his eyes, when she looked to him, had been full of suppressed anger. She wondered how long she must wait before he was to vent his full rage.

Now, in the meager morning light, she could look calmly at her situation. What seemed overwhelming last night did not seem so this morning, for she forced herself to believe she would get away from him, that somehow she would escape. But as her eyes scanned the stretch of beach that loomed before them she had to work doubly hard at convincing herself. From her seat in the small boat, the island had a haunting, primitive look to it. There were no docks, no ships, no buildings, nothing but a white sandy beach that seemed to be reaching out to the sea in search of a safe haven from the clutches of the wild, dense forest that stood ominously behind it. She shivered involuntarily as a feeling of dark foreboding settled over her. How was she to escape this place when the *Real Sangre* looked to be the only way off? Her situation, it seemed, was grave indeed.

"Are you cold, Brittannia?" Sebastian asked, the melodious sound of his voice not fooling her.

"What do you care?" she snapped. It wasn't cold she felt but a chilling fear that crept up her spine at its leisure.

He ignored the tone of her voice. "You might try being civil with me, *querido,*" he said calmly. "We are to be together for a long time to come. We will soon be at the house and I will see to it a fire is lit in your rooms."

Brittannia was going to deny staying with him, but she was weary and so she kept her mouth shut, saying nothing as she felt sand grating against the bottom of the dinghy and as Johnson and another sailor jumped out and pulled the small boat ashore. Strong arms helped her out, arms she tried to avoid, and once on ground she smoothed her crumpled, wet skirts and looked around her.

"Ah, there is Carlos now, always on time that one," Sebastian said as he looked to a clear spot in the dense foliage.

Brittannia watched as a young, dark-haired man made his way down the beach to them.

"*Hola,* Senor Diaz," the young man said cheerfully as he swept a straw hat from his head. His skin was a warm, exotic shade of nut-brown, his words thick with a Spanish accent. His blue black hair was straight and medium length above large, expressive brown eyes. His teeth were perfectly straight and white, showing brightly against his skin when he smiled, which was often.

Brittannia wondered if the handsome young man could be trusted—if he would help her. He was friendly and winsome and since he had walked out of the ominous, dark forest he made it seem a bit less frightening to her.

They followed Carlos to an elegant carriage and two beautifully matched grays that awaited them in the forest. There was a path widened to admit the horse-drawn carriage and Carlos skillfully guided them along that path. Brittannia had the distinct feeling that a dozen pairs of eyes were watching them. She looked around her nervously, jumping at the many bird calls that echoed through the thick growth.

"Brittannia, does my island home frighten you?" Sebastian asked, sweeping his arm wide as merely inviting her into a splendid dining room.

Oh, he was a cool one! Bringing her here against her will and then expecting her to give some cooing response to what he obviously thought of as "his." She didn't answer him, her rage making speech impossible.

"Ah, let me guess," he continued his one-sided conversation. "You feel as if there are many eyes upon us, no?"

She looked to him, her eyes narrowing. What had he in mind for her now?

"Well, *mi querido,*" he said, leaning his dark head toward her fair one, and whispering, "Many eyes are indeed watching us at this very minute. Many *native* eyes."

She moved away from him, moving as far to one side

as she could. She was not going to let him frighten her anymore.

"Natives who will hunt you down if ever you are alone in their jungle," he continued inexorably, his dark eyes looking intently at her for any signs of discomfort. "Be warned, Brittannia, if you do not comply to my wishes, I won't hesitate to set you free in these jungles." He spread his arm wide again, and even though she did not want to look, she did, her eyes scanning the thick growth around them. She could feel the presence of "something" hiding among the thickness and that presence was dark . . . evil. She shivered.

Finally the carriage entered a large clearing, and there, like a glittering white castle, strong yet full of grace, Sebastian's home stood amidst the twisted, hungering jungle. Surrounding it was a sea of well-kept green lawns and nearer to the house were sprays of island flowers, their petals opened to the early light. It was much too beautiful a home for the likes of Sebastian Diaz, yet it belonged to him and was now, Brittannia realized, to become her own gilded cage.

The carriage came to a halt in front of the sweeping veranda of the two-story home and Sebastian was quickly on the ground, turning to help Brittannia from her seat. "Welcome, welcome to my home!" he declared with a curve to his thin lips.

Brittannia ignored him as she climbed down on her own. Her hair was a mass of uncombed curls and her gown was torn and still damp from her time in the sea, but still she brushed by the dark Spaniard with a regalness that put all royalty to shame.

Had she known the effect it would have on Sebastian she would have spit in his face. Sebastian felt his passion rise just looking at her wild beauty and when she swept by him leaving behind her fragrance, he felt a heady sense of ownership. She, Brittannia Denning, was on his island, in his home—and at his mercy. He followed her, holding wide the great door and letting her step inside first.

Brittannia, under other circumstances, might have been awed by the elegant surroundings. But to her, now they meant one thing: Sebastian, whom she despised, along with all that was his. The rooms she entered were done in cool colors, the furniture arranged carefully so as to create airiness. In the center of the house was a courtyard filled with lush, tenderly cared for greenery and a tinkling water fountain. All of the main floor rooms opened onto the courtyard with a wide Spanish arch. The upper floors had a balcony that went the entire length of the courtyard and was enclosed with black wrought-iron grills. To her, all of it was nothing more than a prison.

"Maria will show you to your rooms, Brittannia. I warn you now not to try and escape, for my home is well guarded and you would not get far." With that, Sebastian was gone and she was led up the winding staircase by Maria.

Maria was a young Spanish girl and she reminded Brittannia of a delicate porcelain doll her father had given her years ago. Maria was petite, her movements gracefully slow, as if she were moving to some unheard tune. Her wealth of black hair hung free and it moved about her shoulders like a full, dark cloud. Her eyes were coal black; everything about her was darkly beautiful. Brittannia wondered how the girl came to be in Sebastian's employ.

Her rooms were at the back side of the house and from her windows she could see the thick forest at the end of the mansion's sweeping lawns. Even from her "protective" lair Brittannia felt a feeling of foreboding as she looked out at the twisted dark forest. She didn't yet dare try escape with that route. She abruptly shut the drapes on her western window and passed through the wide arch to the balcony above the courtyard. At least above the courtyard she could hear the comforting sound of moving water and feel that someone was within hearing distance.

Maria directed Carlos to put Brittannia's trunks in the corner of the room then. After he had left, she said, "If you need anything please let me know. Just pull the cord and I will come." She indicated to a silken rope cord with a tasseled edge. It was the same color of the room, a dusty rose.

"Maria," Brittannia said. "You know I am not here of my own will, don't you?"

The young girl did not answer.

Feeling desperate, Brittannia stepped toward her. "I need your help, Maria. I—I need to get away from here. Can you help me?" Her voice was hushed and her words spilled out quickly.

Maria hesitated, then said, "I cannot help you, senorita." There was a note of sadness in her voice.

Brittannia clenched her fists. "But you must!" she insisted. "Sebastian is a cruel man. Look, look what he did to me!" She pointed to the ugly bruise on her jaw. "Look what he has done—and that is just the beginning I am sure!"

Maria's black eyes looked at the nasty bruise and her mouth pursed in disapproval. After long moments of silence, she said in a barely heard whisper, "I cannot help you."

"Maria, please! If you cannot, perhaps Carlos can—"

"No!" Maria cut in. "Do not involve Carlos. He does not know of the cruelties of Senor Diaz and you would do well not to tell him."

"If telling Carlos will insure me of a way out of here, then I have no choice but to tell him," Brittannia said, resorting to manipulation.

Tears were forming in the girl's eyes. "No, you mustn't tell him."

"Why not? I have the feeling Carlos will help me, he has the look of an honest person."

Maria's head shot up defiantly. "Of course he is and he would go to great lengths to help you. He—he would probably be killed in trying to help you! Please, you mustn't involve him."

"I have no choice."

Maria swallowed, looking past Brittannia's shoulder, staring at nothing. "I, too, had thought to seek his help when I was first brought here."

The young girl looked loath to explain further, so Brittannia prompted, "What happened?"

She dropped her head then, her fingers going to the row of buttons along her peasant blouse. "I threatened Sebastian, threatened to tell Carlos of his cruelties to me . . ." She was unbuttoning each button, then she turned away from Brittannia and let the blouse flutter away to reveal her back, "And this is what the senor did to me."

Brittannia heard her own sharp intake of breath as she gazed in wide-eyed horror at the scarred back of the young girl. Ugly welts crisscrossed her brown skin—skin that would never again be smooth. The wounds were thick with healed flesh and Brittannia had no doubt that they had rendered Maria helpless for quite some time.

"But why?" Brittannia heard herself ask. "Why would Sebastian hurt you so? Just because you threatened to escape?"

Maria quickly shrugged into the blouse, securing the front as she turned back to Brittannia. "No, it was not my leaving that angered him, it was my threatening to tell Carlos everything. You see, Senorita, Carlos is like a son to Senor Diaz. It seems, many years ago, in Cadiz, Sebastian came upon a young boy whose parents had just been murdered by thieves. The boy was Carlos and reminded Senor Diaz of himself when he was young. Sebastian took Carlos in and went after the murderers, eventually making them suffer greatly for their deeds. Senor Diaz knows no mercy and it is rumored he killed them slowly." Maria shook her head, her dark hair swaying with the movement. "Anyhow, Carlos, from that day on, has felt nothing but great admiration for Senor Diaz. Diaz revels in such adulation and would never suffer Carlos having anything but for him."

"So Carlos is ignorant of the kind of man Sebastian is."

She shook her head. "And please, do not tell him, for he is a man of honor and would confront Senor Diaz. There would be bloodshed—Carlos's blood!"

Brittannia looked away, trying to digest this new information. "Then what am I to do?"

"I do not know. Perhaps, together, we can find a

way . . ." But even as she spoke the words, Maria knew she would never find a way. Her fear of Senor Diaz was great and it had been a year since she'd even thought of escaping. "I must go now," she said quickly, and darted from the room, shutting the door behind her.

Brittannia looked around the rooms, taking in her surroundings as she tried to form some sort of plan in her weary mind. A huge canopied bed occupied one corner of the room. It was a beautiful bed, she had to admit, the posts being made of rich, gleaming wood, and it was draped on all sides by rose-colored gossamer, the delicate material giving the bedcovers a more silken appearance. So inviting, a safe haven from her unfamiliar surroundings. She was so tired, so very tired from her ordeal. With a sigh, she shed her wet clothing and climbed into the ethereal atmosphere. Drowsiness overpowered her and she fell asleep, the sound of the water falling into the stone fountain filling her ears.

No sooner was she asleep than visions of a stormy-eyed captain with dark hair invaded her mind. Strong arms were around her, soothing her, protecting her, and even though her lips said no, her body shouted yes as he loved her. It was a lovely dream, a blissful escape from reality. And when she heard a foreign voice, she ignored it.

"Senorita, it is time to get up," Maria was saying, pulling back the curtains of the bed.

Brittannia, not quite sure of her surroundings, awoke with a start, trying to remember where she was. "Maria?" she asked, her memory finally serving her. "What time is it?"

"It is late afternoon. Senor Diaz has scheduled the evening meal at an earlier time since you slept through the noon meal," Maria said as she opened the drapes, letting in the slanting rays of the setting sun.

Brittannia quickly rubbed the sleep from her eyes then pushed the tenuous material back from the bed, bringing her slender legs through the opening. "Someone should have awakened me. I—I have to leave this place!" she said with urgency. She crossed the room and opened one of her trunks to retrieve a dressing robe.

"Oh, Senor Diaz would not let anyone awaken you," Maria replied as she helped Brittannia into her robe.

"Do you always obey that man?"

Maria ignored her words. "Your bath water is ready in the other room."

Brittannia looked to her left and saw a door that had gone unnoticed before. A bath might soothe her sore muscles, she decided, so after Maria left she entered through the door and found herself in a spacious room with a large gilt-framed mirror, a vanity with a silver-backed brush, a hand mirror, and many bottles of perfume upon it, and lastly a tub filled with steaming water. She quickly shrugged her silken robe to the floor and stepped into the steaming water.

The smell of verbena wafted to her and she noted someone had scented the bath water. She sank into the inviting warmth of the water, letting it soothe her senses. Such elegant surroundings, she thought. One would think she were an empress instead of a prisoner.

When she was done she grabbed a thick towel from a nearby stand and wrapped it around her body. Her hair hung down her back in thick, dark golden ringlets. She toweled her body dry then set to the task of combing her hair. When she was done, she donned her dressing robe and went out to her western balcony and seated herself on one of the rattan chairs, letting the setting sun dry her hair.

Its rays were warm upon her skin and she leaned back in her chair, content to feel its caress upon her. She sat there, unafraid of the hungering jungle from her high perch. She looked at it, studying it, almost wishing one of the natives would scurry before her eyes. Perhaps *they* would help her. Her eyes scanned the end of the forest for a long while, watching as the dark shadows of the twilight descended and claimed the edges of it. No natives scurried and she was almost unbelieving they were there but for the fact she had felt their presence.

She was about to go back inside her rooms but a flitting shadow caught her eye and she paused to watch it. She saw a small shape come to the edge of the forest and wait. It was the shape of a young man—it was Carlos! She watched as he crouched low to the ground. He looked to his left and right and then scanned the white walls of the house. He seemed to be afraid of what he looked for, and then, certain he did not see it, motioned for someone.

Brittannia watched with curiosity as a young girl ran across the great lawns to the waiting shape of Carlos and entwined her arms around him. Why, it was Maria! Brittannia watched as Carlos scooped the lithe Maria into his arms and hugged her tightly, letting her down easily. She watched as Carlos led Maria into the thick jungle. So that is why Maria did not want Carlos involved. But to Brittannia, the fact the young couple was in love was even more reason to involve Carlos, for surely the young man would not stand for Maria being mistreated.

She stood. *How nice to be in love,* she thought, to have someone wait for you. She turned and entered her room sadly.

As Brittannia was preparing for the evening meal, Sebastian sat in his study sipping slowly from a tall glass of rum, his left forefinger thoughtfully running along his dark mustache. His black eyes narrowed as he stared into the blazing fire within the hearth before him and his thin mouth was set into a grim line. There was a soft knock on the door. Without turning, Sebastian spoke in a cruel voice to the small girl who entered. "Where have you been, Maria?" he demanded. "Close the door."

Maria slowly entered the large study, a look of hatred briefly passing over her delicate features. "I was busy with my work, Senor Diaz," she replied as she gave him the mandatory curtsy.

"Have you brought what I've requested?"

"Si." She held out her hand and in her palm was a small crystal vial filled with a clear liquid.

Sebastian took the vial in his dark hands and looked at Maria. "This is of the same mixture I used on the last girl?"

"Si."

"You have done well, Maria." He stepped toward her and brought his hand to touch her jawline. She drew in a sharp breath and looked down, loath to meet his eyes.

"I shall reward you for this. Maybe tonight," he said. He pulled her chin up, forcing her to look at him. He smiled, his white teeth gleaming against his dark skin. "Perhaps I will give you a drop of this liquid and then . . ." He didn't finish the sentence; instead he brought the bottle before her eyes, causing the liquid to catch the light of the fire.

Her eyes grew large and she opened her mouth to protest but then the look in his eyes stopped her.

"Ah, so you are afraid of the native aphrodisiac? Well, do not worry, for I do not think you need it. You do well enough without it." He dropped his hand from her face. "This is only for those who are not so quick to come to my bed, unlike you, *puta,* who will spread your legs whenever I say." He laughed then.

Maria hated him for what he had made her become. He was right when he called her, *puta,* whore. She always felt dirty when she was around him, she felt used. Oh, how she longed for Carlos and her to be away from Andros, away from the cruel senor. She hated life on Andros and lately she was beginning to hate herself.

"Maria," Sebastian was saying, "go and see if Senorita Brittannia is ready to join me for dinner."

"*Sí,* Senor Diaz." After another curtsy she left the study, closing the huge door softly but wishing to slam it hard, so hard that all four walls would collapse, falling hard and heavy on Senor Diaz.

There was a timid knock on Brittannia's door. Brittannia reached over, swinging it wide as she turned once again to check her appearance in the full-framed mirror.

"Senorita, dinner is soon to be ready and Senor Diaz is waiting for you," said Maria, a mixture of feelings washing over her as she watched Brittannia. She felt sorry for her, sorry that she would become the victim of the aphrodisiac, for she had heard stories of its potency. Yet, she felt a bit of relief too. She was glad that Senor Diaz had this beautiful woman to entertain him, to fulfill his needs. Now with Brittannia here she would be free to do as she pleased at night, free to go to Carlos, free from the senor's cruel ways in the bedroom.

Brittannia debated whether to tell Maria she had seen her with Carlos, but she decided against it. "You can tell Senor Diaz that I have no intention of dining with him this night or any other."

Maria looked shocked. "But . . . he will be furious! I can not tell him that!"

"Maria, I for one do not intend to be a willing prisoner. If he wants to keep me then he must deal with me."

"And he will," Maria warned.

"Just give him my message," she said, not wanting to give way to thoughts of what Sebastian might actually do to her. She would learn soon enough.

It was only minutes after Maria left that Brittannia's door was pushed roughly open and Johnson strode in, a dangerous look on his coarse features. He still wore the same dirty clothes she'd last seen him in. "Diaz wants you. Come with me," he demanded, hooking a thumb toward the hallway.

Brittannia took a step back. "No."

"Y' haven't got a choice, wench." He strode over to her and grabbed her wrist. Then with his other hand he wrenched her other arm up and back between her shoulder blades viciously. She cried out in pain. "Don't make me any madder, slut," he said into her ear, his breath stinking of rot and alcohol. "You've given me enough extra work—work I haven't been paid for yet!" With that he pushed her out the door, still retaining his mean hold on her.

Brittannia could do nothing but stumble ahead of him, so tight and painful was his grip on her. He kept his hold on her the whole way down the wide staircase, through the first-floor hall and straight into Sebastian's study. Once there, he let go of her arm then gave her a vicious shove that sent her sprawling into the study. She fell to her knees, her hands barely breaking her fall, then with venomous eyes she glared over her shoulder at Johnson. He only laughed at her.

From behind his desk, Sebastian spoke. "Maria tells me you have no intention of sharing any meals with me. Is this so, Brittannia?"

She jerked her head toward him while she sat back on her knees. Her palms stung from running across the carpet and she rubbed them together. "Go to hell, Sebastian!" she spat.

"Ah, still fighting me, I see."

"I'll fight you to the end," she said, getting to her feet.

"And you may get there very soon, Brittannia, for I'm losing my patience with you. I find you too unmanageable. I admit a small bit of defiance excites me, but, Brittannia, you take it too far."

She looked levelly at him, squaring her shoulders as she watched him come from around his desk. He came to stand just inches from her and she steeled herself for whatever blow he would give her.

"Did you fight Captain Barclay when he took you to his bed?" He saw the surprise in her eyes. "Yes,

Brittannia, I know of your little tryst with the captain, but do not worry, I am willing to forget that you are a used woman."

Unable to control her anger she brought her hand up to slap him, but he was quicker than she and caught her wrist in a tight grip. "Have you no decency?" she ground between her teeth.

"Decency?" He laughed. "And where was your decency the night on the beach?" His other hand came up to stroke her smooth cheek. "Soon, Brittannia," he began, the "r" rolling slightly over his tongue, "you will lie beneath me and give to me the same fruits you gave to the captain."

Dain! He had been gentle in their lovemaking. She shuddered to think what Sebastian Diaz would be like and with a quick yank she pulled her wrist free of his hold. "Never," she breathed. "Never will I give in to you!"

Sebastian's eyes did not leave her face and she could see the cold fury that crept into those black orbs as he said, "Johnson, take the senorita to the jungle. I think she needs to clear her head this night. Let her sleep with the natives, then perhaps she will be more willing to share my bed."

Brittannia's eyes grew wide as Johnson grabbed onto her and pulled her to the door. "No!" she screamed. "You can't do this! *NO!*"

It was useless, Sebastian was not listening, already he had turned back to his desk. Brittannia struggled violently in Johnson's arms but his hold was tight and she couldn't get away. In minutes he had her outside and was dragging her to the thick line of trees and jungle. The night was pitch-black, not even the moon

113

lent its rays, and Brittannia had to force her eyes to become accustomed to the darkness.

She heard the crunch of foilage beneath their feet as they drew nearer to the line of forest and she could hear strange jungle sounds—or so she thought, she wasn't sure. The only thing she was sure of was her fear.

"Please, don't do this," she pleaded as she struggled in Johnson's hold.

"Shut up," he growled.

He dragged her into the forest, not caring that vines and branches slapped her face and arms, tearing her tender flesh. Her skirts caught on a thorned branch and he merely yanked them free, tearing the delicate fabric as he did so. He said not a word as he dragged her to the trunk of a large mahogany tree, pushing her roughly up against the cool bark and holding her there while he wound a thick cord of rope around her and the tree.

"There, that oughta keep ya till morning," he said, securing the rope with a great tug that caused the braided fibers to bite into her skin.

She bit her lip to keep from crying out, and it was only after he walked away, back to the house, that she let her tears come. She was alone now, all alone in the dark, foreign world. Something moved in the bushes to her right and she felt her heart jump as her eyes strained to discern some shape, and she immediately forgot her tears. She could see nothing in the inky black and that only served to heighten her anxiety. Her mind began to play tricks on her, causing her to see things that were not there; a snake dangling toward her from the branch above, the figure of a man standing only a foot away— her imaginings were great and she thought she would go mad from them!

She stifled a sob of fright as she moved to try and free herself but each move seemed to cause the rope to dig into her skin that much more. "Damn!" she muttered into the dark night, then immediately shut her mouth for the sound of her own voice even frightened her. She stood animal-still, her back tight against the great mahogany trunk as her wide eyes surveyed the darkness around her and her ears became fine-tuned, listening. Minutes crept by and gathered into hours and still she stood, intense . . . listening. This night her mind would know no rest.

The wind that reached her and rustled the jungle leaves was cool and it caused the fine hairs on her arms to stand on end, for it brought with it the sound of native drums—an ominous sound of throbbing voodooism. The sound came from somewhere in the distance and was sporadic, stopping and ending with no obvious pattern. She shuddered wondering what meaning the drums held and if the natives knew she was alone in their jungle. She listened for the sound of their feet, dreading to hear them but wishing they would hurry and come if indeed they were coming at all. Something tiny and spidery fell from a branch above and landed on her bare arm and she had to clamp her mouth shut to keep from crying out in revulsion as the tiny, unseen creature crept along her skin, its thin legs pricking her bare flesh until finally she felt its presence no more. She let out a sigh of relief, the sound of the pounding drums familiar to her now. She waited for sounds of approaching feet. The coarse rope dug into her skin, stopping the normal flow of blood, and the roughness of the bark cut into her back. Every muscle in her ached and her mind was weary from tension.

And then she heard it; a small rustling of leaves, a snap of a twig. She straightened, drawing her breath in with uncontrollable sharpness—they were coming! She peered wide eyed into the velvety black, straining to see a moving object but she saw nothing but dark shapes that swayed as they had swayed all night.

"Who's there?" she demanded, hearing again movement in the bush. Silence answered her and her fear caused her to call out again, "Who's there?" Her voice cracked and sounded alien to her own ears.

Long minutes passed before she heard whispers to her left. She jerked her head in that direction, squinting her eyes to peer intently, trying to penetrate the thick darkness. She heard another whisper, an odd sound of deep native tongue. She froze as she saw something move!

A black shape rose slowly from the thick bush, tall in height, broad in shoulder, and Brittannia could barely discern the dark matting of tight curls on the man's head and the sinewy muscles that covered his near-naked body as he moved cautiously toward her. She swallowed hard as she moved against the constricting rope, trying to break free. What was this native going to do to her?! He stopped with her movements, the whites of his eyes showing starkly against his brown skin, watching her. He mumbled something she did not understand and then he started toward her again.

She wanted to scream but her throat was tight from fear, preventing any sound from coming forth. All she could do was fight against her bonds, wriggling frantically against the great trunk as the native came closer, his unsmiling face clearer. Brittannia shook her head, her mouth working, and when she saw the flash of a knife blade she found her voice.

"Help!" she screamed into the deep night. She thrashed wildly, kicking her legs and moving her body, trying to get away from the native who was now beside her, his eyes unreadable, his full mouth set into a grim line. She screamed again, a shrill cry that split the night. She watched in stunned horror as she saw the native raise the blade in a swift movement then let it drop toward her. Her mind went blank then, terror and fear causing her to forget reason, forget everything as she thought she would soon feel that knife twisting into her tender flesh, would soon feel her own blood gushing out of her body, leaving her lifeless. The last thing she remembered before she fainted was the feeling of freedom as the rope fell away from her body and she fell to the ground, unconscious.

Pale morning light came, greeting her sensitive eyes. She lay on the ground by the tree, the rope that had once held her slack beside her. Tiny creatures scampered by her immobile body, intent on the business of their daily life, birds squawked moving from tree to tree, and she could hear the buzzing of the many insects that were already assaulting her warm skin. No sounds of drums, no signs of natives. Slowly she moved first her hands, then her arms, and then her legs; all seemed to be well and as she pushed herself up from the hard ground, she looked quickly to her body expecting to see a bloodied knife wound. There was none.

She stood then, her body trembling and sore as she stretched her long limbs. Slanted rays of sunlight dappled the strange world around her, reaching the jungle floor through the many leaves and branches, and already the day was warm. She picked up the rope and studied it. What had happened last night? Had the native actually cut her bonds then left her here? Obviously he had and she wondered again at the brown-skinned inhabitants of this uncharted island. She hadn't long to think of it, for she heard voices in the distance—*familiar* voices. Sebastian and Johnson were returning for her! Without hesitation she dropped the rope and broke into a full run in the opposite direction of the voices.

She thought of nothing but escape as vines tore at her face and arms and long grasses whipped around her legs, hampering the speed of her mad flight. She pushed through dense foliage, not caring that she was running through web after web newly spun by industrious spiders. She cared not that the berries she squished splattered her dress and stained her skin, she only knew she must get away from Sebastian, must flee for her life. Perspiration broke out in tiny beads along her flesh bringing more insects to swarm around her. She swatted them away and pressed forward. She heard sounds all around her—jungle sounds that had not been present through the deep night. The world around her was full of life and even though she was in grave danger, that life continued, uninterrupted by her pounding feet and labored breathing. Her lungs burned and her muscles screamed for her to stop, to rest, but still she ran, tripping over roots only to push herself back up and trudge on.

Thick brush hid the grassy bank that lay before her and so, as she stumbled forward, she did not see the sharp slope, did not have time to catch herself before she tripped and fell, tumbling down the wet bank and into the cool, swampy water. She heard the moan that tore from her lips as her right foot, held fast by a jutting root, twisted before she could dislodge it, and as she hit the water she felt nothing but the searing pain. Her head went under and instantly was enclosed by long, entwining water grasses that wrapped around her body and held her tight. She struggled against them and the more she struggled the more entangled she became! Her legs thrashed in the murky water as she fought to get herself free.

Even had she known of the great noise she was making she could not have stilled her fruitless movements, so great was her terror. Sebastian and Johnson, the cut rope in hand, ran toward the commotion.

With quick words Sebastian ordered Johnson to retrieve her.

Brittannia fought wildly against the grasses and against the strong arms that grabbed hold of her, tugging her away from her swaying prison. She was sputtering and coughing as he dragged her up the grassy bank then slung her over his back like a sack of potatoes. She struggled only a bit, but soon her weariness overtook her and she stopped her movements, letting him carry her back to Sebastian's home, resigned for the time to wait until she had another chance to escape. Next time she would be prepared . . .

The moon that had hid behind dark, scuttering clouds last night was in full view this night and as Brittannia sat in her rooms looking out, she saw how its beams silvered and touched all things with its transient light. To think she had spent an entire night in those caliginous jungles . . . She shuddered just thinking of it, then turned from the window and paced her rooms.

Her door was locked, she knew, it had been all the day long. Now, dressed in the evening gown of lime green Maria had placed on the bed for her, she wished fervently she had gotten away this morning instead of having to face yet another night on Andros, in Sebastian's home. She waited nervously for the knock upon her door. She knew Sebastian would soon summon her downstairs to dine with him. She had thought of ignoring his request to wear the gown, of declaring she would not leave her rooms, but he had seen to it no food was brought to her and she was ravenously hungry. She knew she would need to keep her strength up if ever she was to flee this wretched place.

The knock came and the door was unlocked. She followed a silent Maria to Sebastian's first-floor study. It was a spacious room with a huge window that offered a stunning view of the large lawns and line of trees farther away. The adjacent wall was lined with a bookshelf and the one to her right was filled with a huge hearth.

Sebastian stood from his chair and said, "Ah, I had thought you would deny my requests. I am glad you have decided to come to your senses, Brittannia." He strode over to her, dismissing Maria with a curt nod of his leonine head. Taking Brittannia's stiff arm in his, he led her to the hearth and motioned for her to sit in the huge leather chair beside his.

"It is only my hunger that brings me from those rooms, Sebastian."

He nodded, pouring them each a glass of wine from

the crystal decanter that occupied the small table between the chairs. "I see," he said. "Then it is not my company you seek but a warm meal?"

She gave him a metallic look as she took the glass he offered her. "You know I despise you. Whatever it is you want from me I'll not give it!"

He smiled then. "Oh, I think, in time, *querido,* you will."

She turned her gaze to the roaring fire before her, watching as the yellowish flames licked at the pieces of wood. "Think what you wish."

He settled into his own chair, wineglass in hand and after long, silent moments, he asked, "Do you miss your Captain Barclay?"

Brittannia nearly choked. Placing her own glass on the table she said, "He is not 'my' anything—and I know not why you would ask such a question!"

"You are much too defensive when it comes to Barclay," he observed, a feeling of jealousy tightening his stomach muscles. "One would think you have deep feelings for the man, is this true, Brittannia? Is this the reason you refuse me as you do?"

Her turquoise eyes, shining defiantly in the light of the fire, bore holes in the man opposite her. "I refuse you because you disgust me," she ground out. She wanted to say more, but her anger choked any words from coming, so she turned her head and looked back to the yellowish flames of the fire, their movement almost enough to calm her uneasy nerves.

"I am sorry to hear you say that, *querido.* Very sorry indeed," Sebastian said, jealous rage contorting his dark features.

Brittannia did not notice the way Sebastian looked

at her, she did not see the murderous anger in his black eyes. She was too intent on her own anger and yes, the memories of Dain that had suddenly come crashing in to invade her mind. She was too preoccupied to see when Sebastian dropped a few drops of the native aphrodisiac into her glass. She sat there in the huge leather chair, unaware of what was to come in the long night before her. Slowly, without taking her eyes from the fire, she brought the glass to her lips and drank deeply of its contents.

Chapter 6

"Ah, my darling Brittannia, *mi querido*. I can forgive your wandering heart. I can forgive you because I want you so . . . I want to drape you in jewels, and more."

Brittannia took her eyes away from the licking flames of the fire and, with concentrated effort, focused on the dark Spaniard beside her. Her gaze caught with his for a long moment until he leaned forward in his chair and, with a self-assured smile, reached into his dinner jacket pocket and withdrew a blue velvet case.

"For you, Brittannia," he said as one dark hand carefully opened the case and brought it before her. "A small token of my affection."

Brittannia watched without feeling as Sebastian brought the case within reach revealing its contents. On a bed of white satin lay an emerald and diamond necklace, lush and glittering.

She said nothing.

Sebastian flashed her a handsome grin as he scooped the necklace out of its satin bed and flung the case carelessly onto his desktop. "No gift is too extravagant for you, Brittannia," he said as he stood and moved behind her, bringing his arms around her. Holding the white and green blaze of gems in one hand, his other hand moved to gently push small wisps of her hair away from her neck. His touch upon her skin was feather light but it was enough to send ripples of revulsion coursing through her body.

He took one end of the shining necklace in each hand and held it in front of her for a fraction of a second; long enough for her to see the firelight catch and dance inside each perfectly cut stone. Once on, the precious stones felt heavy against her skin and she instinctively brought her hand up to touch the emerald that hung at the tip. She wanted to yank it from her neck.

"Remove it," she demanded as she ignored the display of wealth that hung heavily around her neck.

"Lucky for me your eyes show green tonight," Sebastian said, ignoring her words. "If your gown were to be blue, then I would have to search through my treasures for sapphires." His hands gently massaged her bare shoulders.

She shuddered.

From somewhere beyond the study door soft music could be heard. A soft Spanish melody played with skillful fingers on a guitar, accompanied by a woman's voice, drifted to them. The woman's voice was soft and pretty and Brittannia wondered at what ploy Sebastian would use this night.

He moved in front of Brittannia, the firelight casting a warm, softening light on one side of his face and throwing the other in dancing, unreadable shadows. "If you stay with me, Brittannia, I will shower you with jewels. I will give you whatever you want . . . fulfill your deepest desires." He took her hands in his and pulled her up to stand beside him.

Brittannia said nothing as he put his strong arms around her and pulled her body closer to his. She felt funny—as if she weren't inside her body any longer. Fighting the foreign sensations, she pushed him away. "Don't," she breathed.

Sebastian's dark eyes contemplated her for a moment, then without a word he slipped his hand down to the small of her back and directed her toward the door of the study. "We shall dance this night," he announced, guiding her out of the study.

Brittannia walked beside him only because she felt so odd—a feeling she had never felt, and as they stepped out into the long hall that eventually led to the court-yard, she found herself becoming light-headed. The music that had sounded so clear from behind the study doors now seemed to be coming from miles away. Her footsteps on the stone floor sounded muffled by distance, as if they weren't her own. She felt overwarm and the spacious hall with its high ceiling felt as if it were closing in on her.

"Sebastian?" she heard herself say. "I—I don't feel very well. I need some fresh air."

"The courtyard is but a few feet away. You must have drank too much this evening," he said as he took her elbow in a strong, assuring hold and guided her through the wide arch and into the courtyard.

Too much to drink? Surely one glass of wine could not be considered too much, she thought to herself and doubts began to form in her hazed mind.

Sebastian seemed to be watching her overly close, as

one who expected something to happen soon, and his hold on her was becoming more than gentlemanly as they neared the lantern-lit courtyard.

She shrugged from his hold. "I don't need your assistance," she said curtly, and took a dizzy step to the right, out of his arm's reach.

"But, of course," Sebastian said as he brought up his hand to thoughtfully brush his forefinger along his dark mustache. "You are clearly in control of your movements now."

"Yes, I am."

But her head swam as she took a seat on a stone bench near a string of swaying lanterns. She busied herself smoothing out the many folds of her lime-green evening dress, anything to keep her mind off the dizziness she was feeling.

Sebastian stood before her; his powerful frame towering above her, his gaze dark and piercing. His nearness was unnerving her and she again reached up to finger the precious string of stones he had given her. She should fling them in his face, she knew, but was afraid of the outcome of such an action.

"Brittannia, dance with me."

His request broke her train of thought and she looked up to him, trying to focus her suddenly unfocusable eyes. "No," she replied flatly. But he pulled her up anyway and she found she had not the reserve to fight him. She went slowly, cautiously into his arms, and as they moved about to the sound of the music she kept a safe distance between them.

A few lanterns were lit to illuminate the outer areas of the courtyard but darkness claimed the spot near the fountain where they danced. Sebastian held her lightly, his hand giving more warmth than pressure to the small of her back and, surprisingly, she began to relax, enjoying the melodious sound they swayed and whirled to. A strange sensation was stealing over her body, growing in intensity as she moved about the stone floor. It was a warm feeling that coursed through her veins, lulling her senses, relaxing her suspicious mind. She looked up to Sebastian, her lids heavy from the languorous feeling inside her.

Sebastian smiled and drew her closer. "You see, *mi querido,* I told you you would feel better once we reached the courtyard," he said in a husky voice.

She ignored him, wondering at the odd sensations coursing through her, letting herself be consumed by languid feelings, having no power or desire to stop them. Something was not right, she knew, she should not feel this way, should not be standing in Sebastian's arms, letting him sway her gently to the music. Abruptly she stopped moving, pushing his arms away from her body. "What have you done to me?" she demanded, her voice wavering.

"Done?" he questioned, tilting his dark head to one side. "I have done nothing, Brittannia." His black eyes studied her for a brief moment, then he turned and gave a quick wave of dismissal to the musicians. "Enough music," he said, turning back to her. "Now we shall dine, and then . . ." He let his words trail off.

She felt her body tingle at the huskiness of his voice and she shuddered with revulsion at her own response to the man beside her. What was wrong with her? She could feel her control slipping away and being replaced by—by wanton feelings she'd only felt once before . . . in the arms of Dain Barclay. "I'm not hungry," she

127

replied, not daring to sit through a meal with this man. "I'm going to my rooms." She did not wait to listen to his answer, for she didn't care whether or not he wanted her to dine with him—she had to be away from him, she had to be alone to deal with these strange sensations.

Picking up her skirts she hurried away from the fountain toward the main staircase. Sebastian was right behind her yet oddly enough he did not stop her flight. She no sooner had her foot on the bottom stair when she was overcome by a violent spinning sensation in her head and she fell against the rail, grasping hold of it as she pressed her other hand to her temple. She closed her eyes momentarily and took in a deep breath, trying desperately not to let whatever was in her system overtake her. It was nearly impossible.

"Do you need some help?" Sebastian asked, his voice sounding very far away.

She spun toward him, an accusing look on her beauteous face. "I need *nothing* from you," she spat. "You've obviously done enough as it is!"

"You look absolutely white," he calmly observed. "Perhaps you would like me to help you to your rooms." He took a step in her direction.

"Don't come near me!" she warned, tightly grasping the rail for support. Her head was still spinning and her knees were sure to give way beneath her if she didn't sit soon.

Sebastian ignored the stern command coming to her and sweeping her up in his arms in one quick movement. "Ah, Brittannia, must you always fight me? Be still and relax. This will be a night you will never forget."

Her fists pounded against his chest as she wiggled in

his tight embrace. "No!" she screamed. "What have you done to me? Tell me!" She was fighting an inner battle. Something alien was speeding through her veins and illiciting responses she did not want to give.

In a few easy strides, Sebastian had Brittannia up the stairs and into her rooms. He laid her gently on the canopied bed and walked over to shut the door that led to the balcony overlooking the courtyard.

"Relax, Brittannia. You will enjoy it, I promise," Sebastian said as he walked to the fireplace and poked the logs for a better flame. Someone had conveniently built a fire.

The dizziness was abating but she still felt the strange warming sensation coursing through her veins. "Leave, Sebastian."

He merely laughed, then casually crossed the room to extinguish the light above the bed, then the one near the main door and, lastly, he dimmed the lamp that was on the chest of drawers in the corner.

Brittannia watched as he came to stand at the side of her bed. As he loosened his tie, his night-dark eyes stared down at her.

"Sebastian, what are you going to do?" she asked, although she knew full well.

He didn't answer her. She could see the want clearly in his black eyes as he undid the top buttons of his silk shirt.

"Leave my bedchamber at once!" she demanded in a shaky voice and stood to usher him out.

A powerful arm snaked out and caught hold of her. "What am I going to do?" he asked her as he pulled her close, the tightness of his grip commanding her to look at him. "This," he said and brought his mouth down on hers.

Brittannia's neck was arched back with the force of his lips and she pushed at his chest as he drew her closer still. Her head began to spin again and she had to take a deep breath to still the room. The sound of his lips and tongue upon her skin seemed to come from far away and she was suddenly certain that something besides the wine and the events of the past few days was taking its toll on her.

"N-no, please don't do this to me," she said breathlessly as she vainly tried to fight down the languorous feeling inside her. Her body wanted to drop all defense and let Sebastian do as he pleased, let him caress her and take her, but her mind knew better! Her better sense was fighting a tough battle and as Sebastian showered her neck with searing kisses and laid her down onto the bed, she wondered which would win.

He was too close, his body much too warm, his embrace too personal. Brittannia tried to push him away but she had not the strength, something foreign to her was sapping her strength, making her a slave to Sebastian's passionate assault.

"Oh, God," she cried aloud. "What's wrong with me? Sebastian, can you help me?"

"*Sí*," he replied as he began to undo her many buttons to pull down her dinner gown. "We can help each other," he said as he kissed a trail down her throat to her breasts. He undid her underclothing and pulled them away from her ripe, young body.

His touch was fire on her skin and it was with great effort that she pushed away from him. "Sebastian, don't! You are frightening me," she said and turned her body away from his searching hands. "Please leave me . . ."

"Ah, if I could leave, I would. But I cannot. You are fire in my blood, Brittannia," he said as he reached a dark arm toward her. "I can only bring you pleasure," he said softly.

He ran a warm hand along the curve of her body, reaching around to pull her over to him. She lay on her back now, her body exposed to his hungry eyes. She could feel his black, piercing gaze devour every inch of her quivering body and her face burned with shame. She brought her hands to cover her nakedness but he stopped her with his arm.

"Let me look at you," he said as he moved closer and took one taut nipple in his mouth. "Ah, you are beautiful!"

Brittannia laid her head back and looked up at the dark canopy above her. What was happening to her? she wondered as she felt tears of shame sting the back of her eyes. She felt so weak. She felt as though this weren't really happening. She couldn't really be lying naked in bed with Sebastian Diaz, could she?

"Sebastian, what did you do to me?" she demanded. She pushed his head away from her body.

"I have done nothing," he lied as he quickly stood and began to undress. "But, now I'm going to make love to you, Brittannia. I will soon make you forget about all other men, make you forget about Captain Barclay."

Dain! He had been gentle with her, he had not forced her or drugged her. But, she remembered too well, he had left her side to find fulfillment in another woman's arms. She was tired of being used and then cast aside and when she turned to Sebastian, her eyes were two blue chips of ice as she spat, "Get out! Do you hear me? *GET OUT!*"

Sebastian threw his head back and laughed. "I'm not leaving, Brittannia. I've waited too long as it is." In a second he was beside her again, naked, and her body stiffened as his hand caressed her stomach and moved down to brush her thighs.

"You disgust me!"

He laughed again. "You're going to live with me, love me, and you're going to love doing it," he commanded in a voice deep with desire.

She pushed at him and tried to pull away.

His sinewy fingers dug into the flesh of her arm and she flinched involuntarily. His other hand grabbed her wealth of hair and roughly pulled her head back. He lowered his dark head toward her, his lips parting as they neared hers and kissed her savagely, hungrily.

She fought him, thrashing her legs up as she beat her fists against his back, and when his mouth finally released hers, she brought her hand around and slammed her palm across his face. The force of her blow stunned him for a mere second, then with a slow, sardonic smile, he said, "Ah, *bruja,* witch. You excite me!"

Brittannia quickly threw her legs over the large bed and stood up, fighting the dizziness that tried to claim her again. Sebastian's dark arm shot out and he grabbed her by the wrist before she could take flight.

She screamed wildly. She grabbed the bed post and as she pushed against it for leverage, she pulled her other arm free of Sebastian's tight hold. She ran blindly toward the door that led to the courtyard balcony.

When she threw the door open and ran out onto the balcony, Sebastian was right behind her. She gave no thought to her nakedness as she backed away from the dark Spaniard. Her only thoughts were of escape. She clutched tightly to the wrought iron railing as she cautiously stepped back with each step he took toward her.

"Brittannia, I am master here. There is no one who can help you. Come back inside with me." He spoke in a soft voice as if comforting a frightened child.

"No! Stay where you are!" Brittannia demanded in a shaky voice as she brought a trembling hand to her temple. Her rushing blood was speeding the drug through her body and her head felt as though it might spin right off her shoulders.

"Brittannia, do not fight it. Come, I will help you," Sebastian said and stepped quickly toward her, lunging at her.

Brittannia's arms shot up in defense. "Damn you!" she spat and turned to run.

Sebastian's arms closed around her with frightening strength and she writhed her body as she brought her head down and bit him hard on the arm. His hold loosened and she bolted away in that split second, her head spinning violently as she careened along the narrow balcony.

"Bitch!" he cried as he ran after her, grabbing a handful of hair that flew behind her in her flight.

Her head snapped back and she instinctively reached back to stop her hair from being pulled out of her scalp. Sebastian pulled her to him by her hair and curled one arm around her neck.

"I enjoy taming you," he whispered into her ear.

Brittannia was breathing deeply and when he put pressure on her throat she saw little pinpoints of light in front of her eyes and she knew she would faint if he didn't let her go soon. She dug into his arms with her nails and pulled at it with all her might.

"Are you going to behave now?" he asked, tightening his hold.

She nodded, wanting only to get precious air into her starved lungs. He loosened his hold on her and she quickly turned and pushed away once again. This time as she ran away from him the floor beneath her tipped and the world around her swayed and her vision was blurred by the tiny pinpoints as a loud ringing filled her ears. She heard Sebastian call her name, he sounded so far away that she had to turn and look. She looked at him, he was only a few feet from her, why couldn't she hear him clearly? She was running backward now and, unsure of her way, she turned, intending to put more distance between them. When she did, she tripped over her own feet and her legs gave way beneath her. She fell to the cold stone floor, hitting her head soundly on the wrought iron as she went.

She could feel her head hit as she tried to grab something to break her fall. She let the blackness come, welcoming the oblivion it brought.

Chapter 7

Brittannia fought her way up out of the clutching darkness, pushing with great strength against the heavy slumber that held her down and kept her weak. Her eyelids fluttered slowly open and she finally joined reality.

"Good morning, senorita," a voice said from the corner of the room.

Brittannia turned her head to see who spoke and quickly regretted the hasty movement. From the back of her head a white flash of pain coursed into her brain and she gingerly touched her temple with trembling fingers.

"Be careful, you are to lie still," the voice said.

"Who are you?" Brittannia asked, her own voice sounding strange to her ears.

"My name is Maria. You do not remember?" Maria asked, worry creasing her smooth brow. She stood and then approached Brittannia's bed.

"Remember? I don't remember anything," Brittannia replied, her voice rising in fear. "Where am I? I—I can't remember anything!" she cried aloud as a tear fell down her cheek and she turned to Maria, her blue green eyes large with fright.

"Senorita, please, do not get upset. You'll remember in time. You hit your head and you slept all yesterday and this morning and—" Maria spoke quickly, her mind filling with guilt. Had she given the senor too potent a drug? She racked her mind trying to remember. She had filled the vial half full, like she was supposed to do. But had that been too much? "And that is how this sickness goes," she supplied quickly. "You forget and then you remember after awhile." Her heart wrenched at the frightened look in Brittannia's eyes. She didn't know if she would ever remember but she had to comfort her.

Brittannia listened intently to Maria, searching the planes of the girl's face for something that would make her remember. She said, "I hit my head? How?"

Maria cast her eyes down. "I—I do not know. I wasn't there."

"Who was there? Anyone?"

Maria shifted uneasily. She didn't want Brittannia to remember that night, for surely it must have been a terrible ordeal for the senorita. Senor Diaz had been in a rage ever since, giving sharp orders and punishing anyone who didn't do his bidding quick enough.

"Yes," Maria answered reluctantly, "the senor was with you."

"Senor who?" came the next question.

"Senor Diaz, he—"

"He is here," Sebastian interrupted as he strode purposefully into the room. "And I am most concerned about you," he said as he smiled at Brittannia, and then

136

turning to Maria he said, "Come, I wish to speak with you."

Maria gave Brittannia a quick nod and followed Sebastian out the door. "She does not remember, senor," she supplied once they were in the hall.

Sebastian smiled. "Good, it was a night worth forgetting."

"No," Maria said. "She does not remember anything, not even her name! Do you think the drug was too potent?"

If Sebastian was concerned about Brittannia's loss of memory he did not show it. No emotion passed over his dark features. He said, "You may leave now. I'll personally tend to the senorita. No one is to be near this room unless I say so. And not a word of what happened to her, understand?"

"*Sí*, I understand," she said, and with a quick curtsy, she hurried down the hall.

Sebastian ran a finger across his black mustache and then reentered the room, a warm smile fixed on his lips. "*Querido*, how are you feeling?" he asked as he pulled a chair up beside Brittannia's bed and sat down.

Brittannia pulled the covers up to cover herself. "I do not remember you," she said in a formal tone. "Your presence in my rooms is most uncomfortable."

Sebastian smiled as he sat back and crossed one black-clad leg over his knee. "I see your memory fails you. Not to worry," he said as he waved one hand in the air, "you'll soon remember. Hopefully before the wedding."

"Wedding?" she asked. "Whose wedding?"

"Ours, Brittannia."

Brittannia's mouth formed a small "O" as she looked

137

questioningly to Sebastian and asked, "Married?" and then, "My name is Brittannia?"

Sebastian laughed as he took her small hand in his. "Ah, Brittannia, surely you remember that we are to be married in a fortnight? Why, it was you who wanted the wedding date moved to a nearer day."

"No," she whispered breathlessly as she pulled her hand away, "I don't remember!"

"Give it time, *querido*," he said as he stood. "I'll let you rest now. If you need anything just ring the bell," he finished, gesturing toward a small bell on the bedside table and then with a light kiss to her forehead, he left the room.

Married? Had she really accepted a proposal of marriage to the dark Spaniard? If so, why couldn't she remember just a shred of some feeling that surely a young bride would feel for her intended? It was a terrible thing not being able to remember, and as Brittannia sat there willing herself to remember something from her past, an overwhelming feeling of depression settled over her. Try though she might, no memories came flooding or even trickling back to her. Exhausted from her mental exercises and still suffering the dull, throbbing ache at the back of her head, Brittannia soon gave into the depression and spent the rest of the morning weeping and sleeping.

By mid-day a tray was brought to her and a silent Maria stood by while Brittannia forced herself to eat a few bites of the elaborate fare. Maria had not said two words since coming in and as she was clearing away the remains of the lunch, Brittannia said, "I'd like to bathe. Could you please see that things are made ready for me?"

"Si," Maria replied. "Are you sure you are strong enough to make it to the next room, or do you prefer a sponge bath in bed?"

"I prefer to soak in a tubful of hot water. Please see to it," Brittannia ordered a little more tersely than she should have. The ache in her head was throbbing unmercifully and all she wanted was to relax the tension in her spine and to remember!

Maria went to do Brittannia's bidding and Brittannia threw back the covers of her canopied bed and slowly maneuvered herself to the edge. Gingerly she raised herself to her feet and stood for a moment on shaky legs until she felt she had the strength to move across the room.

She spied two large sea chests in the far corner of the room, and deciding they must belong to her, carefully walked over to investigate their contents. The lid of the first trunk was heavy and cumbersome and she had to get down on her knees, fighting a wave of dizziness, before she could pull the lid up and push it back. The trunk was filled with accessories: ribbons, gloves, shoes, chemises, silk stockings, and other underclothing neatly arranged between layers of tissue. She pushed through the conveniences and came upon a deep box made of gold. It looked to be a jewelry box and on the top, the initials *B.M.D.* were engraved in elaborate scroll.

Evidently the first initial stood for Brittannia, she couldn't recall what the last two initials might stand for. Slowly she opened the heavy, ornate lid and peered into the box. On the top was a tray with four different compartments filled with jewelry. Necklaces and pendants of all lengths, earrings, and bracelets overflowed the small space and Brittannia stared at the array of them, trying to catch any memory that one of the pieces might stir.

No memory fleeted by and she lifted the tray from the box, setting it on the carpet beside her. Beneath the tray the cavity of the box was filled with folded papers held down by a silver, circular dish. She picked up the dish and held it up to the light. It was almost crude in its making, but there was something about it, perhaps its handmade look that made it seem special. She held the top and bottom of it together and turned it over. On the bottom was an inscription that read: To Brittannia, with love, Lord Denning.

This had been given to her? Why couldn't she remember? She turned it back over and lifted the lid. Inside, on a bed of dark blue satin, lay a delicate gold chain and a heart locket with tiny swirls across it. She lifted the dainty chain between two fingers, wondering why it hadn't been packed carelessly into the tray as all the other jewelry had.

"What is special about this?" she asked aloud to herself, and as she studied it, she saw the heart opened to display two pictures of a dark-haired man. Something in his face, perhaps the curve of his full lips, reminded Brittannia of something, but she didn't know what. She sat on her knees for a very long time wondering just what it was about the man in the pictures. She snapped the locket shut, staring forward. Instead of the wall before her she saw storm-gray eyes and a sensuous mouth that tilted up at the corners while they spoke unheard words to her. Why would she keep something so carefully packed? Was the picture of an uncle, a close friend, a love?

There was a knock at the door and Brittannia jumped, she had been so close, so close to remembering. Remembering something, no matter how small was important to her, and as Maria held the door for a young dark-haired man to enter, Brittannia dropped the necklace back in the dish and turned impatiently to them.

"Excuse me, Senorita Brittannia. Here is the water for your bath. It was too heavy for me to carry so Carlos offered his help," Maria said as she cast a fond look at Carlos and then continued. "You will not mention to the senor that Carlos was in your room?"

"No," Brittannia said as she looked to Carlos with curiosity. "But why would he mind?"

Maria shut the door then said, "He would not mind, it is just that he wants as few people as possible bothering you."

"He need not worry about that," Brittannia replied, then turning to Carlos said, "So you are Carlos. I am, so I'm told, Brittannia."

Carlos cast Maria a puzzled look and then turned back to Brittannia. "You do not remember meeting—"

He was interrupted by Maria when she said, "Carlos, please pour the water so the senorita can bathe. I'm sure she is anxious."

"No," Brittannia said, anxious only to hear about her first meeting with Carlos. "I'm in no hurry. Please, go on."

Carlos looked suspiciously to Maria, searching her eyes for some answer to her strange behavior, and when he turned back to Brittannia, he said only, "I'll pour the water now."

Maria avoided Brittannia's eyes and walked quickly

141

behind Carlos, noticeably glad to be out of her close scrutiny.

Carlos poured the steaming water and as he left Maria in the adjacent room sorting fresh linen, Brittannia caught him before he left.

"I'd like to speak with you," she said in an urgent whisper, anxious to hear her story told from someone other than Sebastian or Maria.

"And I with you," he replied with a quick glance over his shoulder. "But not now. I will come when I can." With that he left the room.

Brittannia turned her attention back to the young girl in the adjoining room. "Would you please lay something out for me to wear to dinner? I plan to dine with," she waved her hand in the air, "whoever it is dines with us in the evenings."

In the other room Brittannia slid out of her robe, gingerly touching a toe to the scented water; it was warm and inviting and she quickly stepped into it. As she rubbed the dripping sponge along the curves of her body, she noticed two unsightly bruises on her arm; one on the inside, the other along the outer side. She stared at them, shocked at their presence, and wondered how they came to be. Just by the intensity of their color she knew she had recently received them and she shivered involuntarily, wondering just exactly how she fell.

"Brittannia, how beautiful you look!" Sebastian exclaimed as she descended the wide staircase.

She had a strange case of *déjà vu* as Sebastian took her arm and led her to the dining room and she told

142

him so.

"Of course you have, Brittannia. We are to be married! We've dined together many times. It shouldn't be long until you're fully recovered," he said.

Dinner was another elaborate fare, cooked to perfection. Brittannia ate slowly as she listened to Sebastian recount several stories of their times together. He seemed anxious to supply all of the facts, quite satisfied to fill her mind with his own memories rather than have her remember them on her own. Brittannia instinctively mistrusted Sebastian, though he was an excellent host and did nothing overtly to make her doubt his good intentions.

For Brittannia, the next few days went by as though they were weighted by chains. As she walked the numerous halls of the large house she came upon no one willing to say more than a cordial greeting to her. Granted, they were hired help, but she thought they could at least engage in a bit of friendly conversation. Not even Maria would say more than necessary while fitting Brittannia in what was to be her wedding dress.

She spent endless hours being fitted—standing, turning, and being poked at with pins. As she watched the yards of material being pinned, tucked, and sewed into a grand wedding dress, she began to have second thoughts about marrying Sebastian. She felt no love for the man and wondered if she ever would. She thought about leaving Andros. But where had she come from? The world outside of Andros seemed very dark and lonely, for she had no place to go, no relatives she could remember. And so, with a heavy heart, she let the wedding preparations continue.

As she stood for one last fitting of her dress,

Brittannia turned to Maria. "As my wedding day draws nearer I find I need someone to talk to," she paused then went on, "someone besides Senor Diaz."

Maria looked up from pinning the hem. "I see," she replied, still reluctant to talk to Brittannia lest she reveal something forbidden. "We can talk, we're talking now."

Seeing Maria had finished with the hem, Brittannia stepped off the stool. "But I want to talk as friends do. I need a friend."

Maria brushed an errant wisp of midnight dark hair slowly from her face. Her guilt at having given the drug to the senor had grown in intensity with each day. Especially since Brittannia's memory did not return and the wedding was only a week away. "I will be your friend. What do you wish to talk about?"

Brittannia moistened her lips. "How did I fall? Was it an accident?" she asked in a hush voice.

"I was not there when you fell," Maria replied carefully. "The senor said you tripped and fell. Of course it was an accident."

Brittannia let out the breath she had been holding and her shoulders sagged slightly. Of course it was an accident. And yet—why the bruises on her body, why the instinctive mistrust of Sebastian?

She asked herself these many questions but there were no answers. Instead there was nothing, just like when she tried to remember her past . . . nothing.

As the days wore on and her wedding day drew nearer, she felt a great tension chain her. She felt she might go mad if she didn't soon extricate herself from the situation. She sat in her rooms watching the setting sun and, knowing Sebastian could be found in his study this time of day, she stood and made her way downstairs. She had to tell Sebastian she would not marry him. How could she marry a man she didn't love and knew nothing about?

She gave a bold knock to the study door. At the sound of Sebastian's voice, she entered. "Sebastian, we have to talk," she said.

Sebastian was quickly to his feet and motioned for her to have a seat. His night-dark eyes scanned her face, trying to read her thoughts. "What is troubling you?" he said, taking a seat opposite her.

She folded her hands in her lap and took a deep breath. She looked him straight in the eye. "I can't marry you."

A tight muscle twitched in Sebastian's cheek. After a second of showing no emotion, a smile spread across his thin lips. "You are nervous, no?" He leaned forward and covered her folded hands with his. "It is usually the groom who gets cold feet, but you have been through a lot in the past few weeks and so I understand your mixed feelings."

"No, Sebastian," she said, his closeness unnerving her. "I don't think you understand. I don't love you."

He straightened and leaned back. "Brittannia . . ." His voice sounded tight and hurt. "It tears at my heart to hear such words from the woman I love. Surely, you do not mean that. You are my life, *querido*. I want you for my wife and until your accident you wanted me just as much. We've shared so much, how can you say now that you don't love me?"

"Sebastian, please understand," she pleaded. "I—I don't remember anything. I don't know you anymore. I don't even know myself anymore. Perhaps in time . . ."

"Ah, Brittannia," he said, taking hold of her shoulders. "Of course your memory will soon return and all the feelings you have for me will come rushing back. And that is why I can't let you destroy all of our plans. For your sake I can't let you do this!"

"I don't know," she said uncertainly.

"Marry me, Brittannia," he said. "We'll share the intimacies of husband and wife and I will make you remember." He brought his dark head toward her fair one and his lips claimed hers.

Brittannia arched her neck, letting his lips play over her own. It was a slow, lazy kiss that he assaulted her with and it stirred sensations in her body she wanted to deny. His tongue brushed by her pliant lips and with savoring slowness explored her mouth, fanning the flame of desire that had begun to grow within her.

He gave a slight groan as his lips left hers and kissed a fiery trail to her hair. "Marry me," he whispered, his voice husky.

"Please don't," she pleaded as she pulled away. "You're confusing me."

"Tell me you don't want me now," he pressed.

"I'm human," she said, trying to fight down the growing desire.

"Brittannia, I love you. Please don't deny me. Marry me." His voice was hoarse with desire, and he drew her close again, showering the slender arch of her throat with kisses.

"Sebastian, I—" she said breathlessly as she threw her head back and welcomed his passionate kisses.

"I need you, Brittannia. I could not live without you, I wouldn't want to."

Brittannia felt his strong arms caress her back; his touch was warm and she found herself craving it. Perhaps, she thought, marriage to him would not be so terrible.

"Yes," she whispered as she ran her fingers through his black hair. "I'll marry you."

Chapter 8

The silver moon shone bold and bright upon the lovers as they embraced then drew apart. A sea-borne breeze blew across them, cooling their warm skin.

Maria was the first to speak. "I'm sorry, Carlos. But he ordered me to get the drug and fill the vial half full."

The way Carlos stroked her long hair and the look in his eyes told her he forgave her for the part she'd played. She was glad she'd decided to tell him everything. For the first time since that night, she felt the weight of her guilt leave her slim shoulders.

"I'm worried about the senorita," she went on. "She did not want to be here at first, and if she had her memory I'm sure she would not marry Senor Diaz."

"How do you know?" Carlos questioned, his mind sorting through all Maria had told him. "How can you be so sure?"

"A woman can see these things," she said, not yet ready to tell Carlos of the true Sebastian. "The day she arrived I found her staring at a locket and there were tears in her eyes. One would have to have been blind not to see the pain of losing someone she loved, still loves, written on her face."

Carlos looked to Brittannia's window and his black eyes clouded over. "I'm going to talk to her, perhaps I can find something to jog her memory with. I'll be back, wait here for me."

"Carlos, it is late. You can't bother her now."

"The wedding is day after tomorrow," he said urgently. "We have no time to waste." Then he was running through the darkness to the house.

Brittannia jumped at the sound of the knock upon her door. It was late and she had thought everyone but herself to be asleep. She opened the door cautiously until she saw it was Carlos.

"Forgive me for bothering you, senorita," he whispered. "I must talk to you."

Brittannia pulled her robe about her and tightened the knot around her small waist. "Now?" she asked.

Carlos nodded. "May I come in?"

"I'll get dressed and meet you in the study and we can discuss—"

"No," Carlos interrupted, then with a quick glance down the hall he hurried on. "I don't want anyone to see us speaking together."

Brittannia motioned for him to enter her bedchamber. She quietly closed the door.

He stood in the middle of the room, his blue black hair shining in the gaslamp and as he looked to Brittannia his black eyes were full of concern. "Have you regained your memory?" he asked.

Brittannia shook her head.

"Is there nothing that will help you remember? A piece of clothing, a locket perhaps?"

"No, noth—" she started to say, then caught herself. "A locket, did you say? What do you know of the locket?"

Carlos shrugged his broad, young shoulders. "I know nothing of it. I only wish to help you remember."

"But how did you know I own a locket?" she pressed.

"The day you arrived you wore a locket about your neck and your hand touched it many times, as if it brought you peace of mind to feel its presence."

Brittannia looked to the trunk in the corner. She remembered the moment she had held the locket in her hands and a fleeting glimpse of gray eyes and smiling lips had passed by her.

"Yes," she said slowly, "I came across the locket and it did bring back something. But memory eludes me."

"Could I see it?"

"Certainly," she replied. "It's in this trunk." She crossed the room and retrieved the gold box, carefully removing the upper tray and reaching to get the silver dish. She took the locket from its bed of blue satin and handed it to Carlos.

Carlos carefully opened the heart to study the picture inside. The face, with its rugged contours, looked familiar but he had been in many seaports in his young life and had seen many faces. "Do you know him?" he asked as he looked to Brittannia.

She shook her head. "I don't think so, but there's something about him."

"Is there anything else in the box that stirs a memory?" He took the gold box and pulled the pack of papers out. "Is there no address here, no name of someone you could contact?"

"I've looked through a few," Brittannia replied, fingering the locket. "They are all London addresses and Sebastian has promised to take me there soon after we're married. I'll wait until then to contact them. Who knows how long it would take for a letter to get there in these turbulent times."

Carlos scanned the many letters in the stack. As he neared the bottom he found an invitation written on an elaborate letterhead. The return address was George Street in Nassau! He quickly skimmed the letter to find the name Michael Delving scrawled in bold handwriting at the bottom.

"Michael Delving, do you know him?" he asked.

Brittannia thought hard for a moment. "No, I—I don't think so, but the name sounds vaguely familiar."

She clutched the locket tightly as she willed her mind to remember. She could see a wealth of blazing candles around her and the man beside her had laughing brown eyes. She felt his light hold on her arm and after she turned from taking a glass of champagne from a passing servant, she saw the brown eyes had turned to midnight-black and the man beside her became Sebastian!

"I can't remember!" she cried and let out a breath in exasperation.

"I'm sorry, Senorita Brittannia," Carlos said. "Perhaps in time you will come to remember." He walked toward the door, the George Street address etched in his mind. "I only wanted to help you," he said, "not upset you."

Brittannia held the door for him. "I'm touched that you cared enough to help."

"Good night," he said. With a quick look in both directions, he disappeared down the hall.

Brittannia peered one more time at the face inside the locket and was warmed by the man's face. She didn't know why, but she put the locket around her neck, clasped it, and let it fall between her nightdress and skin. She extinguished the gaslamp and crawled into bed. A feeling of warmth spread through her limbs as she fell into the most restful sleep she'd had in days.

As Brittannia snuggled deeper into her secure cocoon of blankets, Carlos made his way through the night to the waiting arms of Maria. She was sitting beneath a tree twirling a closed blossom between two fingers.

"Carlos, what took so long?"

"I've got an address of someone who, I'm sure, will be concerned about Brittannia's whereabouts. I'm leaving for Nassau tonight."

"But, how will you get there?" She grabbed tightly onto his arm. "If the senor learns of your intentions he'll kill you! I can't let you go, I won't!"

"Maria, please." He took her hand from his arm and placed it gently at her side. "I cannot stand idly by and watch an injustice be carried out. I have a feeling Senor Diaz is not being truthful with Brittannia. I will do what I can to help her."

"But what of us?" Maria demanded. "You promised to take me away from Andros, to build a life together somewhere else. The senor will kill you when he learns of your betrayal and then I'll be without you. Oh, Carlos, I could not bear that!" She threw her arms about his neck and held him tightly to her.

He endured her melodramatics for only a moment

and then he pulled her arms from his neck. "I will be back soon. If anyone asks you of my whereabouts, you know nothing." He cupped her chin in his hand. "I must do what I must."

She nodded her head as a single tear coursed down her lovely brown cheek and Carlos lovingly wiped it away. "None of that, Maria. We are strong." He tipped his head slightly and brought it toward hers, claiming her parted lips with his.

They tasted each other hungrily. Wrapping their arms tightly around each other, they felt their love flow and knew there was nothing they couldn't face together. Theirs was a love borne of respect, trust, and desire.

"Good luck, my love," she whispered as she turned her tear-damp eyes up at him.

With one last caress to her cheek, he sprinted off in the direction of the shore.

The wind borne out at sea brought with it thick, dark clouds as it swept over Andros Island, hiding the bright moon and casting all things in dark shadows. Carlos made his way quickly over the familiar, twisting path to the small, rounded hut that stood near the ocean-lapped shore. A light burned within the small space and he hurried toward it, anxious to secure a boat and be on his way. The ocean roared ceaselessly in the distance. He pushed the door of the hut open, blinking his black eyes against the bright light.

"I need a boat," he said urgently. "Tonight."

A large native man stood, recognizing his friend and the urgency of his voice. He nodded his head in understanding and pointed beyond Carlos to the dark world outside the small hut.

Carlos thanked the man and sped outside to the place beneath the pawpaw tree he knew the crude native boat would be. He dragged it across the white sand, into the cool water, and over the coral shoals to the wide expanse of the ocean. He rowed fiercely and was soon caught by the current that propelled the boat north, toward Nassau.

With the unending push of the current and his furious rowing he slowly made his way to Nassau. In the coolness of the late night perspiration soaked his white billowing shirt and his muscles burned with each lift and dip of the crudely made oar. The night passed slowly. A gray, misty morning was finally revealed as the cool wind whipped across the ocean and sent the dark clouds skirting away. His muscles were worked tight and stung with each thrust of the oar. He wasted no time dwelling on the pain his body suffered; instead he kept his black eyes fixed on the endless stretch of water before him and concentrated on the down, push, up, forward, down, push, up, forward motion of his arm.

The day wore on. The sun climbed high in the now cloudless sky and hung as a great blinding ball of yellow that beat unmercifully down on him. He wiped the sweat from his brow and cursed himself for not having the foresight to bring a supply of water with him. His tongue was thick in his mouth and he scooped water from the ocean to splash upon his brow in hopes of staving off the faintness he felt. By afternoon he finally reached Nassau and docked at the pier.

"Whoa, mate," a stout dockworker said as he grabbed Carlos by the arm. "Where do you think you're going?"

Carlos looked down at the meaty hand that clasped his forearm and picked it off with his other hand. "I've got business in Nassau."

"Ain't to be no one coming or going. Fever's running wild through the city. You best turn around and get to where you came from." The man rudely pushed Carlos back toward the native boat, nearly sending him into the water.

A muscle twitched in Carlos's cheek as he regained his balance and summed up his opponent. In one fluid movement he slammed his elbow into the man's thick stomach and sent him sprawling to the dock. Carlos wasted no time to see if the man got up; he instead had to dodge a few tars and sailors who had witnessed the scene and tried to grab him. He pumped his arms and ran hard up the incline to the streets above the harbor. He had been in Nassau numerous times before and knew his way blindfolded through the maze of littered streets and alleys.

As he went, an ominous feeling settled over him. The usual hubbub of people, animals, drays, and carts was not to be found. Houses, bars, and even hotels were closed tight with shutters shut and curtains drawn. Only a few stalls along Market Street were open for business and the few people who were shopping had their mouths and noses covered with handkerchiefs or scarves and all noticeably avoided contact with anyone else.

Carlos kept to his path. His pace quickened when he had to leave the middle of the road to let a funeral procession pass. He instinctively put his hand to his face as the wagon rumbled by.

He sprinted the last incline and hurried along George

Street, anxious to find the house number he sought. He found it easily enough but painted onto the gate surrounding the manse was a white cross. A sense of dread overcame him as the meaning of the white cross sunk in; it was to let others know the occupants had been overcome by yellow fever!

He peered up at the large, two-story house and hit his fist hard against the black iron railing. So far. He had come so far, only to be deterred by some white paint haphazardly painted on wrought iron.

Yellow fever be damned, he thought savagely. Clutching at the gate he pulled at it with all his might. Finding it was locked tight, he pulled back and thrust himself up and over the unmoving obstacle. He landed lightly on the other side and with a quick glance in all directions he bolted toward the great house. He took the wide steps two at a time and without bothering to check both ends of the veranda, reached for the door knocker.

"Who are you and what do you want?" a deep voice demanded to know.

Carlos spun around and came face to face with a powerfully built, well-dressed man. He was the healthiest person Carlos had seen in Nassau that day.

"My name is Carlos. Please, I must speak with Senor Delving. It is important!"

"Mr. Delving is one of very few who is recovering from a tough battle with the fever. He's not to be disturbed." The man leaned casually back on the wooden ledge of the sweeping veranda.

Carlos had come too far to be deterred and he had no time to waste. "I must see him!"

The man shook his dark head. "No, but perhaps I

can help you. I'm Dain Barclay, a close friend of Michael's." Dain extended a suntanned hand in Carlos's direction.

"I have news of a friend," Carlos explained as he shook Dain's hand. "At least I think she's a friend. She's in trouble and needs his help."

"A woman? That sounds like Michael. He chases anything in skirts. Go on, boy. You say this lady's in trouble?"

"Yes, she was abducted and she lost her memory. Now she is to be wed to the very man who abducted her."

Dain laughed lightly. "Sounds positively cloak and dagger to me." At the intense, sober look on Carlos's face he became serious. "Tell me the lady's name, perhaps I know her."

"Brittannia. Brittannia Denning."

Dain's heart skipped a beat. *Brittannia.* The wildcat he had tamed in a small hut by the ocean, the woman who had come to be the center of his every dream. *Brittannia.* The turquoise-eyed beauty who caused his passion to rise with the mere memory of her creamy skin beneath his hands. He grabbed Carlos roughly by the shoulders. "Where is she?" he demanded, wild thoughts coursing through his mind. Brittannia in trouble? He had returned to Nassau after his run only to find her hotel room empty. She'd left no message. When he went to see Michael to learn her whereabouts he found his friend delirious with yellow fever.

Soon the fever had spread through Nassau and no runs could be made. All he could do was stay with Michael and see he was nursed back to health. There had been no word from Brittannia—and he was just as glad that she was away from the yellow fever plague.

"Where is she?" he repeated, his gray eyes taking on a stormy look.

"You know her, Senor Barclay?" Carlos asked, almost frightened by the mad look on Dain's face.

"Of course I know her and the scurve who took her will rue the day he ever laid eyes on her!"

"Senor Diaz is a ruthless man and—"

Diaz. So that is where she had gone. He'd warned her against seeing that man. Obviously she had been too overwhelmed by the Spaniard's charms to pay attention to Dain's warning. His mind whirled in a confused state of jealousy and anger.

"Sebastian Diaz has Brittannia in his home on Andros Island, I presume." Dain struck his fist hard on the wooden rail as thoughts of Brittannia lying naked in Diaz's arms wavered before his eyes like a lantern show. She had made such a charming show of her innocence. And yet she had gone from his bed right into the arms of a man like Diaz! A muscle twitched along his jawline. How many hours had his mind betrayed him in conjuring up visions of the dazzling Brittannia—how much time had he wasted in remembering the silken feel of her ripe body. No woman had ever haunted him, no woman had ever kept his thoughts prisoner—not until Brittannia. And now, now she was on Andros Island, trapped into marrying that scum Diaz. Well, it was no more than she deserved.

His thoughts were dark indeed as he stood by the rail.

"*Sí,*" Carlos said, interrupting his musings, "she is on Andros. She needs your help."

Dain's head jerked up, his eyes stone cold. *"My* help?" he asked in a ruthless voice. "Brittannia needs no help from me. She's obviously helping herself quite generously—to any man who'll have her!"

Carlos felt his hope slipping away. He had thought this man would help him. "Please, senor, she is in great danger. I can not do this on my own."

"You've wasted a trip, son."

Carlos looked long and hard at the man before him, the man who suddenly looked as if he were filled with demons. "Then if you will not help me I must speak with Senor Delving, ill or no." He turned to walk into the house but a strong hand clamped down on his shoulder and held him back.

"You leave Delving out of this," Dain said in a low voice. "He doesn't need to hear of this, not in his condition."

"Then you will help me? Will you help Brittannia escape Andros?"

There was a long pause in which Dain gave great thought. In the end he realized he hadn't much choice. For the sake of his friendship with Michael Delving if nothing else, he was honor-bound to try and help her.

"Yes," he finally said. "I will help you."

Carlos's face broke into a wide grin for already Dain was making his way down the stairs. "Have you a fast ship, senor? We will need a strong crew too for Senor Diaz keeps his home well guarded."

"I captain the fastest blockade runner afloat," Dain said as he made his way to the stable and threw open the door. "As to the strength—there aren't many who can best me." He quickly saddled one of the three horses. Once on the powerful animal's back he motioned for

Carlos to climb up behind him. Carlos was no sooner astride when Dain spurred the animal into a fast run for the harbor.

They had no trouble rounding up the crew, for most were on the docks passing their idle time with dice and rum. Once on ship they ran into a little difficulty. Officials would not let them leave the harbor as no one was to leave the island until the quarantine was lifted. With a few words to the right people and a large sum of money following, Dain soon had the *Airlee* out of the harbor and under a full head of steam.

Dain stood on the rolling deck of the *Airlee* as she breasted the waves and made a straight course for the northern tip of Andros Island. His thoughts, as he stared out on the endless stretch of blue, were of a night that seemed a lifetime ago. The steady pulse of the engines below decks seemed to say: Brittannia, Brittannia . . .

He could see her golden blond mane of hair fanned out around her exquisite face and her eyes—blue green and full of passion—were only for him. He could see her lips moving and he heard her sweet, honeyed voice say, *Yes, yes, damn you,* . . .

The night they had shared together seemed so long ago and his body craved her, needed her, and damn but he wanted her despite her affair with Diaz. His hands balled into tight, capable fists at his sides. He couldn't wait to squeeze the life from Sebastian Diaz if he had harmed Brittannia. He'd kill him with his bare hands, crush his windpipe, make him pay for anything he'd done to Brittannia.

161

"Land ahoy!" a sailor called from the small cross-trees.

Dain was brought to the present by the shout and he bellowed orders so that all could hear. He had chosen five of his best men to go ashore with him, the rest would stay on board, ready to sail at any time.

They dropped anchor and two small boats were lowered to the turbulent, angry waters of the Tongue of the Ocean.

"You're sure of your directions?" Dain asked Carlos as he surveyed the desolate stretch of sand. There were no signs of civilization and Dain had the eerie feeling he was stepping onto a land from a different time period; a period before mankind where only the elements raged.

"*Sí*, the house is south from here and once in the forest you will find there are many paths that lead to it."

Nearer to land they jumped out of the small boats and pushed them over the coral shoals and onto the sand. The ceaseless roar of water lessened as they made their way cautiously into the dense forest. A black parrot squawked in alarm and with flapping wings left its perch in one of the mangroves. The heat was sweltering amid the thick tangled mass. Insects assailed them on all parts of their bodies as they pushed past wild, scratching briars.

Carlos was unfaltering as he led them through the rich growth, his blue black hair plastered to his head from sweat. Although his muscles quivered from over-exertion he kept a quick pace, leading the group through the jungled maze. When they reached the forest end he held up his arm and stopped. Turning to Dain, he said, "There is the house. I will go first to make sure the way is clear."

Dain stepped up beside Carlos and looked out to the wide expanse of forest-cleared land. Amidst the green sea of grass lay the blindingly white two-story mansion. "Which window is Brittannia's room? I want her out of the house before I blow it sky-high."

"Her rooms are in the back wing. "I'll lead you there but first I must see where the senor and his men are." He motioned for the men to keep low until he returned. Then he sprinted off toward the manse, the huge bell of his sleeves billowing out behind him.

As he rounded the back of the house he nearly toppled Maria and her bundle of island flowers as he ran into her. "Maria! Maria!" he cried breathlessly. "Was I missed? Has the senor asked for me?"

She shook her head, her dark cloud of hair brushing gently across her shoulders. "Did you find someone who can help the senorita?"

"Yes. He's in the forest with five of his men. He will take her by force if necessary."

Maria searched the edge of the dark forest. "By force is the only way he will get her. The senor has never been in a better mood. These flowers," she said, holding up the wild array, "are for the wedding, by his demand. Pah! He never cared before if a single blossom adorned the inside of his home."

"Where is he now?"

"I do not know. I have not seen him since morning."

"Do as usual, Maria, but be ready to flee at any moment. There is sure to be a fight. If you hear any commotion, run to the northern bight and wait for me. If I'm not there in twenty-four hours, leave the island. Flee for your life!"

She gasped. "I will not leave without you!"

"You will," he commanded and with a quick kiss to her cheek, he sprinted away.

He entered the house on silent feet and ducked any servants by slipping into a closet or taking a sharp turn down one of the many halls. Warily he made his way to Sebastian's study. When he pressed his ear to the thick door, he heard the sound of muffled voices from within. The deeper voice, he knew, belonged to Sebastian. He made his way back through the halls and once outside sprinted toward the row of small houses where the sailors and hired ruffians slept. He went around to the main house where he knew the men gathered to gamble and drink to pass the time. Sure enough, the men were there and at this late hour in the afternoon, most were drunk and near to passing out.

He felt his blood quicken through his veins as he furtively picked his way across the open expanse of lawn to Dain and his waiting men. Had he turned and glanced toward the mansion once more he might have seen a shadow standing near the study window, might have seen Johnson part the heavy drapes, and with a suspicious eye, watch him duck into the dense forest and emerge with one man behind him; a man with a gun slung across his back. But Carlos did not turn; instead he kept straight for the spot he left the men. After recounting to Dain where everyone was and giving directions to the five other men to the main gambling house, he again ventured out into the open lawns, this time with Dain right behind him.

Brittannia sat in her rooms looking out at the blue

sky above the mansion. If she had stepped out onto her terrace at that moment and looked to the lawns below, she would have seen Carlos racing into the dark forest. But seated in a rattan chair inside the terrace door, her view was of the sea, of dark pine and mahogany trees, and the darkening blue canopy that stretched above it.

She fingered the tiny gold locket that hung about her neck and wondered again who had given it to her. Tomorrow was her wedding day. She should be excited and happy at the prospect of sharing a life with her new husband, but strangely she dreaded it.

She remembered back to the day in Sebastian's study when she'd said she'd marry him. *What a fool I was,* she thought. She didn't know why she'd said yes. Perhaps it had been her fear of never remembering her past, her fear of having to walk out into a world full of unknown faces, into a world that demanded a woman to have some resources; friends or relatives to support her until she married. With no memory what would she do, how would she survive in such a world?

She knew her fear hadn't been her only reason. Sebastian had proved to be an expert at seducing her. He had ignited in her a flame that had long lay dormant, a flame that licked with abandon and soon burned out of control. Perhaps if she'd had her memory she would not have succumbed to his kisses, his caresses, his sweet whispers. Perhaps she would have been strong enough to pull away, to flee from his tight embrace and potent kisses, but in her condition she was vulnerable and she had been drawn like a moth to a flame when he had pledged his love to her and said he couldn't bear to live without her. She had said one word: "yes," and that had set all the wheels in motion.

And as the days had passed and she was drawn into the flurry of activity in preparation of the wedding, she felt the strength to call things off slip away from her. It was so much easier to let the fates carry her, let them take her where they would.

Carlos knelt beside Dain in the thick forest. "The coast is clear. Senor Diaz is in the study and the bulk of his men are drunk." He quickly gave directions to Dain's men to the barracks and common room.

Dain kept close to the ground as he followed Carlos across the great lawn to the mansion. He pushed the Remington rifle to a more comfortable position on his back and reached instinctively to the knife strapped to his waist. He would leave no escape for Sebastian Diaz. Carlos led the way into the back of the great house, and with each cautious step they marked their ground and listened for footsteps that never came. Dain's storm-gray eyes surveyed the great halls they passed through and with the stealth of a thief he made his way to Sebastian's study. He planned to deal with Sebastian then race upstairs and take Brittannia from her gilded cage.

His plan might have succeeded if Johnson had not already alerted Sebastian and run swiftly to the men's barracks, readying them for a fight.

Dain and Carlos stood, one on each side of Sebastian's study door, guns poised. In one fluid movement, Dain released the door latch, pushed the door wide, and stepped into the study with his gun held in front of him, ready to shoot. Four muzzles greeted them; two pointed at him, the other two at Carlos.

166

Sebastian stepped from the far dark corner of the room, a sardonic smile fixed on his thin lips. "Carlos, you disappoint me. Had I wanted Captain Barclay to attend my wedding, I would have brought him myself."

Dain ground his teeth together and gave Sebastian a dark, warning look. "Where's Brittannia?" he demanded.

Sebastian laughed. "Ah, jealousy. I did not think you were a man to feel such human emotions, Barclay. It seems I have misjudged you on all counts, for I also did not think you to be stupid enough to let the lovely Brittannia slip from your fingers."

A muscle twitched along Dain's jaw and his fingers itched to pull the trigger of his gun. "Where is she?" he repeated.

Sebastian ignored his question and the tone of his voice. "I never did care to bed a virgin," he commented easily, a sardonic smile on his thin lips. "I must say when you break one in you do a fine job. Brittannia has brought to my bed many tricks that please me . . . and I'm not an easy man to please." The lie came easily to him.

A white flash of anger went through the whole of Dain's body. "Damn you, Diaz!" he growled as he swiftly brought his rifle up but before he could fire a shot from its chamber, one of Sebastian's men fired a round and a bullet grazed by Dain's arm, piercing the skin and causing him to drop his weapon.

Dain clutched at the bleeding limb as his stormy eyes turned to flints of steel. "You'll have to kill me before you marry Brittannia!" he hissed.

"And I will," Sebastian said, snapping his fingers, motioning for his men to subdue the two men. "In time,

167

I will."

"To think I once thought highly of you," Carlos said as a sailor grabbed his weapon and bound his hands behind his back. His brown eyes were full of disgust. "You'll pay for this, I swear! You're a dead man!"

Sebastian seemed not affected by the look Carlos cast him. "I'm not dead yet," he said as he rubbed a finger along his dark mustache, and then turning to his small band of cutthroats, said, "Take them below the house. Kill them. Slowly."

The burly men nodded in unison, and as they slung their rifles onto their thick backs, they pushed Dain and Carlos toward the cellar stairs, toward the airless rooms that waited below.

Brittannia stood from the rattan chair and paced the room. She was restless. She felt her nerves being drawn tight as the clock ticked and the hour of her wedding drew nearer. She couldn't sit alone in her rooms any longer. She needed to talk with someone, needed to get her mind off what would take place early tomorrow morning.

She left her rooms and passed quickly through the spacious hall. She was about to descend the wide staircase when she heard a man yell Sebastian's name. She then heard a gun fire and the sound of something clatter to the floor and a man's quick indrawn breath. She instinctively stepped away from the stairs and leaned back against the wall, straining to hear what was taking place beyond the stairs in Sebastian's study.

She heard the stranger's voice again. This time his words were slow and his voice was low. It was a haunt-ingly familiar voice. She heard the stranger say her name and tell Sebastian that he'd have to kill him before he'd allow him to marry her. *That voice*—it brought back a fleeting glimpse of gray eyes and a smiling mouth. She could hear that same voice murmuring something sweet to her. But the total memory eluded her and when her mind returned to the present she heard Sebastian ordering his men to kill him.

She flew back down the hall to the safety of her rooms. Kill who? Her whole body trembled as she shut the door and leaned her back against it. Whom had Sebastian ordered to be killed and why? Her body shuddered with revulsion. She was going to marry the man who had ordered death so casually!

Chapter 9

"Maria, please!" Brittannia pleaded as Maria again scorched her scalp with the hot curling stick. "One would think it were your wedding day instead of mine! If you'll get my slippers, I'll finish here." She took the curling stick from Maria's fingers and placed it on the stone plate atop the vanity.

Brittannia's hands trembled slightly as she stroked a faint touch of pink to her cheeks with a sable-tipped brush. She was nervous. In ten minutes she was to meet Sebastian downstairs and from there they would walk across the lawns to the small chapel. Soon she would speak the vows that would forever bind her to Sebastian, soon she would feel the cold band of gold being slipped onto her finger. Soon she would belong to him . . .

"Senorita, are you ready for your dress?"

Brittannia put a hand over her eyes for a moment. "Yes. Yes, bring it over, please."

Maria silently helped her into the wedding dress. It was a creation of white silk threaded with silver and

171

sprinkled here and there with pink-centered daisies which were veiled with white tulle. The puffed sleeves left her shoulders bare and a white satin sash was tied around her waist. Brittannia slipped her feet into the high-heeled, satin-covered slippers and made her way to the mirror for one last examination. Her silk skirt rustled crisply. As she turned for a view of the back, she felt no joy at the vision of white reflected there.

"You look lovely, Senorita Brittannia," Maria commented as she reached to the vanity to get a small velvet-covered box she had brought in with her. "Senor Diaz has asked that you wear these today." She opened the lid and handed the box to Brittannia.

If given to her by someone else, Brittannia might have gasped at the shimmering diamond necklace and matching earrings. They were a king's treasure. But today she merely glanced at them and put them on without comment.

Remembering the threat she had overheard Sebastian make, she asked hesitantly, "Maria, have you ever known Senor Diaz to be a violent man?"

Maria stiffened at the question. "No," she lied, "never violent without just cause." She abruptly turned to the task of repacking the brushes and porcelain jars into the makeup case.

Brittannia watched Maria's nervous movements. Perhaps the stranger she had overheard last night had been her enemy in the past, she thought, and Sebastian was only protecting her. But why hadn't Sebastian told her. And if the stranger had been an enemy why had she felt so drawn to his voice, why had it affected her so? She had no answers to these questions and as she descended the stairs to the waiting Sebastian, an ominous feeling settled over her.

The walk to the tiny chapel was over too soon for Brittannia. Although the birds sang and the early morning sun threw down its warm, slanted rays, Brittannia felt as though it were the darkest day of her life. In her dread of what was to come, she detached herself from the happenings around her. She went through the motions but her thoughts were far away.

Once inside, Sebastian left her side. As she watched him take his place near the altar, her mind drifted . . . she saw the man whose picture was in the locket, heard him speak to her. She wanted to answer him, wanted to speak his name, but she couldn't remember. She couldn't remember his name or what he had been to her.

Someone nudged her and she looked up from her thoughts. From the front of the church, Sebastian stood staring intently at her. It was time to begin her walk down the long aisle. When she reached Sebastian's side, he smiled down at her. The minister began the ceremony, his words monotone. Brittannia looked past him and focused on the cross behind him. She didn't hear a word he said, just the constant drone of his dull voice.

Brittannia was vaguely aware of a commotion behind her. Before she could turn and see what it was, a voice boomed through the church, so loud and deep it shook the very walls. She didn't need to turn around to know who owned the voice. A small tear fell down her cheek as the memories returned, flooding her mind.

Dain's voice rang out, a voice of pure authority that turned all heads. "Don't anybody make a move or it'll be your last."

She turned to him. He held a brace of pistols, both drawn and pointed at Sebastian. Behind him stood six men, all equally armed. He looked to her and gave her a quick nod. He had come for her! She drank in the sight of his tall, lean body. He stood with his feet planted wide, his stormy eyes surveying the small crowd, daring them to try and pass by. Dark, gold-tinged curls tumbled down his forehead as he gave his dark head a toss. "Move away from him, Brittannia."

She did as he said, yanking the veil from her lustrous head and flinging it at Sebastian's feet.

Sebastian gave her a cold look, then turned to Dain. "Do you think your little band of merry men can overtake us? If so, you're quite mistaken."

He gave an almost imperceptible nod of his head. Instantly knives and pistols were drawn from hidden places and wielded with deadly precision. Soon the church was filled with vicious energy, smoking pistols and wild, demonlike yells.

Brittannia drew back in horror as she watched one of Sebastian's men jump from the back of a pew and land on Carlos. Just as the ruffian drew back his thick arm, ready to plunge his knife into Carlos's chest his body jerked with a convulsive reflex and he fell forward, blood gushing from the bullet hole between his eyes. Carlos rolled quickly out of the way and with quick thanks to the man who had saved him, jumped back into the forage.

Brittannia gasped and turned away, her eyes scanning the smoke-filled room for Dain. She saw him making his way to the front of the church, his pistols smoking. The sleeve of his right arm was blood-soaked and it sagged a little, but he held his gun ready. If he was in pain, he made no other show of it. Brittannia rose from her haven behind the pulpit, ready to run to Dain and pull him from the wild mass of clashing bodies and weapons. Someone from behind grabbed her arm and yanked her roughly back. She spun her head around, her hair breaking loose from its pins as she looked up with frightened eyes into the dark countenance of Sebastian.

He pulled her to him and curled an arm around her neck, nearly cutting off her supply of air. Memories of a similar time came flooding back to her and she remembered, with a strangled cry, the night he'd drugged her and had threatened to squeeze the life from her.

"Take your hands from her, Diaz," Dain demanded in a low, threatening voice.

Sebastian tightened his hold on her neck, bringing her chin up so that she could see only the wooden beams of the ceiling high above.

"I'll kill her if you take another step!" Sebastian vowed.

Brittannia dug her nails into Sebastian's arm, but his hold on her neck only tightened. His powerful arm wrapped tighter around her throat, savagely pressing her windpipe into the back of her neck. She saw the familiar pinpoints of light, heard the cacophony of yells and gun blasts die away and knew she would surely die if he didn't release his cruel hold on her.

"You won't have time, I'll put a bullet through you first!" Dain hissed.

Brittannia heard the bullet break from Dain's pistol with a deafening roar, she heard it whiz by just inches from her head. Sebastian abruptly released his stranglehold and flew back with the impact. Brittannia fell to the floor in a heap, coughing and gasping for air. She looked up through a shimmering haze to see Dain standing above her, his other gun pointed at Sebastian.

"I'll kill the bitch before I see you have her!" Sebastian vowed between clenched teeth.

Dain stood with his back to the scene of human carnage that was spread on the church floor. The fighting had stopped, Dain's men the victors. Without taking his stormy gaze from Sebastian, he asked, "Are you all right, Brittannia?"

Brittannia rubbed her throat. "Y-yes," she managed to reply.

"Kill me now, Barclay, or you'll rue this day!" Sebastian yelled as he held his limp arm, the blood pumping in spurts from the vital area that had been hit.

"You bastard!" a female voice cried out in Spanish.

Brittannia yanked her head up. Silhouetted against the glaring sunlight from outside, Maria stood in the entranceway, feet spread wide, arms akimbo.

She had a wild look about her as she boldly made her way through the thick air to stand in the middle of the church. Her dark cloud of hair hung free about her slim shoulders and a twisted smile of contempt played across her full mouth. "I've waited long for this day!" she yelled, her voice swathed in a thick Spanish accent. She held a primed pistol in her fist and with calculated slowness brought it up, aimed, and fired into Sebastian's heart.

Brittannia kept her gaze fixed on Maria. She didn't want to turn and see the lifeless form of Sebastian. Maria's face went blank after she'd fired the gun and now she stood there with her head bowed and her body

176

trembling. Brittannia's heart wrenched as she watched Carlos gather the weeping Maria in his arms and lead her outside.

"Brittannia," Dain said.

Brittannia looked up to Dain and took the hand he offered her. He pulled her up beside him, and after taking a moment to look into her eyes and lightly brush her cheek, he wrapped his arms around her and drew her into a tight hug. For the moment all thoughts of her in Sebastian's arms left him and all he wanted to do was comfort her.

Brittannia went willingly into his protective embrace. She clung tightly to him as he stroked her hair and murmured softly to her, his words making no sense but calming her nonetheless. She buried her head in the crook of his neck as she wrapped her arms around him. He smelled of gunpowder, sweat, and dirt and to her it was the sweetest smell in the world. It was Dain.

"You came," she murmured.

"Yes," he said. "Are you all right now?"

She backed out of his warm embrace and nodded.

"Good, because we've got to get out of here fast. Only a handful of Sebastian's men were here, the others are sure to be along any minute now. Sure you're not going to swoon on me?"

"Yes," she said emphatically.

"Pity. I'd like to have reason to take you in my arms again."

She looked up into his gray eyes and felt a tug at her heart. She couldn't believe he was really here and she put her hand gently on his arm to make sure he was real. Her fingertips touched the warm, sticky blood that was still seeping through his shirt-sleeve.

"You're hurt," she said, lines of worry creasing her fair brow.

He shook his head, passing it off as a mere cut.

"Captain, we must hurry!" Carlos yelled to them from outside.

Dain grabbed Brittannia by the arm and started for the door. "We've a ways to go before we get to the beach. It won't be easy but it's all we've got."

Brittannia stayed close to him as they made their way over the dead bodies and out onto the sea of green grass. Carlos was there with Maria. She stood beside him, proud and undaunted, a pistol in her hand and a knife tucked boldly into the waistband of her skirt. No sign of the earlier tears remained. The men stood nearby, their guns held loosely, ready in their fists.

"Lead the way, Carlos," Dain said. "We're depending on you to get us out of this place."

They followed Carlos to the looming, ominous forest, and Brittannia remembered back to the day she had first stepped on Andros and Sebastian had told her about the natives, how they watched. She pushed the thought from her head as she ran, not wanting to remember anything Sebastian had done or said.

Once inside the thick growth, the day seemed darker and their fast pace was considerably slowed by the hanging vines and thick bushes that obstructed their way. Brittannia jumped as she saw a tiny iguana scamper from her footpath in search of a safer haven. She tried desperately to keep up with the fast pace of the group, but her billowing skirts were hampering her way. More than once the silk had clung to a briar and she'd had to wait until Dain had pulled the fabric free. Maria, seeing Brittannia's deterred flight, pulled back

178

from Carlos and fell in step with Brittannia.

"Here," she said, pulling Brittannia to a halt. "Dressed as you are, you won't get far." The young Spanish girl withdrew the knife from her waistband and in one swift movement, sliced the hampering skirt from the rest of the dress.

Brittannia gasped as she looked down to see only her lace petticoat bloomers covering her slim legs. Maria threw the soiled material over her shoulder as she gave Brittannia a flashing grin.

"You can run like a man now! Let's go!"

Brittannia didn't give another thought to her appearance as she looked up and saw the group had taken a considerable lead and Dain was lagging behind it, craning his neck to see what Maria and she were doing. She quickly caught up to him and didn't miss the look of male appreciation in his eyes when he viewed her new costume.

"Destination, straight ahead, Captain," she said. The look in his eyes promised heady things to come and Brittannia smiled up at him, tossing her mane of golden hair.

Their progress was hampered by thick swarms of insects, sweltering heat, and masses of cumbersome vines and roots. Brittannia felt the sweat trickle down her back in tiny rivulets. She wanted to brush away the many insects that assailed her body, but she made her mind concentrate on putting one foot in front of the other, of getting to the open span of light up ahead, of getting to the safety of the *Airlee*.

They broke into the full light of day, running quickly from the clutches of the dark forest to the waiting small boats. "Four in one boat, five in the other. Brittannia,

Maria, Carlos, and Smith into the first boat," Dain said as he helped Brittannia to her seat in the middle of the boat.

"No!" Carlos demanded. "I'll stay and help fight them off if they show."

Dain regarded the young man with steely eyes. "All right," he said abruptly. "Draper, you go." After the man had climbed in and grabbed an oar, Dain grabbed onto a side of the boat and helped push it away from land. "Row, row like hell!" he commanded as he stood waist-high in the water, his gray eyes fixed on Brittannia. He watched the boat slowly slip away and out of danger.

Brittannia watched Dain become smaller and smaller as they drew nearer the *Airlee*. She strained to see if any shapes would emerge from the forest and shower the men with bullets. She watched and she waited. None came and she let out her breath with a sigh when she saw the other dinghy making its way toward them.

"Climb up, ma'am. I'll grab yer arm when ye're near enough!" a gruff voice yelled down to her when the small boat had hit alongside the iron hull of the *Airlee*. A rope ladder was dangling in the wind; waiting for them to climb up was a bearded man near the end of the rope. Brittannia looked skittishly at the rope and motioned for Maria to go first. Maria didn't hesitate; in one fluid movement she jumped into the air and grabbed hold of the rope, making her way quickly to the top. Once up, she called down, while her black hair whipped in the seabreeze. "It's easy! Much easier than staying on Andros!"

Brittannia needed no other incentive. She too jumped out and caught hold of the coarse rope.

Without looking down she scrambled up and crawled over the side of the deck with the help of strong arms that reached out when she was near enough. Finally she stood on the familiar deck of the *Airlee*.

"Welcome aboard, ma'am. The name's Erskine, I be the chief engineer," a burly, bearded man said. He was covered with black from head to foot and the only clear thing about him were his brown eyes, the whites showing starkly against his blackened face.

Brittannia smiled. "I'm—"

"No need t' tell me, ma'am. I know who you be, the cap'n couldn't quit talkin' about you. You'll be Brittannia, and I might say, Cap'n Barclay has fine taste in pickin' his women."

"That I do, Erskine!" Dain agreed as he swung his legs over the rail to stand firmly on the deck. "You'd best get below and shove those engines full of coal, I want us to be under a full head of steam as soon as possible."

"They've already been stoked, Cap'n. Just waitin' for you t' give the go ahead," Erskine replied, the pride for his captain evident in his voice.

"You've got it, man, you've got it!" Dain said, a hint of amusement in his gray eyes as he watched the older man make his way, with a limping gait, across the decks.

When he turned to Brittannia, the amusement was gone and replaced with concern. "Let me get you to my cabin, it's already been a trying day and the sun isn't yet high in the sky." He started to sweep her up into his arms but she stepped away from him.

"Captain, I'm perfectly fine and I'm truly not looking forward to spending the rest of the voyage

181

back to Nassau in some small, airless cabin."

Dain's gray gaze took in her form, a sea breeze blowing back the dark, gold-tinged curls that grazed his brow. "At least you might see fit to robe yourself in something more presentable while among my crew. Although they respect my command, they still are, after all, men with men's desires."

Brittannia's cheeks burned at his words and her back straightened. "Well, Captain, perhaps if I had known you were going to sweep me from the altar, I would have packed an overnight bag."

Dain laughed a deep laugh as he threw back his dark head. "Perhaps I could persuade one of the smaller members of the crew to part with his spare set of clothing."

"Perhaps," she replied, a coy look on her beautiful face, "I might prefer my present costume."

Dain gave her a slanted look as he called out to a young boy rolling a coil of rope. The boy quickly came and left to do the captain's bidding and in a few moments Brittannia was handed a neatly folded pair of breeches and shirt.

"Thank you," she said to the small boy and was rewarded with a timid nod of his head and a blush that spread from his neck to the roots of his red hair. "He's very young," she commented to Dain after the boy ran back to coil his rope.

"Yes," Dain agreed. "He's what they call a powder monkey, filling the guns when needed. The *Airlee* has no guns so he mostly serves as a cabin boy. He's too young to see war, but he has the sea in his blood and if he's going to serve on a ship, it might as well be mine. I watch out for my crew, unlike other men."

"I believe you do," she said, following him to his cabin. The room was indeed almost airless and she was surprised to see how small it was. Compared to the cabins aboard the *Real Sangre,* this was the size of a storage closet.

"It's small, but it's clean and serves its purpose," Dain said as if reading her thoughts. "When the *Airlee* sails, she sails to run the blockade, not accommodate her crew with luxuries. This is only a place to change clothes or catch a quick nap."

"I see," Brittannia said, setting the powder monkey's clothes atop the small desk that adorned one corner. She ran her fingers through her hair, pulling out leaves and twigs that were the result of running pell-mell through the jungle. She felt Dain's gaze on her. Oddly enough she felt he was angry with her. She dropped her hands, turning to face him. "Well, Captain," she began levelly, "I've the feeling you have something to say."

"That's very perceptive of you."

His voice had suddenly gone metallic, and to her annoyance she felt her stomach flutter like a young schoolgirl's. "Then say it," she replied tartly.

"I warned you about Diaz. I told you to stay away from the man."

"Yes, you did but—"

"Then why in the hell didn't you listen? My God, Brittannia, I nearly lost a few crewmen back there all because you fell into some stranger's arms and then too late, realized your stupidity!"

She felt her mouth drop open. Did he actually think she went *willingly* with Sebastian? She felt her blood begin to boil. "I did not—"

"I don't want to hear about it," Dain interrupted

icily. "Just get out of those clothes and into something decent."

"*I WILL NOT!*" she said furiously. "This is *my* ship and I can go about it in whatever attire I choose!"

His eyes held their own storm as he looked to her. "Is this the thanks I get for risking my life to save your pretty little neck?"

"And what did you expect for your little show of bravery? A repeat performance of our last night together? You've misjudged me, Captain." Then, in afterthought, she added, "It was not *I* who called for your help!"

His hands were tight fists at his sides, and a muscle twitched along his jawline. "No, Brittannia," he said, his voice deep, "I've not misjudged you." With that he closed the distance between them and scooped her into a tight embrace, one that demanded and made her cry out. "Damn you," he growled into her hair as he placed hot kisses there, "I've missed you . . ." His hands were roughly caressing her back as they moved lower and pressed her half-clothed body against his own lean frame. "I'm hungry for you, Brittannia," he breathed.

With a cry of rage, Brittannia pushed at him. "Stop it!" she demanded, squirming in his hold. "I'll not repay you in this way!"

She heard him laugh. "You little fool," he breathed as he brushed his lips by her ear, sending tingles along her spine. "It is not repayment I seek. I want you, and if you'd stop fighting me, you'd realize you want me too."

Her denial came, weak in its resolve. "No." It was very nearly a whisper, for her traitorous body was melting beneath Dain's bold advances and she felt the familiar tingle between her thighs that only he could

184

evoke. Her anger was slipping away from her as she wrapped her arms about his neck and gently toyed with the dark curls at his nape. They were so soft, so silky. She arched her own neck, welcoming the gentle caress of his full mouth, and as his lips moved over her cheek to take her mouth, a low moan escaped her.

He kissed her with a slow savoriness at first, his lips moving over hers in a gentle caressing manner, teasing her with slight flicks of his warm tongue. She moved and responded to his delicate assault. In his arms she could be nothing but pliant, submissive, and as his fingers slowly undid the row of buttons down her back she made no protest to stop him. The steady pulse of the engines beat a soft rhythm in their ears. He curled one arm around her shoulders and drew her nearer still, his hand reaching down to touch her right breast as his other arm worked her garments to her waist.

She sighed again as she stroked his strong forearm. Running her fingers through the dark hair there, she was overcome by her own reckless passion and she had not the power to tell him to stop.

"You're as beautiful as I remember," he whispered in her ear as his fingers rubbed one taut nipple. It swelled under his touch, turning a deep pink.

She turned her head so her cheek was against his, and when she lifted her eyes to him, he was looking at her through lids heavy with desire. She forgot about his accusations, forgot about seeing Esmée in his bed—this moment her body burned for this man and she was going to meet that burning desire. She pulled away from him and stood back to undress, feeling wanton and desirable under his smoky gaze.

Slowly she pulled the silky material from her body

and it fell around her ankles with a silken whoosh. She smiled a bold, brassy smile, heady with the effect her nakedness had on him. She came to stand in front of him and undressed him, kissing his body as it was exposed. Gently she worked his shirt-sleeve over his wounded arm. Seeing where the bullet had grazed by, taking his skin with it, she gasped. "It needs to be tended to."

"No, Brittannia," he said huskily, "there is a more urgent need to be tended to."

A small cry escaped her as he kissed her and their lips locked together meeting with an urgency, drinking of each other, not able to get enough. He crushed her curved body to him, his strong hands sensually rubbing down her spine to her round buttocks, and he caressed the soft, silken flesh there. He bent down and with one hand behind her back, the other beneath her knees, he lifted her and carried her to the small bunk, tenderly lying her down.

His smoky eyes devoured every curve, every dipping hollow of her ripe, young body as he slowly undid his breeches and pulled them off. In a moment he was on the bed, his muscular arms holding his body just above her, and with a slowness born of desire, of wanting to please her, he bent his dark head and began a path of fiery kisses along her skin. He started at her temples, his lips tender and full, moving lovingly over her flawless skin, tasting her, teasing her.

Brittannia writhed beneath the feel of his moist mouth, her back arching, the crests of her breasts rubbing against the black hair of his chest. He brought her senses to life and filled her with desire. She ran her smooth palms across his tanned back, the muscles

186

there rippling beneath her touch, becoming fuller as his passion mounted.

Passion-bruised lips devoured every inch of her body, and she let herself be carried away by a gentle tide that rocked her, enveloped her in its warm waters, and brushed her skin with a gentle caress. She sighed a low throaty sound when his mouth moved to her breasts. His hands lifted them, caressed them gently as his lips and teeth played with the taut nipples. Her body was burning with desire and as he moved his head lower and lingered between her silken thighs she felt she had never known such rapture. It was such a sweet sensation, one that made her want to open up and take him inside of her.

Slowly, deliberately he tasted her, making her cry out in exquisite pleasure. She caught his night-dark curls in trembling fingers and gently guided him up beside her. She wanted to give him pleasure now, wanted to lay him back and explore every part of him, every nuance.

"Here," she whispered as she gently pushed his shoulders back to the bunk. "I want to please you now."

He looked up to her, his eyes heavy with passion and said, "Everything about you pleases me."

She sat up on her knees beside him and then with a seductive smile upon her lips, she placed one leg on either side of him, holding her body up with her hands. She bent her golden head and planted soft kisses in the hollow of his neck, across his broad chest, and, following the trail of black hair from his flat belly, she found his manhood.

"Brittannia," Dain moaned. "I must have you."

She smiled up at him, her own body craving release from the sweet torment that was building inside her. She slowly moved up to lay beside him, her gentle hands caressing his flesh as she went.

He moved on top of her and she opened herself to him, wrapping her legs about him as he entered with a driving force. She felt him; hard and erect, soft as silk, and she squeezed her muscles tight, not wanting him to leave, wanting more of him.

He moved her, rocked her, and with each thrust she felt her senses tingle and shudder and come together to form a great wave that built higher and higher and soon balanced just above her. She writhed beneath him, bringing her hips up to meet his, begging the wave to crash down on her and cover her.

Her body was covered with a film of perspiration that made them slide and rub against each other all the more. She was close, so close to having that great wave crash into her and carry her away. He thrust deeper and deeper, kissing her ear, and when she heard his low, animal moan she felt the wave let loose and crash onto her, sweeping her higher and higher with tumultuous sensations, rolling her over and over in delicious rapture. She felt Dain's body shudder and then he was still, his breathing slowly returning to normal.

Slowly, oh so slowly, the wave pulled away, leaving her on the warm, golden sands of aftermath. She lay there basking in the warmth, her palms running leisurely over Dain's back. He stroked her hair and murmured sweet words in her ear, and when he rolled away, he brought her with him, cradling her in his strong arms and kissing her hair. They lay there for a while, their heartbeats slowing to a normal pace.

Passion spent, she began to wonder at her actions. Her mind, now clear of her recently burning desire, reflected on the moments past. How could she give herself totally to this man? Why had she felt such a burning need to be in his arms, to give to him, to take from him? She knew the kind of man he was: She was one of many women, he was not one to choose just one woman to love—and, most puzzling of all, she didn't love him. Or did she? Her confused thoughts caused her to pull away from him, but he held her tight.

"Not yet," he whispered. "Lay with me awhile longer."

Brittannia did as he asked, staring into space. What *did* she feel for this man beside her?

"Having regrets?" he asked.

"It's a bit late for those, Captain," she replied, then, not wanting to dwell on her confusing thoughts any longer, she asked, "How did you know where I was? That I needed help?"

Dain stiffened a bit, then after long moments, said, "Carlos found me in Nassau and led us to Sebastian's home. Diaz and his men were ready for us when we came, they overtook us, and Diaz ordered us to be taken beneath the house, into a stinking rotten hold beneath his opulent throne. Things looked grim but early this morning Maria came down carrying a crate full of pistols and knives, no less. She even had a few strapped to herself. She told us where the ceremony was taking place and that the bulk of Sebastian's men were in the common room getting drunk for the occasion. The rest is history, you were there."

Brittannia shuddered just remembering. She must remember to thank Carlos and Maria. "Thank you," she said simply.

"I don't want to think of that now," he said, a huskiness coming to his voice that told of his desire. He pulled her atop of him and brought his lips to hers, kissing her again and again.

Brittannia responded with her lips, her hands, her body—and once again nothing mattered except Dain . . .

Chapter 10

"Cap'n, 'taint gonna be easy gettin' in this time. You paid a fair penny on the way out and they're gonna expect double comin' in," Erskine said in his graveled voice as he rubbed the whiskers along his heavy chin.

"Right again, Chief," Dain agreed. "I didn't think to bring enough funds to cover our way back into Nassau, my only thought was getting out."

"Aye, gettin' your lady was the only thing on your mind, but maybe 'tis just as well. No need risking your lady to the yeller fever."

Dain raised a dark brow as he looked to his chief engineer. He let pass Erskine's referral to Brittannia as "his" lady. He knew better. "And what about you and the crew, Erskine? Are you all immune to the fever?"

Erskine spewed a stream of tobacco to the deck, then squinted his eyes up at his captain. "'Ell, I've lived with death at me heels since I was a lad and no fever is gonna keep me from goin' where I please!"

Dain laughed as he wrapped a strong arm around Erskine's shoulders in a gesture of friendship. "I

191

suspected as much, Chief."

"So, gentlemen, do tell why we're bobbing merrily just out of Nassau port."

Both men turned to see who addressed them, but Dain had no need to turn around to recognize that honeyed voice that held a lilting laugh just beneath it. He smiled as he took in Brittannia's costume. She wore the powder monkey's breeches. Even though they were long enough in the legs, they were too snug at the hips and only served to emphasize her womanly curves. The white shirt billowed at the sleeves but fit her tightly across the chest, the swell of her breasts straining against the thin material.

"I do hope we put into port soon as I am in need of something to wear," she said devilishly as she looked into Dain's smoky eyes.

Dain stepped up beside her, almost shielding the pleasant view of her from Erskine. "Indeed," he said huskily, looking down at her, his passion rising just from the sight of her. "I can't have you going about my ship displaying your womanly virtues to my crew."

"Captain," she pleaded, pretending innocence. "You ordered this outfit and," she added on a more serious note, "the *Airlee* is my ship."

"Ah," he said, his gray eyes smiling, "so I did and so it is." In a mock bow, he extended his arm as if allowing her full reign of the *Airlee*.

She tossed her mane of light hair and it blew over her shoulders and tumbled down her back in a riot of thick golden curls. "But, why are we not entering port?"

Dain's eyes traveled to Erskine and they both shifted on their feet.

"Brittannia," Dain started. "Before I left for Andros,

192

there was an outbreak of yellow fever and—"

Brittannia gasped as she looked toward New Providence Island trying to find some sign that told of the fever.

"Nassau is quarantined. We had to buy our way out of the harbor and I'm afraid I didn't bring enough on board to buy our way back in. I also don't know if I want you in Nassau; it is too risky."

"Yes, it is risky," she replied as she looked over the water to the small speck of land. "Can we go somewhere else? Perhaps another island?"

"Well, I don't know," Erskine cut in. "We don't have enough coal to feed the engines. I 'spose you could sail, but what about provisions?"

Dain eyed his old friend carefully and finally agreed. "You're right, Erskine. We haven't the supplies to go far from here. We might be able to make it to the next port." He turned to Brittannia. "Also," he added reluctantly, "Michael was just recovering from the fever when I left."

"Michael?" she gasped as she looked to him in disbelief. "But why didn't you tell me sooner? I have to go to him, I have to see him!" She drew away from him and once again looked toward New Providence, this time her small hands working together nervously.

"I said he was recovering, Brittannia," Dain said as he took hold of her shoulders and turned her gaze to him. "He was on the mend when I left him, I swear."

Brittannia's turquoise eyes searched his gray eyes frantically. "I've heard so much about the fever; how it picks its victims at random and few survive. Are you sure he's all right? Oh, what a terrible ordeal for him. He is so vibrant, so full of life!"

"Brittannia," Dain said as he massaged her small shoulders with his hands. "He's fine, really. The worst was over when I left. Michael is a fighter and, besides, he hadn't yet had his way with one of the notorious strippers who performs on Bay Street."

Brittannia smiled at the thought of Michael pursuing the skirt of a stripper and she had to laugh. It was so typical of Michael. *Michael*. "Oh but I have to see him!" she demanded, latching her fingers to his shirtsleeve. "You said yourself we don't have the supplies to go far from here!"

Dain looked at this golden beauty and regretted not being able to give what she wanted. "I don't have the money to get us into Nassau harbor. I don't think anyone on board has that much on his person."

Brittannia looked down at her bared feet and the deck. She bit her full bottom lip between her teeth as she contemplated the situation. She just had to see Michael, he was like a brother to her. She couldn't bear to think of him suffering alone. Her blue green eyes lit up. "I have the money!" she exclaimed as she looked up to Dain with a smile on her lips. "The jewels, the jewels Sebastian gave me on the day we were to be married!"

"No, Brittannia," Dain said before she got carried away with the idea. "They're worth a fortune. That's too much to give those greedy men and I don't want you exposed to the fever. We'll make for the next port."

Brittannia stood in front of Dain, her turquoise eyes narrowing as she digested his words. "Frankly, I don't see where it's your decision," she said crisply. Two nights of lovemaking and one morning of his bravery were not enough that he could start to make her decisions for her! "I say we take the *Airlee* into port."

Dain crossed his arms over his broad chest, his stance indicating he would not be moved on his decision. "It's too risky. I won't subject my men to such risks. My decision is final, Brittannia."

Oh, the arrogance of the man! "Must I again remind you who is owner of this vessel?" she ground out.

"It doesn't matter. I captain her and I say to what port she puts into."

His tone brooked no argument but that only made Brittannia all the more determined. "I'm going to Nassau with or without your consent, Captain!"

He shook his dark head. "Not on the *Airlee* you're not."

She regarded him for a moment, her turquoise eyes flashing. Without taking her blazing gaze from him, she said over her shoulder, "Erskine, see to it the small boat is lowered." Without another word to Dain, she turned from him and started back to the cabin to retrieve the jewels.

A strong arm snaked out, grabbing her by the arm and tugging her viciously back. "God damn it, Brittannia!" Dain said angrily, causing her neck to jerk with his rough pull on her. "Do you have any idea what it's like when yellow fever hits a city? The place becomes a charnel house, people drop in the streets, *healthy* people who thought they could never become a victim! It's a frightening thing to behold and once the fever hits, no one knows when it will pass or how many will die. I won't let you go!"

She shrugged from his hold but he was quick to pull her back, forcing her to look in the direction of New Providence Island. "Look!" he nearly yelled. "Look across the water! What do you see?"

Stubbornly, Brittannia raised her eyes to look in the direction he pointed.

"Well?" he prompted, impatient.

"Nothing," she spat.

His look was murderous on her. "I'll tell you what you see. You see an island wilting under smothering heat, the same heat that holds the epidemic over the people like a pall! You're looking at a living hell, Brittannia!"

She was silent for a moment as his words sunk in. Surely he was exaggerating. It couldn't be that bad. She peered intently at the not-so-distant island. It looked the same as it always had. Flying fish, their backs gleaming in the early light, glided along the surface of the pellucid blue water and the smell in the air was clear, clean; all seemed normal. "I'm going," she finally stated, her voice flat. She heard him take in a deep breath and then very slowly, with a control she knew he fought to have, let it out as he released his hold on her. She didn't look at him, didn't want to, for his words of warning had disturbed her but she wasn't about to be deterred now. She was going to see Michael, fever or no!

She strode purposefully across the decks to the place where the small boat was stored and looked at the mass of ropes that ran here and there, wondering which, if any, she should pull. She knew she would not receive any help from the crew, for they would move only on Dain's orders, so she randomly grabbed one thick cord and stood holding onto it, staring out across the water. Suddenly her doubts were growing by leaps and bounds: what if the epidemic really was as horrible as Dain described, what if she herself fell ill with the fever?

196

She shook her head, willing the frightening thoughts away. She gave a hard tug to the rope. Nothing happened and she could feel Dain's presence behind her. She gave another yank, then another.

"What the hell do you think you're doing?" he demanded from behind her.

Brittannia gave a toss to her head, sending her hair flying over one shoulder. "If you'll not take me to port on the *Airlee,* then I'll take myself in!"

"The hell you will!"

She whirled on him. "The hell I won't!"

His eyes were two flints of steel as he beheld her. After long moments of trying to cut her down with his gaze, he finally thundered, "God damn it! Get out of the way!" Then, turning, he yelled across the decks, "Erskine, Smith! Lower this damn thing and put in enough water for two!"

Brittannia regarded him for a moment, her anger not yet in check as she stepped out of the way of the scurrying Erskine and Smith. "You don't have to come, Captain. I'm perfectly capable of—"

"The hell you are!" he bellowed, thoroughly disgusted with her.

"I'll get my jewels" was all she said.

He didn't reply and so she scurried to the cabin. The boat was lowered with much murmuring among the crew. Dain left the *Airlee* in Erskine's command with orders to make for the next port and return to Nassau only when he heard the quarantine had been lifted.

"Good luck, my friends," Carlos yelled from the deck. Maria stood beside him, her dark beauty even more enhanced by the bright day. "Maria and I will make our home far from Andros Island. We wish you well. *Adiós!"*

Brittannia waved good-bye, knowing she would miss the brave young couple. She sat across from Dain, her back straight and her gaze fixed ahead, past Dain's muscular shoulders. He rowed with a steady beat, his muscles bunching with the strain. He hadn't said a word to her and she stubbornly refused to speak first. She tried her best to settle more comfortably on the unyielding wooden seat but the heat of the day was stifling and the sun beat down, unmindful of the damage it was doing to her fair skin. She wrinkled her pert nose skyward and was immediately sorry as she felt the sting of a bad burn across her nose and cheeks.

Dain had not rowed straight for the harbor as she had thought he would, but was rowing in the direction of a sanded shore, perspiration soaking his shirt and covering his handsome face as he raised and lowered the large oars.

Her curiosity at his choice of direction forced her to break the silence. "Why are you shoring us on a deserted stretch of beach?" she asked, flicking her wrist in the direction of the sanded shore. "We'll have to walk into Nassau!"

The look he gave her was grave indeed and it caused an unsettling feeling to descend upon her. "It was difficult enough getting out of the harbor, and I can't be sure the same greedy men will be on watch today. It's best we beach here and walk into town."

"Surely they'd let us *into* town, it's those who want out who the quarantine is for."

He shook his dark head as if she were addled and he pitied her for it. "No, Brittannia, the quarantine is to keep people out as well as in."

She said no more. His voice held none of its earlier anger; now it seemed to be filled with grimness, a grimness that frightened her. She forced herself not to think about what lay ahead. All would be fine, she tried to convince herself. They would go to Michael's home and she would finally be at his side to see to it that he became well. But as she sat back and plopped her feet on the seat in front of her, leaning on one elbow as she brought the other hand up to shield her sunburned face, the sunny day seemed strangely ominous and menacing.

The small boat brushed bottom and Dain jumped out and pulled it the rest of the way to shore. Before he could offer his assistance Brittannia was splashing through the water to the sand, her turquoise eyes scanning the world around her for some outward signs of disaster. There was none. Birds squawked, butterflies flitted by showing off their delicate beauty, and a breeze, slight but still felt, brushed by them. Brittannia carried her dainty slippers in her hand, for they were not made for walking long distances, and then she and Dain walked over the long stretch of beach, stopping on a small patch of sparse grass.

"Here," Dain said, handing her an animal-skin flask filled with water, "drink a little at a time. It should last us to Delving's home."

Brittannia slung the flask over her neck and shoulder and fell into step alongside him. His pace was fast but she kept with him, not wanting to give him the satisfaction of seeing her tire. It wasn't long before they came to a dirt road, covered over by blown sand. Dain, his face set into grim lines, led the way along it. Minutes slipped into a half hour and then an hour. Still they walked silently on.

"Don't you notice it, Brittannia?" he finally asked.

"What?" she asked, irritably swatting at the menacing insects and trudging alongside him.

"The lack of traffic. This is a main road out of Nassau. It should be teeming with wagons and buggies. We haven't seen a soul yet."

"If you're trying to frighten me, Captain, forget it. I'm not about to turn around."

She didn't want to admit he was right but all around, despite the usual noises of the animal-life, she could feel something was wrong. She could feel it in the air, and the closer they came to Nassau, the greater that feeling became.

Dain kept up their fast pace, only sipping at his store of water. As they came closer to the town limits, he withdrew the pistol he'd tucked into the band of his trousers.

"What are you going to do with that?" she asked, taking another long drink from her flask.

He gave her a look of reprimand as he pulled the near-empty flask from her lips. "I told you to *sip* it! That's water from Andros and you won't find anything so clean in Nassau, that's for sure. As for the gun, it's for our protection."

Brittannia capped the flask, giving him a puzzled look. "What do you mean we won't find anything so clean? And why do we need protection?"

He took in a controlled breath, his flint-colored eyes scanning the road ahead of them. "We can't risk drinking the water, it may be contaminated. Same with any raw fruit or vegetables. Stay away from them. No matter how thirsty you are don't drink the water!"

Brittannia was horrified. She tucked her now-precious flask closer to her body, wishing she hadn't been so greedy with it.

"We need protection from looters and people crazed from fever who have no control over their actions," he explained.

She drew in a sharp breath. "They would attack us?"

He nodded. "Some will, and they can be mighty strong in such a frenzied condition."

She swallowed—hard.

"Well, you can let your jewels sink comfortably to the bottom of your pocket," Dain said, breaking the silence between them as they finally entered the far side of Nassau. "I don't see any roadblocks ahead and there were none behind. Either the fever has lessened its fury or the officials are lazy."

Brittannia didn't comment. She was hot and tired and her skin was burned beyond help. Once in town it was evident the fever still raged. The streets were nearly bare, only a few people ventured out, and Brittannia was astonished at how many of the women wore widow's black. Four funeral processions passed them by. She felt her stomach turn as she heard the wood of the crude coffin rub against the wood of the buggy. It was such a hollow, final sound.

They made their way along the nearly deserted streets at a fast pace. Brittannia had never truly seen the building fronts. When she was in Nassau last the town had buzzed with activity and the dust kicked up by the drays and buggies had made viewing the surroundings nearly impossible. Now, the streets were littered with garbage and the heat of the day seemed to hold down the decaying smells and yellow fever. Brittannia imagined she could smell the fever with so many coffins, so many grieving people; it was a stifling, sickening smell, and she put the sleeve of her shirt to her nose and hurried toward their destination.

"We're almost there, how are you faring?" Dain asked as they made their way up the slight incline to George Street. He held his pistol ready, his eyes ever watchful.

"No need to worry about me, Captain," she replied. "It's my skin that will never be the same!" She leaned into the hill and quickened her pace.

When they had scaled the last small hill, Brittannia ran along George Street toward Michael's home. She ran past the wrought-iron gate that stood open and made her way up the lawn to the circular drive and then to the wide veranda. She was about to burst through the main door when she heard a male voice rumble.

"Michael!" She ran to him and threw her arms about his shoulders.

"Brittannia!" he said in astonishment. "I thought you had returned to England! What are you doing here at such a terrible time?"

"I asked her the same. Wild horses couldn't have kept her from you," Dain supplied as he stepped onto the sweeping veranda and took his usual seat along the wooden rail.

Michael looked from Brittannia to Dain, his brown eyes forming all sorts of questions. "Where the hell did you run off to, Dain?" he demanded, then turning to Brittannia and regarding her attire, he asked, "And what poor soul did you roll for those clothes?"

Brittannia grimaced as she brushed her fingers through her tangled hair and looked down at her boyish garments. "Oh, Michael, it's a long story. I'll explain everything, but first I want to know how you are. You look a little pale and, my, but you've lost a lot of weight. Are you sure you're well enough to be sitting out here?"

"You do wonders for one's morale, Brittannia. Personally, I think I look better than I have in weeks."

"You certainly do, my friend," Dain replied.

Brittannia paled at their exchange. She hadn't realized how sick Michael had been. "I'm sorry, Michael," she said as she put her hand on his.

"That's all right." He patted the back of her hand. "I've been well taken care of, you can be sure. Forgive my manners. You both look a little parched. Care for something to drink?"

Brittannia opened her eyes wide. "I'd care for a freezing English river to bask in, but," she said, "I'll take whatever you have."

Michael smiled at her and reached over to ring a small bell on the table beside him. His movements were slow. Brittannia cringed at thoughts of what the yellow fever must have made him suffer. He looked much thinner and his hair lacked the healthy sheen she was used to seeing.

"Michael, when I'd heard what happened to you," she said softly, "I was so worried. I don't know what I'd do without you!" She leaned her head on his shoulder as she held back tears of joy.

Michael leaned his head against hers. "I wasn't a pretty sight, Brit."

"No, he wasn't," a female voice said, a heavy French accent evident in the lilted tone. "It was best that you were away."

Brittannia turned her head to see none other than Esmée make her way across the veranda to a chair opposite her and Michael and very close to Dain.

"Is it really you, Brittannia?" she asked languidly as she spread her satin skirts about her and brought up a delicate fan to flutter femininely in front of herself. "Why you look absolutely," she waved her slim white hand in the air as if trying to catch the word, "boyish!"

Brittannia regarded the perfectly clothed and coiffed Esmée. "And you, Countess," she said in a honeyed voice, "are in the height of fashion as always. But surely those tight stays are uncomfortable in this heat."

Esmée flashed her a tolerant smile as she twittered her fan about. *"Au contraire,"* she said. "I'm most comfortable."

Brittannia gave her a wan smile and turned her attention to Michael, but not before hearing a light guffaw from Dain's place. She seethed at the tone of it.

"Brittannia," Michael explained, "Esmée has been with me since I first fell ill to the fever. Dain and she saw me through the worst of it."

"Oh?" Brittannia questioned as she shot a scathing look to Dain.

"Yes, it seems Esmée has battled with the fever before and, knowing this, Dain hastened to get her when I fell ill."

Brittannia looked to Esmée and for the life of her couldn't see Esmée battling anything greater than a skin blemish. "Well, we're all very fortunate to have had her nearby," she said as sweetly as she could manage. "And Captain Barclay was certainly gallant to venture out and bring her to you."

A maid came and left and sure to Michael's instructions cool drinks were brought for all. Brittannia quickly grabbed the cool, tall glass of lemonade and was about to down its whole contents but Dain's hand snapped up and held it from her dry lips.

"Drink it slowly, Brittannia."

She yanked it from his hold, angry that he hadn't bothered to mention Esmée. Some of the contents spilled and she quickly brushed the wet from her breeches. "So tell me, Countess. What does one do when the fever hits?"

Esmée regarded Brittannia from over her fan for a moment. "Pray it doesn't choose you as a victim."

"And if it does?" Brittannia asked, testing the countess's knowledge.

"Then, my dear, you pray even harder."

Michael could feel the tension and he hastened to get Brittannia and Esmée apart from one another. "Brit, you look near exhausted," he said. "Why don't you help yourself to one of the guest rooms and relax before the evening meal."

"Michael," Esmée said as she stood, "you stay put. I'll tell Dolores to prepare two rooms and I'll see to it that a delicious meal is prepared." Then turning to Brittannia she said, "Come, Brittannia. I see you have no baggage, perhaps I can find something for you to wear. I must say I've been positively bored with this epidemic. All social events have been cancelled and I haven't been to the dressmaker in weeks! It will be so nice to have female companionship again!"

"Sheer, heaven, I'm sure," Brittannia murmured as she followed Esmée into the house, the smell of roses

205

wafting back to assail her nostrils.

The gown Esmée gave her was a bright canary yellow adorned with so many ruffles and sequins it bordered on being gaudy. Having nothing else presentable to wear, Brittannia tried it on, but it didn't fit. She stood in front of the mirror in the guest room, the tips of the sleeves nearly touching her knuckles and the waist and bodice sagging helplessly, and she let out a deep sigh. She'd have to wear the powder monkey's clothes again. She could just see herself at the table, looking boyish and wrinkled, while Esmée showed off her best finery.

"Your bath is ready, Miss Denning," a young maid said as she stood near the outer door of the guest room.

"Thank you," Brittannia replied, then with a glance in the young girl's direction, she asked, "Do you think I could borrow something of yours to wear? I have no clothes and as you can see," she held her arms out to her sides, looking very much like an overdressed scarecrow, "this doesn't fit."

The young island girl's eyes widened. "I'd be very honored to have you wear something of mine, but are you sure you want to?" she asked timidly.

"I'm positive!" Brittannia replied and stepped over to the powder monkey's clothes she'd left in a heap by the bed. "Here," she said, digging deep into one of the pockets. "You can have these if you find something that fits me."

Brittannia held before the young girl the diamond earrings Sebastian had given to her. They shimmered in her palm as Brittannia gestured for the girl to take them.

"Oh, no!" the girl exclaimed. "I cannot. They are much too beautiful, too expensive!"

"Nonsense," Brittannia said, taking the girl's brown hand and plopping them into her palm. "They mean nothing to me. In fact, I despise them."

The girl looked down at the heap of glittering diamonds in her hand and clamped her fist shut tight. "I will get you my best outfit!" she exclaimed. "My sailor-boyfriend brought it back from Mexico. You may keep it. He bores me," she said simply and ran from the room.

Brittannia smiled and turned to get to the task of removing the yellow dress and getting a bath. The first she did quickly, the second not so quickly. She soaked in the tub for a long while, reveling in the clean water, glad to be rid of the sweat and dirt from her escape from Andros. She washed her long hair twice and stepped from the tub feeling clean all over. After she had wrapped a towel around her hair, there was a timid knock at the door.

The young maid entered carrying a fresh laundered outfit over her arm. "I hope you like it," she said, holding up the white blouse and turquoise skirt. Both were embroidered with pink flowers of all degrees and the gathered band around the top of the blouse was embroidered in a deep turquoise. A pair of leather thongs completed the peasant Spanish look and Brittannia was pleased with the coolness and simplicity of the outfit.

"Thank you," Brittannia said as she slipped into the underclothes and petticoats the young maid had also brought. "I think it is lovely." She slipped the blouse over her head and adjusted the puffed, embroidered short sleeves above her shoulders. The skirt came next. It clung to her tiny waist and billowed out over the petticoats. She whirled in front of the mirror; it was a bit too snug but it was definitely better than the yellow creation Esmée had given her.

"It looks lovely," the young girl commented. "But the shoulders are to be left bare, like this," she said as she pulled the sleeves off Brittannia's sun-touched shoulders and stood back to admire it.

Brittannia played with the puffed sleeves and decided they did look better off the shoulder. She pursed her lips as she viewed what the sun had done to her neck and shoulders. They were touched with a light brown, as were her arms. She liked the color and found it most complementing despite what she had always been told about the sun. Her face was another matter; it was a light red and felt warm to the touch. Even though it accentuated the blue of her eyes, she feared what the end result would be.

"I brought these also," the young girl said, cutting into Brittannia's perusal of her own image. "You may borrow them. They're a favorite of mine and I thought they would look especially nice on you." She handed her a pair of large hoop earrings. They were so large that, when on, they nearly touched the tops of her shoulders.

Brittannia tossed her fair head back and forth and laughter pealed from her lungs as she watched and felt the earrings sway with her. "I love them!" she cried. "Thank you, I'll return them tomorrow, I promise." She looked to the clock atop the chest of drawers. "I've got to get downstairs or they'll think I'm not coming." With one last smile to the young girl, she flew out of the room and downstairs.

Dain and Esmée stood near the empty fireplace, Dain holding a glass of bourbon in his hand, Esmée a glass of wine. Michael was seated in a leather chair, the thick sides threatening to pull his frail body inside. Brittannia stopped her mad dash just before entering and ran a hand through her hair. She had chosen to leave it free of any pins as she hadn't the time or inclination to mess with it.

"My dear Brittannia," Michael said as he motioned for the servant to get her a glass of wine, "we had begun to think you would forego dinner for a long nap."

"Oh, not a chance, Michael, I'm famished!" she exclaimed as she made her way into the large room, her leather shoes not making a sound.

"You look stunning," Michael complimented as she took the glass offered and drank daintily of its contents. "Wherever did you come by that outfit?"

"Yes, darling, where?" Esmée asked as she flicked her green eyes over the tight peasant blouse and vivid turquoise skirt. "Was the yellow not to your liking? When I'd pulled it from my chest, I swore it spoke of you."

Brittannia smiled sweetly at Esmée. "Actually," she said, "the dress you gave me didn't fit. I borrowed this from one of the maids."

"A maid?" Esmée questioned. "How quaint."

"You look lovely," Dain said as he raised his glass as if in toast of her costume.

"Thank you, Captain," she replied as she brought her own glass to her lips. She didn't miss how close Esmée and Dain stood. Esmée seemed very pleased with her effect on the men in the room. She wore a ball gown of green taffeta that billowed out over a large hoop skirt. The neckline of her dress was shockingly low, almost vulgar, Brittannia thought, but then something like that would probably interest Dain no end.

"Shall we go into dinner?" Michael questioned as he raised himself from the padded chair.

Brittannia was instantly at his side, worrying over his health. She boiled when she saw Dain offer his arm to Esmée.

Dinner was an elaborate fare and Brittannia found herself cleaning her plate despite the feeling of jealousy that knotted in the pit of her stomach. Esmée kept up a light chatter throughout the meal as she toyed with the food on her plate, rarely putting any of the delicious fare in her perfectly painted mouth. She asked endless questions on Brittannia's whereabouts for the past weeks. When Brittannia would only say she had spent time on a neighboring island Esmée pressed for details.

"Oh, do tell, Brittannia," she coaxed in a sweet voice. "I'm sure there is an adventure in there somewhere! And where does Captain Barclay fit into the plot? The both of you looked like something the cat dragged in."

Brittannia dipped her head, concentrating on stabbing the sweet potato with the prongs of her fork. She certainly did not want to relay any of her episode with Sebastian to Esmée, and by no means would she recount to anyone the tryst she'd had with Dain on board the *Airlee*. That was one thing she wanted to forget! Since they'd arrived at Michael's he hadn't paid any attention to her, he seemed to have eyes only for Esmée.

"Esmée, I really don't wish to discuss it. Perhaps

some other time."

"Certainly, my dear. I didn't mean to pry." Esmée pushed her plate away from her, and after a dainty wipe to each side of her mouth with a linen napkin, she said, "I see Captain Barclay is biting at the bit to depart from the table for his usual after-dinner smoke. Feel free, gentlemen, to leave us ladies to our own conveniences. You don't mind, do you, Brittannia?"

Brittannia set her fork down. *His usual smoke?* "No, of course not," she lied. The last thing she wanted to do was spend time alone with Esmée.

Brittannia and Esmée made their exit from the dining room; Brittannia with a silent step and a slight swish of her peasant skirt, Esmée with rapid heel clicks and the crisp rustle of taffeta.

Once in the sitting room, Brittannia made herself comfortable on a small settee in the spacious room. Her mind was filled with visions of the time Esmée and Dain must have shared together while nursing Michael back to health and she felt herself becoming angrier with every passing moment. It was becoming obvious to her that her dreams of Dain forgetting about Esmée were just that: dreams. How could a man forget a woman who had made herself at home in his bed and then remained by his side to help aid his best friend back to health? Evidently, he couldn't, for all Dain's conversation had been directed to Esmée and Michael during dinner.

"Brittannia, darling, are you listening? I do hope I'm not boring you. You look miles away."

Brittannia blinked her eyes and looked to Esmée. "I—I'm sorry, what were you saying?"

"I was just saying," she began as she picked an

211

imaginary speck from the skirt of her dress, "if anything, this dreadful fever has brought Dain and me closer. We spent many long nights watching over Michael and we talked of many things."

Brittannia seethed. She wanted to pick up the nearest object and hurl it at the far wall she was feeling so jealous. She hated feeling this way, hated disliking the woman opposite her only because Dain found her charms more appealing.

"You know, Brittannia, Dain is a moody person. He keeps things to himself and doesn't very often tell a person how he feels. But one night, when Michael was on the mend and we realized the worst was over, he confided in me. And," she said very softly, coming to the edge of her seat to lean in Brittannia's direction, "do you know what he told me?"

After a long pause Brittannia realized Esmée was waiting for an answer. So Dain had confided his feelings to this woman. She could just imagine the night. It was probably a sultry evening with a thousand stars and Dain had probably bent his dark head to whisper his innermost thoughts into the delicate shell of Esmée's ear.

"No, what?" Brittannia asked, dreading the answer.

"He said he has feelings—"

Brittannia put her hand up, cutting off Esmée's next words. "No," she said in a strained voice. "I don't want to know! Please, don't tell me."

"But, Brittannia, he said—"

Brittannia abruptly stood. "No, I said I do not wish to know. I don't mean to be rude, Esmée, but I'm feeling tired and I'm going to my room. I do hope you'll forgive my bad manners." She quickly made her way from the room, tears stinging the back of her eyes as she went. She wanted nothing but to be away from Dain and Esmée.

"Certainly, Brittannia. I understand."

As she ran from the sitting room Brittannia was certain there was a smirk across Esmée's beautiful face.

Chapter 11

Brittannia wanted desperately to be away from Esmée. She couldn't bear to hear Esmée's triumphant news—not after what Dain and she had shared aboard the *Airlee*.

She was angry and hurt as she threw open the main door of the house and made her way along the wide veranda. How could she have been such a fool to give herself so freely to Dain? He'd gotten exactly what he'd wanted from her and now that they were back in Nassau, he'd go back to loving Esmée just as he always had. She rapped her small fist against the railing as she stared out into the dark night.

"Is something wrong, Brittannia?"

She whirled to see Dain standing a few feet from her. The bright moonlight threw shadows along the veranda and he stood cloaked in the darkness of those shadows. She angrily wiped away a tear that had managed to fall from her lashes and with a deep breath she considered Dain's question. She wanted to tell him she had found Esmée in his bed and that she knew of his affair with her. But she had too much pride. She couldn't let him know that for a brief time she had thought . . . she had hoped . . .

"Nothing is wrong," she said coldly. "Why do you ask?"

"You've done your best to ignore me this entire evening. What have I done to displease you?" He stepped out of the shadows and came closer to her. "I thought your anger would have cooled by now, now that you're with Michael and have seen for yourself he is well." Without a word of warning he brought his hands up to lightly caress her bare shoulders and her body stiffened.

"Don't," she said icily as she stepped away from him.

He ignored her cool manner toward him, once again closing the distance between them. "Have you forgotten the night you spent in my cabin?" he whispered close to her ear. "I haven't."

She felt the tingles along her spine caused by his warm breath in her ear and even though she fought to suppress it, her body quivered thrillingly. She wrapped her arms about her waist, as she stared into the silvery night as if she hoped to protect herself from her own feelings. Visions of the time Esmée and Dain must have shared here flashed before her mind like a light show and she felt her anger begin to boil anew. She shrugged from his hold, stepping away from him.

She heard the sigh he emitted and then could hear the rustle of his clothing as he sat atop the railing, the wood creaking slightly. She kept her back to him, too angry to speak just yet and listened to the sounds of his striking a match, and then she could smell the acrid aroma of the cheroot he'd lit.

"Esmée's done a remarkable job with Michael," he commented easily. "One would never think she would possess the knowledge she does about caring for the ill."

She turned to him, her eyes full of venom. "No," she agreed sarcastically, "one would never believe *that* of her!"

Dain stared searchingly at her. Immediately she dropped her eyes, afraid he would see the jealousy that was eating at her.

"Esmée's not a bad sort," he said slowly. "She enjoys shocking people but at heart she's not nearly as hardened as she pretends. You could do worse than befriend her."

Brittannia continued to stare down at her hands—but this time to hide the tears that filled her eyes.

Dain regarded her from beneath heavy lids for a moment or two and then with a huskiness that Brittannia, even in her anger, found far too appealing, said, "Come here." He motioned for her to come to him with a nod of his head, the dark curls looking boyishly tousled and soft as silk in the moonlight as he flicked his cheroot over his shoulder.

Brittannia fought hard against the impulse to walk into his arms. Her resolve was strong. She stayed rooted to her spot. With a quick arm, Dain reached out and took hold of her, drawing her to him with a quickness that took her breath away.

"Don't be coy," he whispered as he placed her lithe body between his legs and wrapped his arms about her waist. His eyes were unreadable in the dark night, but Brittannia's were not, for they held their own blazing light and when he looked into their turquoise depths, he chuckled—it was a sensuous laugh, one that teased its way along her spine and made her angrier. "Ah, Brittannia" was all he said before he pulled her body to his and brought his mouth down upon hers.

Brittannia instantly fought against him, her hands pushing against his chest as she turned her head away. "Stop it!"

"Why?" he asked, not relinquishing his hold on her.

"Because—I'm not like—" She faltered only a moment, then added, "like your *other* women!"

He raised one brow. "Other women?"

"Yes!" she spat.

"Oh. And what are *they* like?"

Brittannia squirmed in his tight hold, her fury increasing. She kept her mouth shut tight. He was mocking her!

He laughed at her discomfort. "Isn't it a little late to be playing the outraged lady of virtue?"

How dare he! Her fury was just about to storm out of her and in her eyes were daggers. "I—" she began, but Dain gave her no time for denials, for he crushed her to him with a driving force and bore his mouth down on hers with a swiftness that caused her head to spin. His searching tongue pushed past her pliant lips and she tasted the faint sweetness of his earlier cheroot as his tongue probed and searched, eliciting in her responses she did not want to give. His hands moved leisurely, familiarly, down to her buttocks where he gently pushed her body more firmly between his legs.

Finally his lips broke from hers only to start a fiery trail down her neck and then to her bosom.

He spoke between flicking, hot kisses that scorched her skin. "You're mine. You'll always be mine. You belong to me."

She grabbed his head by his hair, tugging him away from her heated body. "I'm not yours, and I never will be," she hissed. "Just because you seduced me with your virile charms doesn't make you my master. I'll never belong to you, Dain Barclay, any more than I belonged to Sebastian!" In the moonlight she saw his face had gone white. She was glad, *glad* she had hurt him as he had hurt her and she pressed her advantage. "And Sebastian was a better lover than you'll ever be!"

Too late she realized her folly. He released her as if she were all that was evil, and when his eyes beheld her they were tombstone cold.

"Forgive me! I won't bother you with my attentions again." His words were clipped, metallic, and they lodged in her heart like a shard of glass.

She held her ground as he bowed slightly and took his leave of her. Not until he was inside and she heard the door shut did she let the tears come. They were heart-wrenching sobs that wracked her slim body with a violent force.

How much time had passed? An hour? Two? She did not know, she only knew she was empty inside, that her victory was no great triumph. She'd finally gotten through to Dain, finally made him realize he had no claim on her, but somehow she didn't feel the elation she'd thought she'd feel on the day she was free of him.

With a sigh she leaned her head against the cool beam of the veranda. She stood there, her eyes staring into nothingness, as moonbeams bathed her bare shoulders and golden cascade of curls. The silvery gray light picked out the slight downward tug of her curved lips, the distance in her gemstone eyes, and the overall sadness in her angel's face. Of a sudden she knew the meaning of the word loneliness.

"Brittannia, are you out here?"

It was Michael's voice that cut gently into the perfumed night and with a quick turn of her head, she replied, "Yes, over here." Her voice was soft, poignantly so, and she chided herself for it. She heard his footsteps as he crossed the veranda and came to stand beside her in the moonlight.

"I'd thought perhaps you retired for the night," he said, leaning against the rail beside her.

She shook her head.

"Anything you'd like to talk about?" he asked, his brown eyes gentle as they beheld her.

Again, another shake of her head as she stared into the distance.

Michael need not have been a seer to determine what was troubling Brittannia and he felt a tug at his heart, for Brittannia was like a sister to him and he wanted to protect her from the harshness of life—of feelings. "Dain's a very complex man," he began, ignoring the way her eyes darted to him, flashing in the night at mention of Dain. "But you won't find a better one, nor could you ever find a truer friend."

Brittannia found it hard to hold her tongue, for she strongly disagreed with Michael. "Your words fail to bring an image of Captain Barclay to mind. Were I to describe the man my choice of words would greatly differ from yours!"

Michael raised one brow. "They would?"

"Certainly! The man is nothing more than a cold,

uncaring, arrogant rogue!"

"I see," he said, then after a long look, he declared, "You're in love with him."

Brittannia was instantly incensed. "Love?!" she raged. "Hardly! I *loathe* the man!"

She saw the knowing smile on his lips, the teasing light in his brown eyes and she opened her mouth feeling the need to further impress upon Michael her dislike for Dain. "Michael—" She no sooner had spoken his name than Esmée burst through the front doors, a worried look on her face.

"Michael!" she yelled. "Michael, come quick! It's Blossom! I fear she has the fever!" Esmée ran toward them, her voluminous skirts held off the ground by her clenched hands. Her green eyes were large and held a frightened look. "As she was clearing the table she fell to the floor and now she is running a high fever!" Esmée quickly explained, looking besieged with guilt and fear. "She had complained earlier of a headache but I thought nothing of it. I should have seen the signs!"

Michael was instantly to his feet and following Esmée into the house. Brittannia was beside him, her anger leaving her as she watched the pair beside her. Their faces were set into grim lines as they nearly ran through the front rooms toward the back of the house and the servants' quarters.

"Michael, who is Blossom?" Brittannia asked as she tried to match their hurried pace.

Michael seemed not to have heard her, his eyes fixed straight ahead, his face etched with worry. Esmée looked with concern to him and, then to Brittannia, said, "She is one of the maids. I believe you've met her, for I instructed her to draw your bath earlier today."

Brittannia nodded her head envisioning the tiny island girl with the expressive brown eyes, the same whose clothes she wore. Finally they came to the young girl's room and Michael was the first to enter, his mind only on getting to the girl's side. Brittannia was about to follow him, but Esmée held her back, shaking her dark head.

"No," she said gently. "You mustn't go near her, Brittannia. You too could fall ill to it."

"But you're going in."

"Yes. I've had the fever once. It seems with recovery comes immunity, so I do not fear contracting it again."

Brittannia looked past Esmée's shoulder to the tiny girl lying immobile upon her bed. "But I want to help."

"Of course you do, and you can, but not here." The dark-haired woman looked over her shoulder then turned back to Brittannia and said in a hushed voice, "We need the doctor to come as quickly as possible. The *Airlee*'s surgeon, Dobbins, is staying at the Boar's Inn. Find Dain and tell him to get word to the man."

Brittannia nodded then watched as Esmée entered the room and shut the door behind her. Turning, Brittannia decided against finding Dain. She had no idea where he'd gone off to and she didn't want to have to face him again. She would go for the doctor herself. She wasted no time in dwelling on the idea of venturing out alone in the dark to find a man she had never met—she wanted only to make herself as useful as Esmée was making herself. Leaving the house through the back entrance, she quickly made her way to the carriage house. After lighting a lantern and saddling the nearest horse, she hitched up her skirts and jumped upon the animal's back spurring him into a quick run toward the lower streets and the Boar's Inn.

The going was dark with only the moonbeams to light her way. The air that whizzed by her was cool on her warm skin, cutting through the thin material of her clothes. The clip of the horses' hooves sounded distressingly loud in the dark night as they hit the earth with great force and Brittannia didn't like the way the sound echoed off the close-built buildings she flew by. She hadn't seen a soul on the streets and as she came off the last incline and the horse galloped onto Bay Street, she became worried, for even here, this close to the harbor, there were only a few people about. She kept to the middle of the street, slowing the animal only a bit as she came into the light of the gaslamps of Bay Street, and her eyes were wary on those she passed. She remembered the pistol Dain had carried when they first entered Nassau and she cursed herself for not having the foresight to bring with her some form of protection. The men who stood along the nearly deserted streets looked the type to do a person bodily harm, and the women, they looked just as evil, just as desperate.

She slowed her mount as the shingle for the Boar's Inn came into view. There was a wagon and horse in front of the building. As she reined her horse in and came beside the wagon, she saw the man who sat atop the buckboard was the worse for wear. His hair was sparse and gray and his body was horribly thin, his baggy, dirty clothes hanging on him as if they had been tailored for a larger person. Brittannia jumped down, quickly brushing her skirts into place, then started in the direction of the inn. The man's voice stopped her.

"Where d'ya think yer goin'?"

Brittannia turned to him. He looked barely able to hold the reins in his hands and she wondered why he was sitting there as he was. "I've business here," she replied, then again started for the door.

"Ain't no one in there gonna let ya in. Ya best get off the streets, lady, orders are for everyone to stay put until the fevah is done ragin'."

"Then why aren't you inside?"

He gave her a hard laugh as he spewed a stream of tobacco through rotted teeth to the ground. "Me? I gots ta do the dirty work. I gotta haul away the dead bodies."

Brittannia felt her blood run cold with his words and with wide eyes she looked to the wagon behind him. To her relief it was empty, but she couldn't help the shiver that ran along her spine with thoughts of the cargo it carried. Were there really that many bodies to have to *cart* away?

"Chances are the person ya came ta see is gonna be my next load," the man said. He seemed to delight in Brittannia's obvious discomfort. "My partner's in gettin' the bit of sticks now."

She cringed at his slang. She heard the door of the inn open and someone came out. She turned to see a stocky man with greasy hair and even greasier clothes step onto the boardwalk; over his shoulder was a corpse slung like so many sacks of flour.

"Just one, Davey?" the man on the buckboard asked, not moving to help the other with his burden.

"Yeah," the husky man said, tossing the limp body into the wagon. The boards creaked as the body hit and Brittannia had to look away as the one called Davey threw a tattered piece of cloth over the dead person.

"Though there be two others we'll probably have to cart away soon. I give 'em no more'n a day." He looked toward Brittannia, his bloodshot eyes looking up and down her slim figure. "Who we got here, John? A friend of yours?"

The man called John spit again. "Naw, she's figurin' ta go inside the inn. Says she's got bizness."

Davey laughed as he wiped his filthy beard with a ratty sleeve. "Maybe her friend's right here!" He hooked his thumb toward the back of the wagon. Both men laughed at that.

Brittannia looked at them in stunned horror, taking an unconscious step away from them and their infected cargo. "I doubt it," she managed to say, but wasn't too certain. Suddenly nothing seemed certain, especially her safety. She turned from them and quickly scurried to the door of the inn. She tried the latch but found it locked and her fear mounted. She pounded on the heavy portal with her fists as she heard the men behind her laugh again and then she heard the reins slap against the horse and the creaking wood as the wagon rumbled on down Bay Street, leaving her behind. She breathed a long sigh of relief, but still nearly jumped from her skin when the portal before her was quickly thrust open.

"What d'ya want?" a gruff voice demanded. "Can't ya read the sign?"

Brittannia blinked in confusion as she looked up to a heavyset woman garbed in apron and a dull flower print dress. Her hair, pulled into a severe bun, was dark as a raven's wing and her eyes even darker. "I—I didn't see any sign," Brittannia stuttered. The woman in front of her had a menacing appearance that would cause the bravest of souls to pause.

The woman jabbed a finger to a sign posted on the middle of the door. "It says no new guests!" the woman bellowed and was about to slam the door in Brittannia's face.

"No, wait!" she said, holding the door from closing. "It isn't a room I seek but a person. I need to see a man staying here."

The woman shook her head. "Ain't no one coming in. I don't even want the ones I got!"

"Please, I must see this person!"

"No, ya heard me!"

The door was halfway closed, but Brittannia pushed hard against it. "Wait! Please, just—just tell this person I need to speak with him. Have him come out here!"

The woman paused, her dark eyes boring holes into Brittannia. "All right," she finally said. "Who is it ya want ta see?"

Brittannia couldn't help the smile of gratitude that lit her face. "Dobbins. His name is Dobbins. He's the surgeon for the *Airlee*. Tell him his captain needs him."

No sooner had Brittannia let the words out than the portal was slammed shut again. She heard the sound of it being locked from within and then nothing. Just silence. It was a deadly silence, a silence borne of fear, of sickness. She stepped away from the door, leaning back against the rough wood of the building as her eyes scanned the street around her. Two men and a woman sat on a curbstone, across the street a few buildings down, passing a bottle between them. Their words were muffled by the distance and none seemed to have any interest in Brittannia. They all looked in need of a decent meal and a long bath. Brittannia trusted none of them and so, while waiting for the woman to return, she kept her eye on them. She hadn't a long wait, for only minutes passed before the portal was again drawn open and this time a portly man dressed in overcoat and trousers, a striped vest and white shirt showing beneath the lined coat, stepped outside. In his pudgy hand he held a black bag, while his other hand rested against his large belly, the thumb hooked into the chain of his watch that dangled from his vest pocket. The door was slammed as soon as he was outside.

"Yes?" he inquired, looking to Brittannia with questioning light green eyes. "I was told Captain Barclay needed me. Is this some sort of game, young lady? Where's the captain?"

Brittannia straightened. "My name is Brittannia Denning. Actually it isn't the captain who needs your help but—"

The old man puffed up like a haughty peacock. "The captain doesn't need me? Are you telling me you've brought me out into the night for no reason?" His eyes narrowed as he leaned toward Brittannia. "Or are you one of the many who's come to drag me to the side of a dying relative? Speak up, girl! My patience has worn thin this day. So many people dying and I can't help— I'm overworked, girl, I need my rest, so hurry and tell me your cause!"

Brittannia was quick to explain. "Captain Barclay has a friend who needs your assistance. She's at the home of Michael Delving. I've come to take you there. We must hurry, she's very sick!" Brittannia gestured to her mount standing patiently near them.

"Is it the fever?"

Brittannia nodded.

"Well, let's go, girl. We haven't a minute to spare!"

Brittannia's face broke into a smile of relief, then she quickly turned and mounted the horse, motioning for the old man to jump on behind her. He was too short and clumsy to be able to mount right from the ground, so she had to walk the horse to the nearest curbstone so the portly doctor could get on from there. As soon as he was behind her on the saddle, she spurred the horse into a quick run toward George Street. They fairly flew through the streets; Brittannia with her body leaned forward, almost one with the horse, the old man behind her, eyes wide, his chubby legs hanging awkwardly over the sides while he held tightly onto Brittannia so he wouldn't topple to the ground.

It seemed no sooner were they astride than they were racing through the front gates and up the slight hill to Michael's home. The house was ablaze with light, each room lit from within and Brittannia wondered if they were too late, if Blossom had already been taken away by the fever. She reined the animal in right in front of the front steps, and after alighting, she helped the doctor down, practically pulling him up the stairs with her and into the house. She led him quickly through the hall and toward the back of the house.

Esmée was just coming out of Blossom's room and her face lit up at sight of the doctor. "Dobbins!" she exclaimed. "Her fever is rising rapidly and—"

Brittannia heard no more as Esmée led the doctor into the room and promptly shut the door behind them.

Feeling totally useless now that her assigned errand had been run, she turned from the door and slowly made her way back through the house and up the wide

228

staircase to her room. She silently hoped tomorrow would be a better day.

Morning came. A dawning that was hazy and unusually warm, promising a hot day to come. Brittannia woke early, the heat already penetrating her rooms, and she quickly donned the garments she'd worn the previous day, anxious to be downstairs and check on Blossom's condition. The house seemed ominously quiet as she made her way down the stairs and through the hall. An occasional clang of pans could be heard from the kitchen but no voices filled the large rooms, no laughter could be heard. She was about to go straight to Blossom's room but she heard a loud expletive shouted in French just as a loud crash came from the kitchen. She followed the sounds and was astonished to find Esmée, on hands and knees, her pretty day frock spattered with flour, picking up broken bits of china. Her dark hair, pulled into a careless bun at the nape of her neck, was falling free of its pins and the strands that kept falling in front of her face were just as flour-covered as were the hands that Esmée reached up to push the tresses away with.

"Esmée!" Brittannia exclaimed. "What are you doing?"

The older woman sat back on her heels, blowing the hair from her brow with a puff of air. "Good morning, Brittannia, if one could call it that."

Brittannia bent down beside Esmée, picking up the scattered pieces that had once been a platter. "Why are you preparing breakfast?" she asked. "Where are the servants?" Brittannia noticed the look of fatigue on

229

Esmée's face and she felt her heartbeat quicken with worry. "What is it, Esmée? What's happened?"

Esmée shook her head, holding the broken bits of china in her apron as she stood and walked to the wastebasket. "Now, I don't want to worry you, Brittannia. Everyone will be fine, we'll see to it."

"Who will be fine? What has happened, please tell me!"

The clatter of the broken glass going into the basket could be heard. "The servants, Dolores and her daughter, Mandy. They—they came down with the fever in the middle of the night."

"Oh my," Brittannia breathed. "Has the doctor seen them?"

"No, he left soon after seeing Blossom. Their conditions are bad, but not—" she paused a moment, going to the huge stove and flipping the many pancakes on the skillet, "not as bad as Blossom's. I'm worried about her, Brittannia. I've never seen the fever progress so rapidly in a person."

Brittannia set the broken bits of glass she held onto the counter nearest, her body numb with the grave news. Only yesterday yellow fever had been a sickness she had just *heard* about but had never had to deal with, and now—three people in the same house as she had it—one possibly not to live through it. "Where's Michael?" she asked, her voice strained.

Esmée sighed, taking the pancakes one by one from the skillet and placing them on a platter. "He's with Blossom. He's been running between rooms, seeing to their every need. He feels guilty, Brittannia."

"Why?"

"He let most of the staff go when he first fell ill to the fever keeping only those he needed most. I believe he thinks it is his fault Blossom and the others are sick," she explained. She moved to a pan that had steam rising from its deep interior and with a ladle she poured soup into three separate bowls.

"Is there anything I can do to help?" Brittannia asked, moving over to the stove and removing the sausage from pan to platter, placing the links beside the pancakes.

Esmée set the three bowls on a large tray along with three spoons. "Yes," she said, lifting the tray, "you can sit down and get something into your stomach, we need to keep you healthy. I'm going to try and get Michael out here to have something to eat while I feed the girls some broth. I doubt they'll be able to keep it down, but I've got to try."

"Esmée, I wish I could go in there and help you. Is there no way?"

Esmée shook her head. "No, Brittannia. I'll not risk it, not when I can do the task myself with no risk."

Brittannia watched as Esmée left the room and then she turned and reached into the cupboard pulling out a plate and cup for Michael. She wished she could do something, anything. She felt useless.

The day wore on, the sun rising to a blistering ball high in the sky and as Brittannia stepped outside she felt the air hit her like a hot breath. Insects buzzed, birds sang, but hardly a breeze touched her. She almost dared not breathe in the air, for it hung heavy around her, filled with yellow fever, and as she walked toward the water pump, the buckets swaying one in each hand, she kept her breathing controlled trying not to take in too much air. Her mind wasn't functioning with its normal coolness, for all through the morning and early afternoon, she'd listened to reports of the girls' conditions—and each one was worse than the first. Esmée tried to explain that things would get worse before they got better, but this did nothing to still Brittannia's wild thoughts, her mounting fear. Why hadn't she listened to Dain when he'd warned her to stay on the *Airlee*? She finally reached the pump and began to fill each bucket. She hadn't seen Dain since last night. Where had he gone? Back to his home on Queen Street? To the wharf? The buckets now filled, she lifted them and walked back to the house. What if Dain were to contract the fever? What if, this very minute, he was falling to the ground, his skin hot and burning? Her mind filled with horrible visions of the two men she had seen last night, John and Davey, heaving Dain into the back of their wagon atop a mountain of other bodies—all dead. With a stifled cry she ran for the house, not caring that the water was spilling from the buckets.

The day wore on and melted into another, but Brittannia had hardly a moment to notice, for her time was completely consumed with caring for the three servants. Although she couldn't enter their rooms, she did make the meals, wash the dishes, sheets, and night dresses Esmée was forever, it seemed, bringing out to her. Sheets and night dresses soaked from the perspiration of feverish bodies, bodies that would grow frightfully hot one minute then turn narcotic cold the next. Brittannia always had a pan of water on to boil and it seemed the tasks of preparing the food were never done. She was constantly paring, chopping, and cutting to create thick broths that were only half eaten and the awful cries and moaning that drifted to her from Blossom's room tore at her heart, making her work all the harder.

It was the morning of the third day when Esmée, looking worn and tired, entered the kitchen. She leaned wearily against the drainboard where Brittannia was peeling potatoes.

"Esmée, you need some rest, won't you please go upstairs and lie down for a while? Michael and I can take over."

Esmée shook her head. "I've just sent Michael to bed, he's exhausted, hasn't slept a wink in two days."

"And neither have you!" Brittannia exclaimed, setting down her paring knife, then wiping her hands on her apron. "Here," she said, guiding Esmée to a nearby stool, "sit and rest for a moment. You're going to be ill yourself!"

"No, I can't. I—I have to go find the doctor. We need more medicine and I have to go to the market as we need fresh food."

"I can do that, Esmée. You need to rest!"

Esmée stood, shaking off Brittannia's help. "No, I'll not have you out on the streets, it's too dangerous, and who knows what outrageous prices they'd try and charge you at the market! No, Brittannia, I need you to stay here and listen for the girls while Michael is sleeping. You wake him if you need him."

Brittannia stood for a moment, regarding the raven-haired woman. She shouldn't let Esmée go anywhere but to bed! But she could see she was getting nowhere arguing with her, so with a nod of her head, she said, "All right, Esmée. I'll stay here, but you must promise me that when you get back you'll go straight to bed!"

"Yes, yes," the other said, already on her way out the door.

Brittannia watched from the kitchen door as Esmée made her way to the carriage house, and as she stood there in the slanted light of the morning, she felt a growing respect for the older woman. Although Esmée had shared Dain's bed and had boldly flaunted the fact in front of her, although she'd been positively unnerving when Brittannia had first arrived at Michael's, Brittannia was now beginning to see her in a different light.

As she turned back to her task, her mind pondering her feelings toward Esmée, she heard a commotion in Blossom's room. Quickly Brittannia raced from the kitchen and into the hall, and with a hurried step, she made her way to the small room, pushing the door open. She would see to Blossom herself and let Michael get some much-needed rest. What greeted her was the sight of the small, island girl thrashing upon her bed, her hands in tight fists pulling at the sheets that were wrapped around her sweating body. She was screaming and yelling words that made no sense.

"Blossom!" Brittannia ran to the girl's bedside, taking her shoulders in a firm grip as she tried to still her wild motions. "Blossom, it's okay, honey! Lie still, Blossom . . . oh dear God!" Brittannia said into the heavy air of the room, fright overtaking her as she looked down at the girl. The once beautiful skin of Blossom was no more the shade of nut-brown, but now colored a sickening, deep yellow, and her long, dark

234

hair was plastered to her sweating scalp. Her body was frail, frightfully thin. Gently she laid Blossom back against the damp pillow, and with tender hands bathed the girl's hot brow with cool water from the basin. Blossom's breathing was shallow, too shallow, and Brittannia's worry mounted. Should the girl be lying so still? Where was Esmée with the medicine? Would the medicine even help?

Blossom was mumbling again, mumblings that soon turned to pathetic whimpers. Brittannia had no idea what she should do, for Esmée had told her there was nothing they could do but see she was comfortable. With trembling hands Brittannia gathered the young girl in her arms, rocking her gently back and forth as she tried to comfort her with soft words that made no sense. The words went unheard, for as she held her, Blossom's tiny body went limp, her breathing ceased . . . all life in her had seeped away on a hot, yellow river.

Brittannia felt her own heartbeat stop for a second as she felt life leave the young girl, then she held her tight willing every ounce of her strength to pass between them. It did no good, still the child was lifeless in her arms. "No!" Brittannia cried, breaking down completely. "Oh, dear God!" Her voice broke as sobs choked her and wracked her body. Finally she knew firsthand the hell Dain had tried to spare her from. It hit her like a blowing, vengeful force. Hot tears, tears for her own obstinacy, tears for Blossom, fell unchecked down her healthy, pink cheeks to land unnoticed on the ashen, sunken hollows of Blossom's cheeks.

"Brittannia?"

It was a male voice that came from behind her, but

Brittannia did not hear it. All she knew, all she could feel was her grief at the loss of a life, so young, so innocent. It wasn't fair and worst of all there was nothing she could do about it.

"Brittannia," Dain said, his voice soft and soothing, "here let her go, Brittannia. Let her go."

She held tightly onto Blossom's body, rocking her back and forth. She struggled against him as he pried her hands from the girl as he firmly pulled her up from the bedside. "Oh why did she have to die!" she cried as he pulled her to him, holding her tightly. "Why? Why?"

His arms were like comforting steel bands around her blocking out all the horror that life now seemed to be filled with. "I don't know," he said, his voice sounding strange.

Brittannia let him hold her as she continued to cry. He squeezed her tight, stilling the trembling of her limbs, helping to thaw the numbness of her brain. Without speaking he lifted her into his arms and carried her from the room, her head on his shoulder, her arms about his neck. And still she cried. Tears for her childish reaction earlier to Dain—tears for her selfishness at dragging him to Nassau, knowing now that it could just as easily have been Dain who died—or even herself.

Dain took the steps two at a time, gently holding his weeping bundle, his mind full of confusing thoughts. He held in his arms the only person who had the power to bedevil him so; she could make him want to strangle her one minute and in the next make him want to die for her, do anything he could to please her. He pushed open the door of her rooms, and striding to the bed, he placed her down upon the cool covers.

Once there, Brittannia curled up like a child, bringing her knees to her chest and turning her head to the pillow, not yet able to still her sobs. Dain stood above her, indecisive. He wanted to stay and comfort her, but he knew where that would lead him. He knew if he took her in his arms again he would not be able to leave her side. His look tormented, he turned to leave.

"Dain?" Brittannia choked, turning a tear-stained, pain-filled face up to him. "Don't leave me yet . . . *please.*"

She said the last word so softly, so sweetly that all thoughts of leaving left his mind. As if under a spell, he sat down on the edge of her bed, one strong hand, of its own volition, reaching over to gently stroke her mussed hair.

Long moments passed in which Brittannia lay animal-still, her sobs not so choking, her tears finally drying, and when she finally rolled to her back, straightening her legs, she took hold of Dain's hand and pulled him onto the bed beside her. He came without hesitation, his gaze intense as he beheld her and brought both hands to her face, gently stroking her flushed cheeks. He kissed each tear-wet eye, ran soft lips across her pained brow, pressed a comforting kiss to each temple, then, with delicate lips, brushed by her full and trembling mouth. She felt her pain begin to ebb as a warm wave washed through her, cleansing her, taking away all the hurt. With trembling arms she pulled Dain closer to her, resting her cheek against his chest as she reveled in the wondrous glory of just having him near.

She needed him and he could sense that need. Despite her earlier tormenting words he wanted to be here with her, wanted to be the one to comfort her in her sorrow. He ran caressing hands through her tangled hair that soon moved lower to run by her neck, over her shoulder blades and down her curved back, rubbing as they went, soothing all her aches from the grueling chores of the past days.

Brittannia closed her eyes, nuzzling her face against his hard chest. He smelled clean and warm and the feel of his body against hers brought her a peace she hadn't felt since the last time she'd lain with him. How was it this man could bring to her such a feeling while no one else could? How was it whenever her need was greatest he was there, there for her to turn to, there to help her? She sighed, willing the confusing thoughts away as she ran her own hands across the broad expanse of his muscled back. His athlete's body was hard and lean beneath her palms causing a tingle of excitement to spread through her.

Expertly he was undoing the buttons of her borrowed day dress, opening the thin material and pulling it away from her willing body. His movements were quick as though he needed release just as much as she, and when finally her swelling breasts were free of their tight prison and his mouth took possession of one pink nipple, Brittannia felt her passion begin to flame. She arched her back, pressing her snowy breasts to him as her nails raked across his back, tugging at his thin shirt. Her insides were boiling now. With each flicking touch of his tongue, each hot caress of his hands she felt herself burning from the inside out. She could feel his quickened breath on her skin, could almost hear his rapidly beating heart as he lifted her skirts to her thighs and his hand quickly moved to the quivering place between them. His questing fingers teased and excited her causing her to gasp and writhe beneath his lean frame. She could barely stand the surging of her blood, the keen wanting that he evoked in her. As her breathing grew ragged and she ripped the shirt from his chest, buttons flying, she heard his deep, sensuous laugh. Gone was all reason, all she knew was this reckless, wild need to be filled—this all-consuming fire that burned white hot within her.

Too quickly he moved from her and when her eyes flew open to see if he was leaving, she smiled, for he stood beside the bed stepping out of his breeches. She held out her arms and the mattress sagged as he once again found the warm niche beside her. His male member was hard and throbbing, pressing against her, causing her whole body to shiver in anticipation. She had waited too long, she could wait no longer. As he showered her neck and breasts with kisses, she pulled him on top of her, wriggling her way beneath his warm body as she opened herself to him. Intense, gray eyes looked down at her for only a moment as he positioned himself between her legs, then as his lips came down upon hers in a deep, passionate kiss she felt him enter her with a steely thrust. A moan caught in her throat at the feel of it and she thrust her hips to meet him, needing to feel him within her, wanting to be where only he could take her.

Brittannia clung to him, letting the fires burn and rage inside her, her body arching to meet Dain's as they each moved and writhed, both slaves to their own wild nature. Higher and higher her senses climbed, coming more and more to life and she thought she'd go mad from the many sensations that were bursting within her. It was almost too much yet she wanted more. He moved on top of her and within her and his lips played sensuously over her hot skin, eliciting responses she was all too eager to give. Finally he took her to where she longed to be and her senses reeled and took flight, rolling her over and over in delicious, reckless rapture. Her head spun from the dizzying heights as she felt the hot river of life speed from his body to hers—and she thought she had never known such bliss.

Later, after his breathing returned to normal and he could finally let reality return, Dain lay there, his thoughts turning dark. Brittannia's words, the words she had so carelessly flung out that night on the veranda, came rushing back to him: *Sebastian is a better lover than you'll ever be.* His body stiffened beside her pliant form. He rolled away from her, quickly standing and getting dressed.

"Dain," Brittannia ventured. "Are you leaving?"

Dain shrugged into his torn shirt, his eyes looking dark and violent. "Yes, Brittannia, I've spent enough time in your bed. I've an aversion to whores this day—and only a whore could pleasure a man like you've just pleasured me."

His words hit her like a stinging blow, and after her initial shock she found anger rushing to fill her. "A *whore?*" she raged, scrambling to get off the bed.

Dain, now fully dressed, turned and walked toward the door. Just as he reached it, he turned and asked, "Did you give as freely to Diaz? No wonder he was willing to kill for you."

Brittannia sputtered with raging fury. She longed to make a withering retort about Esmée but she did not trust herself to speak without revealing her jealousy.

Her face turned a bright red as she reached over to the nightstand and grabbed the nearest object. With a quick hand she threw the tiny vase at Dain, just missing his retreating back. It shattered as it hit the doorjamb, coming to rest in a million tiny pieces where Dain had just stood. She screamed out her indignation then fell upon the bed cursing herself for submitting to—and, yes, enjoying—Dain's vile embraces.

The sun had gone down and still Brittannia lay on the bed. She had pulled her skirts down and fixed her buttons, but she was loath to leave her rooms. She couldn't bear to see Blossom's still form again and she was afraid the other two servants might not make it through this day. She should go down, she knew, and help Esmée with the evening meal. There was a timid knock at the door. Quickly Brittannia sat up, pushing the hair from her eyes.

"Yes?" she called.

"Brittannia, it's Esmée. Can I come in?"

"Yes," she called in reply. As soon as Esmée stepped inside the door, Brittannia hastened to say, "I'm sorry I haven't come to help you, but Blossom, she—uh—I just—" Words evaded her as she felt her tears coming again and she cursed herself for her weakness.

Esmée stepped over the sharded glass and came to Brittannia's side, her slender hand coming to rest softly on Brittannia's shoulder. "I know about Blossom, *chérie,*" she said. "Dain is taking care of the—arrangements. I came up to see if you need anything."

Brittannia kept her head down as she tried to still her sobs. She couldn't let Esmée witness her in hysterics.

241

Wiping quickly at her tears, she looked up and said, "No. And I should be downstairs helping you care for Dolores and Mandy. They—they're not any worse, are they?"

Esmée shook her head, a smile touching her lips. "No, they are holding their own and do not worry, Michael is with them. We don't need for you to come downstairs if you'd rather be alone. If you like, I'll draw a bath for you and then you can retire early. You've been working so hard these past few days."

Brittannia looked to Esmée, beautiful, worldly Esmée, mistress of many men, was offering to draw a bath for *her!* She found it hard to believe. Could it be she had misjudged this raven-haired woman, the same she had found in Dain's bed?

"Oh, Esmée, you don't have to do that."

"But I want to. You—it must have been a terrible ordeal for you to go through what you did today. I am sorry I was not here with you. I would never have left had I known she was so close . . ." She let her words drift off and Brittannia felt her throat constrict as memories of that morning came back to her. Her shoulders shook as new tears formed in her turquoise eyes and Esmée was quick to gather her into a sisterly hug, patting her back and soothing her. Brittannia welcomed the hug, the tender compassion that came with it, she desperately needed a friend this day. Someone she could confide in, someone who would listen.

"Oh, Esmée," she cried, "it was so awful! I didn't know what to do!" Her sobs were making the act of talking very nearly impossible.

"Shh," Esmée soothed. "You did all you could." She guided Brittannia to lie down. Night descended upon the world outside and still Esmée sat with her. Brittannia, her emotions frayed from the many events of the day, finally closed her eyes and not until she was asleep, did Esmée get up. The older woman put a light coverlet across Brittannia's sleeping form and then she quietly left the room, softly closing the door behind her.

A slow, work-filled week passed and then another. Brittannia gladly put every ounce of her strength and concentration into the caring of Dolores and Mandy who were making slow but steady recoveries. She didn't want to let herself slow down for fear thoughts of Dain would invade her mind. She kept out of his distance when he came, which was distressingly often as he wanted to check on everyone's health, or so he said, but Brittannia was of the mind he merely delighted in tormenting her. The next week was already a few days old when Esmée, who had been to the market, burst into the kitchen, a huge smile lighting the whole of her face.

"Brittannia!" she cried. "It is over! The quarantine has been lifted!"

Brittannia, just-baked pie in hand, felt her mouth drop open. "Over?" she exclaimed. "Are you certain?"

"*Oui!* Already people are out on the streets again and the ships are able to come and go! Is it not wonderful?"

Brittannia felt herself smile, then laugh as she set the pie down and she and Esmée clasped each other and danced about the kitchen.

"We must celebrate!" Esmée declared, pulling Brittannia to a breathless stop. "We'll have a party, *non?*"

"Yes! Yes!" Brittannia agreed, tears of joy running down her cheeks. "We'll have a party!"

By the end of the week the two of them had most of the preparations finished and all of the invitations out. With the return of all the servants Michael had released at the outbreak of the fever, Brittannia and Esmée now had the entire week before the party to do as they pleased, which was usually to just sit on the veranda and enjoy the sunshine or to visit the dressmaker to be fitted for their new gowns. Brittannia had ordered a whole wardrobe to be made and so she had to stand and suffer many long hours of fittings.

The day of the affair finally dawned bright and beautiful and Brittannia and Esmée fluttered around Michael's home overseeing the making of a pastry here, the arrangements of chairs there. Everything had to be perfect for this would be the first grand party since the epidemic.

Finally, at eight o'clock, Brittannia stepped from her rooms. Her cheeks were flushed from excitement as she glided down the hall to the front stairs. She had chosen a ball dress of white silk that was covered all over with tiny, turquoise blue flowers. About her tiny waist was a blue velvet sash, and the sleeves, a short puff, were positioned off the shoulders, showing to full advantage her long, slender neck. Her hair, pulled up in the back and allowed to fall in a tumbling cascade of three ringlets, shined in the candlelight as she descended the many stairs. As her eyes flicked over the growing sea of people, she felt her heart tremor. There, standing beside Michael near the main doors was Dain. Just the sight of him could cause her knees to go weak. He was dressed almost entirely in black, only the light thin gray stripes of his vest and the white of his shirt giving any contrast. He looked extremely formal, devastatingly handsome.

Esmée came up beside Brittannia, looking stunning in her brocade gown of deep, deep red. "You look positively beautiful!" Esmée declared as she took Brittannia's elbow and guided her toward Michael and Dain. Another man was standing with them. He was older, probably nearing his late sixties, Brittannia guessed.

Esmée gave her a quick wink. "*Chérie,* I want to introduce you to someone very special to me!"

They came in front of the small group, Brittannia feeling very vulnerable as she stood beside Dain. He turned to her, the look in his eyes unreadable.

"Miss Denning," he said in a most formal tone, "how very beautiful you look this evening." He bowed low over her gloved hand and with a feather-light touch he brought that hand to his lips and placed a kiss upon it.

Brittannia endured the sweet torture of the feel of his lips upon her hand. Even through the material of her glove she could feel his warmth and the familiar tingles he always brought to her began to race up her spine. She felt herself blush as she murmured a quick thank-you and turned her gaze to Michael and the older man.

"Brittannia," Esmée was saying, "I'd like to introduce you to Jacques de Remy, my fiancé. Jacques, this is Brittannia Denning, the same who was such a great help to me during this dreadful epidemic."

Brittannia turned to the gray-haired, older man. Esmée's *fiancé?!* "How do you do?" Brittannia heard herself respond, but her mind was in a whirl as the older man executed a quick bow, the look in his watery brown eyes kind. Esmée, the same who had held Dain's attention, was marrying *this* man?

"You see," Esmée was explaining as she moved over to Jacques and tucked an arm possessively into the crook of his, "Jacques is a speculator and was on his way to New York when the epidemic broke out so there was no way he could return to me. He just arrived today." The raven-haired woman looked with a loving smile to the old man and then placed an affectionate kiss on his wrinkled cheek.

Brittannia nodded, smiling, still not able to believe this of Esmée. Why the woman looked absolutely smitten with the old man! She watched, in awe, as the two left the small circle for the ballroom where the sounds of a favorite waltz were now beginning.

"I think," Michael exclaimed as he too watched the couple leave, "that Esmée has finally found what she's been looking for. Who'd have believed it?"

"Indeed!" Brittannia mumbled, her mind lost in thought. She didn't notice when Michael turned to greet more guests and wasn't aware of the intense look Dain was casting her. At the sound of his voice she came back to the present.

"May I have this dance, Brittannia?" he asked, his voice not at all soft.

She gave him a slanted look, visions of their last encounter springing before her eyes. "I'd rather not," she said icily, then brushed by him. She walked with quick steps into the ballroom and around the many bodies that stood along the side of the dance floor as she made her way to the refreshment tables. She took a glass of punch, only sipping at it. She groaned inwardly as she saw Dain approaching her.

"Can you not even be civil with me this night, Brittannia?" he asked, coming up beside her.

Brittannia set down her glass, intent on getting away from him. "There are many women here who would no doubt die for just one dance with you. Why not seek them out and leave me alone?"

Dain folded his arms across his chest. "It is you I want to dance with."

"Why?" she demanded.

"Because I know how warm your embrace can be," he whispered, leaning toward her.

She felt fury beginning to rise. She wanted to spite him. "Could it be your aversion to loose women is no more? For surely you know you are not the only man to spend time in that 'warm embrace.'"

She saw the storm enter his eyes, saw the muscle twitch along his jaw, and knew that she had achieved her goal. He was angry. She pressed her advantage. "No," she said flirtingly, "I think I shall search for a new conquest this night."

Lightning quick he roughly grabbed her by the shoulder, his fingers digging into her tender flesh as he pulled her to him. Brittannia held her breath, for the fury written on his face frightened her. His eyes, dark and murderous, bore into hers and then, after long seconds, he abruptly released her as though she were a filthy leper. Without another word to her he stormed away, walking swiftly and angrily across the dance floor and then out of the room. Brittannia let out the breath she was holding and her whole body shook.

"Brittannia, what has happened?" It was Esmée standing beside her, green eyes alight with worry. "Whatever did you say to him? He looked positively enraged!"

247

Brittannia shook her head, brushing a stray curl from her brow. "Nothing—everything," she replied, her voice quivering. She was going to cry again.

"Here," Esmée said, taking Brittannia by the arm and leading her away from the table and through the ballroom. The two quickly made their way up the stairs to Brittannia's rooms and once there, Brittannia sat upon her bed, daintily dabbing at her tear-filled eyes.

"Ah, Brittannia, you and Dain had an argument, *non?* I wish he hadn't run off in such a huff. Men can be quite impossible at times, *chérie,* one must learn to deal with them. Believe me, I'm almost on my third husband!" Esmée chimed as she sat down beside Brittannia.

Brittannia gave the raven-haired woman a weak smile. "Yes, we had words, but I'm quite pleased he left!"

Esmée gave her a doubtful look. "I don't think you are pleased he left." Then after a long pause, she said, "I have a confession to make, although I'm sure Dain must have told you by now. The morning you—you came upon me in Dain's bedchamber—"

Brittannia cast her a doleful look, not wanting to remember that morning.

Esmée held up her slender gloved hand. "No, let me finish. I must tell you this, for I now consider you a friend. That morning you found me in Dain's bed—" She hesitated and studied the ruby shining on her left finger, a frown playing across her lips, and her brow knitting together in frustration, "we—we hadn't made love. I didn't know where he'd been all night although I was sure he had been with you and so when—" she looked to Brittannia and in a hurried voice went on—

"when I saw you coming up the street, I quickly ran up the stairs, threw off my clothes, and pretended Dain and I had just parted." She kept her head down, her ebony hair gleaming. As she folded her hands primly in her lap, she said softly, "Dain and I have never made love. He never wanted me. You are the one he wants. He never stops thinking about you."

Brittannia was stunned. The sounds from below—voices, music—drifted to them. She was numb, she didn't know what to say.

Esmée looked up and there were tears in her eyes. "I'm sorry, Brittannia. I tried to tell you that night in the sitting room. I tried to tell you he has feelings for you. That is what he told me the night we stood together on the veranda, the night we knew for sure Michael would get well. We were both very tired and longing for better days. He told me he cared for you, felt feelings he's never felt for anyone or anything before in his life," Esmée said as she took Brittannia's limp hands in hers. "He cares for you more than he does the sea, Brittannia. His own mother couldn't pull him from the arms of that mistress! You must go to him, tell him you understand."

Brittannia turned large turquoise eyes to Esmée, tears threatening to spill from the long lashes. She had been so wrong! "I can't. He won't be back. I've lost him." She hung her golden head and cried silent tears, her body wracking with the force of them.

"So why did you wish to deceive me?" she asked when she finally lifted her head and dabbed at her tear-streaked face with the lace handkerchief Esmée quickly supplied.

"Oh, my dear, don't you know? You are everything I

wish to be; young, fair, and innocent! I hated you and wanted to hurt you. But now . . . well, now it's different. I'm no longer so jealous now that I have Jacques."

Brittannia laughed as she crumpled the handkerchief in her palm. "I understand, Esmée. There was a time when I would have gladly clawed your precious eyes out!"

Esmée smiled at her. "We all know where the grass is greener, *non?* But," she added on a more serious note, "now you must talk to Dain and tell him how you feel."

"Feel?"

"Yes," she said, her eyes glowing with green lights. "You are in love with him, of course—as he is with you!"

Brittannia heard the word: love. Was that what she felt for him? Was that the emotion that had so confused her these past weeks? Suddenly she was sure it was, but that did no good in raising her spirits, for she was sure Dain did not feel the same toward her. "No," she said. "I've—I said things he'll not be able to forgive. He is lost to me."

"Nonsense!" Esmée declared. "Surely he cannot deny his feelings for you."

"He's not a man who is governed by his feelings, he's a man who uses his head in all things, no matter of his feelings," Brittannia replied hopelessly as she stood and began to pace her room. All thoughts of the party left her mind. Now, only explaining to Dain mattered.

"I will not believe that of your captain. He feels too strongly about you, Brittannia. Tomorrow you will go search him out and remind him of what he's been missing!"

Esmée said all of this with such conviction, Brittannia almost began to believe it could be true. She'd find Dain and tell him how wrong she'd been. She'd apologize and explain why she had said all she'd said about Sebastian. She'd make him forget all this ever occurred, at least, that was what she thought as she and Esmée planned what she would do on the morrow.

Chapter 12

Brittannia cut a splendid figure as she daintily stepped out of Michael's carriage, and with the help of the driver onto the dusty road near the wharf. Nassau was once again alive, people dressed gaily and bustling about. The air was filled with the pulverized limestone dust kicked up by the many pounding feet and it stung her eyes and nostrils but she would have it no other way, this was the Nassau she had grown fond of, not the fever-stricken one of a few weeks ago. The surrounding area teemed with busy people, moving drays and stacks of crates packed full with Enfield rifles, ammunition, modest clothing for men and women, and lots of food.

In the previous March, there had been a reorganization of what was to be brought into the southern states. No more did the captains of the blockade-running vessels have the luxury of selecting their cargoes and their methods of operation. Hence, smoother operation of getting to the Southerners things they truly needed.

"Thank you, Davis. I shan't be long. Please pull the carriage out of harm's way and wait for me," Brittannia directed as she put a gloved hand up to shade her eyes. She looked straight to the steamer occupying the wharf. It was the *Airlee*. With the lifting of the quarantine Erskine and the skeleton crew had finally been able to bring the *Airlee* back into Nassau's harbor and Dain had wasted no time in beginning to prepare for another run to the States.

With a quick glance in either direction she lifted her full skirts and made her way to the *Airlee*. Men of all sizes labored in the bright sunlight, their muscles straining with the weight of the cargo. The air was filled with dust and non-stop noise, and Brittannia felt as though she had just stepped into the middle of some great piece of machinery that, although looking ungainly, worked with speed and precision and got the job done.

Brittannia looked up and saw Dain standing, shirtless, on deck, shouting orders and pointing his arm in different directions and then making notations on the pad of paper he held in his hand. She felt her blood rush and her stomach flutter just from the sight of him. His muscled arms and chest looked so very familiar, she could almost feel them beneath her hands. He stood with such an air of authority, his black breeches hugging his athletic torso, his gray eyes surveying every crate that was brought on board that she wondered how she ever got by without him.

She hurried up the plank and onto the deck, anxious to be at his side. She had to dodge sweating bodies in her path and was subject to more than a few bawdy remarks from the men she passed. She ignored them;

her thoughts were on Dain and what she'd say to him once they were face to face.

He stood just a few feet from her, his dark head bent to concentrate on what was scrawled on his notepad. "Captain," she said over the loud din, "may I have a word with you?"

Dain's head snapped up with recognition, his eyes stormy as they passed over her. "If it is finances you want to discuss then Delving is the man to see, not me. You've had your say with me."

His words stung. "Dain, please," she pleaded, then lowered her voice after noticing a few men were lingering to hear their conversation. "I want to apologize. I— I'm sorry for all the hurtful things I said. I never meant them."

Dain stiffened with her words, kept his eyes to the pad in his hand as he scrawled more notes. He no longer trusted her.

"Dain, please," she said softly, coming a step closer. "Can we not talk about this and clear up all the misunderstandings?"

"There are no misunderstandings."

"Dain, forget what I said about Sebastian. None of it was true. It is you I—" She paused for a moment, debating whether she should declare her love for him.

He did not give her a chance, for in the next breath, he said, "I need no explanations. Everything is quite clear to me. You flit from man to man like a bed-minded trollop!"

Brittannia felt her chest puff with anger and she had to clench her hands into fists to try and keep herself calm. When she spoke her words were slow, precise. "What I said about Sebastian was not true. I said those things only to hurt you, to make you feel as mis—"

"Save the explanations," he interrupted. "I don't care to hear them." He looked up briefly from his pad eyeing a crate that was carried by him. She might not be standing there for all the attention he paid her!

"Dain!" she nearly cried, reaching an arm out to touch him.

He took a step back. "You are too late, Miss Denning. I have not the time for a woman-child who says and does things she doesn't mean then expects others to indulge her and forget her actions."

"Damn you, Dain! I came here to apologize, to tell you of my feelings and you just slap me in the face with your stinging words!"

"I don't want your apologies, Miss Denning," he replied calmly.

"Then what do you want?" she asked in a high voice, her tears pushing past her lashes even though she fought them all the while.

"You truly don't know, do you?" he asked incredulously. "Well, I'll tell you. I want you off this ship and out of my sight."

He turned on his heel and left her standing, in all her new finery, in the middle deck with her pride hurt and her heart broken into a thousand pieces. She closed her eyes and after a brief moment of pulling herself back together she calmly turned and, with head held high and her back straight, she descended the plank and made her way to the waiting carriage. She didn't allow herself the luxury of more tears until Davis had helped her into her seat and shut the door. Only then did she bow her head and give into the hurt and humiliation.

*   *   *

Esmée was biting at the bit by the time Brittannia returned from her trip to the wharf. Esmée had a long while to wait before Brittannia recounted the day's events, for Brittannia ran up to her room and kept herself locked there for the remainder of the day. Esmée and Michael didn't see her until the following morning at breakfast and by then she was a sight! Her eyes were red-rimmed from all the tears and her hands trembled as she tried to force a sip of tea down her throat.

Michael kept his silence, sure that Dain was the root of Brittannia's distress, but Esmée was not one to keep silent about anything for overly long.

"Oh, Brittannia, do tell us what happened!" Esmée pleaded as she spread a healthy serving of jam on her muffin.

Brittannia raised her red eyes and with a sigh exclaimed, "He hates me!"

Michael raised higher in his seat and with the assistance of a swift kick in the shin from Esmée he swallowed the last bit of his coffee and mumbled something about the office and departed, leaving the two women alone.

"Go on, dear. It can't be all that terrible," Esmée coaxed.

"Yes, yes it can! He called me a child, said I didn't know what I wanted and I wasn't going to have him again, ever!" she exclaimed in self-pity.

Esmée cut her muffin in half, and after placing the knife to one side of her plate, she said, "Well, you are acting like a child."

Brittannia pushed her tea away, annoyed. "I don't want to hear it, Esmée," she said. "I don't care."

"Oh, but you do and so does he!"

Brittannia cast her a skeptical look across the wide

table. "How can you be so sure?"

"Because he loves you and you love him," she stated simply.

"You're wrong!"

"No, I'm not. Now get some food into your stomach and pack something decent to wear aboard ship. You, my dear," Esmée said with a wicked gleam in her cat-green eyes, "are going to board the *Airlee* and take a ride to the States!"

Brittannia shot up in an instant. "No, I couldn't do that!" she exclaimed. "It's much too dangerous and Dain would be furious with me!"

"But my dear, the *Airlee* is *your* vessel. You don't need Dain's permission to demand passage. And what if he is furious? He will soon get over it."

Brittannia slumped in her chair giving her cup of tea a pathetic look. "No," she groaned, "he would never stand for it. He would probably refuse to remain as captain."

"Nonsense!"

"Esmée, you didn't see his mood yesterday. He's disgusted with me. I tell you, he would not stand for it!"

Esmée leaned forward, placing her elbows on the table and her chin on her folded hands, her eyes sparkling with mischievous lights. "Then, my dear," she began in a conspiratorial whisper, "you have no choice but to stow away on the *Airlee!*"

Brittannia's turquoise eyes went wide.

"Oh Esmée!" she gasped. "How can you suggest such a thing."

"As I see it, you have no choice. How else are you going to talk sense into him? This way he won't have a chance to run away."

258

Brittannia thought on Esmée's words, and slowly they began to make sense. Suddenly, the prospect of stowing away on the *Airlee* seemed tempting indeed. After all, it wouldn't really be stowing away since it was her ship. And once the *Airlee* was out to sea and she confronted Dain she would have time on her side, she would be able to show him the real person she was—not the spoiled woman-child he accused her of being, but a passionate, caring woman who wanted only to love him and be with him. If he could just feel her arms around him, see to what lengths she'd go to be near him, he'd realize her love for him was true. Yes, she decided, once she was on the *Airlee* and she and Dain were alone again in his cabin she would show him what they could have together—what they were *meant* to have together.

"Oh no, Esmée," Brittannia cried for the hundredth time. "That's not at all suitable to wear aboard a blockade-running vessel! How did I ever let you talk me into this?" she exclaimed as she snapped the lid of the small trunk shut. "Perhaps I shouldn't go after all."

"Nonsense!" Esmée replied as she pushed back open the lid and removed the garment in question. "Here, take a simple skirt and blouse, and perhaps the outfit you wore to dinner the first evening you and Dain returned from Andros and this green taffeta is exquisite and this white moiré silk, who could resist? There, that should do it!" she exclaimed, sitting on the lid and forcing the top to latch to the bottom.

Brittannia sat on the huge bed and regarded her friend with a comical look of dismay.

"Let's see," Esmée continued, holding a slim finger to her temple as if in consternation. "Three days up and three days back and we'll add two to unload the cargo. "Yes," she declared, "I think we have packed sufficient clothing for every day you'll be gone."

Brittannia rolled her eyes heavenward. "You're impossible, Esmée. How, pray tell, am I to get this cantankerous chest on board? Carry it myself?"

Esmée put the tip of a long nail between her teeth and thought about that. "Well," she finally said, flipping open the latches of the trunk and flinging out garments. "We'll just have to do the unthinkable. We'll stuff your clothes into one of those ghastly little drawstring bags the maids use for soiled linen. Here," she said, throwing Brittannia a bundle of clothes, "roll these and I'll get a bag."

Brittannia set to the task of rolling the clothes. Once Esmée had returned, they found they had to leave more than a few extravagances on the bed if they were to get the most sensible pieces into the bag.

Once finished, Esmée frowned at the pile of clothing left on the bed. "Ah well," she sighed. "Come, we haven't much time. Michael said the *Airlee* is leaving this afternoon and you'll have to be neatly hidden long before it does!"

Brittannia kept her silence as she followed Esmée out of Michael's home and to the waiting carriage along the circular drive.

"Now you remember what you are to do, *non?*" Esmée asked in a conspiratorial tone once they were seated in the carriage. In her excitement of Brittannia's upcoming adventure, her contrived French accent had returned and Brittannia hid a smile as she listened.

Esmée bent her head, her ebony curls swaying as she did so, toward Brittannia and in a lower voice continued. "I shall board the ship first, you come later, but keep your distance and be certain to keep your head down. You look positively boyish and none will be the wiser if you keep your face from being seen and keep your hat on!"

Brittannia looked down at the ankle-length cape she wore; beneath it she was outfitted in the powder monkey's clothes. Stuffed into her breeches pocket was a tattered old gray cap Esmée had secured from who-knew-where. They would get out of the carriage at Bay Street and from there walk to the docks. Once there, Brittannia would dodge behind a warehouse, remove her cape, and make her way, as a young lad, to the *Airlee*.

"Once we're on board, make sure you get near the passageway leading to the officer's cabins as soon as possible," Esmée said into Brittannia's ear, her eyes alive with the adventure of it all. "I'll make some sort of commotion and then you make your dash. Ingenious, *non?*" she asked, sitting back and inspecting one of her long, shaped nails.

"Oh, Esmée, I hope it works. What if someone should see me scurrying to the officers' cabins?"

"Don't worry. If anyone says anything to you just tell them to leave you be, as any young lad would, and if Dain himself should try to call you to a duty just put on your best slouch and shuffle to do his bidding. It will be absolute fun! I wish it were me!"

Despite the heat, Brittannia pulled her large cape about her. "You make it sound so simple."

"It is! Don't forget, it was your money that built and

first manned the *Airlee*. If you wish to take a ride, why shouldn't you!"

The carriage came to a halt in front of Henry Adderly and Company. Brittannia and Esmée quickly alighted leaving a dismayed Davis who wasn't even off his perch before the two bounded to the ground on their own.

"Here, Davis," Esmée called. "Find yourself a cool place and have a drink!" She threw him a gold eagle which he caught in one fluid swoop of his arm. He smiled a crooked grin at the raven-haired woman and sat back on his seat, glad for the time off.

Brittannia and Esmée made their way to the harbor through the throng of human bodies, horse-drawn carts and drays, and carelessly thrown rubbish.

"I'm going between those two buildings over there," Brittannia said with a slight nod of her fair head in a direction to their right.

Esmée gave a quick glance in that direction and nodded. "I'll walk slowly. Don't worry about me, *chérie,* I'll make my grandest entrance ever! There won't be a pair of eyes that aren't on me!"

Brittannia shot her an affectionate smile. If anyone could captivate a whole crew, Esmée could. Without another word and with one great heave to her sack of clothing, she ducked between two shabby warehouses. She had to step over a pile of rubbish to get out of sight of any passersby and she cringed when she felt her booted foot step in something squishy. Once she was deep in the shadow of the buildings, she reached into her pocket and pulled out the wrinkled cap. She snatched the heavy cloak from her shoulders and flung it into the dark, narrow space beside her. With one swoop, she gathered her long hair to the top of her head, and with a determined yank, pulled the cap down to hold it in place. She quickly tucked in any stray wisps. On impulse she bent down and smeared some dirt on her face. She curled her features into a look of disgust and set about to brushing the remaining dirt from her hands onto her shirt and breeches.

With a deep breath and one last push of hair under her cap, she heaved her bundle onto her back and stepped back onto the street looking for all the world like a young, dirty, unkempt lad. With a shuffling gait and her head hung low, she made her way to the *Airlee*. She shoved one slim hand deep into her pocket and crossed the plank onto the deck. She could see Esmée standing near the rail far to her left; the passageway that led to the officer's cabins was straight ahead. With another deep breath she started for it and was nearly knocked to the deck when a burly man ran into her with the edge of a large crate.

"Hey, mate, get outa the way!" he yelled loudly as Brittannia rubbed her hand along the top of the shoulder where the wood had hit. "There's work ta be done and you'll soon be a man if ya git to it!"

Resisting the urge to give him a piece of her mind, she kept her head down and with a boyish mumble shuffled forward. Just a few more feet and she would be there! Suddenly there was a commotion that outdid all other commotion on deck and Brittannia guessed it was Esmée. Bundles and crates were dropped. Men, eager to help, ran to Brittannia's left. She chanced a quick glance over her shoulder. Esmée had just "fainted" in a dead heap, her white silk skirts just happening to flutter up to expose an enticing view of trim

263

ankle and calf. Brittannia did not linger to see what happened next; instead she ran ahead. It was dark and nearly airless once in the passageway and she heaved a sigh of relief when she neither saw nor heard anyone. She avoided the door of Dain's cabin and with a beating heart stealthily picked her way along the narrow passage and pressed on to the small cubicle she knew Erskine and a few officers used to store a little cargo of their own. Dain had laughingly told her of those private speculations and now she was glad she remembered, for it would serve as a perfect place to hide in!

She carefully opened the wooden door. One look and her heart sank. The space was about as large as a small pantry but it was crammed full with bulging crates and boxes, piled almost as high as the top deck. She should have known—these men were out to make a profit and weren't about to let any available space go to waste.

She chewed on her bottom lip. She might be able to remove a few crates but they looked much too heavy and even if she could move them where would she move them to? Her mind raced and she couldn't decide what to do. The only thing she was sure of was she couldn't stand there contemplating the issue any longer! She shut the door and leaned against it as she looked from left to right. She'd have to find another place to stow away, but where? She thought hard for a moment and realized the only other cabin she knew to be "safe" enough was Dain's. Not that he wouldn't be furious with her when he found her, but she'd much rather have him find her than any one of the brutes she'd passed coming below decks.

With the quietness of a thief, she picked her way back along the dark passage to Dain's cabin.

The small berth was much as she remembered it, but the desk in the corner was overflowing with maps and nautical measuring tools. Her eyes scanned the small space for a place to hide. She couldn't crawl under the bed, for it was solid wood rising from the deck. There was no closet, only a small sea chest which was packed full. The only place she could find to even duck into was beneath the desk and if one should want to sit at the desk she surely would be caught.

She sat on the bunk and fidgeted. Maybe Dain wouldn't come to his cabin. He had said it was only for sleeping and he did very little of that during a wartime run. She decided not to worry about her situation. The chances of Dain coming to his cabin while the *Airlee* left Nassau were very slim. And once they were far enough from Nassau she wouldn't need to hide anymore anyway.

She heard the familiar sound of the engines. After a few moments she felt the ship move and heard the timbers heave and creak with the motion. She hung onto the desk as the *Airlee* broke from its lair and moved toward the ocean. Her heartbeat quickened at the thought of the trip ahead. Soon they would be near the southern states, steaming their way toward Wilmington. She was exhilarated and wanted to be up on deck, wanted to watch New Providence Island become only a speck on the distant horizon. She wanted to feel the salt spray hit her face and behold the endless water around her as the *Airlee* dipped and rose with the swell of the ocean.

"Damn!" she muttered to herself. It was her money

that built this ship, why couldn't she walk up on deck and freely announce she was joining the venture?

She knew the answer even before she thought it; it was a dangerous adventure, one for daring men who knew their way around a ship and knew of the skill needed to raise the sails into the wind, stoke the engines, steer through the storms and high seas, and to load and fire a cannon. It was no place for a lady such as herself. She whipped her tattered cap off her head and threw it to the bottom of the bunk and plopped herself on the bunk beside it. She put her hands behind her head and fell back onto the tightly made berth, bouncing a little with the motion. She closed her eyes. Soothed by the steady pulse of the engines and the beat of the paddle floats, she drifted off into a dreamless sleep.

She came awake with a start, instantly alert. Someone was outside the door. It was too soon—Nassau wasn't far enough behind for her to be discovered! She grabbed her cap and quickly piled her hair atop her head and pulled the cap down on it. She braced herself on the berth, both hands clutching the mattress, ready to spring in either direction. Her heart was slamming against her chest as she watched the latch on the wooden door turn up and the door open. With a sharp intake of breath, she watched with wide turquoise eyes a man enter and make his way to the desk.

Brittannia sat paralyzed on the bunk. The officer stopped in his path and stood peering at her.

"Who are you and what is your business in the captain's berth?"

Brittannia didn't answer him. Instead she eyed the open doorway and then bolted for it. The man's arm shot out like a snake and his hand clamped around her upper arm as he dragged her back.

She turned her face from his view as he yanked her close to him. She didn't want him to see the delicate features of her face beneath the grime she'd smeared on it.

"You'll have to explain yourself to Captain Barclay, boy. All hands on deck or in the engine rooms when we leave port, you should know that!"

Brittannia pulled a small, booted foot back and kicked out at the man's shin. He winced at the force of it, but his hold on her arm only tightened and his temper increased.

"You'll be sorry for that, boy! I promise."

He pulled her roughly forward and out into the dim passageway. When Brittannia dug her heels to the deck the man pulled her with more strength. She doggedly dragged behind him, fighting all the way.

Once on deck, she straightened to look out across the rails. The open ocean abounded on all sides and Brittannia gaped at it as if for the first time. She stood in awe of it all—her ship, the *Airlee,* cutting through the waves on its way to the needy southern states bringing with it desperately needed supplies. She halted the officer with a strong yank as she stared about her.

"What are you, a runagate who's never been to sea before? The captain will have you strung up by your toes!"

Brittannia longed to slap the officer across the face for his callous treatment of her but she only pulled the cap more tightly about her head and shuffled behind him, toward Captain Barclay.

Dain was standing near the crosstrees. He was dressed in gray, despite the heat of day, and he was staring out across the wide expanse of blue before them.

"Captain Barclay," the young officer announced, "I have a boy here. I believe he is a stowaway, sir."

Dain turned his gaze from the water and fixed it on Brittannia. She turned her head down and shifted uneasily on her feet. She hadn't wanted things to turn out like this. How humiliating to be dragged in front of him by an officer of his ship!

"A stowaway?" Dain asked incredulously. "From Wilmington to Nassau I can believe it, in fact, I expect it. But from Nassau to Wilmington? Who would want to travel into a war-torn nation?"

The officer looked first to Brittannia and then to Dain. "I found him in your cabin, sir."

"I see," Dain said. "Why don't you tell me your name, son? What's your business on the *Airlee?*"

Brittannia moved uneasily under Dain's close scrutiny and she bowed her head even further.

The officer beside her yanked at her by the collar of her shirt. "The captain asked your name, boy. You'd better give it to him!"

Brittannia shrugged out of his hold and stood staring at the deck beneath her feet.

The young officer yanked her head back furiously. The tattered cap was pulled free, letting loose her golden curls cascading down her back. Brittannia glared at the arrogant officer, pushed him away from her, and snatched her cap that had fallen to the deck.

The surrounding crewmen who were watching the scene all gasped and there was a loud murmuring among them, a few recognizing her as the lady they had rescued from Andros Island.

She looked defiantly at Dain and was greeted with an unreadable stormy gaze.

"I'll take care of this matter, Thomas," he said, dismissing the young officer. In two strides, he was beside her and his hand closed around her elbow in a painful grip.

Brittannia didn't say a word. She was afraid to say anything for fear of what his reaction would be. She looked up into his dark countenance only to see him jerk his head in the direction of his cabin; then he turned and yelled to the lookout posted on the foremast crosstrees.

"Keep a sharp eye, man!" he ordered. "A dollar for every sail sighted. If it is seen first from the deck, your pay will be docked five dollars!"

With quick strides, he pulled Brittannia along with him to the passageway. She had to nearly run to keep up with his pace. He said not a word as he roughly led her along the airless hall and with a shove he directed her into his cabin.

He kicked the door shut. "What the hell are you doing here?" he demanded.

Brittannia took a shaky breath and met him with a coolness she did not feel. "I have every right to be here. I'm owner of the *Airlee*."

"I'm taking you back to Nassau."

Brittannia folded her arms across her chest and regarded him from beneath long lashes. He stood near the cabin door, his eyes as gray as his clothing. She wanted him to forgive her, to hold her. She wanted him to love her again.

"I'm sorry you feel that way. I'm sorry for so many things," she said as she unfolded her arms and reached a slim hand up to remove the cap on her head. "Please, don't take me back to Nassau. I need to be with you. I need to hear you say you forgive me." Her words were soft and came from her heart. She needed this handsome blockade runner.

She moved nearer to him, putting her hands against his chest as she came next to him. She could feel the beat of his heart; it was nearly as fast as her own, and she ran her palms along his shirted chest, recounting from memory every dip and curve of his muscled form. Dain stood very still as she brought her arms around his neck. When she leaned her slight frame against him he drew in a deep breath.

"Dain, please don't take me back to Nassau. I want to be with you," she whispered. She closed her eyes as she rested her head against his chest. She had wanted for so long to be near him again and to touch him.

"No."

Brittannia's eyes flew open at the harshness of his tone. She turned her head up to look at him and the cold, emotionless look there froze her heart. She felt him lean back, and without taking his eyes from her, he locked his hands around hers and pushed her gently away.

"If you have any, put on some decent clothes. I'm taking you back to Nassau."

He couldn't have hurt more than if he'd slapped her across the face. "No!" she said defiantly.

"You have no say in the matter." His tone was cool,

everything about him was cool. Where had his rage gone? She felt she could handle him better when he was displaying his anger. His coolness made him distant and she didn't know how to handle him.

Suddenly there was a knock on the door and a young man entered.

"Sail ho, sir!" the man said in an anxious voice.

Dain was instantly alert. "Where away?" he demanded.

"To the left, off the bow, sir."

Dain gave a nod of his head then turned to Brittannia. "You stay here. You're not to be on deck."

Brittannia hadn't even nodded her head before Dain was out the door. She wondered if it were a Union vessel sighted. She was not soon to find out, for the next three hours she was left in the cabin alone. In that time she dumped the contents of her drawstring bag and procured brush and comb, and after braiding her hair she quickly donned a more ladylike outfit: a sky-blue jacket and matching skirt.

She paced restlessly about the small space and wondered what was happening on deck. Evidently it hadn't been an enemy vessel, for she hadn't heard any shots fired. There was a solid rap on the door and she fairly flew to open it. The young boy whose clothes she had just taken off stood before her with a tray of food in his hands.

"Cap'n says yer ta eat this," the lad said, his red curls nearly covering his eyes.

"Please, put it on the desk," Brittannia said as she stepped to the side and motioned for him to enter.

The young boy quickly set the tray down with a clatter and was about to leave but Brittannia's voice stopped him.

"What is your name?"

The youth shifted uneasily as his face turned a deep red. "The name's Beau, ma'am."

Brittannia gave him a warm smile. "My name is Brittannia," she said, extending her hand.

Beau took her hand and gave it a quick, nervous shake, then made for the door again.

"Beau," Brittannia said to his back, "could you tell me if the ship sighted was a Union vessel?"

Beau turned to her, eager to relay the excitement of the day. "Well, ma'am," he said, "we're not quite sure about the first ship, but the second was surely Union. Cap'n Barclay has ordered the course altered three times today!"

Brittannia was surprised to hear they'd sighted so many ships and had altered course for each. She hadn't realized they would be in danger this far from Wilmington.

"Why do we alter course for every ship sighted?"

"We're not sure who the enemy is, ma'am. Cap'n says it's best seeing as how we ain't got the equipment ta fight back. All's we got is speed and invisibility to keep us safe! There'll be little sleep for all the crew till we put into Wilmington."

"I see," Brittannia replied. "Thank you, Beau."

The redheaded youth bobbed his head and scurried out the door.

The night passed slowly for Brittannia. She ate little of the food brought to her. She spent the long hours reading the material on Dain's desk. Beneath the mass of maps was a journal, and although her conscience nagged at her for doing it, Brittannia took the journal and made herself comfortable on the bunk. In it, every run the *Airlee* had ever made through the blockade was recorded in vivid detail. Comfortably curled up on the bunk and totally immersed in the journal, Brittannia didn't hear Dain enter.

"Interesting?" he inquired.

Brittannia gave a start at the sound of his voice and quickly shut the journal. "I—I'm sorry," she stammered, feeling like a child caught with her hand shoved deep in a cookie jar. "I was bored and it was so intriguing I just kept reading." She put the journal on the bunk and moved to straighten her rumpled skirts.

Had she imagined it, or had a smile really passed across his handsome features? She watched him cross the short distance to the desk and shuffle the already unorganized maps until he found the one he sought. He made his way to the bunk and sat down beside her, studying the map as the soft light of the lantern smoothed and softened the planes of his face.

Brittannia felt her pulse quicken with his nearness and she absently fingered the leather binding of the journal beside her. She peered over his arm at the nautical map.

Dain's finger ran along an invisible line on the paper and with a shake of his dark head he moved his finger back and started again. After a moment of concentration he turned and looked at her. "You make it near impossible for me to keep my mind on the task at hand," he said.

She smiled, glad there was no note of bitterness in his voice. "Do I, Captain?"

"The thought of a beautiful woman in my cabin distracts me from my work."

"Ah, but, Captain, from reading your journal, I

273

know there is nothing more thrilling to you than running the blockade. You stated that nothing you have ever experienced can compare with it."

It was Dain's turn to smile. "That was written before I met you." He leaned over near the desk, and with a flick of his wrist, sailed the map to the top of it. He turned back to Brittannia and with a slowness that sent delightful shivers up her spine, he reached his hand up and gently brushed a wisp of hair from her face. His fingers ran along her face and traveled her jawline then up to her bottom lip where they lingered and explored the soft fullness there.

"You shouldn't be here," he said huskily. "It's much too dangerous. I should have turned around and taken you back to Nassau as I planned to do."

She brought her hand up and captured his, entwining her fingers through his. "No. I want to be with you."

He sat for a moment, his gray eyes caressing her face and she thought he was going to kiss her. She waited with a beating heart for him to bend his dark head toward her and claim her mouth. But in the next moment he had dropped her hand and stood, his eyes stormy and unreadable.

"Dain, what is the matter?" she asked, for she was so certain she had seen in his face that he wanted her.

"You bewitch me, Brittannia. I can think of nothing save taking you in my arms and loving you." His voice was deep, and as he crossed the short distance to the cabin door, Brittannia could see he was reluctant to leave. He lifted the latch and, halfway out the door, he said over his shoulder, "Stay in this cabin. By late tomorrow we should reach the Gulf Stream and the patrolling Federal men-of-war. Beau will be in periodically to ask if you need anything. If you should wish to take some fresh air, tell Beau, and if it is safe, you may come on deck. Good night, Brittannia."

The door was closed with hardly a sound and Brittannia sighed deeply and grabbing the pillow, she fluffed it and put it between her back and the wall and began reading the journal again.

All that night and through the next day, the *Airlee* steamed steadily northwestward, sheltered by the many Bahamian isles and safely out of sight of any Federal vessels. On the evening of the third day, Brittannia lingered on deck awhile longer than she had the previous night after the evening meal. She could feel the tenseness of the crew members as they went about their duties of screening the engine-room hatchways with tarpaulins; every place where sound or light might escape was covered. All the men were dressed in gray clothing and Brittannia could barely discern them even though they were but a few feet away.

"Ma'am, you best get back ta the cabin," Beau said in a whisper as he came to stand beside her.

"Are we near the blockade?" Brittannia questioned, her senses alive at the thought of slipping by the Federal warships.

"We're about twenty miles north of Cape Fear River. Cap'n's decided ta round the northernmost of the blockaders instead of goin' straight through the line of 'em. We took this route last run."

Brittannia looked over at the coastline. It was low and featureless in the moonless night and the only reason she was sure it was the coastline was because she could see the dim, white line of the surf made by the sea foaming toward the land.

"Yes, I remember this route from the captain's journal," she replied. She'd read the entire journal and now she was familiar with names of the passages. "We'll move south toward New Inlet until we reach the river mouth, is that correct?"

"Yes, ma'am," Beau confirmed eagerly, his excitement at running the blockade evident. "That's where the Federals will be a waitin' for us!"

Brittannia looked about her and felt as though someone had pulled a black hood over her head; she couldn't see much of anything. The thick of the night had descended rapidly as she and Beau had stood talking. She knew Dain was standing on the bridge with the pilot but she couldn't see him. She felt a lump in her throat as she envisioned him standing tall and giving commands, directing the *Airlee* along the southern coast and right through enemy lines.

She swallowed the lump and with an effort forced back the tears of pride that threatened to spill over her lashes for the man she loved. She turned to enter the passageway and make her way back to the cabin.

It was dark, too dark, but she knew she must not light the lantern. With a sigh, she sat down on Dain's bunk, the same one on which they had made love that long-ago morning she'd escaped from Andros. She smiled remembering that time, wishing Dain were with her now, this very minute so she could run her fingers through his hair and draw him near to her. How her arms ached to hold him, how her body cried out to be touched by him—stroked and loved by him!

It seemed it was a night for wanting, for as she sat

276

atop the bunk, her body full of yearning, the latch was lifted on the cabin door and Dain stepped inside, quietly closing the portal behind him.

Brittannia strained to see his features in the inky black but it was near useless. "Dain?" she whispered.

"Hush," he replied softly, slowly closing the distance between them. He stood above her, one leg on each side of her sitting body as he gently cupped her face in his hands, guiding hers to tilt up toward his. His thumbs stroked the petallike skin of her cheeks as he bent at the waist and slowly brought his lips to hers, taking them in a long, searching kiss. When he finally released them, he said in a hoarse whisper, "Just your nearness drives me crazy." He kissed her temples, his hands slipping down to caress the slim column of her throat. So tender, so very slow. "God, but I want you . . . all of you . . . now . . ."

Brittannia closed her eyes, drinking in the feel of his hands on her hot skin, the tender urgency of his kisses. "Yes," she whispered, "I want you too. Oh, Dain." She brought her arms up and wrapped them around his neck, pulling him closer. "Dain, love me . . ." She leaned back on the bunk, pulling him with her until he was on top of her. His kisses were turning passionate, his hands roaming to every part of her, pressing, rubbing, enticing, and she writhed beneath him, wanting him to have her—all of her. One by one she undid the row of buttons down the front of his shirt, peeling the garment away from his skin so her greedy hands could feel him and she could run her fingers through the dark hair of his chest. She planted moist kisses there, dark hair tickling her tender lips. He smelled of the open sea, a clean, virile scent that swirled around her senses wrapping them in a dizzying cocoon of surprising warmth. She yearned to feel flesh to naked flesh. "Here," she whispered into his ear. She pushed him gently to the bunk then sat up to quickly undo her own garments. She stood, shrugging quickly out of every stitch, leaving them in a careless heap on the deck while Dain did the same with his own. She gave a stifled gasp when, in the darkness, his hand reached out and grabbed hold of her wrist, pulling her down on top of him. She heard his indrawn breath as their naked bodies touched and she too felt the wonderful, exquisite sensations that came from their contact. It had been so long, so long since she'd felt the heat of him, the manly hardness of him pressing against her skin, and she reveled in the feel of it, branding it on her memory.

Dain let his hands roam over her, remembering every curve of her elegant body and finding new intricacies and details he had somehow missed in their previous lovemaking. She was like a flirting flame to him, forever burning and dancing within him, teasing him, making him want her all the more. He had tried to stop himself from coming to her, had tried to keep his mind on his work, but found the task impossible. His mind was not working in logical sequence, he was not thinking straight. Forgotten, for the moment, was the fact he still did not trust Brittannia, forgotten were her stinging words of how she'd enjoyed Sebastian's lovemaking—his only thoughts now were of losing himself in her beauty, her charms, her body . . . He craved the release only she could give to him, needed the power that just her wanting fed him. She was opening like a flower to the sun beneath him and when she pushed tendrils of hair from his face and pulled his lips to her own, he heard his own animal growl. His manhood throbbed and filled and he knew he could be nowhere but in her arms, in her sweet embrace.

Brittannia strained toward him, her lips working over his in a hungry kiss. In the total darkness her world was reduced to one of searing kisses and tender caresses. She heard nothing but the sounds of their mingled breathing and the pounding of their hearts—it was all the world she needed; one she never wanted to leave. Each roll of her hips, each arch of her back was met by Dain's hands and lips and when he rolled on the narrow bunk, bringing her on top of him, she felt her passion rising exquisitely, endlessly. She craved the sweet release she knew only he could bring to her.

Their legs tangled together, their sweating bodies moved, slipping against each other's with an earth-shattering intensity while passion-spurred lips devoured hot, pliant flesh. With trembling fingers she felt his hard muscles beneath her, felt their gentle, perfect rise beneath his taut, suntanned skin as he too ran searching fingers over her body, boldly touching her between her thighs, lingering there to bring her pleasure, to bring him pleasure.

She thought she would go mad with her wanting as she moved over him, her full breasts rubbing against his chest, then finally, with a gentle nudge, he parted her thighs and guided his member inside her. She felt her own indrawn breath through her parted lips as he thrust within her, sheathing himself with her throbbing flesh. They moved together, becoming one. Sensations broke free within her, running wild and unbridled, filling her with a torment she enjoyed, for it was on this sweet torture she would ride to great, dizzying heights. She knew the course, yet each time was better than the last, each time she felt some new and wonderful feeling awaken within her and pull Dain closer in her heart. She loved him, loved him as only she could love him: with every fiber of her being and she would give and give and take whatever he would offer.

Dain could feel her womanness surround him, tingling against his entry, and as he thrust deeper within her, he felt all reality slip away from him. He was consumed with his own need to have her, to bury himself deep within her and let go. Only she could cool his desire.

Together they strove for that faraway space that was just within reach, filled with the bright light of passion's own, and as they reached it, breaking swiftly into the brilliant splendor that surrounded and caressed them, rolling them over and over, they each felt a thrilling sense of completion, of utter fulfillment that surpassed any they had ever felt. Together they basked in that realm that can be entered only on wings of passion, together they shuddered from intense feelings, and then together they tumbled gently back down, their heartbeats slowing to normal.

Long, silent moments passed, moments in which Dain rubbed strong hands along the length of her back, his mind filled with conflicting thoughts. Once again he had let thoughts of Brittannia take him from his duties, once again he had been blinded by his need for her. He was suddenly angry at his own lack of willpower.

Brittannia felt his body tense beneath hers as his hands became still on the small of her back. She lifted her head, trying to peer into his face. "What is it?" she asked in a whisper.

He gave her a long penetrating look as if the answers to his problems would be written on her beauteous face, then without replying, he moved her to his side and climbed off the narrow bunk. He found his clothes and put them on, not turning to look at her.

Brittannia lay on the bunk, her mind forming a million questions she knew she must not speak. Dain was once again besieged with his thoughts, and if she were to ever gain his trust again, she had to give him her patience. But as he sat to put his shoes on and still did not look her way, she found it hard not to speak.

"What have I done?" she asked.

His shoes now on, he stood, shaking his dark head. "Nothing, Brittannia. I've got a blockade to get by tonight. Stay here." With that, he left the cabin, making hardly a sound as he shut the portal behind him.

Brittannia felt the frown tug at her lips. What they had just shared was beautiful but she wanted more than just his passion. She wanted his love—she wanted his trust—and now she had to wonder if she'd ever have either . . .

Chapter 13

She couldn't stand to be below another minute, she had to go up on deck and see what was happening. It seemed Dain had left hours ago. The silent darkness was a lonely companion. As she opened the door of the cabin and quietly made her way along the pitch-black passage she cursed the fact she couldn't bring a lantern. Surely they could at least have a light lit below!

The light pad of her feet as she crossed onto the deck was frighteningly loud. She stopped for a minute, straining her ears for any sound of anything or anyone. All she could hear was the steady beat of the engines below, and the splash of the paddles—all of which sounded distressingly loud.

The night was pitch-black. It seemed as though she didn't have her eyes open as she moved along the deck. Her heart hammered against her chest and she felt the pressure of her surging blood build behind her ears. Ahead she could just barely discern a human shape and she made her way toward the dim outline.

Dain grabbed hold of her arm and before she could

cry out he clamped a hand over her mouth. Her eyes were wide as he pulled her head close to his and brought her ear to his lips.

"What the hell are you doing?" he hissed into her ear. His voice was barely audible even though he held his mouth right to her ear. "Get below and be quiet. A Union ship, only a few feet away. We're passing through the line!"

Brittannia felt the tenseness in his strong limbs as he held her close and she felt both fear and excitement surge through her with his words. He was angry with her, but at least she knew where they were. She turned to go back to the cabin but didn't miss the scathing look he cast her. She was angry at him for being angry at her; if he would have only told her what was going on she wouldn't have ventured out on deck. She moved a bit too fast in the darkness. Things happened quickly; she wasn't sure if the loud noise came from her or the other ship. In the inky black, she tripped over a coil of rope and with an audible "Oof," she fell to the deck with a loud thump. She winced at the sound she'd made and lay on the deck where she'd fallen, afraid of what would happen next.

"Cut the engines!"

She heard the command being muttered down the engine-room tube. As it was carried out their worst fear became reality; excess steam blew off the engines, creating a loud enough noise to be heard for miles.

Events followed one another inexorably after that, like a toppling line of dominoes. Brittannia heard a deafening roar and the dark night was lit with the brilliance of bursting powder as a cannon exploded into the foremast. A shriek welled up from her throat as she

284

covered her head from the falling pieces of timber that showered everything.

She looked up; only two men were standing, the steersman and Dain. All the others had hit the deck. Slowly the men began popping back up, scurrying to secure the *Airlee* and get her safely into Cape Fear.

The *Airlee* was not outfitted to fight—her strengths were speed, shallow draught, and a low silhouette. When found and fired upon, her escape depended on the fearlessness and knowledge of the pilot, grim determination, and a lot of luck.

"Erskine!" Dain yelled. "Drive those coal heaves. I want full pressure!"

In a minute he was standing above Brittannia, pulling her up by the scruff of her neck. "Get below!" he yelled as another cannon was fired from the Union ship. This one went through the *Airlee*'s foreward and she rocked with the impact. Brittannia let out another shriek as she watched in horror one of the crewmen fly up with the hit of the shell and fall back into the black waters.

"Damn you, Brittannia! Go! Now!" he thundered and pushed her into the passageway.

He pushed her so hard she fell to the wooden deck. When she turned to him, he was gone. She lurched to her feet and ran for the safety of the cabin. She could hear the shouts from above, men yelling and screaming, guns firing and hitting their targets. She ran to the small bunk and crawled back against the wall, huddling there with her knees drawn up to her chin like a frightened child.

She felt the *Airlee* shudder and pitch and she closed her eyes and prayed. Her mouth worked quickly, forming the silent words as she hugged her knees and tears fell down her cheeks. Another shot was fired and she felt the *Airlee* heave, heard the timbers creak, heard the yells of human pain and the loud curses hurled out in anger.

"Oh, dear God," she cried aloud, "it's all my fault! I made such a terrible noise and now they're dying because of it!" Her body wracked with uncontrollable sobs as she heard the battle rage above and felt the *Airlee* try to break out of reach from the Union shells.

For Brittannia, it felt as if she sat huddled in the corner on the bunk for hours. She couldn't imagine how the *Airlee* could possibly have stayed afloat for this long. Her tears were spent and she sat staring straight ahead, seeing nothing. Her body and senses were numbed with the reality of it all. This is war. This is what had been happening all the years she'd been in England and Nassau. Guns had been fired, men had been bleeding and dying while she'd been spending her days deciding which dress to wear!

She was sick at herself as she sat in the small cabin. Her breathing evened as she realized, with a sort of detachment, the kind of person she was—is. For all her life she'd been concerned for one person and one person only, herself. She'd boarded the *Airlee* because she wanted to, she went on deck tonight after she'd been told to stay below because she wanted to. She did all of this without considering anything or anyone else. She'd made stupid, selfish decisions and because of them men were dying right now and the *Airlee* might never sail again.

She bowed her golden head. She had no fear for herself. She knew she would live through this, she knew it would be her punishment to see another day and yet another and to always remember she had been the reason the *Airlee*'s crew lost their lives.

There was a boom of distant cannons and oddly she heard a cheer from the men above! She lifted her head and turned her ear to listen. Another shot and then another was fired from somewhere in the distance. With a start she realized they were under the protection of the guns of Fort Fisher!

Tears of joy welled up in her eyes at the sound. The rebel men of Fort Fisher were known for their all-night vigil of watching for and helping any blockade runner into port. The *Airlee* had drawn the Union ship close enough for the guns of Fort Fisher to fire on her. They were going to make it into the Cape Fear River after all!

Brittannia wiped her eyes and bounded out the cabin door, eager to be up on deck and help any crew members who would need her aid. The *Airlee* carried one surgeon and she was sure he'd need her help on this night. She held back any tears she might have shed for her fall that started this terrible nightmare and once on deck she entered another world. One of fire, broken bits of masts, and other debris falling from the air and wild men running in all directions doing what they could to keep the *Airlee* afloat.

"Ahh! Help me!"

Brittannia turned her head, scanning the wild scene about her to find the owner of that high-pitched scream. She saw a young boy staggering across the deck, his bloodied hands covering his eyes as he swayed back and forth with the pain he was feeling. Brittannia immediately ran to him, for he was headed straight for a burning piece of wood that had just fallen to the deck.

She grabbed him by his slim shoulders and pulled him to her. "Here," she said, trying not to sound as panicky as she felt. "Let me help you." She took the boy's bleeding hands from his face, and although he was covered with black and his face was badly burned, she recognized him. "Beau!" she exclaimed.

"I—I can't see!" he yelled in a little boy's voice.

Her heart wrenched with the sight of him. She looked around frantically, he needed the doctor, but how many other men needed that same doctor? "Here," she said, "I'm going to carry you to my cabin. You're going to be all right. It's only temporary." She spoke in a calm voice that belied the way she was feeling. She lifted the small boy in her arms and was surprised at her strength. She carried him to the passage and yelled to a passing sailor, "I need the doctor, where is he?"

The war-tattered sailor spread his arms in a gesture that told her he didn't know. "The whole crew needs him!"

She nodded and quickly made her way back to Dain's cabin. She gingerly laid the boy on the bunk. He thrashed wildly about, touching his burned face then convulsing with the pain of the act.

"No!" Brittannia said harshly, then gently pulling his hands away from his face, she said more softly, "I'm going to help you. Lie still. I'm going to get you some medicine."

The young boy grabbed tightly onto her hand and held it, almost crushing it.

She covered his small hand with hers. "Please," she whispered, "lie still and I'll be right back."

Beau released her hand and was motionless. She

hurried from his side and went into the passage and straight for the small cubicle she had first tried to stow away in. She knew Erskine and the officers had packed full crates of medicine and liquor and she planned to get them! She threw open the door and pulled down the crates. She tore lid after lid open. Cigars, satins, hoop skirts were all she found in the first three and she cursed the time wasted. In the fourth crate she found what she was looking for: whiskey, bourbon, and champagne were packed carefully, cushioned one from another. In the next she found bandages and medicine. She took one bottle of whiskey, plenty of bandages, and a bottle of morphine and hurriedly made her way back to Beau.

He remained as she left him. At first, she thought he might have died in her absence but when she set the bottle of whiskey down, he said in a scared voice, "Who's there? That you, ma'am?"

"Yes, it's me. I've brought medicine."

She looked at the morphine and wondered how much she should give him to help relieve his pain. She had no idea. His face was badly burned, as was the skin beneath his charred clothing. She opened the bottle of morphine and poured a few drops into the cap.

"Drink this," she said as she lifted his head enough so he could drink the few drops. She put the tiny cap gently to his lips and poured the precious draught in his mouth. He swallowed it and lay back, being very brave about his situation.

She waited awhile, waited for the drug to take effect. She decided the best thing was to cover the burns with clean bandages; clothing and all. She talked softly in a calm voice. He was suffering from shock and so she covered his bottom half with a blanket and waited until

289

she felt he would be numbed to the pain of her applying a dressing. When she thought it had been time enough, she gingerly wrapped around the top of his head and bridge of his nose with thick bandages. His breathing was deep and even and she felt a bit of relief. She next wrapped his chest and his upper arms, making sure not to remove any of the clothing that stuck to his burned skin. When she had bandaged every burned part of him, she covered him the rest of the way with the blanket and asked softly, "Can you hear me?"

He did not answer; he lay there breathing evenly. With a sigh of relief, Brittannia walked to the corner of the cabin and opened the lid of Dain's sea chest. She removed the drawstring bag she had brought on board with her. Grabbing the unopened bottle of whiskey and the small bottle of morphine she ran from the cabin, back to the place where the crates of medicine were. She stuffed the bag full of bandages, medicine, and whiskey and turned and ran back on deck.

The same wild scene greeted her yet now she didn't hear any cannons firing, all she could hear was the sound of wood burning and the yells of crewmen in need of help. She pushed her fragile bundle to a better position across her back and determinedly set out to help who she could.

Finding crewmen in need wasn't difficult at all. Men lay about the deck, most suffering bad burns or injuries sustained from flying debris. She quickly bent down on the deck and administered to the nearest man. She opened a bottle of whiskey. The man managed a smile as he took a great gulp, then another. She quickly withdrew some bandages from the bag and covered his left arm where blood flowed. He suffered a gash above his eye and she dabbed gently at it while he took another healthy swig of the whiskey.

"I'm all right now, miss," he said as he handed her the bottle. "You're an angel in the night, you are."

"Hardly that, sir," she replied as she remembered her fall that had brought on this whole terrible ordeal.

She capped the bottle and left his side, certain he was well enough to leave. She walked only a few feet when she saw a man to her left holding his right arm up in the air, the blood spurting from the torn mass of skin where his fingers had once been. She ran to his side and quickly sat him down. He was talking a nonstop flow of words, obviously suffering from shock. She tied a tight bandage halfway up his arm worrying at the amount of blood he had lost. She wondered what her next move should be. She looked around her, hoping to find help among the chaos. She saw Dain making his way along the decks; he was staggering and holding his left shoulder.

"Dain!" she yelled, glad to see him. She wanted him beside her, wanted to make sure he was all right. "I need help!"

Dain made his way over the fallen debris to her side. He took in the scene before him; Brittannia was kneeled on the deck beside the wounded man, her skirts blood-spattered and her hair a tangled mass. At her side was a cloth bag filled with medicine and bandages. "Dobbins!" he yelled into the smoke-filled air behind him. "We need your assistance, now!"

The portly Dobbins, black bag in hand, came running out of the flame-lit night. He had a determined set to his face and his green eyes were clear and sharp in the night.

"Dobbins," said Brittannia. "This man has suffered a great loss of blood. I didn't know what I should do."

The doctor was at the man's side immediately and he surveyed the injury, telling Brittannia she did well in the bandaging. Brittannia showed him the bag of medicine and bandages she had brought with her and his eyes grew large at the sight.

"I have a boy in one of the cabins. He was badly burned, he can't see," she said in one long sentence. "I bandaged his burns and gave him a drop or two of morphine. Could you go below and see him?"

The doctor glanced up from his task at hand for only a brief second. "That's all anyone could do for him. You've done well, he'll have to stay put until we get into port. Now take yourself and your bag and help the other men. Leave me some bandages and a few bottles of morphine and whiskey. If you come across any extreme cases of amputation, call me."

With a quick jerk Brittannia pulled the drawstring on the bag shut and made her way across the decks. She didn't see Dain again for the next hour or so. She was too busy tending to the wounded to worry about him. It seemed like an eternity that she bandaged, cleaned, and administered to the wounds of the many crewmen who were hurt. She would just finish with one when she would sight another who needed help.

The *Airlee,* battered but not near giving up, limped into New Inlet and once in the safe waters near Wilmington, lights were lit and the injured crewmen made more comfortable until proper help could be had.

With a wipe across her brow with the sleeve of her soiled blouse, Brittánnia heaved a sigh of relief to finally have lights to see by and to be far from the angry guns of the Federals. Her back ached from bending and as she massaged the small of it at her sides with her hands, she surveyed the decks for Dain. She saw him standing near the steersman, his left shoulder and sleeve blood-soaked and his face and neck black from coal. He must have been in the engine rooms, she thought. She quickly made her way to his side, her brow furrowed with worry. "Dain, you're hurt!"

"Brittannia." His voice was almost a rasp. "Get to the cabin before you're hurt!" he ordered, his voice sounding peculiar, almost strained. He moved away from the steersman and swayed as he went, walking slowly toward Brittannia.

Brittannia caught her breath as Dain fell forward, his large frame collapsing toward the deck. She reached her arms out and grabbed him by the waist, trying to break his fall. It took all of her strength to hold him and ease his body gently onto the deck but she did and without a moment's hesitation, she gingerly pulled back his bloodied sleeve and looked at the gaping hole in the meat of his arm near his shoulder.

The steersman left the wheel, and looking over Brittannia's shoulder, he exclaimed, "He's been hit with a Minie ball! Best get Dobbins over here and fast!"

Brittannia's hand flew to her mouth. If it were anyone but Dain she might not feel so worried. She had never witnessed him not in control and the sight tore at her heart, causing her to lose the cool head she had had when administering to the other crewmen.

She ran a nervous hand through her hair as she looked frantically about. "Steer, man! Shouldn't you be steering?" she shouted, completely overwrought with the events of the night. "I'll get Dobbins."

She fairly flew from her spot beside Dain's immobile figure and in a few short minutes she led Dobbins back to him. The portly doctor quickly tended to the wound, and with the assistance of two other sailors, carried him to the wardroom where he would stay until the *Airlee* was put to anchor at Wilmington.

Time crept by for Brittannia until the *Airlee* was finally docked and she could disembark. The wounded men were allowed off first, those who couldn't walk were carried, and Dain was one of them. Brittannia followed behind him, shivering in the cool air. The first faint streaks of dawn etched the wide expanse of sky as she stepped on solid ground and she couldn't believe the hubbub of activity that went on about her. Did these people never sleep? Half a dozen ships, similar to the *Airlee,* hung at anchor. Steam cotton presses at a flat across the river labored without stop, compacting thousands of bales of cotton.

Tiers of tobacco, stacks of compressed cotton, and barrels of turpentine lay on the wharf. Men around her heaved the prime cargoes onto the ships, only glancing at Brittannia and the wounded men. It's a normal thing, she thought. Blood, pain, and destruction are not new to these people. She numbly made her way with the others to a low, makeshift building where warm food was served and bunks were available for those who couldn't stand or sit.

After accepting a warm broth from a kindly old woman, Brittannia found Beau's bunk where he was still under the effect of a heavy dosage of morphine the doctor had administered once on shore. Evidently his burns were worse than she'd thought. She held his small, freckled hand and marveled at the frailness of it.

He was always so full of spunk and vigor, one would never think the lad to be so frail. He was bandaged nearly from head to foot. She sat beside him, willing every ounce of her strength to pass from her hand to his.

Dain had gone into surgery awhile ago. The Federal's grape had found its mark in his arm and even now the Southern doctors were removing the small iron ball. Brittannia prayed for both Dain and Beau as she sat beside the youth's bunk. She felt the weight of the world upon her shoulders and knew it was because of her the men were hurt.

"Miss Denning, mayhap ya might like ta go outside and get a breath of fresh air?" Erskine stood near her, his face and clothing covered with the black dust of anthracite coal, as always, the black broken in spots by the sweat of heavy labor.

"I—I don't know, Erskine," she answered. "I think I'd like to stay here."

"I'd say ya done all ya can, Miss Denning. How 'bout sharin' a nice brew of tea with me in the Carolina sunshine? I brought some in from Nassau."

Brittannia managed a smile to him. "Among other things."

"Ya should know, ma'am," he said, spreading his face into a near toothless grin. "Me whiskey was about gone and all the medicine and bandages were gone! Ya got a might cool head on yer shoulders when ya need ta!"

"Hardly, Erskine," she admitted miserably. She needed to tell someone of her fall on the deck, the fall that prompted the Federal shots of grape and cannister spewing across the *Airlee*'s decks. "I fear I am the reason the *Airlee* was fired on. I—I tripped and fell and made a terrible noise on deck."

Erskine ran the back of his hand along the bottom of his nose. "Come with me, Miss Denning. We'll have our tea and talk outside."

Brittannia rose with his help and followed him outside into the dewey North Carolina morning. They sat on a compressed bale of cotton. To Brittannia's surprise, Erskine revealed a shiny pot full of soothing tea. He even had two mugs as if he'd planned the whole outing days ago.

"This should soothe yer nerves," he said, handing her a steaming mugful of spicy tea.

Brittannia sipped at the hot liquid, leaving it near her lips so she could breathe in the spicy smell. "I was the reason the *Airlee* was fired on."

"That's not the story I heard," Erskine replied as he gave her a sideways glance. "I heard a crewman named Bobby lit a light. The others were wary of him from the start. He was believed to be a Northern sympathizer. The Federals saw the light and directed their shots toward us."

Brittannia gave him a surprised look. "No," she said. "Are you sure?"

"Yeah, I am. It's hard ta say whether ya fell first or if the young sailor lit his light first," Erskine said sympathetically. "My guess is, the Federals could more easily fix their sights on a long lit light than on a blurted groan as you fell to the decks."

Brittannia thought for a moment, then said, "But we can't be sure, it could have been either incident or both."

Erskine nodded. "But we'll never know, will we? My

296

bet is on the open light. Don't ya agree?"

Brittannia set her mug down. "Oh, Erskine, I hope so. I don't want to be the cause of such—such devastation!"

Erskine brought a black-covered, stubby hand over and patted her knee. "Yer not, ma'am, I'm sure of it. This is a war and the *Airlee*'s made many a successful run. We were bound ta get hit sometime. Cap'n Barclay did a fine job bringing the *Airlee* through it. Many a captain would've run to shore and gave up."

"Yes, he did do a fine job, didn't he?" Brittannia said with pride. "I wonder how the operation is going."

Erskine took a healthy gulp of his tea and looked up into the bright early sunshine. "I wouldn't worry about him. He's tough as nails, the captain is."

Brittannia smiled a nervous smile then brought her mug to her lips with trembling hands. It had been an eventful night and the full effect of it was just now settling in on her. "So, where does one stay after running the gauntlet into Wilmington?" she asked, eager to be out of her soiled clothing.

"Most of the crew finds a place along the waterfront. Me, I stick with the cap'n. He's always welcomed by the town's elite families. But seeing as how he's being patched up, I don't know where we'll be stayin'."

Brittannia breathed a deep sigh. She was bone-tired and wanted only a clean bed to lie on until she could see Dain. "I guess I'll go back on board and get a few things, then I'll look for accommodations," she said as she handed Erskine her mug and started toward the water.

"No need, Miss Denning. Yer clothing has been unloaded. I hope you don't mind but it's in with the cap'n's since we couldn't find an empty chest."

She gave the older man a warm smile. To look at him, she thought, one wouldn't think he could be so considerate, not with his grimy appearance and toothless grin and gruff voice. But Brittannia knew that beneath that coarse exterior was a heart, large and made of gold. "Thank you, Erskine. That's fine."

Brittannia went back inside the already stifling room where the injured crewmen lay dealing with their pain. She made her way past the many cots to the far end where an older woman was rolling clean bandages. It was the woman who had given her the warm broth on her arrival.

"Excuse me," Brittannia said to the gray-haired woman. "I am in need of a place to stay, could you recommend a place, and also could you tell me anything about Captain Barclay? He was taken into surgery awhile ago."

The older woman turned to her and gave her an understanding smile. "Miss Denning. Youah Miss Denning?" she asked as she placed a neatly rolled bandage onto a small table beside her.

Brittannia nodded dumbly, surprised the woman knew her name.

"Captain Barclay is over near the far wall. He asked for you as they took him into surgery," the older woman said, a kindness showing in her watery blue eyes. "I'll take you to him. Mah husband and I have had the oppurtunity to entertain the captain and his officers on previous runs. We would be honored if you would accept the invitation to stay with us while the captain recovers and the *Airlee* is repaired." Her voice was soft and draped with a southern accent. Brittannia liked her immediately.

"If you're sure it would be no bother," she replied.

"Of course not, deah," the older woman said, waving her slim hand as if taking in new guests was all she ever did. "As soon as the captain is better we'll have him brought to our house and we can all mend him up right." Her full skirts rustled as she led Brittannia toward the far wall. "Mah name is Mrs. Dulcie Roberts. Mah husband, John Roberts, helps pahtrol Fort Fisher. He and Captain Barclay are close friends and we wouldn't heah of youah stayin' anywhere but in our home."

"Thank you, Mrs. Roberts. I appreciate your hospitality."

Mrs. Roberts led her to Dain's bedside and pulled a wooden chair near so Brittannia could sit beside him.

"Do bring that fellow Erskine with you, he's such a charming man!" she said as she gave Brittannia's hand a pat and with a whish of her skirts was gone to administer to the other wounded men.

Brittannia looked down at Dain. His face was ashen and his breathing shallow. Gingerly she reached her hand across and touched his fingers with hers. He looked so vulnerable lying there with his eyes closed. His dark hair still had bits of timber and debris caught in it and she gently, tenderly picked each from the curls.

"Oh, Dain," she whispered, half choked by her sobs. "I'm so sorry."

The bandage along his arm was soon becoming blood-soaked and she realized the wound hadn't set properly and he needed attention right away.

"Mrs. Roberts!" she cried as she stood, the chair tumbling backward with her swift movement. "He needs a doctor! Come quick!"

Dulcie Roberts was by her side. She held the trembling Brittannia as a doctor came and checked Dain's wound.

"Come, deah, you need youah rest," she soothed as she led Brittannia from the smothering wardroom and out into the sun-splashed street.

"Here, we'll take mah carriage. Have you any baggage?" she asked as she motioned for a black carriage to pull up beside them.

"Yes, near the docks. I believe Erskine is there too."

"Good," Mrs. Roberts replied, climbing into the carriage on her own, then helping Brittannia to alight. "We'll give him a ride and dinner should be delightful with youah company!"

Once seated in the worn buggy, Brittannia sat back against the padded seat and let her body rock freely with the motion. Soon Erskine and the baggage was packed aboard and they made their way to the Roberts home. Brittannia was surprised to see such a grand house in the South. She had envisioned the people to be homeless and wearing rags, but not so in the Roberts home. Although the furnishings were sparse, they were well dusted and of fine value, there were a few servants, and the evening meal was adequate if not grand for the circumstances of the South.

Erskine made his entrance dressed neatly in a dark blue suit with a bow tie and Brittannia was surprised to find he had even shaved his face for the occasion. He kept up a hearty conversation, entertaining the two women with fanciful tales of long-ago times. He seemed to revel in being the only man present while Mr. Roberts maintained his post at Fort Fisher.

Sleep came quickly for Brittannia that night. She was exhausted from the events of the past twenty-four hours and it seemed she had just climbed between the clean sheets of the large bed in the Roberts's guest room and she was asleep. It was a deep sleep, void of any dreams, and when the early morning sun filtered through the white-curtained window, she arose, awake and fully refreshed. She was ready to see Dain.

Breakfast consisted of ham, eggs, and freshly baked biscuits. Brittannia ate her fill and waited patiently for Mrs. Roberts to finish. She was anxious to see how Dain was and she would have skipped breakfast altogether if only the older woman hadn't insisted that she sit down and eat something.

"Are you ready, Miss Denning?" the silver-haired woman asked as she gently dabbed the corners of her mouth with a linen napkin.

Brittannia nodded eagerly.

The older woman smiled warmly as she rose, her graceful movements the result of years of being in the public eye and entertaining guests as wife of one of the most prominent men of Wilmington. "The carriage should be waitin' outside. Now you must promise me, Miss Denning, that you will eat right and take care of yourself. Youah captain needs you to be in the best o' health."

"Yes, I will," Brittannia promised.

During the ride to the ward near the waterfront, the early morning sun was warm and comfortable and the birds chirped merrily from a distance. It was hard for Brittannia, as she sat in the rocking carriage, to imagine guns being fired and men lying bleeding and dying on such a beautiful morning. Yet she had wit-

301

nessed the results of war aboard the *Airlee,* and even though it was hard to imagine, she knew it was happening.

When they reached the small ward it was a scene of bedlam that welcomed them. Men were being carried in the narrow door and a cluster of men stood outside, bedraggled in the early light, all with grim looks upon their faces. The carriage had no sooner come to a halt than Mrs. Roberts was on the ground and making her way to the men.

"Hereah, is there no room inside for you to find a place to rest?" she asked in a concerned voice as she gently took hold of one man's blood-caked arm and inspected it. "What happened?"

Brittannia was right behind Mrs. Roberts and she winced as she looked at the man's wound.

"We were runnin' in supplies when the Federals spotted us and our pilot got scared and ran us ashore. We were lodged tight on the sand, just like sitting ducks! We were carryin' ammunition and just as I jumped overboard the powder blew! Only half the crew made it here, the others are either dead or soon to be sittin' out the rest of the war in some Yankee prison!" the man quickly supplied.

"I see," Mrs. Roberts said. "Is there no room inside?"

The man shook his head. Dulcie Roberts quickly entered the ward with Brittannia following closely behind. The room was filled, every cot occupied. The smell of sweating bodies, torn flesh, and the overpowering smell of medicine assailed Brittannia's nostrils and she instinctively put a hand to her mouth until she could get used to her surroundings. Dulcie Roberts seemed unaffected by it all as she briskly made her way to the back of the wardroom where a doctor stood giving instructions to a young woman. Brittannia took her eyes from Mrs. Roberts and, picking up her skirts, she went to the far corner of the room to Dain's cot.

His eyes were closed and when Brittannia put a gentle hand on his brow, he opened them, the gray orbs focusing slowly on her.

"Dain, it's me, Brittannia," she said softly as she brushed a dark wave from his forehead. "How are you feeling?"

He closed his eyes then opened them again as his tongue rubbed over his dry lips. "F—feel lousy," he managed.

"Are you in pain?"

The corners of his mouth lifted slightly. "C—can't feel any—thing." He closed his eyes and was asleep, obviously under a large dose of medicine for his pain.

Dulcie Roberts came to stand beside Brittannia. "We are terribly understaffed, we need youah help, Miss Denning."

For the next few weeks, Brittannia was caught up in the flurry of tending to the sick and wounded. She changed dressings, prepared meals, fed those who couldn't feed themselves, changed sheets, bathed and shaved the men, and through the long nights when nightmares would keep a sailor from sleeping, she would sit beside his cot and read to him, her voice soft and calming. Dain was never out of her mind and rarely out of her sight. Throughout the long hot days and even longer nights she would keep a close eye on him. When he took a turn for the worse in the first few

303

days and his body burned with a high fever, she refused to leave the ward. She took all her meals there and slept in a chair beside him. She left the ward only when she absolutely had to and that was to change clothes or to bathe.

Once, after a quick change of clothes, when she'd passed the large gilt-framed mirror in the Roberts's front hall, she had stopped to survey her appearance. She looked five years older. There were deep shadows under her eyes and the bright, shining turquoise color was dulled from lack of sleep. She looked skinny, too skinny, as she turned to the side, but she told herself she didn't care. Nothing mattered to her but Dain. She snatched up her bonnet and quickly left the house, eager to be back to Dain.

She found him in the same state he'd been in for the past two days. He was running a high fever and mumbling incoherent words.

Gently she wiped his hot forehead with a cool cloth. His dark hair was plastered to his skull and she realized she'd have to change his sheets again.

"Brit—Brittannia?" he asked, his voice faint and rasping between his fever-cracked lips.

"Yes, I'm here, darling," she answered as she put the damp cloth to his dry lips.

"Dan—dangerous. Take you back to Nassau. Don't want to lose you, too precious," he mumbled as he opened his gray eyes. They were fathomless pools glazed over and Brittannia's heart wrenched with his words.

"It's all right, Dain. We made it through the blockade. The *Airlee* has been unloaded, we're waiting for you to get well," she managed, while trying to hold back the threatening tears.

"I—I need you," he muttered as he drooped back onto the cot.

She sat with him for a while and at last, at long last, he lay sleeping peacefully, his breathing even and unlabored. One of the doctors made his rounds in the early morning, and after checking Dain, he smiled a tired smile at Brittannia.

"The fever is finally breaking," he said. "He's through the worst of it. With plenty of rest and proper food, he should be well enough to be up and around in a week or two."

With the doctor's words, Brittannia felt a heavy weight leave her shoulders. He was going to be all right! She went about her duties with a light step. Toward noon she served Dain a rich soup. He ate every drop, then fell back to sleep.

Beau wasn't faring as well as Dain; his burns were severe and his eyes would be bandaged for a while to come. There wasn't much Brittannia could do for him but make sure he was comfortable. She always made sure to be there in the evenings to read to him.

The days went by and Brittannia was glad to see a few of the men able to leave the ward. Erskine and a few officers came by to talk to Dain and to check on Beau and the other injured crewmen. Erskine brought the good news that the repairs to the *Airlee* were almost complete and in a day or two the men would start loading the cotton.

A week passed and the next was already a few days old as Brittannia made her way along the dusty street toward the ward. It was a warm, late-summer day and she had just changed into a clean day frock. Dain was on the mend and the doctor had said he could leave the ward at the end of the week. He hadn't spoken to her in the last few days, but then she'd been busy and hadn't had the time to sit with him. She had not thought much of it until she entered the wardroom and saw his cot empty. He was standing and buttoning the front of his gray shirt as she walked over to him.

"Dain, what are you doing getting dressed? The doctor said you should rest until the end of the week!"

Over his bandaged shoulder, he shot her a cold look. "I'm leaving. If you want to return to Nassau, pack your bags and give your thanks to Mrs. Roberts. The *Airlee* leaves tonight."

She was taken aback by his brusque manner. "Of course I want to return to Nassau. What is the matter with you?"

"The matter?" Dain asked mockingly. "The matter is you nearly had the crew and myself killed."

"Why I—I—"

"Your little fall on deck nearly cost us all our lives! I knew I should have taken you back to Nassau, but once again, your beauty, your charms—everything about you—blinded me to reason!" With one arm he quickly tucked his shirt into the band of his gray trousers.

"I was told a crewman lit a light—the American you shipped in Nassau. It could have been his light that alerted the Federals of our position."

Dain gave her an odd look, as if hoping she spoke the truth, then with a shake of his dark head, he said, "I don't know of any crew member lighting a light. They all know they'd be shot instantly if they did!"

She wanted to deny him, but she couldn't. It very well could have been her stupidity that brought the shower of grape from the Federals.

"Dain, I'm sorry!" she cried. "I—I'm so sorry." She willed herself not to cry, but it was useless. His anger with her was more than she could bear.

"Save your theatrics, Miss Denning. Just hurry and pack your bags. On the outbound trip you have strict orders to remain in my cabin, is that clear?"

He didn't believe her! He wasn't even willing to consider her story of the American! Where had his feelings for her gone? When he had been locked tight in the throes of fever he had said he needed her, didn't want to be without her. Where were his feelings for her now?

Even as the questions sailed through her tormented mind, Brittannia knew Dain was a man of reason and did not take his position of captain lightly. He was responsible for the lives of all his men. She knew the guilt he felt for bringing her into Wilmington was great and now tenfold with the disaster that had occurred. He was blaming her for the attack, but she knew that deep inside him, he blamed only himself. If he hadn't wanted her, desired her, he would have taken her straight back to Nassau and the *Airlee* might not have been fired on and nearly sunk.

She reached her hand out to touch his arm. "I'm sorry," she repeated.

"The *Airlee* will steam down the Cape Fear River tonight. Be ready to go or we'll leave without you," he said brusquely.

She drew her hand back as if he'd slapped it.

Chapter 14

Brittannia angrily wiped the tears from her face as she made her way back to the Roberts home. She didn't know what bothered her more, the possibility that she may have been the reason the Federals spotted the *Airlee* or the fact that Dain was treating her so cruelly. He was so full of pride and never one to let his thoughts or actions be directed by his heart. If she'd been a man, she was certain Dain would have ordered her strung up by her toes to the yardarm by now. And she wasn't too sure he still wouldn't do it.

At the Roberts home she packed her few belongings into the valise Dulcie Roberts had given her. After a quick cup of tea, she left for the docks. She could have had the carriage readied to take her the short distance but she decided she'd rather walk. Too soon she would be kept tight in Dain's cabin aboard the *Airlee* for the entire trip back to Nassau and she wanted to get all the fresh air she could. She had said good-bye to Dulcie Roberts before she left the ward that day.

"Good luck to you, deah," the older woman had said

as she embraced Brittannia. "Take care of youah captain. He needs you."

Brittannia didn't tell Mrs. Roberts about the conversation she and Dain had had. "Yes, I will. Thank you so much for your hospitality," she replied. Then she hurriedly made her way through the ward. She stopped at Beau's bunk and looked down at the young boy. He was still covered with bandages and Brittannia wondered if he would ever see again.

"Beau," she said softly, "it's Brittannia. I—I've come to say good-bye to you." Beau wouldn't be going back to Nassau on the *Airlee*.

"I know, I heard" came the small voice from beneath the many layers of bandages.

"We'll miss you, Beau. I, especially, will miss you," she said as tears spilled from her eyes.

"Don't cry, ma'am. I may not be able to see but my ears are sharp," Beau said, and with a pat of his hand motioned for her to sit beside him on the narrow cot.

Brittannia sat on the very edge of it and gently took his hand in hers. "You're a strong young man, Beau."

"I know. I gotta be," he stated simply. "I'm gonna be just like Captain Barclay when I get older!" He said the words strongly, as if daring her to tell him he couldn't be just like Dain. "He doesn't let anything stop him. I'm not gonna let any burns or temporary blindness stop me! I'm gonna own me a ship and sail the world and I'm gonna choose a fine lady, like yerself, to be my wife. And," he added in a conspiratorial whisper, "I'm gonna love her as much as the captain loves you, only I'm gonna show her a little better."

Brittannia gave his small hand a gentle squeeze. He had been the second person to tell her how Dain felt about her. Why was everyone but she so sure of Dain's feelings?

"I'm sure you will, Beau." She had stood and, after getting him to promise to sail and see her when he owned his ship, quickly made her way from the wardroom, never to see it again.

"Miss Denning!" Erskine shouted, bringing her out of her reverie as she came closer to the docks. "Let me take that for ya. Ya shouldn't have ta carry yer own baggage!"

"Nonsense, Erskine. I don't need to be coddled."

"Maybe not, but a man enjoys doing those things for a lady."

Brittannia smiled at the chief engineer, who was now growing back his stubby beard along his double chin. "Now that we are no longer in the Roberts home I see you're back to your old ways," she remarked.

Erskine rubbed his thick hand along his chin, savoring it, and said, "Aye, I can put up with tight ties and a clean face for only so long."

Brittannia laughed, the light, tinkling sound filling the warm Carolina air. "May I be the first to welcome the old Erskine back?" she asked as she handed him her valise.

"You may," he said and very gallantly offered her his arm.

She took it, not at all caring that his sleeve was caked with coal dust. They walked arm in arm onto the *Airlee*. Neither noticed the dark scowl of Dain as he stood on deck and observed the merry couple.

"Erskine!" Dain bellowed, bringing both Brittannia and the chief engineer out of their light mood. "Haven't you work to do, man? I'll take Miss Denning's bag." He

311

strode across the decks, took the small valise, and turned stormy eyes to Brittannia.

Erskine gave Brittannia a wink. "Aye, sir," he said and sauntered away.

"Really, Captain," Brittannia remarked, ignoring his dark look. "Must you be such an old goat? Erskine was just being a gentleman, something you've obviously forgotten how to be." With a flutter of her wide skirts, she swept by him and proceeded toward the familiar passageway ahead.

Within an hour, the *Airlee*'s engines throbbed and the sleek blockade runner slowly left the quay at Wilmington. They were cheered on by their brother blockade runners who were either still loading with cotton or unloading the provisions they'd brought past the Federals. Caught up in the excitement from the hurrahs, Brittannia lifted her arms and waved to the men on the docks.

"We'll steam a short distance along the Cape Fear, then we must stop and let the officials search for runaways," said Dain, next to her. His manner toward her was cool.

"May I stay on deck while the search is conducted, or must I go to the cabin?" she asked, her voice as formal as his.

One dark eyebrow raised, Dain studied her face then turned his attention back to the now-distant quay. "You may do as you please until this evening. We'll take the *Airlee* down the Cape Fear River as far as a small town called Smithville. The town is located equidistance from the two exits we can run through. I won't be certain which exit we will use until we get to Smithville, then I'll choose the most favorable."

Brittannia looked nervously at the Carolina shore that passed by. She would be doubly nervous passing through the blockade this time. Her fear must have shown on her face, for she heard a soft chuckle from Dain.

"Don't worry, Miss Denning." He crossed his arms in front of his chest. "No Yankee bullets will find their mark this time." He said the words with such confidence that she almost believed them. In her opinion, however, running the blockade was as much a matter of luck as it was skill and determination.

The search of the *Airlee* was conducted with no stowaways found. She wondered where anyone would be able to hide; the cotton was stacked all around the decks. So tightly were the bales side by side that the skinniest of beings would barely be able to fit between them.

They dropped anchor near Smithville and waited for the moon to set. Brittannia stood on deck near the bridge. The air was cool and a steady breeze blew up the fringe of the light shawl she held tightly about her. Dark clouds skirted across the night sky playing a sort of peek-a-boo game with the small sliver of moon. As she stood, she surveyed the scene around her. Anchored in the lee of the island, the *Airlee* rocked ever so slightly on the water. The crew, scattered around the decks, waited for the order to take the lead-colored steamer out to sea. Dain had gone ashore to Fort Fisher to speak with Colonel William Lamb. From the seaward parapet of Fort Fisher, Dain could survey the blockade fleet and then decide which passage to take to sea.

It was a long wait for Brittannia in the cool night air and it was near ten o'clock when Dain finally returned

313

from Fort Fisher. With his arrival, Brittannia could immediately feel the tension in the air as the crew stood at attention and waited for their orders. Dain's brusque, commanding manner brought back to the sailors the realization of what waited for the *Airlee* beyond the protecting guns of Fort Fisher.

"High tide on the bar is eleven o'clock," Dain said. "By the look of these clouds it will be a pitch-dark night and by that we know the Federal's will close in tight as they can on the very ends of their half-circle blockade."

Brittannia waited patiently near a stack of compressed cotton that looked black in the dark night. She had goose bumps running rampant along the skin on her arms but she was loath to go to the cabin. She wanted to stay on deck as long as possible. Even though she was frightened, she could feel a trickle of the excitement she had felt when first running into Wilmington. She was sure she wouldn't do anything foolish again—she'd make sure she kept her balance. But she did plan to be on deck when the *Airlee* and its brave crew ran the gauntlet.

Dain slowly made his way toward her, his tall, lean frame only a dark outline in the night. Her heartbeat quickened as he neared her. She pulled her shawl even tighter about her and turned her face into the breeze, letting the stray wisps of hair flutter out of her eyes.

"Brittannia, you should be in my cabin. I don't want you on deck when we pass the cordons."

"I promise I'll be careful," she said. He had called her by her given name again and it made her heart quiver a little with pleasure at the sound of it. Without knowing why, her mind brought back to her the night at Michael's party. She was in Dain's arms and he was kissing her with an urgency that had frightened her then. A smile unbiddingly came to her face as she realized that now she would give oh so much to have him kiss her and desire her like that again.

"I can't take any chances with the lives of my men," he replied coldly.

Brittannia stared into the dark night, wishing the Federals didn't wait beyond the bar, wishing there was no war, wishing things could be different between them.

"Very well," she said, almost in a whisper. "Good luck, Dain." She turned from him and slowly made her way to the passageway that led to the captain's and officer's cabins. She stopped just inside of it and leaned against the cool, hard wood. She didn't want to go into the cabin, she didn't want to miss out on what transpired on deck.

At a quarter to eleven when the *Airlee* weighted anchor and the order was given for full speed ahead, Brittannia still stood listening. She felt the engines throb, felt the ship move and slice through the dark water, she heard the paddle wheels splash and the swoosh of water as the *Airlee* made her way toward the open sea. It seemed almost immediately that she heard the panicked, hoarse whisper of one mate.

"Rowing barge, Cap'n!"

Right after she heard the words spoken a rocket flared up into the dark night and lit, with brilliance, the ebony sky. The light not only provided illumination to aid in locating the *Airlee,* but served as a signal to other vessels of the blockading squadron. Two more rockets immediately followed, both thrown in the direction of the *Airlee.* Brittannia's breath caught in her throat.

Heart pounding she steadied herself against the wooden wall, braced for the onslaught of Federal grape. She waited with eyes closed, then after a few minutes when none came, she opened her eyes. She watched a familiar, dark figure bend down and set light to first one calcium rocket, then another. The two rockets went up into the air with a hiss followed by a train of sparks, then both burst into a glaring light, one after the other. Brittannia guessed the reason Dain was sending up the calcium rockets. He had directed them at left angles of the *Airlee*'s true course—thus if any of the Federal cruisers should follow the rockets, which they undoubtedly would, they would be led away from the *Airlee*.

She breathed a sigh of relief as she felt the *Airlee* push forward. She prayed the *Airlee* would get enough steam to outrun all the Federal cruisers. Reaching her head around the opening of the passageway, she saw to her horror two black shapes looming up on either side of the *Airlee*. They were passing right through the blockade! No human sound came from the *Airlee*. The only sounds were mechanical and those were distressingly loud as they passed by two enormous Federal men-of-war. No sooner had the *Airlee* passed by these vessels than shot was fired across her bow. The shells whistled by but surprisingly none found their mark. The *Airlee* broke free, finally out of the choking hold of the Yankees. Brittannia sank to the floor of the passageway, breathing deeply of the Atlantic sea wind that whipped through the narrow space. She felt she had never breathed anything so heavenly. With shaking limbs she pushed herself up and made her way to Dain's cabin. In the darkness, she undid her buttons and crawled out of her dress. She was shaking from cold as well as from excitement when she crawled between the cool sheets of the bunk. There she huddled into a tight ball and willed herself to go to sleep. Slumber was long in coming.

Much later she heard the latch on the door being lifted. She fluttered her eyelids shut and pretended to be asleep. Dain crept silently into the cabin, his footfalls on the wooden deck nearly silent. Brittannia held her eyelids shut and her body tensed beneath the woolen coverlet. She hoped he would climb into the berth beside her, hoped he would cradle her in his arms.

Dain stood above her, and Brittannia opened her eyes just a crack, peering through her thick lashes at the gallant sea captain. He stood there in his gray clothing, his shirt unbuttoned revealing the dark hair upon his broad chest, his gray eyes looking inquisitively down at her. She shivered involuntarily under his intent gaze and hoped he hadn't noticed. She held her breath as he eased himself out of his sweat-sodden shirt. He tossed it into a heap in the corner of the cabin and procured a clean linen shirt from the sea chest. He hurriedly buttoned it and with one last look in Brittannia's direction, he left the cabin, the virile smell of him still lingering in the cool air.

Brittannia awoke the next morning to the throbbing sounds of the engines below and her stomach grumbling. She hadn't eaten anything since the cup of tea at the Roberts home. She quickly threw off the coverlet and donned a day dress. It was very flattering with all its gatherings and fullness and her slender body seemed to stem elegantly from it.

The dawning day was gray and ominous as she stepped on deck. With the restless water hitting from all sides, she wondered if the water wasn't as much to fear as the Union vessels. Dain stood near the stacked bulwarks, his back toward her. She approached him warily. His hands were clasped behind him and his head was turned at a slight angle.

"Good morning, Captain," Brittannia said. The cool morning air cut through her skin and she could taste salt spray on her lips. It was a refreshing, glorious feeling.

"Sleep well?" he inquired without turning toward her.

"Well enough. You handled the situation last night very well, I congratulate you." She stepped beside him. He kept his head forward, his gaze directed out across the gray waters. She studied his handsome profile, wondering what thoughts were filling his mind. Finally after long moments of silence, he spoke.

"It seems," he said slowly, "I handle all but one thing well." He turned to her then, and the look on his face was dark, his eyes as stormy as the early morning weather. He had the look of a man tormented, a man at war with his emotions.

"And what would that one thing be, Captain?"

"Emotion, feelings. You're forever on my mind, Brittannia. You call me a liar, stow away on my ship, fall on deck when we pass through the blockade, but the worst thing about you is you make me weak. I should push you from me, but I have not the strength. You have a great hold on me, like no one ever has!"

He spoke the words with great conviction and he

should just as well have pierced her heart with a knife. It would have been far kinder and much quicker. He had turned his head back and gazed straight ahead again. Brittannia kept her silence. She hadn't known she caused him such pain.

"My own mother," he continued, "couldn't keep me from the sea. My father even kicked me out of their home because he said I broke her heart leaving for weeks, sometimes months at a time. I would never tell them I was leaving, I would just go and sign on some sailing vessel. I was only thirteen the first time I left home. I slept in the bowels of the ship, way below the water line. There was little room, only one light, and the hammocks were coarse and uncomfortable. I had to fight off rats and pick the cockroaches out of the food, but I endured it all. I learned the rigging and the sails and eventually navigation. When I returned home, my mother would welcome me with open arms, tears streaming down her lovely face."

He stopped then, swallowed hard, his eyes taking on a distant look. Brittannia stood very still, holding back the urge to reach out a hand to comfort him. She knew she mustn't do that.

"I'm her only son," he explained. "She would have given me the moon had she been able to grab hold of it. Even though I knew how much it tore her apart, even though I knew she wanted me to learn to do the work my father did, I left again, and again and again. Until one day when I was fifteen my father told me I either stayed at home with my family or I lived at sea." He drew in a great breath. "I chose the sea, Brittannia. I vowed to never love anything or anyone more than the sea. And then you come into my life and for the first time I tell a woman I love her and she throws it back in my face, she tells me to get out of her life, just as my father did. And yet, I could walk away from my family, but I can't walk away from you!"

Brittannia stared up at him. When she'd told him to get out of her life, she hadn't meant it, they had just been words hurled out in anger.

"Dain, I didn't mean th—"

"You're a sickness with me, Brittannia," he cut in. "Like a fever raging inside of me; I burn with memories of holding you, loving you, and God help me but all I want is *you*."

"Is that so terrible?" she asked softly. "I, too, suffer when I'm not near you. I'd do anything to be by your side, Dain. I need you."

He ran a suntanned hand impatiently through his ebony hair. "No, Brittannia, you don't need me. You're young and impressionable. I took your virginity and now you fancy yourself in love with me."

Her turquoise eyes flashed like two blue chips of ice. "That isn't so. You think of me as a child, perhaps I was when we first met. But not now, not after all I've been through. I don't fancy myself in love with you, Dain. I am in love with you. So much so, that once we dock in Nassau I plan to go back to England. I won't be around to torment you anymore. Perhaps if I'm not near, the pain I cause you will lessen and eventually disappear."

She was angry as she whirled away from him and the sharp tap of her heeled boots sounded loudly in the cool morning air as she strode away from him. She heard him thunder her name from where she'd left him, but she didn't turn around, nor did she stop her fast pace. Once in the cabin, she slammed the portal shut.

The rest of the voyage back to Nassau was uneventful. Brittannia chose to stay in the cabin, venturing out on deck only once a day and then only for a very brief time. Dain made sure he wasn't in the vicinity when she took her breath of fresh air and she told herself she was glad. She planned to forget she ever knew such a man, she planned to return to England and get on with her life, something she should have done a long time ago.

The *Airlee* reached New Providence Island on the afternoon of a beautifully sun-filled day. Erskine had come to Brittannia's cabin to tell her they would soon be making port. She came on deck with him, eager to be off the ship and away from its captain. She breathed deeply of the warm air and raised her face into the sunlight, not caring if it would freckle her fair skin. It was a wonderful feeling. Reluctantly, she put the bonnet she'd brought from the cabin on her head. She wasn't about to get another nasty burn like the one she'd received after the escape from Andros Island.

Flying fish glided along the surface of the pellucid blue water, their wet backs glistening in the light. To the left of the *Airlee* stood Fort Montagu, the low-lying stronghold gleaming white in the bright sunlight. Nassau port was dead ahead. As usual the skyline above it was matted with the timbered masts of the many ships that lay at anchor there.

"It won't be long till we dock," Erskine said, squinting his small eyes as he looked toward the island. He ran a thick tongue along his lips, no doubt thinking of all the rum he was going to drink that night. The men clustered around the bow of the ship and even the lookout climbed down from the crosstrees, glad to be relieved of his duty.

"Erskine," Brittannia said, "I want to thank you. You had kind words when I needed them most on this trip. You're a true friend."

The old man looked at her as if she were slightly addled in the head. "Pah," he spat. "Yer a fine lady, Miss Denning. You deserve nothing but the best." He jammed his coal-blackened hands into the pockets of his trousers and rolled on the balls of his feet. "Don't let the cap'n's mood get to ya. Don't do anything foolish like runnin' back to wherever ya come from. Give the cap'n time to come around, he'll see the light soon enough. And when he does," his small eyes grew large, "look out! He'll come stormin' in after ya!"

Brittannia smiled warmly at the grisled old man. He was kind and friendly and she would miss him dearly. "You're sweet," she stated simply. She leaned over and placed a friendly kiss to his coal-dusty cheek. Even beneath all that soot she could see his face redden. "I don't think the captain will be coming for me," she said sadly. "I'm returning to England as soon as I can find a vessel headed that way. I want to wish you well and hopefully we'll meet again someday."

They stood side by side as the *Airlee* made port. Erskine helped her off the ship, taking her valise in his meaty hand. There was no sign of Dain as she disembarked. It seemed a terrible way to end it all, but then endings weren't meant to be happy she scolded herself.

She hired a carriage to take her to Michael's home

and waved to Erskine until her hand hurt and he was hidden from her view by passing drays and busy people. With a sigh she leaned her head back against the seat and let the carriage take her away from the *Airlee,* away from Erskine . . . away from Dain.

Had she been on the other side of the *Airlee* she would have seen him, seen him as no other had. He stood with his back to the wharf, his sea-storm gaze directed out across the open water. His hands were clasped behind him and the slight breeze ruffled his already wind-tossed curls. His full mouth was set in a determined line and his eyes were full of pain.

"Brittannia, must you leave so soon? Can't you stay and visit for a while?" Michael asked. Brittannia was following Michael's maid around the guest room and throwing things into the huge sea chest she had recently purchased. "I barely had a chance to visit with you since you arrived in Nassau a few months ago. First I was too busy with business, then you were held on Andros, and then you take off for the States without even telling me! I must admit I was most upset when Esmée told me of your harebrained little scheme!"

"Yes, Michael, I must go. Perhaps when this horrible war is over you will come and visit me. There is nothing in Nassau for me. My home is in the Cotswolds and I do miss it terribly." With that she tossed a brush and comb on top of the now-filled sea chest.

"Are you sure there is nothing I can say to make you stay?"

"I'm sure. Are you sure there is nothing I can say to persuade you to come back to England with me?" she asked. "Surely you must miss the foggy weather as much as I?"

Michael grinned at her, his brown eyes dancing merrily. "Ah, yes, the fog-filled streets of our fair London! As much as I'd like to go, I can't. A much greater profit is here for me. I won't leave Nassau until the end of the war."

"I'm sorry to hear that. I cannot wait to be far away from this pitiful war."

"Pitiful yes, but profitable. I fear I am forever pursuing the all mighty power: money."

Brittannia flicked her slim hand in the air. "As so many are," she commented. "Perhaps if I weren't born with enough money, I too might constantly pursue it."

Michael cocked his head to one side, his rich brown hair moving with the gesture. "I doubt that, Brittannia. I think you and Dain could find happiness in a one-room shack on a hillside and it wouldn't matter to either of you if you were dirt poor."

Her fair head shot up at his comment. "Don't talk to me of Dain," she said brusquely. "How can you say that, Michael? Dain would never be happy with me!"

"Yes, he would," he stated simply. "He loves you."

Brittannia diverted her eyes from him, studying the pattern of the paper on the walls. "Have you spoken to him since we docked? I think, if you were to ask him, he would tell you differently."

"He probably would, yes," Michael agreed. "Over the years Dain has erected a great wall around him, loath to let anyone affect him. But you, Brittannia, you've the power to break down that wall. You *have* broken that wall. And now, for the first time in his adult life, he's vulnerable."

"But have you spoken to Dain of this since our trip to Wilmington?" she pressed.

"No, I haven't. I spoke to him only when he reported the *Airlee* safely in port. He asked me if I'd seen you and I told him no."

Brittannia sighed. "You don't understand, Michael. Things happened on that voyage and now we'll never be . . . be together," she replied. "I told him I'd leave Nassau and that's exactly what I plan to do."

"Is there nothing I can say to make you change your mind?" he asked.

"No."

She looked one last time around the large guest room for any article she or the maid might have missed in packing. There was none. She planned to stop at the Royal Victoria Hotel to say a quick good-bye to Esmée who was staying there with Jacques. The two had been quickly wed while Brittannia had been in Wilmington. Then she was going to board the next ship out for England. She took one last glimpse in the large looking glass hung on the opposite wall. Her traveling costume was a deep, deep sapphire blue that accentuated the blueness of her eyes. The full skirt billowed out and fluttered around her trim ankles as she turned to pick up the serviceable blue hat that matched the outfit. She fixed it atop her fair head. Tilting her head to one side, she tipped the brim of the hat to a more slanting angle. It dipped low near her left eye now and the sloping angle gave her a slightly daring, most provocative look. She smiled sadly at her reflection.

There was a knock at the door. Her hand stopped

in midair as she looked into the mirror and saw Dain standing just inside the door in his striped gray trousers, matching vest, and light gray jacket. He looked dapper and far too handsome as he stood surveying her reflection in the large mirror.

Her blood surged and her throat constricted. Damn him. Why must she always react this way around him? She didn't speak, didn't trust herself to speak. With a coolness she did not feel she dropped her hand and turned to give him a level look.

"Brittannia." His voice was husky, soft, and it caused her spine to tingle. "Brittannia," he repeated, taking a step toward her.

She instinctively took a step back. "Why are you here?" she asked, her voice quivering from the strong emotions welling within her.

"Don't you know?"

She swallowed. "I've no idea."

He took another step toward her. "I think you do."

If she stepped back any farther she'd be flush with the mirror. His eyes, they were too soft, too tender, and the smile that lingered on his handsome mouth—the same mouth that had known her so intimately—caused her knees to go weak. She had to force herself to speak, had to work doubly hard to make her voice sound normal. "I haven't much time, Captain. My ship leaves within the hour."

He shook his dark head, coming to stand before her, inches away. "I almost made a terrible mistake, Brittannia. I almost let you walk out of my life."

"You—you're too late. I'm just about to leave." She made a pretense of smoothing her belled skirts, and then took a deep breath. She had to be careful where

Dain was concerned. She would go to the ends of the earth and jump off if that's what he wanted but she had to suppress those feelings. She had to leave him, had to let him go and leave him in peace. She'd upset his life and hers by letting herself fall in love with him.

"You can't leave. Not now."

How could he just waltz in here and tell her she couldn't leave after all he'd said to her? She felt her temper rise. "I'm leaving, Captain. Today. *Now.*"

She started to walk toward her chests, but his arm stopped her, holding her in front of him. Her eyes flashed. "What game is it you intend to play now, Captain?" She tried to jerk her arm free of his tight hold.

The pressure he exerted only increased, and after a quick second of letting his now-stormy eyes devour her, he yanked her body to his and crushed her lips with his in a hard, demanding kiss. Brittannia gasped and struggled against him. She fought viciously but his embrace only turned more savage, his hands roughly caressing her back as his tongue thrust in and out of her mouth. Splendor exploded within her and quickly spread throughout her trembling body. At last she ceased to fight him and wrapped her arms about his neck, running her fingers through his silky, night-dark hair. She was a captive of her own passion, of the power this man held over her. With just one word or one gesture he could bring her to dizzying heights or just as easily let her crash to a rocky, dark world. She should have known better, should have realized she could never leave him, could never make herself forget him. As their lips parted she heard the quivering moan that escaped her as her body still tingled from the touch of his lips.

"Damn it, Brittannia. How could you ever think we could be apart? I—I love you. It's what I've been denying these past weeks."

Brittannia felt her knees buckle with his words as she felt a strange happiness within her, one she had never before experienced. One that took her breath away yet gave her more. He loved her. How she had longed for those words!

"Is this all I get for finally declaring my love?"

Brittannia looked up, a tremulous smile on her lips and glistening tears in her turquoise eyes. He smiled back at her, then, with tenderness and desire showing in his dove-gray orbs, he brought his lips to hers. This time his chiseled lips worked slowly, deliberately over hers, his tongue moving lazily to search out the moist recesses of her mouth, probing gently and causing small shivers of delight coursing through her. She pulled him closer to her body, melding her hips against him until she could feel the hardness of him through his handsome suit. She pressed her body even closer.

"Ah, Brittannia," he said in a husky whisper, breaking his lips from hers only to kiss her cheeks, her temples. "Love me, Brittannia. Marry me." His voice was husky and low, a very seductive voice. "Marry me."

She stepped back and looked at him, her turquoise eyes large and bright. "Marry you?" she asked incredulously.

He smiled engagingly—the white of his teeth showing starkly against his tanned visage, the smooth, handsome lips turning up at the corners. "Yes, tonight. Today. Right now!"

"Are you sure? Only the other day you wanted me out of your life."

He stepped nearer and ran a gentle hand along the side of her face and lovingly down the slim column of her throat. "Never that, Brittannia."

She caught his hand in hers just as he was running it teasingly close to the hollow between her breasts. "Captain," she said coyly. "We aren't married yet!" She smiled up at him. "Yes, I'll marry you, but where and what shall I wear?" She had forgotten her earlier passion and now she was aflutter about what to wear and whom to invite and if perhaps some of her friends from England might be able to attend the ceremony.

"The dress you have on is quite nice, I know of a friendly minister who would be most honored to conduct the ceremony, and it just so happens he's free this afternoon."

Brittannia's full lips formed a small "O" as she surveyed his clothing. "You planned this, didn't you? You came here dressed for your own wedding! You knew I'd say yes!"

"Me?" he asked, feigning a look of innocence that didn't fool her. "You're soon to be my wife and a man should be able to predict what his lady will do."

"Yes," she murmured and went into his arms. She stood for a moment, reveling in the feel of him, the smell of him and then her eyes flew open. This was to be her wedding day! She had a million things to do! She must find a suitable dress, she must tell Michael she wanted him to give her away and she wanted Esmée there and she wanted to gather a large bouquet to carry and . . . Her mind raced on and she backed out of Dain's warm embrace. "We haven't a moment to dally," she exclaimed. "We have a wedding to attend!"

He gave her a swift smile. "I, my beautiful lady, am ready."

She gave him an exasperated look. "Shoo!" she ordered. "Go to the Royal Victoria and see if you can find Esmée. I want her to attend the wedding—and tell Michael of our plans. Meanwhile I'll find a suitable dress to wear."

Dain shook his head and gave her a loving smile. "Haven't even spoken our vows and already you're ordering me about!"

"Go, before I change my mind," she teased and then turned around and strode to the sea chest, flinging the lid back.

Chapter 15

Married! She could hardly believe it—then again she'd known for some time that she wanted nothing out of life but Dain. He'd said he loved her. No matter he'd been too stubborn to admit his love before now, hearing him say the words made her want to sing with joy.

She'd no sooner found the dress she wanted to wear then there was a knock upon her door and Esmée burst into her rooms, a radiant smile lighting her face.

"Oh, Brittannia!" she cried. "Dain has just told me the news! I am so *happy* for you! Did I not tell you stowing away aboard the *Airlee* would do the trick?"

Brittannia whirled toward the raven-haired woman, her turquoise eyes sparkling. "Stowing away is *not* what prompted Dain to ask me to marry him, nor did it prompt me to accept his proposal. In fact it very nearly was the cause of his death!"

Esmée's green eyes grew large with curiosity. "His death?"

Brittannia waved a slim hand in the air. "I'll tell you all about it some other time, I promise. But this is to be my wedding day and I want no dark thoughts to cloud its beauty."

Esmée forgot her curiosity at mention of the wedding. "Ah, yes!" she exclaimed. "Your wedding day! How I love weddings!"

Brittannia smiled wickedly. "So one might comment upon hearing of your marriage record."

The two laughed at that.

They were soon immersed in choosing the finery Brittannia would wear for the ceremony. They finally decided upon a beautifully simple gown of white moiré silk, the skirt trimmed very lightly with fragile lace flounces. The V-shaped neckline enhanced Brittannia's swelling bosom and the rivière—a single row of perfectly matched pearls—she wore about her throat. The long drop pearl earrings that matched the rivière was the only other jewelry she planned to wear. The simplicity of ornamentation and color, Brittannia knew, would create an elegance that would be stunning, and this day she wanted to be more stunning than ever before for her handsome captain.

It was late afternoon when Michael called upon Brittannia and Esmée to see if they were ready. When Brittannia opened the guest-room door her eyes grew wide as she took in Michael's form. He was dressed impeccably in black top hat, brown cape with velvet collar and light gray satin lining, striped gray trousers, lemon gloves, and a purple tie.

"Michael!" Brittannia exclaimed. "Look at you—you'll outshine the bride!"

He gave Brittannia and Esmée a quick leg, then a sly wink. "Never, Brittannia," he replied, his brown eyes turning full of admiration as he looked to her. She was a vision in white. Beautiful. "You look—lovely," he finally said when he could find his voice.

Brittannia felt tears form in her eyes. Here she was, standing before Michael, her wedding ceremony about to take place.

"I'm very proud of you, Brittannia," he said softly. "Proud to be the one to give you away to a man like Dain." Then he quickly closed the distance between them and took her in a strong brotherly hug.

"Oh, Michael," she said, sniffling a bit. "It means so much to have you with me on this day!"

"Your parents would be so proud of you. Their little girl all grown up and getting married . . ." He let his words trail off as he gave her another tight squeeze.

"Michael, if you cause her to cry before the ceremony I'll personally box your ears!" said Esmée. "Enough of this. You can get maudlin *after* the ceremony. Dain won't be pleased to see his bride with puffy eyes."

Both Brittannia and Michael had to dab at their eyes, Michael a bit shyly as though he didn't cry often and knowing this Brittannia very nearly was in tears again. Esmée was quick to usher them out of the guest room and down the stairs to the carriage that awaited them outside in the circular drive, her gold skirts rustling with her movements. "We'd better hurry," she said over her shoulder as she led the way down the stairs and out the opened door, "or there'll be a wedding without a bride!"

"I doubt that," Michael commented. "Should Brittannia keep Dain waiting too long, I'd be the first to wager he'll come after her on charging horses and drag her to the altar."

Brittannia smiled beneath her veil, knowing full well what Michael said was true. The three of them climbed into the carriage, Brittannia, in her skirts, taking up one whole seat.

The late afternoon air was warm and filled with the scent of exotic island flowers and the ever-present smell of the sea. As they neared the wharf Brittannia's excitement grew. The busy day had yet to end for the men who worked along the quay. Drays from the warehouses and drays from the discharging ships banged along in a cloud of limestone dust. Local Negro roustabouts shouted above this racking clamor and drivers and other workingmen shouted back. Steam donkey engines still ran and the noise coupled with screeching axles and the hoarse yells of the many men about created a wild cacophony that oddly enough was sweet music to Brittannia's ears. Nassuavian police armed with carbines walked along the wharf, their job to maintain order among the rowdy lot that worked there.

Brittannia could think of no better place to be married to Dain than right here at the wharf where she had first met him those weeks ago. The same wharf that had then too been alive with the throbbing activity of blockade running, that growing industry that had come to be known simply as "the business."

"You are nervous, *non?*" Esmée asked as the carriage was pulled to a stop near the docks.

Brittannia waited for the driver to open the door, her heart already beginning to pound at a fast rate. "Yes," she admitted. "But I love the feeling!"

The two climbed out of the carriage with the help of Michael and the driver and Esmée looked around her in astonishment. There to their left was the *Airlee* looking long and lean as she bobbed on the moving water. She looked sleek as a cat, the lead color of her hull only enhancing her mystique. The sails were rolled and tied about the poles that shot skyward and almost looked as if they could touch the belly of the blue sky above. Along the halyards were hung unlit lanterns that would soon glow and chase away the surrounding darkness as the wedding ceremony began. Paper streamers of different colors also hung along these ropes and their brightly colored ends waved snakelike in the light sea breeze that fanned all things.

Just off the ramp that led up to the *Airlee* were tables of all sizes, some makeshift built upon overturned crates, tables that were overflowing with an abundance of food and drink. On the upper deck of the *Airlee* was another table, this one covered with white linen and adorned with delicate crystal goblets and a many-tiered wedding cake decorated with white and silver icing. Nearby musicians were gathering, tuning their instruments.

"Mon Dieu!" Esmée breathed. "Your captain certainly has outdone himself."

Brittannia looked about her in awe. And to think she had thought they would be quickly wed without much ado! A smile lit her face and she felt her heart swell with love for Dain.

"I quite agree with you, Esmée," Michael was saying. "For the *Airlee* is neither discharging cargo nor loading cargo and yet there she sits, occupying the wharf alongside other ships being readied for a run or unloaded from a run. How Dain has succeeded in allowing the *Airlee* this spot is beyond me. He must have paid quite a bit to one of the custom house officers."

"Did I hear someone mention my name?"

It was Dain's voice they heard behind them and, as one, they all turned toward him.

"Dain!" Brittannia exclaimed. "You're not to see me before the ceremony! It's bad luck!"

Dain came beside her, putting one arm possessively around her slim waist. "Seeing you looking so beautiful couldn't possibly give me anything but *good* luck the rest of my days." He bestowed upon her a handsome smile. Then as he dipped his head toward her, he whispered, "You look stunning. I cannot wait to slip that gold band on your finger."

She felt the familiar tingle along her spine that just his nearness caused. "You've certainly been busy today," she said, gesturing to the *Airlee*.

"Only the best for my wife-to-be," he replied with a sly smile that caused her heart to sing. With a wave of one strong arm he motioned to Erskine who hobbled over to the small group.

"All set, Cap'n?" he asked in his gruff voice, giving Brittannia a wink when their eyes met. "A true angel ya look this night, Miss Denning."

"Thank you, Erskine," she replied, then with a smile added, "I see you've shaved for the occasion."

Erskine ran a scrubbed hand ruefully along his bare chin. "The cap'n thought it best seein' as how I'm gonna be holdin' the ring for 'im."

Brittannia's fair brows raised at this news. It seemed this day was full of pleasant surprises and she was sure before the night was finished she would find innumerable pleasures that would make this the happiest in her memory.

"Enough talk, Chief," Dain broke in. "We've a wedding to begin."

"Aye, Cap'n!" Erskine hurried away to do his captain's bidding.

Within a few minutes, a loud horn was blown and the unending noise and commotion that surrounded them began to slowly die down. Sailors, dockworkers and roustabouts, pilots and officers alike ceased their labor and all, with loud shouts, converged on the wharf beside the *Airlee*. Gaily dressed women joined the men, their laughter and perfume filling the air.

"What—?" Brittannia began, but Dain quieted her as he led her up the plank and onto the *Airlee*.

A loud cheer erupted from the crowd as they ascended the plank and Brittannia's curiosity grew. "What is this?" she asked as they came to a stop on deck near the rail.

Dain gain her a quick smile as he drew her near to him and then he turned to the crowd and yelled, "You've all been invited here to help Brittannia and me celebrate our coming together as man and wife." He spoke with a clear, deep voice that echoed across the wharf, bouncing off the warehouses and coming back over the silent crowd. "This night you shall partake in a wedding unlike any other before it. A 'blockade runner's' wedding is what will take place tonight, and you will all be a part of it!"

Another cheer erupted from the rowdy crowd. Some of the sailors threw their hats up into the air, and a few men threw their ladies into the air to catch them in strong arms as they came back down.

Dain laughed with the crowd. "Eat, drink, and be merry, my friends. This night I pay all costs!"

The crowd went wild then as bottles of spirits were quickly passed around and three local innkeepers and their staff hustled about to serve the many people.

Brittannia looked to Dain. "You're very generous!"

"Only because I'm so full of love for you," he said, squeezing her slim waist. "And to think I almost let you walk out of my life." He shook his dark head then. "I've been a fool, Brittannia. Can you forgive me?"

"Forgive you?" she asked, rubbing a gloved hand along his smooth cheek. "A thousand times and more."

Dain's head dropped a bit as he lowered his lips toward her veiled face and Brittannia stood very still, waiting for him to lift her veil and claim her mouth. But the kiss was not to come, for Esmée and Michael were behind them, and with a quick hand Esmée pulled Brittannia away from Dain.

"You won't get another kiss from her until she's your wife!" Esmée exclaimed, holding Brittannia at arm's length from Dain.

Brittannia and Dain laughed, their eyes never leaving each other's.

"Then for heaven's sake let us get this wedding started!" Brittannia said.

"I agree," Michael said, observing the crowd below. "Already the celebrating has started!"

Dain too turned to look at the crowd then he turned to Brittannia. "My cabin has been made ready for you and Esmée to prepare before the ceremony which," he said, looking to the gold chain watch he pulled from his vest, "should begin within the hour."

"Can I possibly wait that long?" Brittannia asked

aloud, her turquoise eyes shining brightly with the evidence of love in their blue green depths.

Dain took a step toward Brittannia. "If you feel as I then you cannot," he said, his hands coming up to clasp tightly with hers.

Esmée intervened again. "Come along, Brittannia. Already you've lingered too long at your groom's side. I must say this is the oddest wedding I've ever attended!"

Brittannia allowed Esmée to lead her away from Dain and Michael and toward the passageway that led to the officer's cabins. Together they entered the small cabin that was Dain's. The whole cabin smelled of Dain, every object she looked to seemed to proclaim his beautiful name. She recalled the morning she'd escaped Andros and Dain had brought her here and made love to her, and then there was the night just before they ran the blockade, the night she'd been so full of wanting for him and he had come to her . . . Finally, they were to be married, here aboard the *Airlee,* aboard the very ship that had brought them together.

It wasn't long before they heard the musicians begin their rendition of the wedding march: that was Brittannia and Esmée's cue the ceremony was to begin. Nervously Brittannia looked to Esmée.

"This is it," she breathed, her eyes going wide.

Esmée nodded, her green eyes filling with unshed tears. "Oh, Brittannia, I am so happy for you!" The two came together in a heartfelt, sisterly hug. "I know you and Dain will be happy together!" They hugged for long, emotion-filled seconds, then quickly drew apart, each dabbing at the corners of their eyes. "It is time to go up now," Esmée said, clasping Brittannia's gloved hand in hers. "I have something for you," she said, as with her other hand she pressed something into Brittannia's palm.

Brittannia gasped as she looked down at the tiny diamond crescent made to be worn as a hair ornament. "Oh, Esmée, it is lovely. Thank you so much. Will you put it in my hair? I'm afraid my hands are shaking too much for me to do it on my own."

"Certainly, I will." Esmée lifted Brittannia's veil and very carefully placed the diamond crescent among the mass of curls beneath it.

The two looked at each other, and then Brittannia said, "Let us go, before I start to cry!" With that they quickly left the small cabin.

And so it was a "blockade runner's" wedding was held that night aboard the *Airlee*. The sun had gone down and the night-dark sky was filled with thousands of glittering stars. But none outshone Brittannia's dazzling beauty as she walked across the rolling deck on the arm of a resplendent Michael, the second best "catch" for a husband in all of Nassau. The first best "catch," Captain Dain Barclay, stood on the bridge of the ship, his smoky gray eyes fixed on Brittannia as she walked toward him.

Dozens of lanterns hung on the halyards, swinging gently with the warm sea breeze, their light playing soft shadows across Dain's handsome visage as he stood waiting for his bride. She looked ravishingly beautiful in her dress of white silk moiré, a white veil fine as cobweb draped over her delicate features, and long white gloves that reached all the way to her elbows. She was truly a lovely vision as she walked, chin held high, turquoise eyes shining, and as she took her place beside Dain and their hands clasped together, a murmur went throug the large crowd that had now quieted. They exchanged vows; their eyes locked, shining turquoise and stormy gray. A cheer was given by the crew as the minister pronounced them man and wife, and when Dain took Brittannia in his arms and kissed her, another cheer erupted, this one led by a proud Erskine.

Bottles of champagne were opened and quickly laced with rum. Brittannia turned, and from her position on the bridge threw the large bouquet of island flowers up into the air. The long white ribbon that held them together fluttered in the wind as the bouquet soared through the air, and when it came down it landed in the open arms of Esmée who, with a bright smile, held it up for all to see. Esmée laughed as her husband drew his arm more tightly about her waist. Then she favored him with a loving peck upon his wrinkled cheek.

The night went by quickly. There was dancing on board the *Airlee* and soon the celebration grew larger as other sailors from other ships came along and joined in the merriment. Dain gave orders to the local inn-keeper to keep the food and drink flowing, and with desire showing in his gray orbs, he scooped his lovely bride up into his arms and carried her to a waiting carriage. Once inside the dark interior, he moved close to her and showered her neck, the tops of her breasts, and her rounded shoulders with kisses. Brittannia leaned back into the soft leather and welcomed his arduous assault. She was his wife now, she belonged to him and he to her; it was a wonderful feeling and she touched the warm band of gold that he'd so lovingly placed on her left hand. She twirled it once around her slim finger and then with an audible sigh, wrapped her arms around him and drew him closer, returning his ardent kisses with ones of her own.

Too soon, or not soon enough, they were at their home on Queen Street. The house was ablaze with lights and Brittannia silently hoped no gathering of well-wishers waited beyond the doors. She wanted to be alone with Dain on this night, she wanted to have him take her clothing off piece by piece and plant kisses on every part of her body. Dain jumped out of the carriage and before Brittannia could jump down, he had her in his arms again and carried her up the stone steps and over the threshold of their home. No party greeted them indoors, only a single maid who quickly scurried out of their way, leaving them alone as the captain had ordered all to do.

"We're home, my wife," he said, caressing the word "wife" with his timbered voice.

"Mmmm, my husband," she said, trying out the words.

He looked to her as he unbuttoned the dove gray overcoat he wore. He dipped his head a bit and a tumble of rich, night-dark curls fell jauntily over his brow. "I love you," he said huskily.

Brittannia reached up and lovingly pushed the unruly curls back in place. One suntanned hand reached up and caught her gloved hand before she could draw it back.

"Come," he said, "I've something to show you upstairs." There was a devilish look in his eyes as he led her toward the wide staircase that led to the second floor.

"I'm sure you do, Captain," she replied, a wicked

gleam lighting her turquoise eyes.

The hall was ablaze with lights, but in Dain's bed-chamber only a single lantern burned, the flame very low. The room was cast in a warm, golden glow and the bedcovers on the huge four-poster bed were turned down, making the bed look very inviting.

Dain closed the door and stood behind Brittannia, his arms reaching around her light frame and pulling her back against his chest. She could feel her heart beat wildly, or was it his? She wasn't sure as she ran her gloved hand along his muscular forearm.

"Alone at last," he murmured into her ear. The soft whisper sent delightful shivers up her spine. He took his arms from around her and slowly, oh so slowly, began to undo the many hooks of her gown. He planted soft, moist kisses wherever her golden skin was revealed and she stood still, her eyes closed as she reveled in the feel of those feather-light kisses.

He slipped the gown from her shoulders, her chemise and petticoats followed, and soon she stood naked in the dimly lit room. He turned her around, his eyes turning stormy with desire as they devoured every inch, every nuance of her beautiful body. He reached his hands into her rich, golden hair and pulled the pins from it. It fell in lustrous waves around her shoulders, the fine tresses burnished by the lantern light.

"You're overdressed for the occasion, sir," she said, pulling the overcoat from his muscled frame. Then she undid his tie and the many buttons of his pristine white silk shirt. She moved the shirt back from his chest and as he shrugged out of it, she nuzzled her face against his dark hair, breathing deeply of the smell of him. She stood very close against him and could feel the erectness of his manhood, straining against the thin cloth of his breeches. She smiled wickedly at him as she undid them.

"Your slowness is torture—exquisite, but nonetheless torture," he said, his voice rich with desire as he took a step back and pulled off the rest of his clothing. In a quick second, he had her in his arms and laid her gently onto the great bed. Her hair fanned out in a spill of golden tresses on the pillow and she opened her slim arms, beckoning him to come to her. With a groan of pleasure, he nuzzled the creamy skin of her throat. His attentions strayed to her unguarded breasts and gently he kneaded the soft flesh of them, his tongue playfully nipping each taut nipple.

Brittannia writhed beneath him, rubbing the hard muscles of his back then moving her hands lower to gently caress his buttocks. She loved the feel of him, the strength of him, the smell of him. The masculine hardness of him excited her and when she closed her hand around him, she heard his intake of breath, felt his muscles flex with excitement.

He brought his head up from between her breasts and she could see his gray eyes were heavy with desire. He parted her thighs with one knee and as he gazed deep into her turquoise eyes, he entered her. She drew in a deep breath as she felt him move inside her, hard as steel, smooth as velvet. He thrust deep and she moved to meet him, wanting more of him.

They moved and melded as one, his maleness filling her as her womanness surrounded him and held him. He whispered words of love into her ear as his fingers ran through her silky, scented tresses. She kissed his neck, his face, and always, returned to his mouth, his soft sensual mouth that had the power to render her helpless.

His tongue entered the warm moistness of her mouth and a moan welled up inside her as he loved her, kissed her, and took her senses higher and higher. She moved beneath him, wrapping her long legs about him and pulling him even closer. He pulsated within her and thrust deeper. She reveled in the sensations that burst within her and as she cried his name she felt herself rise to the highest peak ever and then tumble thrillingly back down. He let go within her and she hugged him tight as he too slowly tumbled back to earth.

They slept in each other's arms and Brittannia dreamt of smoky eyes and warm embraces. Before the light of day, he took her again and then again. When they finally crawled out of bed, she felt sore, but it was a wonderful feeling which she enjoyed thoroughly as she prepared for the day ahead. It was a gentle reminder of her wedding night, reminding her she was a woman; Dain's woman.

"So, do tell," Esmée coaxed as she and Brittannia sat on the veranda of Brittannia's new home sharing a cup of tea, "where are you going to honeymoon? Will you be returning to England or do you plan to make your life in Nassau?"

Brittannia sipped her tea and thought before answering. She wasn't sure where they would make their home, although she certainly hoped it would be at the manor house in the Cotswolds, and as to a honeymoon, well they'd not discussed it.

"To both questions, I must say I do not know," she

finally replied as she replaced the delicate china cup on its saucer. "Dain and I really haven't had time to make plans. Why, only a few weeks ago we were married and before that day, I hadn't even known I was to be his wife!"

Esmée's green eyes lit as she remembered with what haste the wedding had been carried off. "Ah, it was so romantic, *non?*" she questioned. "I do so envy you, Brittannia. I love my Jacques but truth be said, he doesn't hold a candle to your handsome captain!"

Brittannia smiled at Esmée. She had been surprised Esmée had married such an older man. He was past his prime by a score of years, but he doted on her and they seemed to be a very happily married couple.

"I guess with the war still going on you and Dain will have to wait before you can take your honeymoon," Esmée mused.

"Why?" Brittannia asked. "There are many places to honeymoon and, war or no war, I would not choose the States as one."

"Be that as it may, Brittannia, Jacques told me just this morning that your husband plans to make another run in the coming week."

Brittannia stared at Esmée in surprise. She hadn't known Dain was going to make another run. True, he'd been busy these past days, but she assumed he was making plans to find another captain to take his place. Surely he wasn't going to run the blockade, not now, not when they were married. But one look at Esmée's face and she knew her friend spoke the truth.

"You look surprised, Brittannia. Did you not know of Dain's impending run?"

Brittannia passed a hand across her brow. Suddenly

she'd lost her appetite and wasn't feeling well. "No, I did not know. I—I thought once we were married he'd give up his dangerous job, but I guess I'd misjudged him."

Esmée tried to console her good friend. "Do not worry, Brittannia, your captain is very skilled at running the blockade. He will come back safe, you will see."

"I don't want him to do it. It's much too dangerous. I know, I was through it!"

Esmée was sorry she brought up the subject. She was even more sorry when she saw Dain striding up the stone steps two at a time. She turned to Brittannia and didn't miss the blaze of her turquoise eyes. "I think I had better take my leave now, *chérie,*" she said and stood. "Please keep your anger in check. I'd hate for you two to have an argument so soon after your wedding."

Brittannia smiled at her, but Esmée could see she was angry. "Thank you so much for coming today, Esmée. Perhaps we can get together sometime soon, maybe have lunch at the Royal Victoria." Brittannia walked with Esmée to her waiting carriage.

She waved as the carriage pulled away and then she turned and made her way toward Dain. He was leaning casually against the doorjamb, his wind-tousled dark hair falling in unruly curls about his head. He smiled a lazy smile at her.

"Miss me?" he inquired as his eyes raked over her in a familiar way.

"Dain," she said brusquely, "are you planning to make another run to Wilmington?"

"Of course," he said, surprised that she would ask

347

such a question. "The dark of the moon is next week and the *Airlee* yearns to be at sea again."

"Dain, how could you?" she nearly screamed. "How could you plan to do such a dangerous thing? You're my husband and I'll not have you riding into the face of death!" She stood with blazing eyes fixed on him, her feet planted wide and her arms akimbo. "You'll find someone else to captain the *Airlee*," she shouted, warming to her subject. "I'll not have my husband risking his neck every dark of the moon!"

"Oh?" he inquired, still retaining his deliberately casual stance. "I didn't know you had such strong feelings about this. I also didn't know that, as my wife, you would affix a leash around my neck so as to always have me in your sight."

Brittannia stamped her slippered foot as she stood looking up at him. "You're being unfair, Dain. There is no rope about your neck. You can do as you please, just as long as you don't please to run the blockade!"

"Come here." His timbered voice was soft yet demanding.

Brittannia regarded her husband for a moment, not yet ready to end their argument, but when his dark head beckoned her and his chiseled lips tilted up into one of his engaging grins, she reluctantly climbed the stairs and crossed the short distance to stand before him. He took her in his arms and held her tightly as he stroked her hair.

"You mustn't ask me not to run the blockade. I have to. It's getting tighter all the time and only the best can make it in you know." He pulled her head gently back so he could look her in the face, "I'm one of the best."

Brittannia didn't reply. She just let him hold her close. She was his wife and she would back him in his decisions, even though it hurt her to let him go.

The days sped by too quickly and too soon Brittannia was standing on the quay waving good-bye as the *Airlee* steamed out of the harbor toward the open sea. She knew it was something he felt he had to do and she didn't ever mention to him again that she didn't want him to go.

"He'll be back before you know it," Michael said as he squinted into the sun and watched the *Airlee*'s sails become small specks of white. He put a hand to her elbow and guided her away from the harbor and toward his office on Bay Street. "Would you do me the honor of accompanying me to lunch?"

"No, I'm sorry, Michael. I prefer to be alone."

Michael frowned. "He'll only be gone a few days."

Brittannia didn't reply, she kept her silence as they made their way along the teeming streets. She was trying her best not to be discouraged but she absently wondered if she would always feel this depressed when Dain made a run. There was some nagging feeling in her that said all would not be well with this run. *I shouldn't have let him go,* she thought to herself as she walked alongside Michael under the warm rays of the sun.

"Brittannia," Michael was saying, "are you listening to me?"

Brittannia shook her dark thoughts from her mind and tried to concentrate on the idle conversation Michael was so determined to have with her. He was a dear friend, Michael was, but he didn't understand that nothing would make her feel better, nothing save Dain returning alive and well.

The next three days dragged by as if weighted with heavy chains. Dain didn't return on time, nor did he return the next day or the next. Visions of the *Airlee* being blown apart by Federal grape and canister filled her thoughts and she found herself jumping at the slightest sound she heard. The sound she heard this time was a knock at the door, and even before the servants had a chance to let the caller in, Brittannia was at the door and opening it, hopeful that someone brought news of Dain to her.

"Esmée," she exclaimed dishearteningly. She'd hoped it to be Michael or some sailor.

"Well, I daresay, my dear, I've received warmer welcomes from relatives of my long departed last husband, and all they wished to do was scratch my eyes out for having inherited all the old man's money!"

"I'm sorry. I'm so worried about Dain, I'd hoped there would be news about him by now."

Esmée entered the large room and gave her parasol to the young maid who stood near. "You look absolutely terrible, Brittannia! Have you eaten anything since your husband left?" she asked, then not waiting for an answer, plunged on. "No, I don't think so. You look near a skeleton. I've made an appointment for you with the doctor. Now I don't want any complaints from you. You're going to go and that is that. Now hurry and fix yourself up, my carriage is waiting."

Brittannia looked wide-eyed at Esmée and was about to protest, but she thought better of it. She hadn't been feeling well lately and perhaps the doctor could give her some sleeping draughts. She couldn't be of much help to Dain if she was dead on her feet!

If Esmée was surprised that Brittannia came along so willingly, she didn't show it. The ebony-haired woman kept up a lively one-sided conversation all the way to the doctor's office. Brittannia waited her turn patiently in the waiting room, all the while nodding her head and smiling in the right places as Esmée continued to talk to her.

Finally it was her turn to see the doctor and she succumbed to his thorough examination and barrage of personal questions. Wearily, when he was done, she smoothed her skirts and patted her hair back into place.

"Well, Doctor, do I pass the test?" she inquired as he stood regarding the notes he'd scrawled on a piece of paper.

The old man looked at her from over the rim of his spectacles and said, "You need rest, Mrs. Barclay, and plenty of it."

"Yes, I quite agree with you, but I'm going through some dif—difficult times," she stammered, remembering Dain. "I find it near impossible to sleep. Perhaps you could prescribe some sleeping draughts for me."

"No, Mrs. Barclay, you'll have to make yourself sleep on your own. It is imperative that you eat and sleep regularly for I've good news for you," the man said, placing the paper on a nearby stand. "You are with child."

Brittannia looked to him in disbelief. "Are you sure?" she gasped, unable to believe it. She didn't feel as if she were carrying a growing, living thing inside her.

The old doctor smiled. "Yes, very sure, Mrs. Barclay. In April of next year you should, if you follow my advice, give birth to a healthy baby."

Brittannia was shocked. Expecting? Why, they'd only been married a few short weeks! Her mind mentally recalled the date of the night Dain and she had shared aboard the *Airlee* after leaving Andros; nine months from that date would be April. "Well, thank you, Doctor. I'll be sure to follow your instructions to the letter," she assured him as she bade him good-bye and made her way back to the sitting room where Esmée was waiting.

Esmée stood and accompanied her out the door. "Well," she said. "What did the doctor say?"

Brittannia squinted her eyes against the bright sunlight. Did it never get cloudy here, she wondered as she recalled her beloved Cotswold Hills where rain would replace bright weather with the wink of an eye. "Nothing," she told her friend. "Nothing other than I must eat better and get more sleep."

Esmée breathed an audible sigh of relief. "I am so glad to hear that. You've been looking much too pale. You must promise me to do as he says," she told her.

Brittannia nodded, her thoughts on other things. Expecting! She was going to have Dain's baby! What a glorious feeling to know she carried her husband's baby. Instinctively, she ran a hand along her stomach as they climbed into Esmée's carriage. She would have to take better care of herself, she vowed and settled back into the seat. Her mood lightened considerably with the news that she was pregnant.

The days passed by and still there was no word about Dain. Brittannia had gone to Michael's office earlier that morning but there was no information to be found there. Michael had looked haggard with deep circles beneath his once smiling brown eyes. Brittannia felt her heart go out to him, he was just as much affected by this whole ordeal as she was, she thought as she left Henry Adderly and Company.

In the past few days she had made a conscious effort to take care of herself and she had to admit she was feeling a little better. She didn't want to tell anyone she was expecting, she was afraid they'd hold back news of Dain thinking it would upset her in her delicate condition.

Once home, she made herself comfortable in the sitting room. She had found reading kept her mind off the things that bothered her most and so she had brought a book from the library to the sitting room. The book was old, its binding used and its pages coarse, but she loved to read poetry and so, with careful fingers, she began reading.

"Oh, Brittannia! Jacques has just told me the news!" Esmée cried as she burst into the sitting room where Brittannia sat reading. Her ebony curls bounced as she quickly made her way to Brittannia's side and her green eyes were full of concern.

Brittannia placed the book of short poems on the table beside her and looked questioningly at the flustered Esmée. "What is the matter, Esmée? What news?"

Esmée's back straightened perceptively as her eyes grew large. "You do not know? No one told you?"

"Told me what? Has something happened to Dain? Tell me," she pressed, "what has Jacques learned?" In a minute she was out of the chair and grabbed Esmée by the shoulders. "Tell me!" she demanded in a frantic voice.

"Oh but I don't want to be the one to tell you. Please, sit back down. And do not worry, everything will be fine."

"I don't want to sit!" Brittannia nearly screamed. She was half out of her mind with worry. She was certain something terrible had happened to Dain. When she had spoken earlier with Michael his manner had been strange. She should have known something happened. "Tell me!" she demanded again.

"Oh, Brittannia, the *Airlee* was sunk!" Esmée blurted, her green eyes misting over with tears.

Brittannia felt as if she'd been slapped hard, felt as if a heavy dark curtain had descended around her and would never lift. "Sunk?" she whispered, her turquoise eyes staring blankly ahead. "Dain, what of Dain?" she asked as she gripped Esmée's arm.

Esmée hesitated, deciding whether she should say anymore, but Brittannia's hand closed around her arm with more forcefulness and the look in those turquoise eyes could not be denied.

"No one knows yet. A few crewmen made it to shore. Those who didn't perish would have been taken to a Yankee prison. Brittannia," she said, taking hold of Brittannia's shoulders and forcing her to sit down on the chair, "Erskine made it to shore and he was down in the engine rooms, Dain would most assuredly have been on deck so he should be safe somewhere. Perhaps he is on his way back to Nassau this very minute."

Brittannia shook her golden head, her eyes wide with dread. "No," she said, tears starting to well up and push past her thick lashes. "I don't think he's coming back.

Oh, Esmée, I knew he should never have made this run. Why did I let him go?"

Esmée gathered the young girl in her arms and rocked her gently, letting her cry out her pain and sorrow. "He's alive, Brittannia. You've got to believe that!"

Brittannia pushed open the door of Henry Adderly and Company and ignored the bell that jangled sassily above her. There was a determined set to her delicate chin and her turquoise eyes were two chips of ice, belying the calmness she tried to affect.

"I'm going in to speak with Mr. Delving," she informed the young man sitting at his desk as she opened Michael's door and strode in.

Michael was seated behind his desk. His overcoat was thrown casually over a chair and the sleeves of his silk shirt were rolled up to his elbows. His brown-haired head was bent over a pile of papers.

"Damn you, Michael, why didn't you tell me?" Brittannia demanded as she stood over the desk and glared down at Michael with a venomous look.

Michael looked up then leaned back in his chair and threw down his reading glasses as he regarded her. He exhaled deeply, then said, "Sit down, Brittannia."

"I'd rather stand, thank you. Now you had better tell me any news you've received about Dain, or I swear I'll squeeze your neck until you do!"

"Brittannia, I know you're upset. Dain and I go back a long ways and I too am upset over this incident. Please, sit down and calm yourself."

"Calm myself?" she nearly shrieked. "He's my

355

husband! I have a right to know what has happened to him, now tell me!"

"I have no other news other than the *Airlee* was sunk off the Cape Fear, and I gather that you have learned that much. What we have to do now is wait."

"Wait? Wait for what? To learn of his death? He might be lying along some deserted stretch of Carolina beach somewhere. A lot of good we do him, sitting in Nassau waiting for news!"

"Brittannia, I seriously doubt that," Michael said, standing, and then coming around the desk to stand beside her. "We have to wait until the next runner comes in from sea. They should have news for us, that is how we learned the *Airlee* was sunk. A brother blockade runner spoke to one of the crewmembers from the *Airlee*. Quite a few men were hauled off by the Federals."

"How long until another runner makes port?"

"The same vessel that brought news of the *Airlee* left this morning for its second run, they should return in a few days."

A few days. She would have to wait a few days to know of anything more and that was only if the men aboard the vessel heard any news—if they even made it back to Nassau themselves! She clasped her hands tightly together and forced herself not to cry. She had to be strong, for Dain's sake she had to keep herself together.

"Thank you for the information," she murmured and turned to leave, her eyes glazed over, her movements slow.

"Brittannia, are you going to be all right?" Michael questioned as he helped her to the door.

She inhaled deeply. "No," she answered. "Not until I have Dain beside me." She placed a sisterly kiss on Michael's cheek and then without another word, she left his office.

The commotion, the noise, the glaring sun, the smell of freshly baked food mingling with the smell of human bodies seemed not to exist for her as she climbed into her carriage and bade the driver to take her home. Home? Where was home without Dain? Where was anywhere, what was anything without the man she loved beside her? she asked herself as she stared out the window. The motion of the carriage stopped for a moment and she watched a small island boy smile up at his dark-skinned companion. She wondered how he could smile on such a day.

It had been three days since she'd spoken with Michael and her nerves were frayed past the point of repair. But all she could do was weep and wait.

"Brittannia."

Her head shot up and her heart lurched at the sound of the male voice. She so wanted to look up and see Dain striding up the stone steps of their home toward her. But it was Michael who was taking the steps two at a time. The look on his face was grim.

"I've news of Dain."

Brittannia was instantly out of her chair, instantly alert. "What, what have you learned?"

"As much as I suspected. He's being held in a northern prison."

"Where?" she pressed. "Was he hurt?"

He shook his head. "I don't know. My sources told

me only that someone saw him being taken by the Federals."

Brittannia's face clouded over and she felt the earth sway beneath her feet. She was overjoyed to hear Dain was alive—but in a northern prison? She'd heard of what the war prisons were like.

"Brittannia, get hold of yourself," Michael said as he grabbed her by the arms. "He was walking when anyone last saw him, be thankful for that!"

Brittannia shook her head as if to clear it. "Yes, you're right. You say you've no idea where they might have taken Dain?"

It was Michael's turn to shake his head and Brittannia thought long and hard for a moment. She had to help Dain get out of prison, but how? Perhaps she could buy his way out, but first she must find where he had been taken. Who could give her such information? She thought a moment longer, her gaze fixed beyond Michael's shoulder, seeing nothing in front of her.

"Brittannia," Michael was saying, "we'll get him out. Don't you worry."

She looked to Michael and said, "I'm not worried. I know we'll get him if I have to do it myself!"

Michael's brown eyes narrowed. "You? No, Brittannia. Get whatever schemes you've conjured up out of that silly head of yours. Let me handle this."

"I can't sit idle any longer! I must do something for him!"

"There is nothing you can do. I will try to bargain him out of wherever he's being held. Please," Michael pleaded, "let me try before you do anything foolish."

She didn't even know where to start to look for Dain

and so with a heavy sigh she said, "Very well, Michael."

He gathered her in his arms and gave her an affectionate hug. "I'll get him out," he promised.

The weeks slipped into a month and still no word was to be had as to Dain's whereabouts. Brittannia grew more tense with each passing day. She couldn't eat and her nights were long and sleepless. She had to do something. Michael had not been able to learn for sure where Dain had been taken. She was afraid Dain would die before anyone could help him.

The morning was bright and warm as Brittannia made her way down the stairs toward the carriage that awaited her outside her home on Queen Street. The weight of chests held down the conveyance that was to transport her to the wharf. She had purchased fare to New York on an outbound steamer. She couldn't wait any longer for someone to bring news of Dain to her, she had to go to him herself, she had to do what she could.

With the help of the footman, she climbed into the carriage and then sat back, her mind on all that was before her. She hadn't slept a wink in the past twenty-four hours, her mind had been filled with thoughts of what she planned to do. She mentally recalled every acquaintance her father had had in New York. They were all well-to-do men who were very much interested in politics. She planned to go to New York and look up every name that came to her mind. Surely among the many names she would find someone who would know where blockade runners were imprisoned. She would coax, beg, or plead—or more, if she had to. Anything to find Dain and get him out of prison.

The carriage came to a halt on the wharf of Nassau that had become so familiar to her and she boarded the nondescript steamer. Once in her cabin, she sank to the hard berth, exhausted and a little dizzy.

She heard the familiar sound of engines starting, felt the ship tremble then give. She stared at the ceiling of her cabin as the steamer broke its lair from the dock and made for the open ocean. Soon, oh so soon, she would be in the northern states and close to Dain. She passed a slim hand over her brow. Closing her eyes, the slight rolling of the ship rocked her into a deep, dreamless sleep.

Chapter 16

The trip to New York was a long and difficult one. Her cabin at night was cold and although the steward had given her two extra blankets, they weren't enough to keep the chill from her body. She fought down the bouts of nausea in the cool mornings. There were days when it was all she could do to make it to the dining room for a warm meal.

At last, at long last, the large, bulky steamer made its way into New York harbor. Brittannia stood near the rail watching the land of New York loom closer. A black cloud of smoke hung above the city, a product of the many industrial stacks that shot skyward. Brittannia stared about her as the steamer made port. A forest of masts choked New York's waterfront, a symbol of the Union's commerce.

Slowly she disembarked, not half as anxious as the other passengers seemed to be to leave the ship. Until now she had thought Nassau's wharf was the busiest in the world—but that was before she had been to New York. All around her were throngs of people, heading this way and that. The choking air was filled with the discord of a thousand different sounds: the racket of large machinery, the sharp blow of a policeman's whistle, the rumbling of carriages and drays, the shouts and curses of the dockworkers and sailors, the raucous laughter and loud screech of the many prostitutes who plied their trade near the docks. The imperfect cadence was enough to make Brittannia turn around and demand the captain of the steamer to return her to Nassau, but the thought of Dain held her back. With an involuntary shiver, she put her chin up and continued along the wharf.

She hired the first carriage that came along and ordered the driver to take her to the most respectable hotel in the city. The driver merely tipped his hat and then clicked the reins.

Brittannia passed a hand across her brow and vainly tried to block out all the noise that surrounded her. A flash of bright gold caught her eye and she gasped as she brought her left hand before her. Her wedding band, the same Dain had so lovingly slipped on her finger that long-ago night, sparkled with warm light. If she were to be presenting herself as Brittannia Denning then it had to come off. Slowly she drew it from her finger, not able to help the tears that sprang to blur her vision. Such a small act—to remove a ring—but for Brittannia a bit of her heart fell away as she dropped the symbol of love into her reticule.

It was a wet fall day that greeted her eyes as she looked out the window. The chill of the air seemed to seep between her clothing. The clothing she'd brought from Nassau was hardly appropriate for this weather. She'd heard fall was beautiful in the northern states, but at that moment she wondered how anything could be beautiful in this dirty, industrial city. She made a mental note to see a dressmaker as soon as possible and purchase some suitable clothing. After all, she must be dressed in the height of fashion if she was to woo the upper echelon of New York's society. But first she would have to write a few carefully worded letters to each of the various influential men her father had known.

It wasn't long before she received responses from her many letters. Soon Brittannia was caught up in the whirl of New York's elite society.

"Please hurry," she said to the young maid she had recently employed. She had moved into a modest townhouse preferring the privacy it offered over the large hotel.

The young girl nervously curled and pinned the last of Brittannia's tresses.

"Thank you," Brittannia said curtly. "You may leave now." She was a jumble of nerves. She was to attend a large party this evening escorted by a young man by the name of Brian Keyes. Her evening dress of sea green velvet fit snugly across the bodice and the skirt belled out in three generous tiers. The vibrant hue of the gown set off the color of her turquoise eyes, and as Brittannia reached for her cloak she chanced a look in the mirror before her. The woman who stared back didn't look at all like the young woman who had traveled to Nassau, New Providence Island, a few months ago. She looked a stranger. Her coiffed hair, bleached by the sun, was a stunning light blond, her cheekbones looked much higher than she remembered, much more pronounced by the slight hollows that had appeared in her cheeks from lack of proper eating. The woman who stared back was pretty, in fact, she was stunning, but she was not happy and anyone who knew Brittannia would need only to look into her eyes. They didn't sparkle, they didn't smile, they weren't alive with lights and shadows as they had been only weeks ago. No, tonight they were two hard chips of blue green ice, not giving, never telling, only searching.

With a deep sigh she left her rooms to go downstairs and greet her chaperon. She carried herself regally down the stairs, steeling herself for the night ahead. Her chaperon's father was a high government official who spent most of his time in Washington, D.C. Perhaps she could bribe the son into helping obtain Dain's release. She wasn't sure what she would have to do, but she knew that whatever was necessary, she would do it.

"Miss Denning?" The young man who stood at the end of the stairs smiled warmly up at her. His handsome looks nearly took her breath away. He was tall and broad of shoulder. His thick blond hair was the color of the high autumn grass of her beloved England. His brown eyes were soft and amiable.

"Yes," she said as she left the bottom step and came to stand beside him. "But please call me Brittannia." She extended her gloved hand and her chaperon placed a chaste kiss upon it.

"And you must call me Brian," he said with an engaging smile.

"I hope I haven't kept you waiting overly long." She turned and allowed him to place her cloak upon her bare shoulders. "I found myself a bit behind time this evening."

"Not at all, Miss—Brittannia," he replied, correcting himself as he opened the door and allowed her to proceed before him. A smart-looking carriage awaited them at the end of the walk, the two snowy white steeds biting at the bit, ready to move and warm their blood in the cool, wind-whipped air.

Inside, Brittannia folded her hands on her lap and looked out the window. She was nervous but she must not let anyone know it. She had to remember to mingle with the many guests this evening and listen with sharp ears to all that was said.

"Will Major Keyes be joining the festivities this evening?" she asked casually.

Brian Keyes cast her another of his handsome smiles. "No, my father has been in the capital these past many months. My mother received your note and hastened to invite you to this dinner party. Our fathers were very close and Mother was quite fond of Lord Denning."

Brittannia felt her hopes fall. So Major Keyes would not be at the gathering. She wondered if she could pull herself through the evening if it were to be only a gathering of the very wealthy who were happy enough discussing trivialities instead of anything pertaining to war and prisoners of war.

"Yes, our fathers were certainly close," she agreed absently.

At long last, the carriage came to a halt in front of the Keyes home. It was a grand structure of three stories, with impressive straight lines. The front was very square, supported and adorned by large white pillars. That evening it was ablaze with lights. As Brittannia and Brian alighted the carriage, a throng of guests filed in through the huge double doors.

"My mother loves to entertain," said Brian, guiding Brittannia through the entrance of his home.

Brian's mother was standing at the door receiving guests. At the sight of her son and Brittannia her brown eyes—so like her son's—lit up. "You must be Brittannia." She grasped Brittannia's gloved hands. "Lord Denning was such a dear man. We miss him terribly. But we're so pleased you could travel from your home and visit with us."

Brittannia squeezed Mrs. Keyes's hands and murmured her thanks for the invitation. If Dain hadn't been taken to a Northern prison, if the Yankees hadn't fired on the *Airlee* and burned Beau terribly, she might have felt some friendliness toward this woman, but as things were, she could feel nothing. Her father had found the Keyes family to be magnificent hosts and gracious people, but to Brittannia they were Yankees—Northerners—the people who had taken her husband away.

The night wore on bringing ever more guests flowing through the double doors, their cheeks bright from the biting northern wind outside, their eyes flickering across the crowd even as they spoke to the effervescent Mrs. Keyes.

Brian introduced her to many of the guests and she made a great effort to remember each of their names; she might need their help in the future.

She endured the elaborate dinner. Throughout the meal she couldn't help but think how much food was heaped on everyone's plate while Dain probably hadn't had a decent meal since he'd been taken captive. Afterward, a small orchestra began to play a lively tune and Brittannia eagerly accepted Brian's invitation to dance.

The young man held her lightly in his strong arms and swept her across the dance floor with ease. In his arms she found herself relaxing for the first time.

"May I compliment you on your beauty?" said Brian as they executed an intricate step and then whirled in a circle. "I must admit I wasn't too eager to accompany the daughter of an old friend of the family."

Brittannia smiled up at her escort. He was so very truthful in all that he did and said. "And I must admit I had some reservations as to who would be my escort!"

They shared laughter and he took that moment to draw her closer to his body. Brittannia breathed deeply, but did not pull away, her body held rigid, the sweet smile frozen on her face. She was determined to woo this young man in order to glean every ounce of information from him.

"I feel the need for a cool bit of air," she said, her turquoise eyes discreetly darting to the outer doors before returning to Brian's handsome features.

Brian instantly offered her his arm and led her beyond the doors into the dark, very cool night outside.

"This is much better," she said, breathing deeply and letting her full bosom strain against the velvet material of her dress. "I was beginning to feel a bit closed in by all those people."

Brian didn't miss the strain of her full breasts against the material of her bodice. He snaked an arm around her waist to guide her into the shadows, away from the searching eyes of the many guests. "Is this better?" he said as they stood in the shadows, away from the guests, away from the cool wind.

"Yes, much," she murmured, taking a small involuntary step away from him. "So do tell me, Brian, how are you involved in the war?"

"My last fight was down in Virginia. I was wounded and my father saw to it I was brought home to recover." He said the words with mixed feelings and Brittannia sensed the young man beside her wished his father hadn't intervened. But perhaps the same channels that kept Brian home and out of war could be used to obtain Dain's release.

"How very hard for you, just as you were in the thick of battle to suffer a wound," she said, looking up into his eyes through her thick dark lashes. "Just think how the rebels must feel in the Northern prisons, most with wounds, all suffering from homesickness."

Brian moved nearer to her, his hand circling around her waist. "It wasn't hard, Brittannia. I was up and around before I knew it. As for the rebs in our prisons, I must say they are faring a lot better than our soldiers in the Southern prisons; I've read articles and have seen proof in pictures of men who are held in the Andersonville stockade in Georgia."

"Yes, so I've heard," Brittannia lied. "It seems you know quite a bit about the prisoners brought north," she said, averting her eyes so he wouldn't see the interest in the turquoise depths.

"What is there to know? Other than they are fed, clothed, and housed. There has been much ado about how the North should treat its prisoners. Some say we should treat them brutally, inhumanely as they do our men, but others maintain that all humans should be treated as humans."

Brittannia tried not to shudder, tried not to think

about what Dain endured this very minute. "I see," she said, then raising her thick lashes, she looked deep into Brian's eyes. "Perhaps we could dance again," she offered, leaning ever so slightly toward his tall frame.

The rest of the evening went by in a whirl for Brittannia as did the next few weeks. Brian was her constant companion. He proudly escorted her to innumerable plays, balls, dinner parties, and fall outings. Brittannia could see, as could any casual observer, that Brian had become enamored with her.

Her conscience nagged at her as he led her, one chilly fall night, into the home of his parents for yet another of his mother's elaborate affairs. His touch on the small of her back as they walked was personal, much too warm, much too comfortably placed. She wondered for the hundredth time if she was doing the right thing when so far she was no closer to finding Dain.

As the night wore on with the usual bright chatter, the fashionable couples strolling in their silks and uniforms through the doors, Brittannia wanted desperately to end her charade. She wanted to tell Brian she was married, she couldn't bear to lead him on another night. But as she chanced a quick glance up at him, she knew she couldn't tell him the truth. The truth would devastate him. He was so unsuspecting, so full of trust; she couldn't tell him she had no feelings for him other than those felt for a good friend. No, she thought as she let him seat her at the elegantly laid table, it would be kinder to just let him think she'd returned to England. She would just leave without any explanation.

"So pray tell, Miss Denning," a bald man near her

right was asking, "what brings you to our city in such turbulent times?"

His question, the question Dain had asked of her that long ago night at Michael's party, caused a tingle up her spine. She looked demurely down at her still-full plate before answering. She swallowed hard as she remembered that warm summer night, the night Dain had said he needed her, wanted her. Oh dear God, how she wanted and needed him this very minute!

"I desperately felt the need to meet with acquaintances my family has had in New York," she said as she finally looked up, meeting his watery blue eyes.

The old man smiled at her but the smile was devoid of warmth.

"Well, it shouldn't be too long until this war is over and the rebs are finally crushed. Soon we can all enjoy peace and put our minds to healing and unionizing this country of ours."

"Yes, dear," his wife inclined, "something that should have been done years ago."

There was murmuring and agreement among the dinner guests: women, poised with wineglass in hand, nodding their perfectly coiffed heads, men giving a distant look to their eyes, seeing other times, other places while they too nodded.

"I think 'crush' is a very harsh word to use, sir," Brittannia said. "I think the Southerners wish for the same end." She was remembering Dain was a Southerner and that he had brought supplies to the south and was no doubt dying this minute for doing so.

There was a hush along the elongated table and Brittannia could feel all eyes on her. She sat straight in her chair, unwavering beneath the old man's critical eye.

"I didn't know we had a Southern sympathizer among us tonight."

Brittannia didn't flinch, although from the corner of her eye she could see Mrs. Keyes fan herself vigorously. Brian looked like a stallion biting at the bit, ready to plunge in the conversation for Brittannia's defense.

"I sympathize for *both* the North and the South," she said, her turquoise eyes meeting watery blue eyes. "I'm for living side by side and respecting your neighbor's opinions, with both sides compromising."

The old man ruffled up like an angry hen. "Are you for slavery, Miss Denning? Are you for no tariffs on imports? We are an industrial nation, our bread is buttered from the money of our industrial goods, our people are paid fairly for a hard day's work!"

Brittannia looked about her, all eyes were on her, she drew in a large amount of air. She hadn't realized her quick remark would bring on the judgmental stares and pregnant silence. She wondered what her next words should be.

Brian came to her rescue. "Miss Denning is far removed from this war and most influenced by what she hears spoken around. Shall we get on with the dancing and merriment?" He leaped from his seat and, with a motion to the musicians, extended his arm to her.

"What a lovely idea," Mrs. Keyes chimed in with an affectionate smile at her son.

Once on the dance floor, Brian apologized for the predicament she'd found herself in. "If I were always clever, you would never find yourself in such a corner," he said, his brown eyes smiling down at her.

"No, Brian," she said, wanting to finally speak some truth to him, "I fear you would always find yourself in such a corner as I always speak my mind."

Brian smiled at her, a wheat-colored wave nearly covering his right eye. "I am glad you do. I'd want you no other way." He pulled her close as they dipped to the music and she felt the leanness of his young body, smelled the cleanness of him.

She smiled mechanically up into his handsome face and curled her arm around his neck.

The music ended and Brian guided her to the punch bowl set upon a long table at the end of the ballroom. Many couples stood along the side of it watching over the rims of their glasses the scene around them. Brian left her near the end of the table as he went to get them refreshments. Brittannia proudly stood her spot, refusing to bend beneath the many stares pointed her way. Apparently she hadn't yet been forgiven for her outspokenness.

"Ah, there you are, Miss Denning." The old man with the watery blue eyes came to stand beside her. "Are you truly for humanity or are you just a Southern sympathizer come to plague us Yankees?"

Brittannia turned to him, her turquoise eyes flashing. "I am not 'just' anything, sir!" she exclaimed, her anger rising at the old man's tone. "I am a believer in living side by side with your fellow man, of giving and taking. It takes but a boy to lift his gun, it takes a man to lower that same gun and come to a compromise."

The old man regarded her. "And if you can come to no compromise, what then?" he said after a pause.

Brittannia averted her eyes from his piercing gaze. *Indeed,* she thought, *what then?* She didn't know "what then," but surely not all this bloodshed! She was saved from her dilemma as Brian returned with two glasses of punch.

"Mr. Ewell," Brian proclaimed, "had I known you would take such a profound interest in Brittannia's sympathies I would have been more prepared," he joked. "I would have ordered dueling pistols at fifty paces."

The surrounding crowd tittered with the appropriate laughter but Brittannia knew very well they would have loved to hear her comment to Mr. Ewell's question.

"Shall we call a truce?" Brian persisted. "This is a gathering for merriment, not for discussing war policies." He pressed a cool glass of punch into Brittannia's hands.

"Yes, of course, Brian," Mr. Ewell said. "I can see I've upset your guest and you have my apologies."

Brittannia managed a smile at the old man. The way his eyes bore into her at that moment, she could feel his dislike toward her. *Well,* she thought, *I've made one enemy this night and I'd better not make anymore. I won't get Dain out of prison that way.*

Mr. Ewell turned to speak to a group of men to his left and Brittannia was glad to be out from under the scrutiny of those piercing eyes of his. Brian stood beside her, regarding her over the rim of his glass. His soft brown eyes were full of concern and something else.

"A penny for your thoughts, Brittannia. Your secrets are safe with me."

She shook herself from her reverie. "Brian, you must

know," she teased, "a woman never reveals all her secrets." She shifted uneasily under his smoldering gaze as she took a large swallow of her punch.

"Ah, Brittannia, I would reveal all of my secrets to you if you would but ask. You must know," he whispered, leaning closer, "I have very strong feelings for you."

Brittannia took another healthy swallow from her glass. She should have known it would come to this. "Brian, we have to talk."

"Yes, we do."

"But this isn't the time or place," she said, her turquoise eyes darting around the room.

"Perhaps we could stroll outside," he offered, hopefully.

Brittannia inwardly blanched. She didn't want to be alone with him in the dark. She couldn't give him any opportunities to declare his love for her, as she knew he longed to do. She quickly swallowed the rest of her punch. "Perhaps. But first I would like some more punch. I have an unquenchable thirst this evening."

Brian took the glass from her hand, brushing his fingers lightly along hers as he did so. Brittannia breathed a sigh of relief as he left her side to refill her glass. She would have to keep a distance from Brian from now on, she vowed to herself. As she stood waiting for Brian to return and wondering on what pretense she could cancel their date for the next evening, she overheard Mr. Ewell speaking of the blockade. She couldn't help but overhear since the old man was so caught up in the telling of his story his voice was loud and excited. Had she imagined it or had Mr. Ewell said something about the *Airlee?* She leaned closer.

"I guess she was quite a sight," Mr. Ewell was saying to the small cluster of men around him. "Captain Wilkinson said she burned like a beacon in the night. It was a proud day for him when he had the most successful blockade runner hauled into Fort Lafayette! Captain Dain Barclay will have plenty of time to figure where he went wrong on that night!"

Brittannia felt her blood rush.

"Brittannia, are you all right? You look as white as a sheet!" Brian said as he set the two glasses down and then lightly held Brittannia's shoulders in case she would faint.

"I—I am fine, really I am."

"You don't look fine. Let me help you to a seat and then I'll order the carriage brought around and I'll take you back to your town house."

She allowed Brian to help her to a nearby chair and then endured the ministrations of Mrs. Keyes, who insisted on fanning Brittannia and ordering one of the servants to bring her smelling salts.

But at the mention of smelling salts Brittannia immediately stood and assured everyone that she was all right and didn't need anything more than a good night's rest, which she planned to get as soon as she got home. Brian finally returned, and after she thanked her hostess, she walked, with an eager step, out the door.

"I'm sorry to do this, Brittannia," Brian said once they were seated in the carriage, "but I must insist that we cancel all of our engagements for this week. I can see I've tired you out by escorting you to every social event scheduled. Why didn't you say something to me? I've been terribly selfish taking up all of your time."

Brittannia gave a sisterly pat to his knee. "Don't

blame yourself. I merely felt closed in, perhaps it was all the people in the room. No matter, I feel fine now."

The carriage rocked gently to and fro and Brittannia felt tears of self-pity sting her eyes. Brian must have sensed her sadness, for he moved closer and gently put an arm around her. Brittannia drew in a trembling breath as her thick lashes fluttered downward self-consciously at the tender look in Brian's eyes. She was suddenly feeling very emotional. She felt guilty for sitting so close to Brian, felt deceitful at the thought of letting him think she was single and open for amorous pursuits and at the same moment she felt all alone in the world. She was in a city whose ways were foreign to her, her husband was in some prison far from the people who loved him and could help him—and on top of it all she was pregnant. Her world seemed dark indeed. She needed a friend, she needed a shoulder to cry on, she needed to be held. Her tears came and she quickly wiped them from her cheeks. She mustn't give in, she had to be strong!

"Brittannia," Brian whispered in a caressing tone. "What is the matter?" His fingers lightly brushed her jawline as they traveled to her chin, and with a tenderness that tore at her heart, he lifted her face to his. "It grieves me to see you so hurt. I would do anything for you," he proclaimed, his soft brown eyes so full of trust, so full of love, baring his soul to her.

His words, his eyes, the moment, all proved too much for Brittannia and she felt her body tremble as new tears sprang into her eyes. He was so sweet, so very, very sweet and she was cold and manipulating, not worthy of his feelings! She tried to hold back her sobs, but she couldn't and in the dark, cool interior of the carriage, she found herself wrapped gently in his strong arms as he stroked her hair and shushed her sobs with soft murmurs.

She stayed in his arms, not able to push him away, not wanting to leave the safe, warm shelter of them. She needed him this night, she needed him to rock her gently as she cried tears of shame, hurt and sorrow.

Slowly and oh so gently, he pulled her from him only to bend his blond head and cover her lips with his own. His lips moved slowly, caressingly, as they claimed and moved over hers. She shouldn't be doing this, she shouldn't be letting him kiss her, but as the thoughts whirled in her head his arms pulled her closer and she felt her body go pliantly toward his. His lips were soft, tender in their assault and then there was no reason, just the feel of his warm body, the touch of his soft mouth, the forgetfulness his embrace brought her. She lost herself in his arms, forgot all of her dark worries. There was nothing but the silken feel of his lips on hers, nothing but the golden warmth that he brought to her. It was like some great yellow ball of light at the end of a long, dark tunnel and she ran blindly toward it, heedless of the consequences.

After a blissful eternity, it seemed, he slowly released her, his full mouth smiling down at her, his brown eyes lit with desire. At that, her senses returned and she moved away, her cheeks flaming with the realization of her folly.

"I—I'm sorry, Brian. I shouldn't have let that happen," she said, her voice wavering from her wildly beating heart.

Brian quickly closed the distance she had so determinedly put between them. "Don't be sorry. I enjoyed it thoroughly."

She looked miserably out the carriage window into the darkness that was lit only by an occasional street-lamp.

"You enjoyed it too," he persisted. "I know you did. Forget what I said earlier, I must see you tomorrow. Tell me you'll see me tomorrow."

Brittannia glanced at him as the carriage came to a stop in front of her rented town house. His handsome features were bathed in the soft light of the lamp outside the window and a blond wave had tumbled down to just above his right eye. He was very good-looking, and Brittannia was certain he had broken many hearts in his young years. She wondered how he would fare after she'd broken his heart. Sooner or later she would have to leave his social circle or tell him she wanted nothing more to do with him. But for now something inside her couldn't let her speak the words that would crush his heart.

"Yes, I'll see you tomorrow," she finally said as he helped her out of the carriage. "Perhaps we could visit prisoners of war in one of the forts."

Brian nearly choked on air. "Well, that was certainly sudden!" he exclaimed. "What makes you want to visit with prisoners of war? Surely we can find something more interesting and far more appealing to do!"

She was quick with a response, her quickness surprised even herself. "Why, Brian, I can sympathize with all those Southern women who must be worried sick about their husbands, sons, or relatives biding time in the Northern prisons." She could see the look on his face, his lips were turned down at the corners and there was a furrow between his blond brow. "You know,

Brian, that if you were in a Southern prison I would hope some kind, Southern lady would visit you and bring provisions. I think it is only right that we help these men, console them, and bring them what they need."

He stood for a moment, regarding her in the lamplight and cool night air. Then he said, "The sights of prison life are not pretty. Are you sure you want to go?"

"Yes," she said firmly. "Perhaps to some near prison. Are there any near us?" she questioned, careful to hold her enthusiasm in check.

"Well, there is one near the harbor," he replied reluctantly. "It's called Fort Lafayette."

Chapter 17

All these weeks Dain had been so near. How much precious time she had wasted traveling Brian's circles for some bit of information only to find Dain had been within walking distance. She could have been taking provisions to him, she could have spoken with him by now.

She chewed nervously on her bottom lip as she once again checked the basket she planned to take to Fort Lafayette with her. Mentally she recounted all the items she'd placed in it: a blanket, a few shirts, candles, matches, salt, fresh baked breads and ham, and on impulse she had thrown in a bottle of spirits. She remembered how Dain enjoyed an after-dinner drink. She didn't know if the prison officials would allow her to bring all of this, but she was determined to at least try.

She fought down a feeling of nausea as she lifted the heavy basket. The last few mornings had been difficult for her; she'd felt sick and not at all like going out and facing the world. With her basket hefted on one arm, she let the other arm stray to her stomach. There was a soft bulge beneath her dress and in just the few weeks she'd been in New York, she'd noticed a visible difference in her appearance. She'd been very careful to wear concealing clothes but soon that would be near impossible. At the rate she was showing, soon nothing would be able to hide her condition from the people around her. She cringed at that thought. Hopefully by then Dain and she would be far away from New York and comfortably settled in the manor house in the Cotswolds. Then she wouldn't care if she puffed out as far as one of the hot air balloons that scouted the war regions.

She gave Brian an affectionate smile as she descended the stairs. He was quickly at her side, taking the basket from her hold and looking down at her with those concerned soft brown eyes. She gave into him, letting him dote over her as they walked to the waiting carriage outside. It was a cold rainy day. She drew her cape more closely about her.

"You're positive you want to do this? Fort Lafayette isn't a place I'd boast to my friends about taking you to!"

"Yes, Brian, I'm sure," she replied, annoyed. "Please don't press me on the matter." She pressed the back of a slim hand to her mouth as nausea threatened to overwhelm her.

"Brittannia," Brian said as he stared at her with acute awareness, "you're not well. I'll order the driver to turn around and take us back to your town house. You need rest. You shouldn't be out in this damp weather and you certainly shouldn't be near any sick prisoners."

Brittannia's hand flew from her mouth to land in her

lap and clasp tightly with the other. "I'm perfectly well. But did you say that all the prisoners are ill, Brian? Surely they are receiving medical care?"

Brian waved one hand nonchalantly in the air. "They're being treated far better than any of our boys down in the rebel prison camps! No need to worry about them. They deserve whatever they get and probably worse."

Brittannia's turquoise eyes flashed. "They deserve to be treated as human beings," she spat. "How can you say such a thing? They fight for what they believe in, the same as the Northern men are doing!"

Brian shifted uneasily under her angry stare. "I'm sorry if I've offended you."

Brittannia closed her eyes and drew in a deep breath. She knew the spirit of patriotism that inspired Brian to fight for his country also bred a fierce antagonism toward the enemy in him. His life and his world had been thrown into chaos because of the war, as had the Southerners'. No wonder he was bitter. In his mind the South had caused the war all on its own.

"I'm sorry, Brian. I've been very testy. Please forgive me."

Brian softened under her contrite gaze. "I could forgive you anything, my dear."

Brittannia smiled at him, knowing there would come a time when the truth of that statement would be put to the test. The carriage rolled on and Brittannia sat numbly, listening to Brian as he spoke of the times he'd spent fighting the South, his childhood antics, and the latest gossip about the people she had met in the past few weeks. She nodded her head, laughed, and gave the proper "oh" in all the appropriate places. Brian was chattering on like he never had before—perhaps he could feel her nervousness and was just trying to make her feel better.

The carriage came to a halt in front of a squat drab building.

"This isn't going to be a pretty sight," Brian warned. "I don't know why I let you talk me into this, you look absolutely peaked today. Are you sure you wouldn't rather turn around and go home?"

"Quite sure," she said firmly. She motioned for him to bring the large basket beside her. They alighted the carriage and quickly headed for the shelter of the building ahead.

"Are you sure we'll be able to visit with the prisoners?" Brittannia asked as they stepped inside and brushed rain droplets from themselves.

"Surely you only mean to drop off the provisions you brought! If you wish to look at the prisoners that can be arranged, but visiting with them is another thing!"

Brittannia looked up to him with large eyes. "Brian, I mean to speak with them!"

"Whatever for?" He was visibly shocked.

"Be—because, I must! My mission will not be complete unless you see to it that I can visit with a few of the men."

"Brittannia, really. I've let this come far enough," Brian protested. "We will leave your basket and then be on our way. I don't want you subjected to anything as terrible as a war-time prison."

Brittannia gave him an angry look as she grabbed her basket from his hands. She wasn't going to let him deposit her so-carefully-packed basket and then quickly usher her out without ever seeing Dain. "I want to visit with a few of the men," she said, trying to speak calmly. "I—I must let them know someone cares."

Brian regarded her, a shuttered expression in his eyes. "Very well. If it is what you want, I'll arrange it."

Brittannia released the breath she'd been holding. Now all she had to do was make sure Dain was among the men she would be allowed to see.

"My—my father had a friend in the Southern states who was a privateer," she lied, "and was somewhat of a raider. He died, of course, at the hands of a Northerner. Perhaps if you could bring in a man who sailed, a man who chose his field upon the high seas, I would feel comforted knowing I had helped at least one man who had the same dream as the young privateer." Her turquoise eyes grew large and moist as she looked deeply into Brian's handsome face. "I heard Mr. Ewell mention a Captain Dain Barclay. Perhaps he could be brought out and I could visit with him. Do you think you could arrange that for me, Brian?" she asked ever so sweetly, her bottom lip trembling slightly.

"Certainly," Brian said coolly. "Captain Dain Barclay, did you say?"

She was sorry as she watched him walk over to the seated corporal and make arrangements, sorry that she had deceived him so, sorry that she wasn't able to nor could she ever fall as deeply in love with him as he had with her. Her conscience nagged at her as she was led to a connecting small room and seated upon a hard wooden chair. She had requested that each prisoner be brought before her alone and, surprisingly, that was what she was going to get. Obviously Brian had powerful connections and a rich purse to obtain this for her.

Brian, she thought as she sat there waiting for the first prisoner, how sweet he had been, how very thoughtful. She must one day tell him the truth, he had done so much for her.

The door opened and a man, tattered and limping, came into the room. The odor from him was nearly staggering and his face was as pale and gaunt as a very sick, dying invalid.

"I heah you'd like the privilege of starin' at a dying man," he said through teeth that were beginning to decay.

Brittannia held back the urge to cringe and replied, "No, not at all. Here," she said, pulling out a clean shirt from her basket. "Take this. I'll send more, I promise. I'm so sorry you're here."

The man regarded her through bleary eyes then slowly drew his hand out to accept the welcomed garment. "That's mighty sweet of you—considerin' you're a Yankee woman."

"I—I'm not a Yankee. I'm from England, I'm only here for a visit."

"Now fancy that—you takin' the time to stop off and look in on us."

"Please, sir, I only wanted to help. I only wanted to offer you my sympathy . . ."

"Sympathy? Sympathy don't mean nothing to a dying man."

Brittannia looked away and pressed her hands to her mouth as the prisoner stood and knocked on the door for the corporal to let him out. It was so unfair. How could anyone lock a human being up like this? It just wasn't fair, and what of Dain? Was he also dying?

She didn't have long to wait, for the next prisoner

ushered in was none other than he. She sat glued to her spot on the hard chair. She saw nothing, felt nothing, but Dain standing before her! His gray clothing, the last she had seen him wearing when he'd departed Nassau on that long ago day, was tattered near shreds. His face was covered with a scraggly growth of beard and his eyes were a faint, faint gray. Almost the color of the thin dew upon a meadow flower. They filled with anguish at the sight of Brittannia.

"Oh, dear God, what's happened to you?" she exclaimed as she ran to him, her arms held open, ready to take his tattered body in her arms.

He stepped back as she came to him, his hand reaching up to keep her away.

"Dain, it is all right! I've come to take you home!" she cried.

"You shouldn't be here," he said savagely. "I'll get myself out."

Brittannia looked up to him, her heart breaking a thousand times. "Oh, Dain, I've missed you so!" She wanted so badly to tell him of their child, the child that was this very minute growing within her. The words to tell him were on the tip of her tongue but she held them back, knowing that they wouldn't help him in his situation. He would only worry about her and demand that she return to Nassau. No, she wouldn't tell him, not yet. "Look at yourself! You're weak, you need medical attention, and you haven't decent clothes to wear."

"I shall wait for either the war to end or for my exchange to be offered," he replied, his gray eyes drinking in the beautiful sight of her. "I've missed you, Brittannia," he said, his tone softening. "I'd take you in my arms this minute if I weren't so covered with filth and vermin. I hate for you to see me like this. Please, return to Nassau and wait for me." His words were soft, almost a plea, and Brittannia had to fight to hold back her tears.

"No," she whispered as she closed the distance between them and placed her hand on his forearm. "I'll not go back to Nassau without you."

He tensed under her touch. "You need an army order to have a prisoner released. Let it be, Brittannia. Why the hell did Michael let you come? I'll wring his neck when I see him next!"

"Michael had no say in the matter. I'm here because I came to see you freed. I'm not about to let my husband sit out the war in some squalid prison. You might not live until the end of the war. Even if you do they'll just open these doors and let you on your merry way, you without decent clothing and money. No, I'll not wait for that nor will I wait for you to be exchanged. I'll find someone to issue an army order, I'll take you out by force if I have to, but one way or another I'm going to get you out of here!"

Dain looked down at her, his gray eyes so soft, so full of pain as he lifted her hand to his mouth and placed a tender kiss upon it. "Go home, Brittannia. I'll be there soon. All the forces of hell—and this place must surely have them—couldn't keep me from you."

The tears she'd fought so hard finally slipped past her thick lashes and down her cheeks. "Dain, please—"

He put a finger to her full lips, stopping her words. "Hush. You must go back to Nassau. When you see me next I will be clean and healthy and then I will take you in my arms as I've longed to do these past weeks."

She went toward him, wanting to throw herself in his arms. She wanted to hold him, she needed him to hold her, but his arms held her back. "No," he said. "Promise me you'll return to Nassau."

"No, not without you. I—I can't." She ignored the dark look that came to his handsome visage with her words; instead she turned and went to the basket she had brought with her. "Here," she said, handing him the heavy bundle. "I've brought you this. Tell me what else you need—I want to bring it all to you."

Dain took the basket without looking at its contents. "I need nothing save my peace of mind knowing you're safe in Nassau where Michael can watch over you until my return."

Her turquoise eyes flashed. "I don't need a protector! I need my husband alive and with me!"

There was a knock at the door and the young corporal entered. He motioned for Dain to return to the barracks as his eyes looked to the basket Dain held.

Brittannia saw where the man's gaze was directed and she said, "I have brought a few provisions. Surely you won't deny this man of these meager victuals?"

The young man shrugged his shoulders as if it didn't matter to him. Brittannia looked to Dain before he walked out. Their eyes met and held for a long moment and she felt a great tug at her heart when he smiled at her. Those sculpted lips, the same that had so intimately explored her body, turned up at the ends, revealing strong, even white teeth. He might not be walking back to a filthy barrack, she thought, but might be leaving her side for a quick jaunt to town and would soon be returning. She returned his smile with trembling lips. She watched him leave the room. His

389

stride was the same he had always had, powerful, sure of himself, and all about him exuded an aura of pride.

She stood watching the empty doorway, her mind on other times, other places, her tears falling unchecked down her face.

"Brittannia," Brian said as he came to stand in the doorway.

Brittannia blinked away her blank stare and quickly brushed away the tears.

He came quickly to her side. "I knew I should not have brought you here today. You'll be seeing no more prisoners. It was foolish of me to let you have your way. I'm taking you home."

Brittannia let him fuss over her and before she knew it she was back in Brian's carriage and Fort Lafayette was only a dim, gray outline in the distance. The air was filled with a chill and the drizzle had become a downpour as the carriage took them away from the noisy, dirty harbor and to higher ground. Brittannia had wiped the last of the tears from her face before she finally spoke.

"I'm sorry for my behavior today," she apologized. "It is just that I wish there were something we could do to help those men."

"You brought them provisions, that is enough. Now put them out of your mind, you don't even know them, they should be of no concern to you."

Brittannia listened carefully to Brian's words. If it would take an army order for Dain's release, then Brian was the man who could help her. He certainly had proven he had enough pull, as the corporal at the fort had let her speak with two prisoners and he even let Dain have the basket of provisions. But her problem was how to get Brian to obtain Dain's release? Brian didn't think she even knew Dain. Perhaps if she told him the truth, told him Dain was her husband and she was expecting their child, but that would crush Brian and make him hate her. What was she to do?

"So it is best if you just forget what you saw today," Brian was saying. "Brittannia? Are you listening to me?"

Brittannia shook her head and turned her gaze to him. "Yes, yes of course I am. But, Brian, did you know that one of the men I spoke with was a very dear friend of my father?" she asked. It was of course a lie, but was the only way she could think of to get Brian to obtain release papers for Dain. "Yes," she continued when she saw the surprised look on Brian's face. "That is why I was so upset. You see, this man is a good friend of the family and I had no idea he was being held at Fort Lafayette, you see he changed his name. Barclay is not the name I knew him by, otherwise I would have gone to see him long before this."

She paused for a moment and with baited breath awaited his reaction.

"Captain Barclay?" he asked astounded. "You know him?"

"Yes!"

"Why, Brittannia, he is a notorious blockade runner. I'm surprised your father would have even conversed with such a scoundrel! He's an outlaw!"

She spoke slowly, choosing her words carefully. She had to be careful, for Dain's future depended on Brian's willingness to help her. "Oh, no, not an outlaw," she said, smoothing the velvet fold of her skirt. "He is just doing what he thinks needs to be done. Now, mind you, I'm not saying my father would approve of Captain Barclay's role in this war but he would not disapprove either. He would respect the man's courage and strength." She paused for a moment. "Is there nothing we can do for the captain?" she asked, her eyes wide. "My father and he were such close friends."

"What would you have me do?"

Brittannia looked him in the eye and said, "Oh, whatever it is one does. Perhaps see to it he is exchanged or obtain a release for him."

"Brittannia, what you ask of me is no small favor!"

"I know that, but it would mean so much to me to see the captain released. Is there nothing you can do?"

Brian looked at her for a long moment then turned his gaze out the carriage window. Brittannia held her breath, waiting for an answer. Finally he said, "There may be some way I can see the captain released. I'll look into the matter and let you know in a few days. Now, can we forget about the prisoners, Fort Lafayette, and the war? I want to spend a pleasant day with you and I fear the possibility of that has been greatly reduced by our outing this morning!"

A few days, Brittannia thought to herself. That was a lifetime to her. Dain needed medical attention now. Despite her thoughts, she managed to reply, "Thank you, Brian. I appreciate your willingness to help. Perhaps we could salvage the remainder of the day. We could start by having lunch at our favorite restaurant."

Brian smiled at her, obviously pleased that she was willing to forget about the prisoners for the time being.

"That is by far the most pleasant idea you've had all morning!" he said, then leaned out the window and shouted directions to the restaurant to the driver.

Brittannia heaved a sigh and wondered how she could ever be able to keep lunch in her stomach let alone the meals that were to come in the following days. Her worry for Dain was great.

The days dragged by and still Brian had not mentioned anything more of obtaining Dain's release. Brittannia frantically wondered if he'd decided to forget the whole idea. Through the long dark night the first snow had fallen and had covered the city with a fine white blanket. The air was chilled and the mid-afternoon sky lead colored. Brittannia sat at the large table of her town house sipping tea. She absently rested her free hand on her rounded belly. The dress she'd donned earlier did little to conceal the fact that she was with child, but she hadn't even thought about that when she'd dressed. Her thoughts had been of Dain. When the outer bell rang and the maid discreetly rushed by to let in the caller, Brittannia still sat, clutching her cup of tea and staring into nowhere.

"Brittannia," Brian said, ignoring the maid and hurrying to the dining table. "I've come to say good-bye."

"But where are you going?" Wasn't he going to stay and see Dain released?

"I'm going to Washington, D.C. I'm going to see my father and," he said, lowering his voice as the maid passed by on her way to the other room, "talk to him of obtaining an army order for Captain Barclay's release."

Brittannia drew in a deep breath and smiled. It was

the first smile Brian had seen in days from her.

"Oh, Brian, that is good news!" She stood and poured a cup of tea for him, her hands shaking slightly. She forgot the swollen look of her body as she handed Brian the cup and missed the look on Brian's features as his brown eyes lingered on her full belly and breasts.

"Are you leaving today?" she asked, dropping two lumps of sugar into his cup of tea.

He drew his eyes up to her face and smiled. "Yes," he said softly. "I'm leaving within the hour. I wanted to let you know of my plans. Are you sure you'll be all right while I'm gone? I should be gone a number of days." He spoke as if talking to a small child who just skinned her knee.

"Of course I'll be all right." Brittannia thought how odd he was acting but she quickly forgot about his behavior with thoughts of Dain. "How do you intend to get an army order?"

Brian stirred his tea with the small spoon, his brown eyes never leaving her face. "My father will see to it. Don't worry, Brittannia. I'll see the captain released and then you can put your mind to rest and start caring for yourself."

Was her lack of proper rest and food that much evident? she wondered. She'd been trying her very best to eat right these past few days, for the baby's benefit.

"I must be off," Brian said as he put his half-empty cup on the table. "Promise me you'll take better care of yourself and not worry over any prisoners." He took a step toward her and wrapped his arms around her, drawing her full body close to his.

Brittannia opened her mouth, ready to protest his

holding her so close but before she could speak he had his mouth on hers and was kissing her tenderly, his mouth moving slowly over hers and his tongue flicking in and out, gently probing the recesses of her mouth. His hands slowly caressed her back and she could feel the pounding of his heart against her chest.

"I'll miss you," he said huskily, a thatch of wheat-blond hair nearly tumbling down to cover his eyes. "You know I'd do anything for you."

Brittannia held back the threatening tears as she smiled up at him. Suddenly she had no doubt he would return with an army order for Dain's release and now what troubled her most was how to leave him once Dain was freed. How would she say good-bye to him, how could she thank him, how could she leave him without breaking his heart, without making him hate her?

"I wish you Godspeed, Brian. Be careful," she said softly.

He gave her one of his crooked smiles as he brushed the back of one hand along her cheek, then he turned and was gone, the manly smell of his cologne lingering in the air behind him.

Brittannia busied herself the next few days with daily visits to Fort Lafayette. She spent many long hours sitting in the anteroom of the fort, her fingers clutching the handle of the large basket. She had no idea if the supplies she'd sent the preceding days had made their way to Dain or not. The officials had not allowed her to see Dain the previous days and she was sure they weren't going to allow her to see him today. She wished Brian were with her. He would surely have been able to make arrangements for her to visit with Dain.

Brian arrived back in New York on a sunny early November day. His face was set in a happy smile and when Brittannia greeted him she felt her heart leap. By his attitude, she was sure he had obtained the release.

"It's so wonderful to see you!" she exclaimed as he entered her sitting room. "Please sit down." She motioned to a full, cloth-covered chair.

He leaned back into the padded softness of the chair and crossed his legs, his brown eyes drinking in the sight of her.

"Well," she coaxed, nearly bursting at the seams for news of what his trip brought. "Did you get the captain a release?" She bit her lip as soon as the words were out. She shouldn't have sounded so excited, she should not have asked so quickly! "How is your father?" she added, hoping to tone down her earlier question.

"He is well, and Washington is buzzing with activity. I thoroughly enjoyed my visit. I've missed you, Brittannia. You look beautiful and have put on some weight. It befits you," he commented.

"Yes, I took your advice and have had three square meals every day since you left," she said. "Your mother must be anxious to hear of your visit with your father."

"Not so anxious as I am to hear of all that you did while I was gone," he said as he leaned forward and took her hand in his. "Truly, I missed you."

Brittannia smiled at him. "And I missed you, Brian."

Brittannia felt a twinge of guilt when his face lit up at her words. Well, she *had* missed him, she thought defiantly. She'd missed him when she went to Fort Lafayette!

"You'll be pleased to know I've obtained a release order for Captain Barclay."

"You did?" she asked, trying not to sound too excited. "That is wonderful. How soon can he be released?"

"Tomorrow, if that is soon enough. All I have to do is give the documents to the official in charge and Captain Barclay is a free man."

Brittannia felt a heavy weight lift from her shoulders and the sunny day outside her window seemed ten times sunnier. "Thank you, Brian. I appreciate all of your help."

"Anything, anything for you, Brittannia."

She looked away from his intent gaze.

"Will you join my mother and me for dinner tonight?" he asked.

"Oh, Brian, your mother and you will have family matters to discuss. She'll want to hear all about your visit with your father."

He squeezed her hand gently. "To me, you are family."

She withdrew her hand and stood. She crossed the room and gazed out the window, trying to concentrate on the snow-dusted landscape there.

"Brittannia." He stood and came to stand beside her. He put his hands on her shoulders. "Just when I feel I am getting close to you, you turn away and deny the feelings that are between us. What is the matter?"

She stiffened at his words, tormented by the truth. "I—I'm sorry," she whispered as she hugged her thick waist and continued to stare out the window.

His lips inches from her ear, Brian wrapped his arms around her and drew her back against him. "Who is the father of your baby?"

She whirled around, tearing herself from his hold. "What?" she exclaimed incredulously, her eyes wide.

"The father, Brittannia. Where is he, who is he?" He cupped her chin in his hand.

She pushed his hand away and turned to again stare out the window.

"Why, what are you talking about? I'm not with child." The lie came with difficulty to her lips and she had to force the words out.

"Ah, Brittannia. Do you think me blind? I've held you in my arms since the first night we met. I could feel your body swell with child and I could see your moods change. The day I came to tell you I was leaving for Washington, D.C., your dress did little to conceal your full figure."

Brittannia took a deep breath, ready to disagree, but she couldn't. She couldn't lie to Brian anymore. "I—I'm sorry," she said again.

"Sorry?" Brian asked. "Why should you be sorry? I think you are beautiful, more so because you are with child. The man who begot you this way should be sorry. What gentleman would let his lady travel alone when she is with his child?" he demanded. "You obviously deserve better than what you've had in the past and I intend to give it to you. Marry me, Brittannia. I'll love the baby as if it were my own and no one need ever know. We'll tell my mother tonight that you are carrying my child. I've already told my father."

"You what? How could you?" she exclaimed. "Brian, I can't marry you!"

"The man who planted his seed in you is not worthy to be the father of your baby. If he were, he would have married you!" he thundered.

"Brian, please," she begged. "I don't wish to discuss this any further."

"What kind of a man plays with a young woman's affection, gets her with child, and then abandons her to have the child on her own?" Brian went on. "I'll tell you, a man who is a coward and a scoundrel. He isn't worthy of your loyalty!"

Brittannia grew angry with his words and was ready to tell him so, but she held herself back.

"Brian, please. Don't upset yourself," she pleaded weakly.

"I love you, I can't help but upset myself! I want to marry you, I want to raise the child within you as my own!" He moved toward her and as he spoke the words he ran a hand gently across her midsection.

Brittannia pushed his hand away. "I can't marry you," she said. "I am already married."

The silence in the room seemed too much to bear and she slowly chanced a look at him. He stood staring at her, his brown eyes filled with hurt, tears near brimming over his lashes.

"Truly, I didn't mean to hurt you," she said. "You've been so kind to me."

Finally, after an eternity it seemed, he spoke. "Kind?" he asked. "Kind is what I've been to you? Brittannia, you've been much more than that to me! You've been the woman I want to marry, the woman I want to share the rest of my life with! Is that all I've been to you, *kind?*" he asked, cruelly grabbing hold of her arm and squeezing it tightly, waiting for an answer.

"Brian, you are hurting me!" she gasped as he yanked her to him with his savage grip.

"Hurting you?" he asked, his voice growing with hysteria. "What about the father of your child, the man who used you and cast you aside? The man whose whore you were?"

Brittannia brought her hand back and then slapped him with all the force she could muster. The blow brought a sting to her palm but had no effect on Brian.

"Who is he?" he demanded. "Who is the father of your child?"

"Don't do this, Brian," she pleaded. "Don't do this, please!"

"Who is he?" he thundered and nearly brought her to her knees with his vicious hold on her wrist.

"He's—he's Dain. Captain Dain Barclay," she gasped.

Brian's brown eyes opened wide and with one great shove he pushed her roughly away from him, as if she had the plague.

"Barclay!" he roared. "You had me traipsing across the country to obtain his order of release!"

Brittannia, not knowing what else to do, nodded her head. She had never seen Brian like this before. He frightened her.

"Barclay!" he spat. "Barclay is your lover, your husband, the father of the child within you?" He reached into his jacket pocket and withdrew a packet of papers. "I'll be damned if I'll see him released now! He can rot in that fort for all I care!"

"No!" Brittannia screamed as she lunged for the papers, those precious papers of release that she'd waited so long for. "Please, Brian. Please reconsider!"

"Go to hell, Brittannia!" he yelled and strode angrily from the room, shoving the papers deep into his pocket, out of her reach.

Chapter 18

Brittannia fell to the floor in a heap, her sobs uncontrollably convulsing her body. How did things turn out this way? How did she let things become so mixed up, so terrible? She'd planned so long for the day when Dain's release papers would come and now it was all for naught!

She lay sobbing on her knees for a while until, with concentrated effort, she stood and wiped the tears away. The sun had long since gone down and the room had become dark and cold. She didn't care, she wanted darkness, she wanted the black night to hide her shame, hide the tears that spilled from her lashes. She'd done Brian a terrible wrong. Dain would probably never be released if Brian had his way and no doubt he would!

"Damn!" she yelled aloud as she hit her fist on the back of the padded chair near her. "What am I to do? I've got to get Dain out of there!"

She stood for a moment longer in the darkened room, her fists clenching and unclenching. Then with an iciness in her turquoise eyes and determined set to her chin, she took a deep breath and left the room for the warmer rooms upstairs. She walked like a sleep-walker, her gaze fixed straight ahead, her mind filled with what she was about to do. Once in her rooms, she opened her sea chest and dug deep into it, pushing a few articles of clothing from her way.

The small handgun felt heavy in her hand as she moved it up and down, testing its weight. She slipped her finger near the trigger, and aiming the revolver to an imaginary object on the far wall, she pulled it. The click as the empty chamber fell into line with the barrel was loud, metallic, and deadly. She shuddered. She hoped the prison guards would accept her bribe of money and release Dain into her custody. But if they didn't, she would be quite prepared to use force. Carefully she placed the revolver on a nearby chest of drawers and went to her closet. She rummaged through the many clothes until she found a large, fur-lined cloak. It would help conceal her weapon and if she and Dain must flee on foot, it would provide warmth in the night.

She took the cloak and draped it across the bed. The maid had turned down the covers and a fire burned in the hearth, but Brittannia ignored both of these luxuries and instead crossed the room to the chair beside the window. She sat down and waited for the sunrise. She had a long wait.

At long last the sun peeked above the horizon, its rays sending down light but no warmth. Brittannia left her window seat, and tucking the revolver into the waistband of her skirt, tied a bag heavy with money around her wrist, and drew the heavy cloak about her, securing the strings of the hood beneath her chin. Slowly she descended the stairs and left the town house. She didn't expect to ever see it again and she didn't care whether she did or not. Her carriage was waiting as she had instructed, and with a sort of detachment, she climbed into the conveyance.

She wasn't tired from her sleepless night, her body was tense, ready to spring while her mind was calm as if she watched an interesting play and she was the main character. The biting wind whipped into the carriage and she breathed deeply of it, wanting to feel the cold, wanting to feel something.

The carriage came to a halt at the sentry box outside Fort Lafayette and the sentry, half awake, ambled out to see who wanted in. Brittannia was quick to explain she had important business, she needed to see a prisoner. The guard was loath to let her in, but when Brittannia pressed a few bills into his palm he quickly consented and her carriage passed into Fort Lafayette. Getting to see Dain wasn't as easy. The young corporal, the same who had let her visit with the prisoners on the long ago day with Brian, was not willing to let her visit with the captain today.

"Sir," she said, interrupting the man for the fifth time. He was sitting at his desk seemingly absorbed with the paper that lay in front of him. The same paper, Brittannia noticed, that had lain in front of him for the past forty-five minutes. "I do wish you would let me see Captain Dain Barclay. It is very important that I do."

The young man regarded her for a moment, his small

eyes darting up and down her cloaked form. "The captain is to have no visitors today, ma'am. That's my orders."

"Why?" she demanded. Had Brian seen to it that she would never be able to get to him? Surely he could not have had those orders issued so quickly, she thought, but as the minutes ticked by and the corporal did not answer, she was not so sure. "Why can I not speak with Captain Barclay?" she pressed.

The man threw his writing utensil onto the stack of papers in front of him. "I'm trying to do my work, ma'am. Please take a seat and when the prisoner you request to see is available for guests, I'll let you know!"

Brittannia drew up with his words. She whirled from him and made her way to the crude bench that ran along the wall. She'd sit until she had blisters, she vowed to herself!

Slowly the minutes turned into hours. She was stiff and sore but she wasn't willing to get up and leave, nor was she willing to doff her heavy cloak. She still had the revolver tucked into the waistband of her skirt. She ran a hand along the back of her neck, massaging the tight muscles there and as she looked toward the ceiling she heard another man enter the small anteroom. He was dressed the same as the young corporal and it was obvious the two were good friends. Greeting each other, the newcomer had a tray of food in his arms. He set it upon the desk, covering the all-important papers the young man had been stewing over for hours. The papers were of little importance to the two men now as they shared a hearty noon meal and washed it down with a bottle of rum. Brittannia watched the pair and did not miss how their eyes darted to her and then how they would smirk at each other.

"Who's the lady?" the newcomer asked.

"A friend of the notorious blockade-running captain," the younger man supplied. "She claims she has important business to discuss with him."

The two laughed jovially as they again looked to Brittannia. She seethed under the sound of their laughter. They acted as if she were deaf and dumb and couldn't understand they were talking about her. Her fists clenched and unclenched with anger as she stared at the two young men. They were just boys sent to do a man's job and they were making light of the situation, not at all seeing to their duties. They should have allowed her to see Dain or at least have taken the basket of provisions she'd brought along for him.

With a determined set to her chin, she stood and once again approached the corporal. "I'd like to speak with Captain Barclay now."

The young corporal looked to his friend, and as he took a healthy swig of the rum and passed it across the desk, he smiled. "He isn't allowed any visitors," he finally said. "I told you that before. But," he added as he gave his friend a sly look, "if it's a man you need, I'm available."

The two men laughed uproariously and Brittannia wondered where their superiors were. "I demand to see Captain Barclay," she said as she stood her ground.

"You can demand all you want," the young corporal said, "but you aren't going to get it."

The two again erupted into a fit of laughter and Brittannia stood regarding them, her hand straying inside her cloak to the hidden revolver. She sized up the two men: They were both small and obviously besotted with rum. Her eyes darted to where both their rifles had been carelessly laid and she judged the distance not too far. She could easily bound over there and with a swoop of her other arm she could encircle the young corporal's neck and hold him at gunpoint. What she would do from there she wasn't sure. She just knew she had to do something to get Dain freed.

"Oh?" She sauntered nearer the corporal. "Are you quite sure I'll not get what I want?" She swayed her hips, and although she was covered by the voluminous folds of her cloak, the movement was evident. She tossed her head and carelessly lifted her hand to undo the bun of hair at the nape of her neck. Her insides turned at the sickening display she was giving these lewd men.

"Are you trying to vamp me, ma'am?" the young corporal asked as he nervously licked his lips. "I'm to keep an eye for vamping women."

"Me?" she asked innocently, resting one hip on the desktop. "Why, I only came here to see an old friend. But if I can't see him," she said, waving a hand in the air, "then why should I deny myself?" She thrust her shoulder forward and rested her chin near it, all the while smiling provocatively at the young man.

He blushed and looked nervously to his friend.

"Well, Corporal," she began huskily, "when does your shift end? Surely you don't work all the day long?"

The young man stood, a grin on his pocked face. Brittannia felt her heart sink as she spied the gun in a holster on his person. She chanced a look at the other man and was relieved when she saw no holster. He saw her looking at him and he smiled at her, his young face moving into a leering grin. She shivered beneath her warm cloak and turned her attentions back to the man with the gun. She would have to get close enough to get his gun away from him.

"I'm off duty as of now," the young corporal said as he reached a hand up and ran it along Brittannia's arm. "There's a room a few yards down. We could do it there, then John here could have a roll with you too."

Brittannia felt her stomach turn. She'd take the young corporal to this room, get his gun away from him, somehow render him unconscious, then come back for the other man. If he didn't take her offer of money to release Dain then she'd hold him at gunpoint until she got what she wanted.

"Well," she said coyly, "are you one to keep a lady waiting?" She pushed a strand of hair from her face and moved away from the desk, being sure to make her cloak and skirts sway. The young corporal was right behind her as she made her way to the door of the anteroom when the portal was thrust open and a tall figure barred the doorway.

Brian Keyes took in the scene before him and his brown eyes rested on Brittannia. Her hand flew to her heart. She was sure he was going to give her away and have her arrested for conspiracy! She stood waiting for him to give the orders and when he finally spoke, she was surprised by his words.

"I have an order for the release of Captain Dain Barclay into my custody," he said, the authoritativeness in his voice ringing through the room. "See to it, Corporal," he ordered. "I want the man brought out and put in my carriage. Now!"

The young corporal was suddenly all business, straight and at attention. He took one look at the papers Brian thrust under his nose and then he hustled to bring Dain out. Brittannia stood rooted to her spot wondering what had changed Brian's mind, what had made him come to Fort Lafayette.

"Brian," she started, "why did—"

"Hush," he ordered. "Get into my carriage and wait for us."

Brittannia nodded her head dumbly and quickly left the anteroom.

She was breathless by the time Brian climbed into the carriage. Dain had to be helped into the conveyance, and once on the padded leather seat, let his head fall against Brittannia's shoulder.

"Brittannia," he managed through his cracked lips.

Tears pushed by her thick lashes and fell unbidden down her cheeks as the carriage pulled away from the squalid confines of Fort Lafayette. Brian yelled directions out the window to Brittannia's town house to the driver.

"Why?" she finally asked Brian as Dain drifted in and out of consciousness, his head still leaning against her shoulder. "Why did you come?"

Brian looked at Dain and then at Brittannia. His words were slow and full of pain. "Because I love you, Brittannia. And if Barclay loves you half as much as I, then he deserves to be with you. If his love for you is near as much as mine, then his life without you has been hell."

Brittannia was silent and the carriage rocked to and fro, gently moving its riders. She listened to him, not interrupting.

"I realized I could never have you, your heart belongs to him, and so I reasoned that one of us should have you, my love. If not me, then Barclay. He is a very lucky man. I wish it were my baby growing within you."

Brittannia swallowed hard. "Brian, I am so sorry," she began. "I've done you wrong and I only hope you can forgive me. I should never have lied to you but—"

He leaned over and put a finger to her lips, stopping her words. "But you love Barclay. Please, Brittannia, I don't want to hear you say those words. Although I know it's true, I couldn't bear to hear you say it."

Brittannia nodded her head, her golden hair brushing her arms. She took his hand in hers and held tightly onto it. "You are a very dear friend," she said. "And if I'd never met Dain, I know you'd be the man I'd choose to marry."

He gave her an understanding smile. "I know and had I known that years ago, I would have made tracks to the Cotswolds to claim your heart."

"I love you, Brian. I do."

"But not the way you love him."

Brittannia nodded as a tear trickled down her cheek and she lovingly caressed Dain's unshaven cheek. He looked so pale, so gaunt. Would she ever be able to nurse him back to health? Gently she eased him away from her shoulder then quickly slipped her cloak off, covering the front of Dain's body with it, then bringing his head back to rest on her shoulder as she entwined her arms around him, holding him tight. How she had missed him! She felt her tears sting her eyes as her hands massaged his body, letting her love and strength flow into him. She put trembling lips to his ear, she whispered, "God, how I've missed you. When I first heard the *Airlee* was hit I thought I'd never see you again!" She stopped talking then, tears making it impossible to speak anymore.

Dain reached a strong hand up, grasping tightly onto one of hers. He gave it a reassuring squeeze. "I've been dead inside these many weeks without you but we're together now," he whispered hoarsely, his eyes drinking in the sight of her. He closed his eyes then, as he brought her hand to his lips and placed a kiss upon the palm of it. "My strength is coming back into me with just your touch, your scent."

Brittannia leaned her fair head against his dark one, a lustrous rain of curls falling against his cheek. He sighed contentedly as he breathed in the sweet fragrance of her clean locks.

Brian watched the scene uncomfortably. "I requested my family doctor to meet me at your town house." His voice was barely audible in the small confines of the moving carriage. "He'll tend to Dain and to you if he feels you need medical attention."

The bright moon rode high in the night sky, casting the shimmering snow in a bluish light and illuminating Brittannia's town house bedroom with soft radiance. Dain lay sleeping naked in the huge bed, his body

412

washed and cleaned of all vermin, his face shaven, his breathing even. Brittannia sat beside him, content to just look at him. Every now and then she would let gentle fingers stray from her lap to caress his face or outline his lips.

When they had arrived at the town house the doctor had prescribed a hot meal, a hot bath, medicine, and plenty of rest, all of which Dain had received promptly and in that order.

Slowly Dain opened his eyes and when he saw her, he spread his lips into a smile. "You are a vision to wake up to," he whispered.

She gave him a soft smile as she entwined her fingers with his. "How do you feel?"

"Better than I have in weeks!"

"Hungry?"

"Mmm-hmm," he murmured. "But not for food."

Brittannia moved back in her chair a bit as she recognized the light of desire that lit his soft gray eyes. "The doctor prescribed plenty of rest and that is exactly what I plan to see you get."

One dark eyebrow lifted skeptically. Brittannia ignored it as she stood.

"I'll get some hot soup for you and there is fresh-baked br—"

Dain sat up in bed, all evidence of his prison stay gone as he reached a strong arm out and grabbed hold of Brittannia's wrist before she could get away.

"Later," he said as he pulled her gently down on the bed beside him.

"Captain," she gasped. "Your strength surprises me!"

How many sleepless nights had she spent in this large bed, alone, afraid, her body aching for want of his touch? Now he was beside her, holding her. She felt a wave of peace wash over her as he slowly undid the fastens of her large robe with one hand while the other ran gentle fingers through her unpinned hair.

She stopped his hand before he had a chance to slip it through the opening of her gown and caress her body. "I've something to tell you," she whispered as she drew his searching hand away from her midsection to her lips. "Something very special." She planted a moist kiss on each of his fingertips. "I'm—we're going to have a baby."

"Mmm-hmm, I know," he said, planting a sweet kiss upon her pert nose.

"You know?" she echoed. "How do you know?"

"I know," he started as he ran a tracing finger from the hollow of her throat down and over her protruding belly, "every dip and curve of your beautiful body." His fingers pushed her night robe out of his way until the rounded curves of her were exposed to him, the tenuous material of her nightdress hiding nothing from his gaze. "I can see you are with child in your eyes, in the flush of your cheeks. You wear it like an invisible raiment. I could tell from the moment I awoke, from the moment you smiled down at me."

He rubbed his large hand across her full belly as his eyes looked deeply into hers and she was moved by the naked emotion in those gray orbs. Oh dear God, how she'd missed him!

She wrapped her arms around his neck and clung tightly to him, not wanting anything or anyone to take

414

him away from her ever again. "Oh, Dain," she cried, showering his neck with kisses, "my darling, darling Dain."

"Shh," he soothed, easing her gently down on the bed. "I'm here now."

"Love me," she whispered.

He helped her to ease out of her nightdress and slowly, delicately he explored her body, so new to him now that she was filled with his child, their child, the product of their love. With his hands, with his tender mouth, he brought her pleasure, bringing her to the highest peaks.

He held her with a fierce, sweet tenderness that caused a tear to spill from her lashes down her smooth cheek where he kissed it away as he kissed away all the pain and hurt she'd experienced in his absence. His lips, those same soft lips she had dreamt about so many times in this big, empty bed, blazed intimate trails across her milky flesh, always coming back to her mouth. Always he would return there, lingering, enticing, giving, and Brittannia responded as never before. His slow, gentle caresses brought forth from her a flaming passion that burned bright within her. She loved this world only they shared, this world where only he could bring her: it was bright, yet seductively dark and it was where yearnings of the flesh were met, where their bodies came together and became one.

She entwined her fingers through the silky, black curls at the nape of his neck as he ran teasing, flicking kisses down her throat and then to the hard peaks of her full breasts.

"So beautiful," he murmured as he massaged their

fullness and showered them with kisses. "God, I've missed you. Night and day my thoughts were filled with you, visions of you lying beneath me . . . Never again will we be apart!"

"Never!" she echoed, arching her back and rubbing her body against his.

"All those long days of wondering if I'd ever see you again, ever be able to hold you in my arms . . ." His voice broke as he brought his mouth to hers and crushed it with an intense kiss.

Brittannia could feel the love flow from him and the feel of it caused a tug on her heart as she entwined her arms about him and held him tight, wishing she could erase all the hurt his time in prison had given them. "I'm so sorry," she whispered, breaking the kiss and placing her lips to his temple. "So sorry you had to go through what you did."

He lifted his head and let his eyes gaze down to hers for long, tender moments as his hands came up to caress her cheeks and run gentle fingers through her hair. "I thought I'd never again see the sunlight catch in your hair, or see this beautiful mouth that can pout just as beautifully as it can smile." He ran the forefinger of one hand across her full, bottom lip as he spoke. "Brittannia, you are everything to me and I'm the luckiest man alive to be given one more chance at happiness with you . . . and our baby."

"Oh, Dain—how I love you! How happy you make me!"

Their bodies came together then, meeting with great urgency as love spilled from each and they clung to each other as never before. Caught up in a fever of bared emotions and passion they were soon lost in the whirlwind that swept them upward and blew away all the pain of the past weeks. It was a storm wind that cleansed them and fed them, making their wanting keen and undeniable.

Unable to hold back any longer, he rolled on the great bed, bringing her on top of him and soon it became a bed of ecstasy as he gently entered her and took her to soaring heights, moving within her, ever mindful of the life now growing within her—the life they created . . . their love created.

Brittannia's long locks cascaded waterfall-like down around their locked bodies, covering them like a tenuous rain of bright, sun-touched gold. It was a world of splendor they entered, one where only beautiful things could be found, one where darkness never touched, one where every desire would be joyously met. And Dain, expert lover that he was and one deeply in love, brought to Brittannia fulfillment such as she had never known, fulfillment that made her sigh in contentment and caused a tear of joy to slip from her closed eyes. She felt him let go within her, felt his body shudder as he held her tightly. She nuzzled her face against his neck. *Together at last,* she thought. *And never again to be apart* . . .

When finally their passions were spent they lay in each other's arms, Dain's hand possessively covering her rounded belly, and they both slept—the first peaceful sleep either had had in weeks.

"Rise and shine," Dain yelled in a booming voice as

he entered the bedroom. "Early to bed, early to rise, the early bird gets the worm and all that!" he added as he whipped open the heavy drapes to let the blinding sunlight pour into the room.

"Ohh," Brittannia moaned as she snuggled deeper into the downy softness of the warm bed. "Don't speak to me of worms or food! And shut those drapes, I'm trying to sleep!"

Dain ignored her sleepy protests and yanked the warm covers from her body. "Sleep?" he bellowed jovially. "You've done nothing but all morning long. Now get up, we're leaving for Nassau today. Our ship leaves in a few hours."

Brittannia sat upright. "Leaving? Today?"

Dain nodded his dark head as he offered her his hand and pulled her up from the cozy bed. He had recovered rapidly in just a few short weeks and now he was his former self again. His dark hair was brushed away from his face, the curly locks looking a luscious black, enhanced by the golden highlights that touched most of them. His face was freshly shaven and Brittannia could smell the spicy scent of his cologne as he moved about the room with a quick, light step. Somewhere he had purchased a new suit of the darkest blue that looked nearly black. He wore his top coat open and his vest had yet to be buttoned as did the top buttons of his pristine white shirt. He did indeed look handsome.

Brittannia rubbed the sleep from her eyes as Dain drew a warm dressing robe about her shoulders. "But you didn't tell me we were leaving."

"You didn't ask."

She smiled at him as her sleepiness began to leave her

and she sat down in front of the vanity to brush her bed-tangled hair. She had a lot to do before leaving New York. She had to see to the packing and she must not forget and pay Brian one last visit. She hadn't seen him since the day Dain had been released.

"I have someone to see before leaving," she told Dain as she ran the brush through her golden tresses.

"If you're speaking of Brian Keyes," Dain said knowingly as he met her eyes in the mirror, "he's downstairs. He and I breakfasted together, in fact, he is the one who obtained our passage. You don't think any Northerner would allow me to go right back to Nassau, do you?"

So Brian had come to their aid again. "He's a fine man, isn't he, Dain?"

"Yes, but I would never leave you two alone for very long. It doesn't take a seer to realize he has deep feelings for you."

Brittannia's brush stopped in mid-stroke.

"But he has a level head," Dain added. "And once we are out of New York he will begin to come to terms with his feelings."

"Yes," she agreed. Brian would be fine once she was out of his life.

The sun rode high in the cloudless sky and Brittannia was beginning to feel the heat as the large steamer made its way past the landmarks that had become so familiar to her: the Narrows, Potter's Cay, Hog and Athol Islands. She stood on the rolling deck, her arm through Dain's as they watched the Nassau harbor loom closer.

The familiar mast-matted wharf was a glorious sight indeed.

"Just like an old and dear friend," Dain remarked as he gently squeezed her arm in the crook of his. "Forever there to welcome you."

Brittannia agreed and was surprised to feel the lump of emotion form in her throat. Nassau! After cold, gray, war-drab New York, New Providence Island seemed like a paradise, a small jewel filled with never-ending sunshine, long, lazy days and moon-drenched evenings—beautiful!

"Happy to be home?" Dain inquired.

Brittannia turned her face up to him, her turquoise eyes bright, rivaling the brilliant sunshine. "Home is wherever you are, my love."

He leaned his dark head toward her and as he lifted her chin with his free hand, he placed a sweet kiss upon her mouth.

"You are beautiful," he said. "Even if your dress is a little too tight," he added on impulse as a teasing smile touched his lips.

"Dain," she said, drawing out his name, and looking around her to see if any of the other passengers were staring at her. "You are not to remind me! Can I help it if all the clothing I purchased in New York is too warm for this clime and that all the things I brought to New York are now too tight?" Then after she made sure no one was staring outright at her she chanced a quick look down at herself. "Is it very evident? I mean, do I look as if I'm with child?"

"Of course it is and of course you do."

She gave him a crestfallen look and then her eyes

420

quickly scanned the crowd to judge how many people would notice if she fled pell-mell to her cabin.

"You look lovely," Dain assured her. "In fact, you have never looked healthier. You have a radiant glow about and I love you."

She eyed him carefully. "Are you sure?" She had become very self-conscious of her body. Perhaps she could stay in hiding until the baby was born, she thought. Oh no, that would never do. She wanted to see Michael and Esmée and tell them the good news and then she wanted Dain and her to go to her home in the Cotswolds so she could give birth there. She would, she finally decided, have to get used to the idea of being big and ungainly.

"I'm positive," he replied and gave her a wink.

The steamer finally made port and Brittannia and Dain were nearly the first passengers off. The familiar smells and noises greeted them with a rush and Brittannia felt herself step into another world. One made of strong, daring men and free-spirited women. The ill wind that blew the States such sorrow blew untold riches to Nassau and those riches were ever evident on the quays and in the warehouses. Brittannia breathed deeply and smiled up at Dain. It felt wonderful to walk beside her husband, the most successful blockade runner, the most daring captain, not to mention the most handsome man she had ever met. She held her head high and was proud to be on the arm of the once-most-sought-after man in Nassau. He probably still was, she thought as she met the eyes of a passing woman. The bold redhead swung her hips and gave a provocative thrust of one bared shoulder as she passed by and Brittannia didn't miss the look of rivalry in her green eyes. Brittannia smiled at her, thinking they had one thing in common: good taste in men.

"Should we stop in and see how Delving is faring?" Dain asked, oblivious to the provocative stare from the redhead. "He's probably worried half out of his mind about where you ran off to."

"About me? What about you? You are the one who was hauled off by the Federals!"

Dain chuckled good-naturedly as his hold on her tightened and he led her through the throng of people to Bay Street and the offices of Henry Adderly and Company. The small bell atop the outer door jangled sassily, as it always did, when they entered. Michael stood near the desk in the corner, his back to them. He was seemingly engrossed in conversation with the man seated there.

"Michael, ol' boy!" Dain said in his timbered voice. "How the hell have you been?"

Michael whirled and in a moment was across the room and taking Dain in a bear hug.

"How did you make it here?" Michael asked.

"By steamer, naturally," Dain replied, a twinkle in his gray eyes.

"I mean, how did you get out of prison?"

"Oh, that. Well, it's a long story. It was all Brittannia's doing and we'll tell you later."

"Yes, over dinner," Brittannia added.

"Of course, over dinner," Dain replied. "Right now if you've the time."

"Yes, now," Brittannia said excitedly. "I'm starved!"

Michael looked from one to the other, his brown

eyes smiling. "I knew from the beginning you two were a match!" Over his shoulder, he said to the young man still seated at the desk, "I'm off to lunch. And you have my blessings to wet your tongue and fill your belly also." He drew his money clip and tossed back a slim wad of bills. "Today is a celebration!" he exclaimed as he turned back to Dain and Brittannia. "My two favorite people are with me once again and, I daresay, one of them is with child!"

Brittannia instantly blushed. "Michael!" she exclaimed, embarrassed that he had announced it so loudly and that he had noticed so soon.

"Brittannia," he replied. "You look lovely and the baby will be lovely and I will make a lovely godfather!"

"How very subtle of you," Dain remarked good-naturedly.

"Indeed," Brittannia said, "you will make the best godfather a baby ever had!"

"I knew it," he said as he straightened his tie and winked one brown eye.

Dain wrapped a strong arm around the back of Michael's neck and guided him toward the outer door.

"I, my friend, would love to stand and discuss your redeeming qualities and all that but the fare on that poor excuse of a steamer that brought us here was even a poorer excuse for food and I've been thinking about nothing but the delectable shrimp the Royal Victoria dining room serves. Shall we go?"

Out on the sun-splashed streets of Nassau, Michael questioned, "Now, how did Brittannia manage to get you out of a Federal prison? No, no, don't tell me. Let me guess." He thought for a moment, then after a long look in Brittannia's direction, he said, "She stormed in brandishing a gun and demanding your release!"

Both Brittannia and Dain laughed. "Yes," they chimed as one, "that's about it!"

Michael rolled his eyes heavenward, shaking his head.

When she was able to stop laughing at the vision of herself charging into the barracks with a loaded pistol and screaming like a banshee, Brittannia said, "It wasn't really like that. We did have some outside, or should I say inside help."

"I've a feeling your story is going to make an interesting conversation piece over lunch," Michael commented as they stepped onto the veranda of the Royal Victoria and entered the large hotel.

The days passed slowly, each one spent leisurely and enjoyably. Brittannia could feel the baby grow within her with each passing day and she was anxious for Dain and she to be off for the Cotswolds. A few more weeks and she wouldn't be able to travel. Her doctor had informed her that she really shouldn't travel at all, but she wanted to give birth to her firstborn in England. She liked their home on Queen Street, in fact, she loved it, but it just wasn't where she wanted to give birth to their baby. She wanted to have their baby at the manor house, the same house she was born in, the same house her father was born in. It meant a lot to her to return to the Cotswolds at this most important time of her life.

"How was your day, love?" she inquired as Dain entered the large bedroom.

He gave her a warm smile as he discarded his frock

coat on a nearby chair and began to undo the buttons of his white lawn shirt.

"Very well," he replied. "I've made a few business decisions that I am happy about."

"I'm glad," she replied, deciding that now was the time to bring up the subject of their returning to the Cotswolds. "Dain," she began, "I've something I wish to discuss. I know you've never approached the subject but as time goes by I feel the need to return home. I want to have our baby in the manor house. I want to return to England."

Dain stopped his task, his fingers still, as he held one button between its buttonhole. "What?"

"I want to return to England."

"Brittannia, this is our home."

Brittannia's mouth opened wide. "No, this is not our home. Our home is in the Cotswolds. I—we own a vast estate there and I wish to return to it."

"You said home is wherever we are together. We are together here in Nassau."

"Yes, I said that, but I meant that home was with you and, well, I just assumed that once you quit running the blockade we could return to England."

Dain stood regarding her, a surprised look on his face. "Quit running the blockade? Is that what you think I've done? Just because the *Airlee* was sunk you think I'll quit running?"

It was Brittannia's turn to look surprised. "Yes, of course!"

"Brittannia, I'm planning a run for the coming weeks. A new ship, another cargo. Surely you must have realized that is what I've been doing all these past days."

"No," she said breathlessly. "I did not."

Dain forgot his task of unbuttoning his shirt and crossed the room to stand before her. She sat perfectly still; the small quilt she was making for the baby lay on her lap, forgotten. Dain looked down at her, his gray eyes turning stormy.

"Brittannia, you never mentioned you wished to have our baby in England."

"Did I have to?" she asked in a whisper, tears beginning to spring into her sad eyes. "You never said you planned to make another run."

"Did I have to?"

She sat and pondered his question. She should have known he would make another run and then another. Why had she not realized that? Why had she fooled herself? A single tear coursed down one lovely cheek.

"Do you have to go? Can't you stay? Can't you take me home?" she asked, her voice quivering, her heart aching because she knew the answer to her questions.

"Brittannia, darling," he said as he knelt beside her and gently took the half-finished quilt from her. "It is something I feel I must do. I've explained all of that to you."

"But our baby, what if something should happen to you?" She was crying openly now, her voice choked with her sobs. "Please don't go. Please."

Dain stood and she could tell her plea was a great strain on him. She knew how much running the blockade meant to him, how he needed to help his family, the family that was lost long ago to him. She felt terrible for asking this of him, but she had come too close to losing him, he had come too close to dying for running the blockade.

"I have to do it," he finally said as he looked out the sheer-curtained windows, toward the water. "You know that, don't you?"

"Yes," she sobbed. "I know. But do you know that I feel you should make the sacrifice and come to England with me? Don't you know I want you there when our baby is born?"

"Come to England with you?" he asked incredulously. "Be there when you have my baby? Of course I'll be here when you have my baby!" he thundered. "For you'll give birth here in Nassau. You won't be going to England! You're my wife and I'm telling you to stay in Nassau with me!"

Brittannia, in her dejection, became incensed with his words. He was demanding her to stay in Nassau. How could he do such a thing? It was so very important for her to have this baby in the Cotswolds, in her own bedchamber, with Ella beside her. "No!" she cried, coming quickly to her feet. "I'm having this baby in England."

Dain's stormy eyes clashed with her blazing turquoise ones.

"You are my wife, you'll do as I say!"

"I may be your wife, Dain Barclay, but I am still my own person and like all the Dennings before me, my baby will be born in the Cotswolds. With or without your consent I'm going home to England!"

Their eyes held for a long tension-filled minute until Dain consciously tried to cool his temper.

"Brittannia," he began, "I've things to do. Important things. Please try to understand."

"I cannot understand you wanting to make another run to Wilmington. It is foolishness. The blockade has become so tight and there are rumors that Fort Fisher will be overtaken soon. Please, please," she begged. "Don't do it. Please come with me."

He stood for a moment, his eyes staring into hers. Finally, he said, "I have to, Brittannia. Don't you see?"

She shook her head. "Not at all. You are soon to be a father. You have a family to think of. Your child—our child deserves a father. What will I ever do if the Federals kill you this run?"

"No one will kill me. I know what I'm doing!"

"I'll not have you risking your life anymore."

"My decision has been made."

"Why?" she asked. "Why would you want to risk your life for a dying cause? The South is nearly choked as it is. Will you leave me a widow and your child fatherless for some debt you feel you owe to your family? They threw you out, remember? You owe them nothing, you don't need to risk your life!"

Dain grabbed her roughly by the shoulders, his reason gone from him with her words. "I owe them. I owe them my life!"

"Hah!" she spat, pushing him away. "You don't! You owe this baby inside of me. You owe this child a happy home, a secure future, a place upon your knee and in your heart."

"I know that," he said. "And I'll give it. I'm leaving now, Brittannia and when I return I hope to find you in a more congenial mood."

"If you walk out that door now, I swear I'll return to England without you!"

"I'm leaving," he repeated and crossed the room to retrieve his frock coat. He quietly left the room.

"Damn you!" she cried as she hurled the nearest

object at the now-closed door. The delicate vase shattered into a thousand jagged pieces, just as her dream had shattered. The dream of Dain and she living a happy, carefree life in the Cotswolds.

"Damn you," she sobbed again as she picked up the tiny quilt and hugged it to her heaving breasts.

Chapter 19

Brittannia felt nothing as she stood near the rail of the steamer and watched New Providence Island become smaller and smaller. She seemed not to notice the brilliant display of color as the sun dipped low on the far horizon and cast the few clouds in a glorious reddish gold light. She was numb, she was dead inside, she was leaving Dain.

"Brittannia," Esmée said, trying to draw her friend out of her reverie. "You've made your decision, now live with it. He will soon learn he cannot live without you and he'll leave Nassau, you will see."

"Thank you, Esmée," Brittannia said. "You are a true friend. I don't know if I agree with you but I am most grateful you consented to come to the Cotswolds with me."

Esmée waved a slim, gloved hand in the air as if it were no bother to leave her Jacques in Nassau and accompany Brittannia.

"I couldn't have you traveling alone, now could I? I still cannot fathom why your doctor would allow you to travel. Why, in four short months the baby is due!"

Brittannia turned away and for the first time that evening noticed the sunset. "He didn't give his permission. I didn't tell him." She could hear the sharp click of Esmée's tongue. "I feel fine," she assured the raven-haired woman, "truly I do. My baby will be born in England and nothing will stop me from getting there!"

"You are positively the most stubborn person I've ever met, *chérie,*" Esmée commented. "That husband of yours is just as bull-headed and I can see clearly that it will be totally my job to watch over you and your baby."

The dinner gong sounded from somewhere along the deck. "At last," Esmée said. "I'm near starving. I do hope the food is decent enough to pick at."

Brittannia walked with Esmée to the dining saloon and absently wondered if anything would ever taste good or look good, or feel good again. Her heart was heavy and she felt a terrible void in her life. She felt miserable.

A light snow fell from the sky and the whole world outside the carriage was covered with the white stuff. Brittannia knew that beneath that pristine blanket lay the English country that, during cool summers, gently rolled with green pastures and sylvan glades. She pulled her lap robe more closely about her legs and then reached a slim hand up to push an errant blond curl back into the hood of her ermine-trimmed cape. She was cozy and comfortable for the first time during the long trip from Nassau to England. The familiar landscape that passed slowly by the carriage window

432

brought back memories of other times, other faces and she felt she'd been gone too long.

"We're almost there, Esmée," she said excitedly as she turned to her friend. Esmée sat beside her, her red lips pursed as she surveyed the scene outside the window. She was a vision in white: white cape lined with white fur, white gloves and white, soft leather boots. Her ebony hair and cat-green eyes looked all the more startling and beautiful against the simplicity of color.

"Brittannia, dear," Esmée said hesitantly, "I do so hate to be the one to bring the curtain down on your play, but are we actually going to live this *far* from civilization?"

"Far? If you ask me this isn't far enough!"

Esmée shot her an astonished look. "Surely you jest."

"You will love it here, I promise!"

"But what does one do to pass the time?" Esmée asked, the look on her pretty face holding no hope.

"Trust me, Esmée. You will soon learn to love the relaxed way of life."

"Ah, *chérie,* I doubt that. But for our friendship I will give it a try."

The carriage came to a halt. "I won't be able to make the small hill, Miss—I mean, Mrs. Barclay," the footman said as he jumped from his perch and opened the door.

Brittannia had sent word earlier that she would be returning today and she realized it was unexpected news for all at the manor to learn she was a married woman, with child and without her husband.

"That is fine," she told him. Then turning to Esmée

she asked, "Are you in the mood for a winter walk?" Her turquoise eyes were bright with anticipation.

Esmée gave her a slanted look. "Walk up that hill, in your condition? Certainly not!"

"Oh, come! It will be fun!"

"Fun? Ha! It will be cold and wet and oh so tiring!"

Brittannia threw her own lap robe from her and bounded out the carriage door. "Nonsense!" she cried as she danced about in the snow. "It isn't a *hill,* it is just a slight incline."

Esmée rolled her eyes heavenward, and then with an audible sigh, she too climbed out of the conveyance. Together they made their way up the snowy incline to the manor house. They were both breathing hard by the time they crested the small hill and their breath made little puff clouds in front of their mouths.

Brittannia led the way and with a loud yell she burst through the wide oak doors. "Ella! I am home!"

A little old woman, rounded and gray, ambled to the foyer from some adjacent room. "Brittannia!" she exclaimed, and without a moment's hesitation gathered Brittannia up in her arms and hugged her tight. "Oh, my baby, you've been gone too long and just look at you!" The older woman held her back and took in Brittannia's full form. "Where is your husband? What have you done, Brittannia?"

Brittannia let Ella begin her many questions. She had been expecting Ella's disapproval. She knew Ella would say she should have stayed in Nassau with her husband, but she would deal with Ella later.

"Ella," she said, "this is a very dear friend of mine, Esmée de Remy, formerly Countess Esmée Rougeaux. She will be visiting with us until my baby is born, then

434

she will travel to London and meet her husband there."

Ella smiled a warm smile at Esmée. "So very pleased to meet you. You must forgive my manners. I just worry about my Brittannia, I feel responsible for her."

Esmée nodded.

"Has a guest room been prepared for Mrs. de Remy?" Brittannia asked as she slid her heavy cape from her body. She smiled warmly at the maid who took it from her.

"Yes," Ella confirmed, "rooms have been prepared and a hot meal also. Now, Brittannia, I want you to go upstairs and don fresh clothing, the hems of your skirts are wet from the snow. I just can't imagine what kind of a man would let his wife travel when her day of delivery is so near!"

"Ella, I do not wish to discuss it," Brittannia said, her tone brooking no argument. "This is my homecoming, the day should be merry. I'll hear no further remarks or questions about my husband."

Ella set her mouth into a straight line and nodded her gray head. "Very well," she sniffed. "You'll not hear another word about it this day from me."

"Good," Brittannia said, leaning over and planting an affectionate, quick kiss on the woman's sagging cheek. "Then I shan't worry about it until tomorrow when you will no doubt barrage me with a million questions and opinions."

"No doubt I will!" Ella opined. "Now, the both of you get along and I'll see how the evening meal is progressing."

Brittannia motioned for Esmée to follow, and side by side, they climbed the wide staircase to the second floor.

"I suspect they prepared the nicest guest room," Brittannia said as they made their way along the highly polished, gleaming wood floor. "It is just down the hall."

"Ella seems to already hold an innate dislike for Dain. I think, when he comes for you, he will have to summon up all of his charm to win her to his side," Esmée commented as Brittannia opened the door to the guest room.

"You seem overly confident that Dain will choose to come to England for me. I, myself, am not so sure."

"Ah, *chérie,* he will come, believe me. Before the babe is born your husband will be with you."

"I hope so, Esmée, for I don't look forward to giving birth without my husband near."

There was a short silence between them as they stood just inside the large guest room that was warmed and lit by a roaring fire in the hearth and the slanted rays of the setting sun through the windows.

"I am afraid," Brittannia finally said.

Esmée reached for Brittannia's hand and she clasped it tightly, reassuringly. "There is no need to be afraid. Ella and I are here and soon so will be your husband."

"I'm afraid of—" Brittannia paused as if speaking her fears would make them come true. She crossed the room and after closing the door, Esmée followed her. "My—my mother died in childbirth. My father blamed himself, you see, he was away at the time, on business in London. My mother had begged him not to go, she said she might go into labor early and she would need him to be with her. He—he," she closed her eyes tightly shut and, after swallowing, continued, "he told her that was nonsense and he would be home long before the babe

436

was born. He wasn't though. It was a black March day with howling winds that my mother called me to her side. She was frightened to death, for her water had broken nearly a day before. She knew she would die in labor and even though I was only seven years old, she called me into that dark, candle-lit room that smelled of sweat and impending birth. Oh, Esmée," she said, her face wet with tears, "I thought I would gag but I could see that she needed me and so I went to the bedside and held her shaking white hand. Her whole body was covered with sweat and she was swollen and blotched and I wondered why anyone would ever let such a thing happen."

"I'm so sorry," Esmée whispered.

Brittannia brought a tight fist to her mouth, trying to still her sobs. "She and the babe died that night. I would have had a brother or a sister, I don't know which, I never asked." She was crying openly now, her shoulders rising and falling with each ragged breath she took. "I am so afraid!"

Esmée gathered her in her arms and as she stroked Brittannia's hair, she soothed, "There is no need to worry. I am here and Ella and soon Dain will be too."

"No," Brittannia sobbed, finally giving in to all the grief she'd felt since leaving Nassau. "I don't think he will. Something tells me he won't!"

"You are being silly, Brittannia. Stop worrying."

"Oh," she exclaimed as she stepped out of Esmée's hold, "I truly don't think he will be here!"

"Brittannia," Esmée exclaimed, distraught at seeing her friend like this. "If he isn't here it is no matter, for you *will* survive. You are a fighter, you've been nothing but since we met and you will fight this battle as you

437

have fought all the others. You wanted to have your baby in England and here we are, in the dead of winter and in the middle of nowhere, but nonetheless here. Now pull yourself together!"

Brittannia continued to cry. She didn't want to be strong, she didn't want to do this alone. She felt terribly vulnerable. "And if I live through it then I will have all the years of raising my child alone. Oh, Esmée, I can remember nights when I would creep downstairs to my father's study to say another good night to him and he would be weeping and when I asked him why, he said he missed my mother and felt so very guilty that I had no mother to teach me the ways of a lady."

Esmée stood, waiting patiently. She was moved by Brittannia's story, true, but she realized if she were to help her, she must not succumb to the tears that stung the back of her green eyes. "You have done very well as a lady. Your father taught you well, and if Dain does not return, which he will," she added, "then you will raise your child just as well as your father raised you."

Brittannia stood for a while, staring at the fire as she contemplated Esmée's words. Her father had raised her well. He had weathered the worst storm, the storm of turbulent human emotions after losing a loved one. He had gone beyond his grief, had done well.

"Yes," Brittannia finally agreed. "You are right." Her father had been a fighter, her mother as well, and she wasn't about to let a fear, no matter if it were the fear of childbirth or the fear of never seeing Dain again conquer her. She would rebel against those fears, she would fight them.

"Thank you, Esmée," she said as she wiped away the tears. "I'll see you downstairs for dinner in thirty minutes. Is that too soon?"

Esmée's eyes grew large then returned to a normal size. "No, that is fine," she said with a smile.

"Good, for I'm starved!"

"Yes," Esmée agreed. "I'm quite ravenous myself!"

"It must be the country air. It makes one feel things."

"That it certainly does," Esmée mumbled as Brittannia bounded out the door. She turned to look at the long expanse of white-covered ground that lay outside her window. "It makes one want to rush back to civilization, even London with all its crowded streets and stench-filled air! Only Brittannia could drag me away from the social season," Esmée said aloud to herself, and she turned from the window and took a seat near the huge fire until her trunks were brought to her.

The months slipped by slowly, with Brittannia and Esmée occupying their time with walking, chess playing, reading, and hand crafts until the baby was born. Brittannia thought she might go mad waiting for the babe to arrive, and with each passing month as she grew larger and larger and the day drew nearer, she became more downhearted when Dain did not return and no word was heard from him. She had thought that once inside the walls she had grown up in, once inside her own bedroom, she would feel safe again, she would feel comforted and strong, but that wasn't so. The four walls proved to be nothing more than a gilded cage. She couldn't venture beyond them because of her delicate condition nor could she stand to stay within them because of all the solitude. Her thoughts soon became her worst enemy. She would leave one room in search of another, but her thoughts were always the same, her mind always determined to bring visions of Dain.

And her nights! All too often they were near endless and filled with the same dream: it seemed no sooner would she close her restless eyes then he would come to her. Always the place of meeting was the same, a place she had never been before yet was strangely familiar . . . comforting. It was always night, a warm summer night touched lightly now and then with a gentle breeze that brought the scent of blooming greenery and delicate petals. The moon would be full and heavy, suspended in the black heavens, hanging just above the black silhouette of the distant horizon. She would be standing beneath a huge oak whose twisted, creaking branches had seen so much life beneath them, her hair would be free, falling down her back in silky waves, catching the light of the moonbeams that softly bathed her. About her shoulders would be a dark blue cloak that billowed behind her covering only partially the white gauzelike dress she wore beneath it. The dress was like no other, like nothing she had ever seen or worn. It was draped about her body Grecian-style, its fabric glistening like a newly spun web and radiating with a silvery twinkling only stars possess.

She would stand beneath the oak, her heartbeat quickening with the sound of distant hooves, the sound she had known would come. A smile would touch her lips as the pounding grew louder and she would become anxious. He was coming.

Upon a great, black steed whose powerful legs hit the packed earth with a charging force, he rode, his dark cape flowing behind him caught in the rushing wind man and beast created with their speed.

She would stand utterly still, watching with passion-filled eyes as the black beast broke from the darkness, it and rider one as they thundered toward her. He looked the demon astride his mount, his dark curls blown back from his chiseled features, his gray eyes intense. The whites of his eyes and that of his strong teeth, when he smiled, were the only contrast to his black clothing . . . clothing that fit him closely like a lover's embrace. He would rein in the fiery steed, pulling on the reins as the proud animal danced a bit before settling, and as he did all of this his flint-colored eyes would never leave her face, always he would watch her, thrill her with the smoky, lazy look in them. It was a look that told of his passion, told her how he wanted to lay her down and please her.

She would lift her arms then, the cloak slipping over her shoulders with the gesture as a flash of silvery-white from the sleeves of her dress lit the night. In a moment he would dismount, swinging heavily muscled legs over the animal's back then come to land easily beside her, a strong hand reaching up to gently caress her creamy cheek.

The beginning of this nightly vision was always thus, the ending would vary greatly, but still the outcome was the same, still they would come together and love as never before.

This night, with the blowing of an early spring wind outside her window, the sounds of it filling her ears, the dream again materialized, and this night, the force of it, the all-too-real feel of it, left her feeling empty in the morning light. For this night, when Dain came, her yearning was keen and she wanted this dream to be more than just a dream, she wanted Dain to be beside her when she woke, wanted him to be with her when she opened her eyes to greet the new day. Knowing he would not, she tossed in the huge bed and let the visions come, let them sweep her away to another world. A world that was warmed by the strength of their love. A world she longed to be in.

This night, as he caressed her cheek, his fingers warm on her skin, he spoke loving words, words that soothed her, made her recall the trust and unequaled sense of peace she had always found in his embrace. A single tear fell from one eye as she looked up to the man she loved more than life itself. *Why must he come only at night? Why could he not be with her always?* The words were nearly out of her mouth but he quieted her with just a look and he brushed away the tear with a soothing stroke of his hand. No, this night was not for words that made explanations. This night was for loving and holding and comforting . . . His arms came around her then, pulling her tight into his warm embrace and she went willingly, a sob breaking in her throat as her head rested against his chest and the smell of him surrounded her. *How she missed him!* His hands were gently caressing her cloaked form as he rocked her and she slipped her own hands beneath his billowing cloak and rubbed them along his lean sides, her cheek resting over the place where his heart beat. The sound of the beat was strong, just as he was strong, and she marveled again at how the steady rhythm of it could soothe her.

After long moments their bodies broke apart as Brittannia moved to his side and, arm in arm, they walked a few feet to a makeshift bed of soft grasses and fallen leaves situated beneath the bending boughs of the huge oak and those of another nearby. The two trees' branches formed a sort of arch above the inviting nest, an arch that created coziness but also let in the light of the moon and stars. Brittannia looked to Dain as they stopped just beside the makeshift bed, and her turquoise eyes sparkled in the moonlight as his hands undid the clasp at her neck that held her cloak together. The material fell away from her body, hitting the leaf-covered earth with only a rustle. He undid his own cloak then, and after a moment of looking lovingly into her beauteous face, he gestured toward the bed at their feet. As one, they both dropped slowly to their knees, their eyes locked, their hands clasping each other's. The leaves rustled beneath them, the branches above them creaked with a passing breeze, and Dain's black steed moved to a nearby patch of grass to graze. Nature moved but for Brittannia time stood still. From the moment she had heard the sounds of Dain's approaching until the time she knew they must part, time would be still and she was glad of it. Glad that morning would not come until they were finished here. Secure in that knowledge she let him gently guide her back and down upon the soft makeshift bed and she entwined her arms about his neck as he nuzzled his face against the long column of her throat. His breath was warm on her tingling skin, his roving hands even warmer. She could feel the fires in her begin to burn, could feel that unnamed thing within her that was wild and chained and only broke free at this man's touch. She could feel it breaking loose, could feel it coming to life and growing stronger with each kiss his chiseled lips planted on her body, with each gentle touch of his

443

hands and fingers. And she reveled in the feel of it, loving the way its wildness filled her, the way it fought to possess her and make every nerve of her body slave to its fury of passion.

His searching hands moved along her curved side and down her legs where they pulled the tenuous material of her dress higher and higher, until the hem was up past her thighs and the silvery light of the moon gleamed on her slim legs. She moved on her side, fitting her body nicely against his and she undid the many buttons of his shirt and then peeled it away from his sun-darkened skin that looked even darker in the dappled night.

His sinewy fingers were on the closures of her own clothing expertly undoing and soon her breasts were free of the silvery material and touching the fine hairs of his chest. She shivered involuntarily at the contact and her nipples hardened as his hands came up to knead her rounded bosom. It seemed she could not get close enough to him, could not have enough of his lean body beneath her palms, so keen was her desire for him.

She could hear the quickening of his breath, could feel the delightful shivers that ran up her spine as naked flesh touched naked flesh. She could feel his manhood pressing against the silken triangle between her legs and her eyes came open at the feel of it. He was totally naked beside her—as naked as she was—but she couldn't recall when they had stripped off their clothing, couldn't remember letting him out of her embrace long enough for him to do it. But it didn't matter, for she soon ceased to wonder where their clothing had gone, ceased to marvel at the magic of their meeting, for she was caught up in the enchantment of Dain's embrace and at the moment nothing else mattered. Nothing but the silken feel of his roving hands on her hot skin, the sweet moistness of his lips as they moved along her skin with flicking, light kisses, nothing but the secret wells of feeling brimming over within her.

Her whole body tingled with rapturous delight as his hands played along her sensitive skin and when he pulled her over him, fitting her body atop of his, she went quickly, loving the feel of his masculine body beneath her. She showered his face and neck with ardent kisses as she moved over and down upon him, helping him to guide his manhood inside her. His rigid shaft penetrated her throbbing flesh with a driving force that drove deeper and deeper within her, causing wondrous sensations to spring forth in every part of her passion-crazed body and with each thrust she felt more and more like a snowflake that was caught in a turbulent, rushing wind. A wind that bore her thrillingly up and up, then just as quickly sent her spinning toward the earth only to come beneath her and once again take her high, high above everything seen and felt, high into a realm that held only rapturous, charming delights. Again and again he thrust within her and her body moved to meet his, wanting to become one with him. The sound of his warm breath in her ear became the sound of that rushing wind that swept her away, and tumbled her over and over. She felt his manhood fill her, throb within her, and a sudden, sharp excitement filled her as she felt his hot flow pour into her. And that wind that had so whipped her about slowly began to subside as a great ray of sunlight poured upon her and she felt herself begin to melt, melt as a snowflake would beneath a warm sun, and as she melted, she gently floated back to earth, back into the arms that had always held her, back to the arms she had never left, for it was in these arms only that she could take such flight. She heard her own deep sigh of contentment as Dain held her tightly and then she closed her eyes and knew no more . . .

Brittannia awoke, feeling languorous at first but when she realized she was in her huge bed, alone, that languorous feeling soon turned to one of deep despair. *It had only been a dream.* Dain was not with her, loving her, caressing her . . . She was alone. She felt the happiness her dream had brought flee as she sat up in her bed, the sheets twisting about her swollen body, and she angrily kicked them away. Would she never be free of wanting Dain? Would she never find peace without him? She grabbed her pillow and punched it hard, then brought it to her chest as tears began to fill her turquoise eyes. *It had seemed so real.* Every caress, every kiss, every touch of his hand had seemed so real. She had felt every part of him, had felt him move within her. How could her mind play such tricks on her?!

Her tears soon flooded her eyes as a spring wind whipped the world outside her window. It was not yet dawn. She had to get through another day without Dain . . .

"I feel like a spring walk," Brittannia commented as she and Esmée sat finishing their breakfast of eggs, ham, and fresh baked bread with jam.

"You will be doing no such thing!" Ella exclaimed as she gave Brittannia a strong disapproving look. "You are much too far along to be traipsing across the countryside. You will stay right here until the baby is born, and I must add again that man of yours is no man. Look at you, he has gotten your belly full of child and he is nowhere to be seen. He wanted one thing, a quick toss in the bed!"

"Ella," Esmée cut in, "please, leave it be." Esmée and Ella had become good friends over the past few months but Ella still spoke aloud of her ill feelings toward Dain, whom she'd never met.

Brittannia threw down her linen napkin and pushed her chair away from the table. "Ella seems to be the only one who can look at Dain objectively. Perhaps she is right."

Esmée sighed. "Brittannia, Fort Fisher fell to the Federals three months ago. He should be on his way to you."

"And did it have to take Fort Fisher to fall to bring him to me? Couldn't he come because *I* was the most important thing in his life? Do I stand second to the damnable fort?" She abruptly got up and stormed from the room, her heart pounding and her eyes wet with tears.

It was near the middle of April and any day now she should give birth, any day now her baby would be born and still Dain was not with her, she had heard not a word from him. She slowed her pace and with awkward steps made her way slowly up the stairs, her body heavy with child. She was breathing hard as she finally reached the top and crossed through the large hall to her bedchamber.

Bright morning sun filtered through the sheer curtains and warmed the large expanse of her room. It had been a long winter for her, she thought as she waddled over to the window seat and eased her frame onto it. She had thought once she returned to the Cotswolds all would be well. She thought she could make herself forget about Dain, but as the days wore on the reality of Dain never returning hit her full force. It was one thing to think you could forget about the man you love, but it was totally another to actually have to do it, she thought to herself.

She looked out across the wide expanse of lawn and felt pride well up in her. These vast lands belonged to her and one day would belong to the child still nestled in her womb. As far as her eye could see lay the sweeping meadows and escarpments covered with the deep, lush green grass of spring. The sunny morning did not fool her, for she knew if there were sunshine in the early hours there was sure to be rain in the afternoon.

A dull ache began to throb in the small of her back and she stood, thinking she should move about to ease the pain. The white puffs of clouds outside the windows, skirting across the sky, played a kind of peek-a-boo game with the sun and it helped Brittannia to keep her mind off the pain. She paced the room, watching as the sun's rays would grow bright then lessen in intensity just as quickly.

She felt low, nagging cramps claim her belly, growing stronger as she paced her room. She tried lying on the bed, sitting up, nothing seemed to help. The pains remained.

"The baby's coming," she said aloud to herself and

then she waddled quickly to the door, her heart hammering with thoughts of what was to come. She tried to get near the top of the stairs so she could call down to Ella, but another pain took her, this one more like a mild contraction. She squeezed her eyes tightly shut and willed the pain to go away as she doubled over. It left as quickly as it had come and Brittannia straightened herself up, and after taking a deep breath, yelled for Ella. She yelled once, twice, and on the third time was overcome with a sharp cramp that hardened her stomach to rock and was followed by a warm rush of liquid between her legs.

Ella came running up the stairs, pushing back the sleeves of her dress. Esmée was right behind her, her green eyes wide as she took in Brittannia's state.

"Chérie!" she cried. "You are going into labor!"

Of course I am! Brittannia thought to herself, what a silly thing to say, but then she saw more fright in Esmée's eyes than she was feeling. She let the two women help her back into her room and Ella quickly pulled the covers down then turned to help Brittannia onto the bed.

"I don't want to lie down!" Brittannia said, fear gripping her as did another spasm of pain. She was breathing heavily and perspiration was breaking out on her smooth skin. "I—I can't, Ella. I must move about."

Ella drew her lips into that so-familiar, straight line as she eyed Brittannia. She knew it could be anywhere from a few minutes to a few hours before the baby came. Turning to Esmée, she said, "I'm going downstairs to get the necessary things and to let the servants know what is happening. Clean linen is in the chest at the foot of the bed." The old woman left, her legs carrying her heavy body at an incredibly fast pace.

Esmée threw open the trunk and pulled the birthing sheets from it. Her hands shook as she unfolded the clean linen. "Brittannia, dear, wouldn't you feel better if you sat down. Your pacing is making me nervous!"

Brittannia clenched and unclenched her fists as she recovered from the latest pain. They were getting closer together now. "*You* are nervous!?" she panted between breaths. "Esmée, I've the feeling you are as green as I when it comes to births!"

Esmée turned away from Brittannia's blue green gaze and once again busied herself with the linen. "Ah, *chérie,* I don't think this is a good time for confessions and all that. I'm here to help you and that I will!"

"Ohhh! Then you'd better start, this is it!" Brittannia doubled over as another contraction, this one harder and stronger than the last, bent her to its power. Her eyes were wide when it finally abated and with Esmée's help she moved to the bed, her limbs shaking as she positioned her heavy body upon it.

Esmée kept up a running chatter as she helped Brittannia from her clothes and into a clean night-dress. Through the haze of her discomfort, Brittannia tried to listen, tried to conjure up the images Esmée was creating with her words, but she couldn't. She could think of nothing but the sharp, twisting knife of pain that threatened to rip her apart.

Ella was soon back in the room and setting things onto the small bedside table. From the washbasin she brought a cool cloth to Brittannia's cheeks and bathed her perspiring brow. "How close are they?" she asked Esmée.

"Close" came the quick reply.

"This is it!" Brittannia cried again. She was brought up with another contraction. Another contraction followed, this one fierce, angry, and strong. Brittannia could not hold back her scream and somehow it made her feel better, though not much.

Ella was soon into motion, directing Brittannia on what to do and when. "You must push, Brittannia. That's it, dear, easy, easy."

It seemed an eternity to Brittannia that she lay there, her belly growing rock hard at intervals and Ella ordering her to push and bear down. She felt she had no strength in her body and she so wanted to cry out for Dain. She wished he were beside her, wished it were his hands she was clutching so tightly instead of the hard, cold headboard.

"I see the baby's head." Ella spoke to her, seemingly from miles away. "You must push again, Brittannia."

"I—I can't," she managed to say, but even as she said the words, she bore down again, her face contorted into a grimace of pain. She felt the baby's head slide from her and she relaxed for a moment, breathing heavily as she waited for another wave of pain to wash over her. She felt the baby move from her and she pushed with all her might while Ella pressed a hand to her belly and with the other guided the baby out. Brittannia felt her pain wash away, felt the baby rush out as if on a warm tide. She heard a loud cry, a cry she had never heard before and she wept as she realized it came from her firstborn.

"It's a boy!" Esmée exclaimed.

Brittannia blinked away her tears as she looked lovingly at the small baby in Ella's arms. Her baby,

Dain's baby. The tears sprang quickly back as she looked at the tiny pink hands, the tiny pinched face. He was bellowing loudly and Brittannia thought it the most beautiful sound in the world as Esmée and Ella cleaned up and fluffed her pillows and then finally brought him to her. She weakly put him to her breast and peered wonderingly down at him. She felt sad and happy at the same time. If only Dain were here to see the product of their love. If only . . . She didn't finish the thought. She drifted off into an exhausted sleep.

"Pah! You run for the mail as if you awaited a written summons from the good Lord bidding you to heaven!" Ella commented as Brittannia shuffled through the few letters the maid had just brought to her. One of the servants had traveled to London and among other things had returned with a few letters. Brittannia's turquoise eyes quickly scanned the letters for a familiar scrawl. There was only one, but she knew it to be Michael's handwriting. She paused before she opened the letter. She had a feeling it brought ill news to her.

"Here, Esmée," she said, handing two envelopes to her. "These are for you."

Esmée took the proffered letters and tore them open. Her eyes glowed brightly as she read first one then the other. "Ah, my Jacques, he is in London. He's been there for a few weeks and is now ready to move on. My dear," Esmée exclaimed as she held the letter in front of her and waved it up and down, "this only verifies my opinion that we are much too far from civilization."

"Why is that?" Brittannia questioned as she fingered

452

the still unopened letter from Michael.

"Because Jacques says that President Lincoln was shot while attending a theater party at Ford's Theater! He died the morning of April 15. My dear, that was nearly a month and a half ago and we hadn't yet heard!"

"Murdered?" Brittannia asked, the shock evident in her voice. Would she never be far enough from the haunting memories that damned war brought to her? Now the man who had strived for so many years to see the states bound together was dead. Was Dain also dead? Had a bullet claimed him before he could return to her? With shaking fingers she tore open Michael's letter and with anxious eyes she skimmed over the words he'd written. She caught only a few sentences from each paragraph, enough to know that it did not tell her Dain was dead.

Brittannia closed the letter with mixed feelings. Michael had said nothing about Dain, that was good and that was bad.

"What is it, Brittannia? Is the letter from Dain?" Esmée asked.

"I hope it is from that man!" Ella said loudly. "I've got quite a bit to say to him. What kind of man is he? His baby is nearly two months old and he is nowhere to be found. If I were you, Brittannia, I'd hire a couple of London brutes to go look for him and bring him back by the scruff of his neck and then I'd—"

"Well, you're not me." Brittannia cut in. "And I'll do no such thing. My husband knows exactly where I am and when he is able or ready, whichever the case may be, he will come!" She took a deep breath to steady her nerves, then walked to the far side of the library where she had ordered a small cradle to be put so she could have the baby beside her while she read. She looked down at her sleeping son. Jeremy Edward Barclay, she'd named him, after his grandfathers. He looked so precious lying there, his little fists clenched and his pink lips slightly parted. She knew he was God's gift to her, for her husband wasn't returning. At least she had Jeremy. Already he looked like Dain, the little bit of hair on his crown was dark and she was sure his blue eyes would turn to gray.

"Did you receive bad news, Brittannia?" Esmée questioned softly as she came to stand beside her.

"No. The letter was from Michael. He says he's coming to visit as soon as he returns to London. He made no mention of Dain."

"Don't worry, Brittannia. He *will* return."

Brittannia hugged her own waist as she stared down at Jeremy. "Esmée, you've been saying that for months. I just—I don't believe it any longer."

Esmée put a comforting hand to Brittannia's shoulder as she too looked down at the sleeping baby. "Perhaps I should not leave yet. Would you like me to stay with you a while longer?"

"Nonsense. You've been away from your husband for far too long and I can see that you are biting at the bit to attend a party. You've been a good friend, Esmée. Jeremy and I will be fine. You have a life to live and I must learn to cope with raising Jeremy on my own. I can't have you for a crutch for the rest of my days, now can I?"

"But—"

"Hush, not another word. Come, I'll help you pack your things. There is no reason why you can't leave for

London in the morning." With that Brittannia guided Esmée from the room and upstairs to pack her many things.

The morning of Esmée's departure dawned fresh and bright and Brittannia decided she would wear one of her prepregnancy outfits instead of one of the garments she'd been wearing since her delivery. To her surprise the jacket and skirt of sea-foam green velvet fit her nicely. All evidences of her pregnancy were gone, there were no ugly marks as she was told there would be, and as she stood in front of her large mirror, she thought she looked better than she ever had. Her hair was fuller with added length and her body was slightly more voluptuous, more womanly. How beautiful motherhood makes one feel, she thought to herself as she left the room and headed for the adjoining nursery.

Jeremy was lying awake in his crib and he kicked his little feet and pumped his little hands as she bent over his cradle.

"Hello, precious," she cooed to him as she ran tender fingers over his smooth cheek. He smiled and gurgled and she smiled back. "Auntie Esmée is leaving today, but soon you'll meet your Uncle Michael. Oh, he'll spoil you, I'm sure."

"Brittannia," Ella said softly from the doorway. "Esmée is downstairs and waiting to say good-bye."

"Yes, I'm coming. I wanted to get Jeremy and bring him outside for a while. Is it chilly out?" she asked as she picked him up.

Ella nodded. "I'll bring his blankets, it is a bit cool out yet."

Esmée was standing near the carriage, her numerous bags strapped to the top, threatening to topple off if the conveyance should sway to one side.

"Oh, you brought little Jeremy down. I crept in your room this morning, didn't I?" she asked Jeremy as she took him from Brittannia's arms. "He was much too interested in his toes to pay me much mind."

Brittannia laughed and felt very proud as she watched Esmée and Jeremy together. "We shall both miss you terribly. Promise me you'll write and perhaps you can drag that husband away from the city life and the both of you can come visit us."

"I will, I will," Esmée promised as she planted an affectionate kiss on Jeremy's forehead. "I think Jacques plans a trip to Paris for the summer season. Paris is lovely this time of year." She handed Jeremy back to Brittannia then peered up at her luggage and lastly to the long stretch of road. "Who is coming up the way? Surely it couldn't be Michael, could it?"

Brittannia quickly turned her head to see. A carriage was making its way toward the manor and her heart sang, Dain! She felt her heart begin to hammer in her chest and she thought she might explode with the waiting.

"Here, Ella, hold Jeremy for me." After placing him in Ella's care, Brittannia picked up her skirts and ran to meet the carriage. She ran along the side of the road, her high-heeled boots hitting the damp earth. She felt tears sting her eyes but she didn't care, she just wanted to see Dain. Finally she reached the carriage and the driver pulled the horses to a halt.

"You came!" she cried as she pulled open the door.

"Of course I came, I told you I was coming in my letter," Michael said, a puzzled expression on his face as he jumped down out of the carriage.

Brittannia looked up to him in surprise. She felt as though she'd been slapped hard in the face.

"Brit, you look as if you've seen a ghost. What is the matter?"

She passed a hand across her brow as she tried unsuccessfully to still her beating heart.

"Nothing is the matter, Michael. Nothing at all," she assured him as she forced a smile to her lips.

"Good, for I would hate to be the cause of your distress," he said, then pulled her into a brotherly hug.

She hugged him back. She *was* glad to see him, it was just that she wanted to see Dain more.

"You are looking very dapper!" she complimented as they walked hand in hand back to the manor. He did indeed look handsome in his off-white vest and trousers that were bound and banded in blue and a dark coat that displayed expensive satin lining.

"So do tell, the suspense has been killing me!"

"What?" she asked as she looked up at him, then realized what he meant. "Oh, a boy, Michael! A beautiful boy! Jeremy Edward has been told all about you and now only awaits your arrival."

Michael puffed with pride. "I see him in Ella's arms. My, she looks the same as when I last saw her," he said as they continued on in the cool morning. "Ella, dear lady," he exclaimed as he took Ella and Jeremy in a hug. "You look as lovely as ever and this—this is my godson!" His eyes looked for Brittannia and she smiled up at him at the expression on his face.

"I was never one to think a baby is beautiful, but Jeremy *is!* May I hold him?" he asked softly.

Ella gave over the wrapped bundle and Michael held his godson for the first time. His movements were awkward and he held the baby as if Jeremy might crack from just the pressure of his arms around him. After a few minutes of surveying him, Michael carefully returned him to Ella's arms.

"Where is Dain?" he asked. "Did he finally make it home for the blessed event? He was on his way when we last spoke."

Brittannia felt as though a dark gray cloud had blown in from angry seas and blocked the sunshine from her.

"What?" she whispered.

"Don't mention that name around this home!" Ella demanded as she rocked the now-sleeping Jeremy in her heavy arms. "That man is no man!"

Michael looked first to Brittannia then to Ella and lastly to Esmée. "Is something the matter? What does she mean Dain is no man?"

"Where is he, Michael? When did you last see him?" Brittannia questioned as she gripped his arm in a desperate hold.

Michael looked surprised. "You mean he isn't here? But I thought—"

"Michael, when?"

Michael thought for a moment then said, "It must have been early January or possibly late December. It was just before Fort Fisher was overtaken by an army-navy team. Brit, he told me he was coming here for you, said he wanted nothing more to do with war."

Brittannia stared blankly at him, she was numb. Dain was planning to come to her? "He—he never came. That was months ago, what do you suppose happened to him?"

"The good Lord no doubt gave him his due, that's

458

what!" Ella added, then pursed her lips and stared off into the distance.

"Shush, Ella! Please, take the baby in out of the cool air. I have to think."

"There is no point in you getting upset all over again. Whatever became of him is—"

"Ella," Brittannia cut in, "Michael said Dain was planning to come to me in late December. Esmée and I hadn't left Nassau long before that so he probably made one last run, right, Michael?" she asked, turning her blue green eyes to him. "He told me he had to make another run and that was all he made, is that correct?"

Michael nodded. "That was all he made, to my knowledge. He said he had important matters to tend to and I assumed he meant you and the baby. When I asked him where I would be able to reach him he said in the Cotswolds."

"Oh, I should have waited. I should not have been so bull-headed."

Ella gave an exasperated sigh that told all she did not understand Brittannia's feelings then she turned and took Jeremy inside. Esmée turned worried eyes to Michael then tried to comfort her friend.

"Brittannia, perhaps the important matters he had to tend to were not you and the baby. Perhaps he is still tending to those matters and that is why he hasn't yet come."

"Yes," Michael agreed as he stepped over beside Brittannia and wrapped his arms around her trembling shoulders. "He does have family in the South."

"He left home when he was a boy. Why would he choose to go back now?"

Michael shook his head. "Who knows. War has different effects on people, maybe he felt he'd been gone too long."

Gone too long. Michael's words brought back memories of that snowy day she had returned to the Cotswolds. She felt then she'd been gone too long and she remembered how she'd longed to be in England when she'd been in Nassau.

"Yes, perhaps he did go home. Let us pray he is safe." She straightened her slim shoulders and brushed away her tears. She would hope for the best. Maybe Dain wasn't lost to her after all.

Chapter 20

"*Chérie,* are you sure you'll be all right?"

"Yes, Esmée, now climb into that blasted carriage and be on your way! You've dallied here quite long enough."

Esmée gave Michael an uncertain look. "Go, Esmée. I'll be here with her for a while. You should get back to your husband."

Esmée finally gave in and after a lot of hugs and more good-byes, she climbed into the carriage and was gone. Brittannia waved until her hand hurt and the carriage was out of sight. She would miss Esmée. Turning to Michael, she said, "My life has been nothing but a series of meetings and partings lately."

Michael smiled. "I wouldn't use the word 'nothing.' And whose life is more than a meeting and a parting, beginnings and endings?" He took hold of her arm and guided her into the manor house. "Shall we go into the library and talk for a while?"

Brittannia nodded. "Is it too early in the day for a good stiff drink?" she asked, knowing full well it was.

"Yes, but let's have one anyway."

Once in the library, she sank into a huge leather chair as Michael walked to the secretary and, recounting from memory, procured two glasses and a decanter from it. He poured them each a glassful of brandy, taking a great gulp from his, then refilling it before he crossed the room and took a seat across from Brittannia.

"You've heard the president of the States was shot?" she questioned.

Michael nodded.

"What more tragedies can befall that young country?"

Michael studied her for a long moment. "It is not as though you were never touched by the war, Brit. You and Dain suffered a lot. You still are suffering."

"I'm trying so very hard not to."

"I know. When Dain returns all will be well, eh?" he asked, then when he saw a shadow of doubt cross her delicate features, he added, "He has nine lives, you know. I don't believe he's used up half of them yet."

Brittannia swirled the amber-colored liquid around the small space of her glass, then brought it to her lips and took a long drink. "I should have stayed in Nassau."

"Maybe," Michael said. "Who knows. You did what you did and Dain did whatever he did. Things have a way of working out. They'll work out for you and Dain, I know they will."

She smiled at him but she wasn't so sure he was right. Suddenly she felt very old, weighted down by the responsibility of her own actions.

"Well," Ella announced as she entered the library

462

bearing a large tray, "I thought you might enjoy an early lunch." She was followed by a silent maid wheeling in a cart ladened with silver-covered dishes.

"What is this?" Ella exclaimed, her eyes setting on the glass in Brittannia's hand. "You'll be drinking none of that this time of day! You barely touched your breakfast!" The old woman snatched the half-empty glass from Brittannia's hands and then took Michael's glass as well.

"It is so nice to be in your company again, Ella," Michael commented as he watched Ella put the glasses and decanter on the bottom of the serving cart. "I can see you are still your charming self."

"Of course I am," Ella confirmed as she gave them each a linen napkin and began to place the plates on the table in front of their chairs. "You'll get your stomach full of warm food and then you can drink until your eyes pop out of your head for all I care."

"Good," Michael said as he lifted his fork and speared a hot buttered green bean.

The days passed and Michael continued his stay. Brittannia could see he longed to be in London. She knew how much he thrived on working sun up until sundown, knew how much he loved the excitement of handling large sums of money.

"Michael," she said one evening as they sat in the library sharing an after-dinner drink. "Why don't you return to London tomorrow? I can see you miss it. Please don't feel you need to stay with me. It is becoming quite clear to me Dain is not returning. He would have sent word by now. You know that, you're just not admitting it."

Michael considered her words. "I don't know. I thought he would be here by now."

"He's not dead," she stated simply. "I know he isn't dead. If he were, I would feel it here." She laid a hand over where her heart beat in her chest. "I remember when he was taken by the Federals. I could feel his danger then and I knew something had happened to him. I don't feel that now. Wherever he is he has found a peace. I can't explain it, but I can feel it in my heart. He is where he wants to be and isn't soon to be coming to me."

"Brittannia, I wish you wouldn't talk like that."

"No, Michael, it is the truth. I've got to live up to that. I have to admit to myself so I can give up this anxious waiting and devote myself to my son and to the business that needs tending to. I have to learn to live without him."

Michael said nothing, for he agreed with her and Brittannia felt a heaviness leave her shoulders. Oddly, it felt good to finally and truly realize she had to go on without Dain. She had to turn her thoughts to living and to raising Jeremy alone.

The leaden sky looked ominous with its dark, angry-looking clouds and a great wind was picking up and blowing across the wolds.

"Are you sure you want to travel in this weather?" Brittannia questioned for what seemed to her the hundredth time that day.

"Yes, I'm sure," Michael assured her. "I love a storm and perhaps the rain will hold off for a while and give us a good head start."

Brittannia looked skyward and doubted the rain would hold off for anything. "I wish you would reconsider," she said.

"Oh, poppycock!" he said, then placed an affectionate kiss upon her forehead. "Bring Jeremy to the city soon and you and I can discuss finances and all that interesting stuff. Perhaps I'll even spring for a dinner and a night on the town." He gave her a quick hug and then he was gone, gone as were the other people she'd met over the past months. She sighed a heavy sigh as she pulled the hood of her deep blue cloak about her head and turned from the manor house, making her way along the rolling expanse of green and didn't stop until she had reached the long narrow belt of beech trees.

Their light green leaves blew to the side with the powerful force of the wind, their branches bending, but Brittannia kept to her course. She wanted the wind to blow, wanted to hear it howl. Her soul was in the mood for a storm, a storm so great that it would wash away her hurt, thunder out her pain. Dain. How she missed him. How would she live without him? She had to live without him! How long had she been standing there, thinking of him, wanting him? Too long, she decided and then the rain began to drop from the sky. First in splashes, a few here, a few there, then, as the wind picked up, the rain became harder and soon it was whipping about her, stinging her face with the force of its drops. She didn't care, she didn't care about anything at this moment. Her heart had been broken and she felt the force of her sorrow constrict her chest.

The wind swirled about her, carrying with it leaves

and dust, bending the trees and grasses with its force. Her hood flew back from her face and she let it go, not caring that the rain plastered her hair to her head or that it stung her scalp with its fury. Dain. Why hadn't he come for her? Why hadn't he sent word? Her cloak was heavy about her now, weighted down with the rain. She picked up the hem of her skirts, stumbling over an unseen rock as she made her way beneath the meager shelter of the large beech trees. Her breath came in shuddering gasps as she leaned against the hard, wet bark of one of the trees.

Was it tears gushing down her cheeks in rivers or was it the rain? She wasn't sure, she wasn't sure of anything but the knife twisting hurt that engulfed her.

"BRIT-TAN-NIA!!"

Her head shot up as her eyes searched the storm-ravaged landscape. Had she really heard Dain's voice yell her name? She looked about her, the rain poured down, and she couldn't see far. The day was a dark, dark gray and the wind and pelting rain made visibility near impossible. No, it couldn't have been Dain. How silly. She leaned her head back against the tree, pulling up her hood to shield her ears against the mean trick the wind played on her.

"BRIT-TAN-NIA!!"

There it was again! "No!" she cried into the howling wind. "Stop it!" She couldn't stand to hear that voice. It was so familiar, too missed. It sounded full of pain as it called her name and she covered her ears, not wanting to feel any more pain, she couldn't endure any more pain, any more loss.

Thunder boomed in the distance, seemingly rolling

across the landscape in deep tones and was followed by a flash of not-so-distant lightning. Brittannia sank to the ground, not at all afraid of the elements that raged about her. She welcomed them, welcomed the fury, needed to have the rain drench her, needed to have the thunder and lightning shake all memories of Dain from her. She brought her knees to her chest and hugged them tight, sobbing as she released all the pent-up sorrow and anger.

"Brittannia!"

"No!" she cried. She couldn't bear anymore. She had to be rid of him once and for all.

"Brittannia. Look at me!"

She felt herself being shaken, felt strong fingers digging into her shoulders with great force. She didn't want to look. She knew the image her mind's eye would give her. It would be Dain. She would see Dain's face, his eyes, his lips. No, she couldn't bear to see that now, not ever again.

"Leave me be!" she cried. She turned her head, her sodden cloak pressing into her cheek. She was crying uncontrollably now, her hurt and anger surfacing, spilling over, and there was nothing she could do, nothing she wanted to do to stop it.

"Ah, my darling, please, look at me! Don't cry."

That voice! Would it forever haunt her? Would she never be free from those timbered tones, those southern-accented words? The hold on her arms was increasing and she thought she was going mad. The wind whipped about her, lifting her skirts and the pelting rain stung her face and hands.

"Get away!" she cried, trying for one last time to still

the demons inside her. The demons that demanded she remember him, hear him and forever want him.

"Brittannia, open your eyes! Look at me! I've come for you. I've come home if this is where you want home for us to be. I've come for you and Jeremy!"

Jeremy! She opened her eyes. How could that voice repeat the name of the child she'd borne alone, without him? "Dain?" she asked. Was he really standing before her, holding her, smiling down at her. "Dain?" she repeated.

"Yes, love," he answered. "I'm here."

Timidly she reached up and stroked his rain-splattered face. She ran trembling fingers along his smooth face, that handsome face that was now drawn and creased with pain. Pain. That is what she felt, that is what she could see he felt. Without another word, she went into his arms, the arms she'd longed to be cradled in, the arms she'd needed all these past months.

"Dain," she sobbed as new sheets of rain splashed down on them. "Oh, Dain, it is you!"

His arms were around her, caressing her, warming her. The ominous darkness around her seemed to lift, the rains seemed to lessen their fury and the thunder sounded miles away.

"Where have you been? Jeremy? You've seen Jeremy?" She had a thousand questions but he quieted them with his kisses and for the moment she was glad enough to just have him with her, holding her. She went willingly into his embrace, returning her love with each kiss, each caress.

"Hush," he soothed, "hush and just let me hold you." He gently rocked her, his arms squeezing her, not being able to get enough of her.

"Dain, I'm so sorry I left Nassau. I should have stayed, I should have listened to you."

He put a silencing finger to her lips and as he gazed down at her she could almost feel the tumultuous emotions within him, they were so much like her own. Around them the storm still raged but they were oblivious to the howling winds and pelting rains. It was just the two of them.

Wordlessly he lifted her into his arms and carried her back to the manor house. Brittannia didn't protest, she circled his neck with her arms and placed her head on his shoulder, glad to have him with her again.

With one large hand, Dain opened the double doors of the manor and with his booted foot kicked them open wide enough to carry his precious bundle through. "Ella!" he called as the wind blew in sheets of rain behind them. "Have you ready dry clothes and a fire in the hearth of our room?"

Had Brittannia imagined it or was Ella actually nodding to Dain. Did the old woman actually look like she was glad Dain was here? With a gentleness that tore at her heart, Dain set her firmly on her feet and Ella was right there to help her out of her wet cloak.

"Upstairs with you, Brittannia," Ella ordered as she took first Brittannia's cloak, then Dain's. "I'll not be having you catch your death. Imagine, you staying out in this kind of weather! Lucky for us Dain is here, else you'd still be out there doing who knows what!"

Brittannia looked in astonishment to the older woman. Obviously Dain had done something to win her approval or she would not have let him step foot inside the manor house. She looked to Dain and he wore one of his handsome grins on his face.

"Just what did you say to—"

"No, my love," he interrupted her once again and lifted her into his arms, "I shall answer all of your questions only when you are out of these wet clothes." He took the stairs two at a time and before Brittannia realized, he had her in her bedchamber.

"How did you know these are my rooms?" she questioned as she tilted her bright head to one side.

"No questions answered until you are—"

She put up her hand as he let her down in front of the warm hearth. "I know, I'm getting to that," she said, and slowly began to undo the many buttons of her ivory taffeta dress. It was soaked through to her skin and the color was no longer ivory but a deep pearl gray. She watched, through thick lashes, as Dain stripped off his sodden shirt and then began to undo his trousers. How long had she wanted for him to be near, to be here in this room, undressing? Too long.

"Damn!" she muttered.

He regarded her, his hands still holding onto the opening of his trousers, one dark brow raised inquisitively. This is unbelievable, she thought to herself. There he stands undressing as if nothing has happened between us!

"Where have you been?" she demanded. "And why is Ella acting like the cat who got away with licking the cream?"

Dain threw his dark head back and laughed a deep laugh.

"I fail to see the humor in all of this!" she said,

incensed. "Well, are you going to stand there laughing or are you going to tell me what's happened?"

His laughter near stopped. "Where I have been is nothing to laugh about, but what has Ella 'moon-eyed' as you put it is funny."

"Well, where and what?" she pressed.

"Actually, it is not what but whom has Ella starry-eyed."

She forgot her many buttons and put her hands on her hips. "Well?" she questioned, her wet hair beginning to curl as it dried from the heat of the hearth.

"Erskine," he stated simply and then began again the task of undoing his trousers.

"Erskine? He's here?"

Dain nodded. "And Beau too."

"Erskine and Beau?" She was surprised but very pleased. "Why?"

Dain brushed wet curls from his forehead as he approached her. "Erskine goes where I go and Beau needed a home. I was hoping he could live with us."

Brittannia felt tears coming to her eyes. Beau was all right and he was here, here in England! "Of course he can live here, but what kept you from me?"

Dain's eyes clouded as he took a seat near the hearth. The dark hair of his chest was just now beginning to dry and she realized, with a start, just how defined his body was, how much she'd missed having him near. "I made that last run to Wilmington as I had planned. I did it more for Beau than for anything else. He has no family and he'd been with me for a few years. I felt he needed me and truth to tell, when I'd learned you left for England, I needed someone to need me." He turned his gaze to the fire that crackled in the hearth and continued. "When I returned there was still no word from you so I loaded up ship for another run, but this time I ran for Charleston. I knew I'd come to England after the last run and I just felt this overpowering need to see my family one last time. Brittannia, I would have left by the end of December as I had planned, but my mother had died of a heart ailment and my father," he faltered for a moment then continued, "he was just a skeleton of a man. I'd never seen him so defeated, so ready to die. I had to stay with him, he needed me."

Brittannia was silent as she too turned to stare at the burning logs within the hearth. Poor Dain, the mother he had left so long ago was now gone from him forever.

"Your father, he's—"

"He's—he died," Dain answered without hearing the question. "I was beside him and he said he forgave me for leaving like I did. But, oh, Brittannia," he said, turning his face up to her, "I felt so guilty, I felt as if I'd killed them both!"

"No," she said, kneeling beside him, taking him into her arms. "Don't blame yourself."

"I could fill my journal, but when it came to writing a letter, I couldn't. My father didn't pass away until the beginning of April. I came to you as soon as I could."

"Oh, Dain let's just put it all behind us, please?" she asked as she pulled him closer and stroked his drying hair. Finally when she could wipe away her tears, she asked, "Have you seen him—Jeremy?"

Dain's gaze slowly turned from the fire toward her. "Yes, he's the most beautiful baby I've ever seen. He looks just like his mother." He ran teasing fingers along her jawline and she smiled.

"He looks like his father and you know it!"

Dain smiled back, knowing full well Jeremy resembled him the most. He was eager to acquaint himself with his son—their son. But first, while the boy slept, he would reacquaint himself with his wife, this beautiful, golden woman, so strong-minded, the same he had first seen aboard the *Airlee* with her hair streaming down her back and her breasts straining to be free of their cloth prison. His wife, Brittannia, who had ignited his desire from the first. Brittannia, with her indomitable spirit and her warm, welcome embrace . . .

"Now," he said huskily, his gray eyes turning stormy with passion as he stood and gently brought her with him, "you have got me to answer all of your questions and you are barely out of your wet clothes."

Brittannia backed playfully away from his searching hands. There were tiny goose bumps along her cool skin as she walked to the bed. A sly smile played across her full lips for today was to be a day of rediscovery, a day when she would once again be free to explore Dain's body, be free to feel the wonderful touch of his hands on her.

Tomorrow they would catch up on the time they had spent apart, tomorrow would be soon enough to show Dain the vast estate they would call home. But today—today would be for loving. Today, with the blazing fire of the hearth to warm their skin, they would rekindle their passion, they would once again soar to the ancient heights they had come to love.

Dain cast her a heady smile, one that promised an intoxicating afternoon as he walked toward her, his head slightly down, the look on his face intense, passionate. She returned his smile with a bold, promising one of her own as she gave her fair head a flirting toss that sent her wet locks flying over her shoulder. She pursed her lips, the smile still playing on them as he came before her and slowly began to finish undoing the tiny buttons of her gown. She stood there, her eyes locked with his, her heart beating within her chest as the buttons one by one came free and the material fell away from her body, exposing her tingling skin and the delicate material of her feminine underclothing. Without speaking he peeled the wet taffeta away, and when her upper body was free of its wet clinging and the dress fluttered to her feet to land in a glistening pile Brittannia stepped out of the damp circle and raised her arms to her handsome captain. She ran her hands along the smooth skin of his back feeling the bunching muscles that were so familiar to her. His skin was warm and his own masculine scent wafted up to surround her as she tilted her head to one side and looked lovingly up to the man she would always love, always need to be near.

"You know, my love," she whispered, "once you crawl between these covers you'll not be apart from your son and me ever again."

He gently nuzzled the crook of her neck as his hands ran along her body. "I need not crawl between the covers to tell you I'll never leave you and Jeremy. Forever and always I'll be by your side."

As he spoke the words she knew them to be true, knew there was nothing that could keep them apart again. They had come a long way, these two, since that long ago morning aboard the *Airlee* when they had first

474

come face to face, when she had first felt the thrill this man could bring to her. And she knew she would always find this thrill when she was in his arms, would always feel this quickening of her heart when he was near, for he was the man of her dreams, the man of her future. He was everything to her, and now that he was here in the Cotswolds with her she knew peace at last . . . her world was now complete.

His questing hands were once again on her garments unhooking with a finesse that made her smile. With a whispered *swoosh* her delicate undergarments fluttered away from her body floating gently to a silent heap on the floor and once she was free of their confining hold, Dain swept her lithe body up in his strong embrace then gently laid her on the bed—their bed. Brittannia's arms were out to him, opened for him as she waited for him to climb out of his breeches, and then he was beside her, going into the embrace she gave him.

And in that embrace he found the wonders of the universe, found an enchantment that would not let him be, not until his desires had been met.

Arms and naked limbs entwined, moist lips searched and teased, giving, taking, and through it all their love flowed from one to the other, flowed as a rushing river would, wide and deep, current never-ending.

In the great bedroom of the Cotswolds manor Brittannia and Dain once again conveyed to each other the deep love they felt, once again they soared on that rushing wind they knew so well. And when their passions had been met and their bodies broke apart only to come back together to snuggle deep within the covers in each other's arms, they each knew a wonderful peace.

"Welcome home," Brittannia whispered.

Dain kissed the tip of her nose as he watched her drift into a peaceful sleep as he heard the stirrings of his son in the next room. *Home*. Yes, that's where he was. Home with the woman he loved and their son.

Finally, home.

THE ECSTASY SERIES
by Janelle Taylor

CAPTIVATING ROMANCE
by Penelope Neri

CRIMSON ANGEL   (1783, $3.95)
No man had any right to fluster lovely Heather simply because he was so impossibly handsome! But before she could slap the arrogant captain for his impudence, she was a captive of his powerful embrace, his one and only *Crimson Angel*.

PASSION'S BETRAYAL   (1568, $3.95)
Sensuous Promise O'Rourke had two choices: to spend her life behind bars—or endure one night in the prison of her captor's embrace. She soon found herself fettered by the chains of love, forever a victim of *Passion's Betrayal*.

HEARTS ENCHANTED   (1432, $3.75)
Lord Brian Fitzwarren vowed that somehow he would claim the irresistible beauty as his own. Maegan instinctively knew that from that moment their paths would forever be entwined, their lives entangled, their *Hearts Enchanted*.

BELOVED SCOUNDREL   (1799, $3.95)
Instead of a street urchin, the enraged captain found curvaceous Christianne in his arms. The golden-haired beauty fought off her captor with all her strength—until her blows become caresses, her struggles an embrace, and her muttered oaths moans of pleasure.